MARVEL

SUPER HERO ADVENTURES

SPIDER-MAN

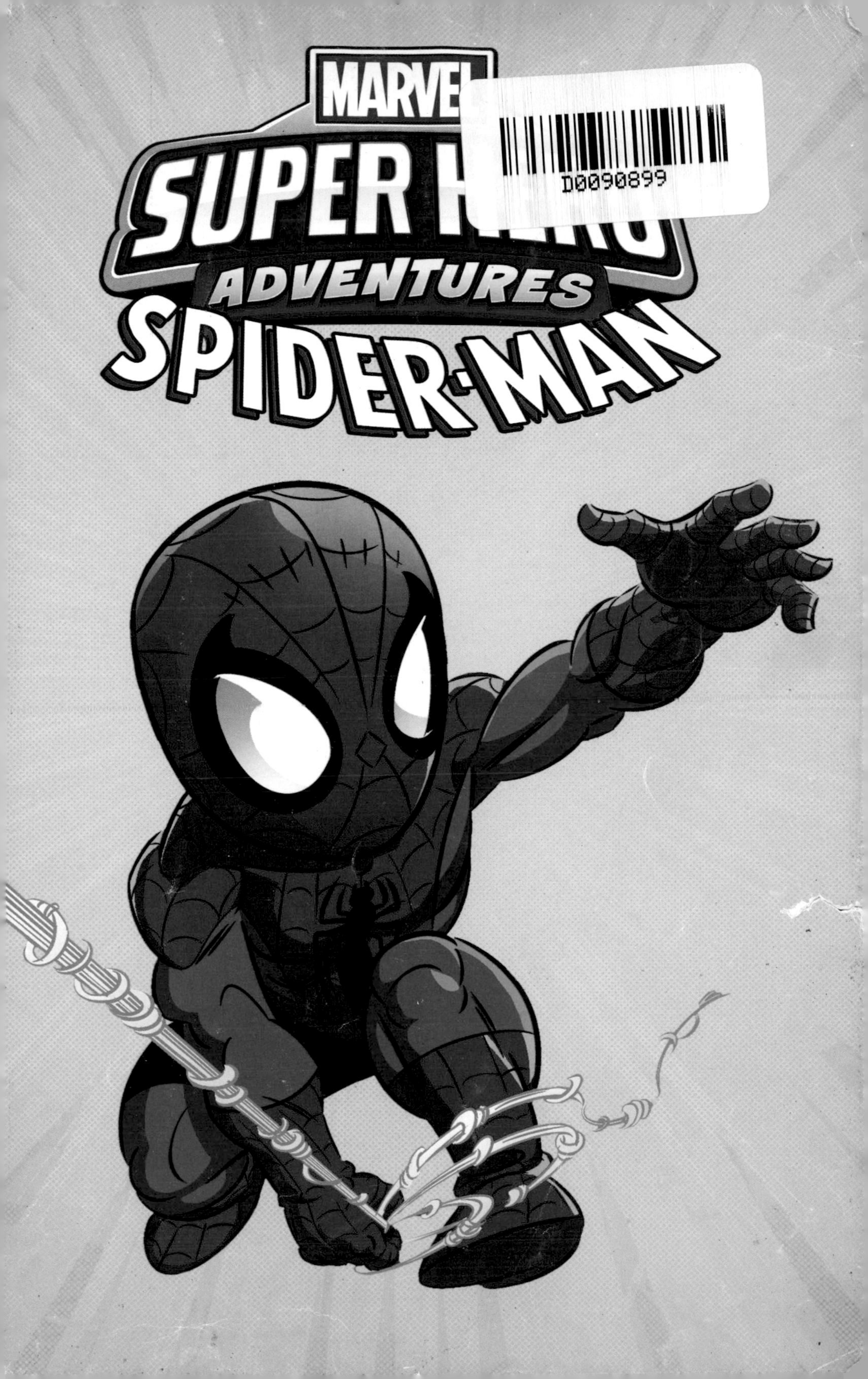

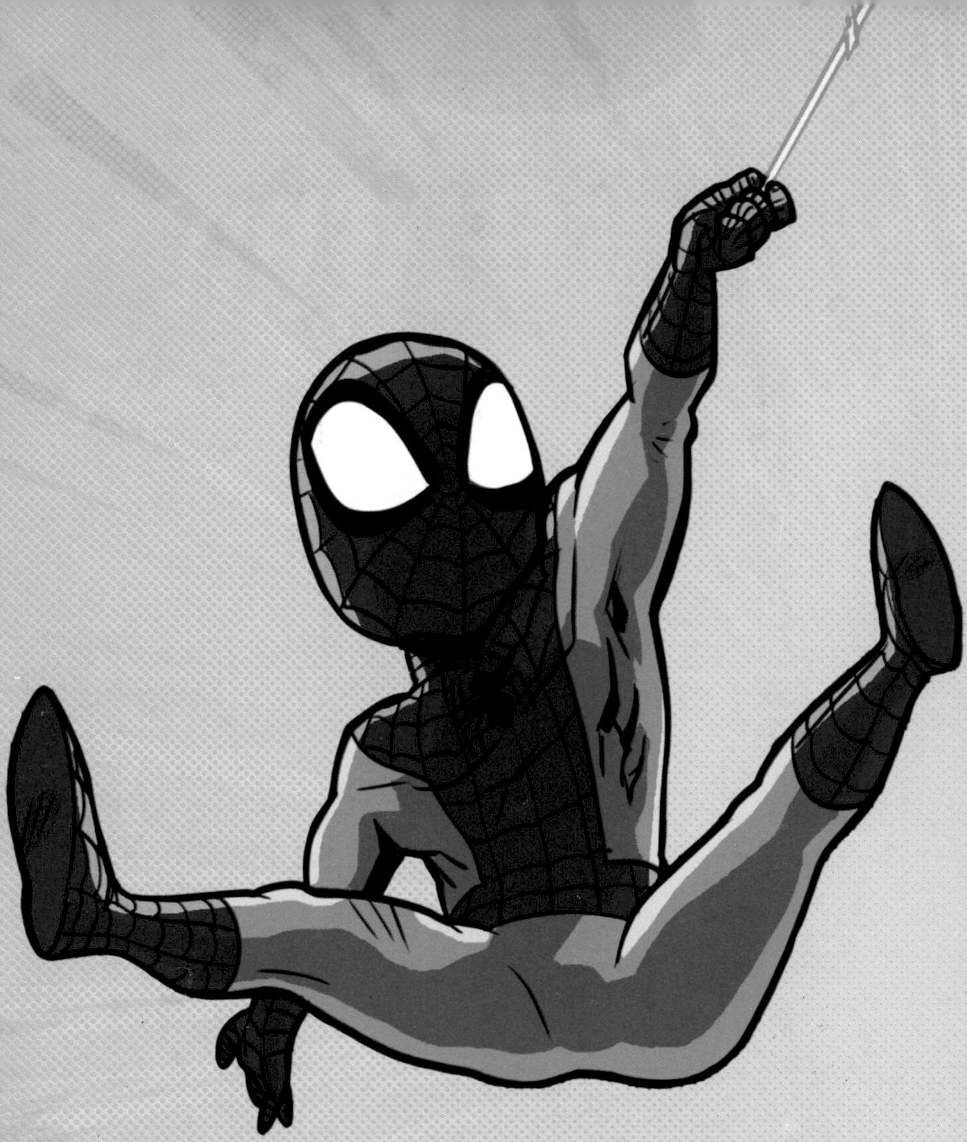

Spider-Man created by Stan Lee & Steve Ditko

collection editor Jennifer Grünwald
assistant editor Caitlin O'Connell
associate managing editor Kateri Woody
editor, special projects Mark D. Beazley
vp production & special projects Jeff Youngquist
book designer Salena Mahina

svp print, sales & marketing David Gabriel
director, licensed publishing Sven Larsen
editor in chief C.B. Cebulski
chief creative officer Joe Quesada
president Dan Buckley
executive producer Alan Fine

MARVEL SUPER HERO ADVENTURES: SPIDER-MAN. Contains material originally published in magazine form as MARVEL SUPER HERO ADVENTURES: SPIDER-MAN — ACROSS THE SPIDER-VERSE #1, MARVEL SUPER HERO ADVENTURES: SPIDER-MAN — WEB OF INTRIGUE #1, MARVEL SUPER HERO ADVENTURES: SPIDER-MAN — SPIDER-SENSE OF ADVENTURE #1, MARVEL SUPER HERO ADVENTURES: SPIDER-MAN — WEB DESIGNERS #1 and MARVEL SUPER HERO ADVENTURES: CAPTAIN MARVEL — FIRST DAY OF SCHOOL #1. First printing 2019. ISBN 978-1-302-91732-6. Published by MARVEL WORLDWIDE, INC., a subsidiary of MARVEL ENTERTAINMENT, LLC. OFFICE OF PUBLICATION: 135 West 50th Street, New York, NY 10020.

Printed in Canada. DAN BUCKLEY, President, Marvel Entertainment; JOHN NEE, Publisher; JOE QUESADA, Chief Creative Officer; TOM BREVOORT, SVP of Publishing; DAVID BOGART, Associate Publisher & SVP of Talent Affairs; DAVID GABRIEL, SVP of Sales & Marketing, Publishing; JEFF YOUNGQUIST, VP of Production & Special Projects; DAN CARR, Executive Director of Publishing Technology; ALEX MORALES, Director of Publishing Operations; DAN EDINGTON, Managing Editor; SUSAN CRESPI, Production Manager; STAN LEE, Chairman Emeritus. For information regarding advertising in Marvel Comics or on Marvel.com, please contact Vit DeBellis, Custom Solutions & Integrated Advertising Manager, at vdebellis@marvel.com. For Marvel subscription inquiries, please call 888-511-5480. **Manufactured between 3/29/2019 and 4/30/2019 by SOLISCO PRINTERS, SCOTT, QC, CANADA.**

10 9 8 7 6 5 4 3 2 1

MARVEL SUPER HERO ADVENTURES SPIDER-MAN

ACROSS THE SPIDER-VERSE

"Bad Influence"
By Daniel Kibblesmith,
Mario Del Pennino & Jim Campbell

"Who's Got Game?"
By Sholly Fisch,
Arianna Florean & Andrew Crossley

WEB OF INTRIGUE

"Spiders Everywhere!"
By Sholly Fisch, Mario Del Pennino,
Arianna Florean & Jim Campbell

"The More the Merrier"
By Jeff Loveness,
Mario Del Pennino & Jim Campbell

SPIDER-SENSE OF ADVENTURE

"Panic Island!"
By Sean Ryan,
Mario Del Pennino & Jim Campbell

"Spidey Bugs Out!"
By Leah Williams,
Irene Strychalski & Jim Campbell

WEB DESIGNERS

"Don't Get Mad"
Parts 1-2
By Sholly Fisch,
Mario Del Pennino & Jim Campbell

Daily Bugle Funnies

Written & Drawn by Ty Templeton
Colored by Keiren Smith

Amazing Spider-Maze!

Written & Drawn by Owen McCarron
Colored by Andy Yanchus

FIRST DAY OF SCHOOL

By Sholly Fisch, Mario Del Pennino & Java Tartaglia
Special thanks to Derek Laufman

Letterer: VC's Joe Caramagna
Assistant Editor: Lauren Amaro
Editor: Devin Lewis
Consulting Editor: Sana Amanat

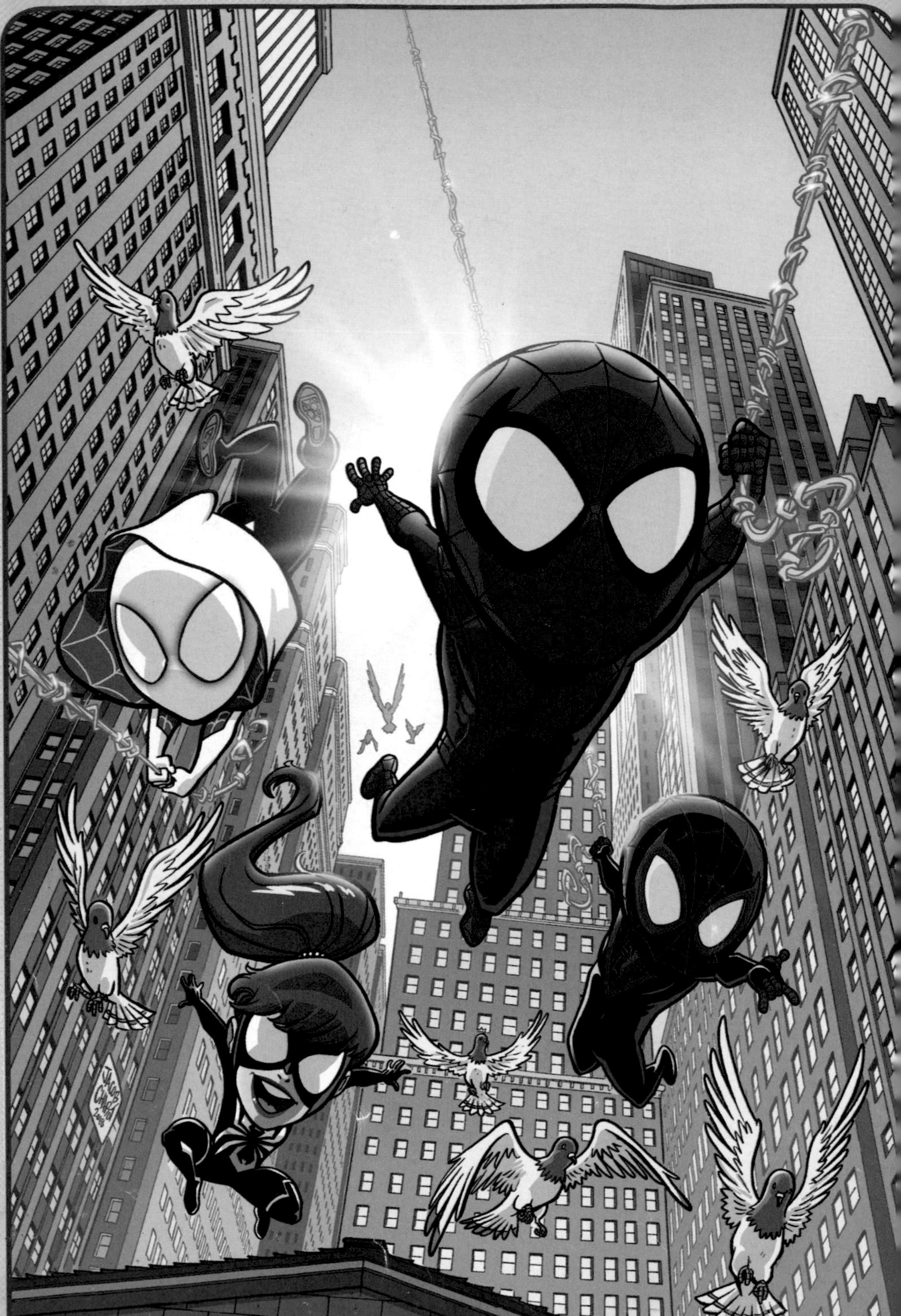

Across the Spider-Verse

cover by Jacob Chabot

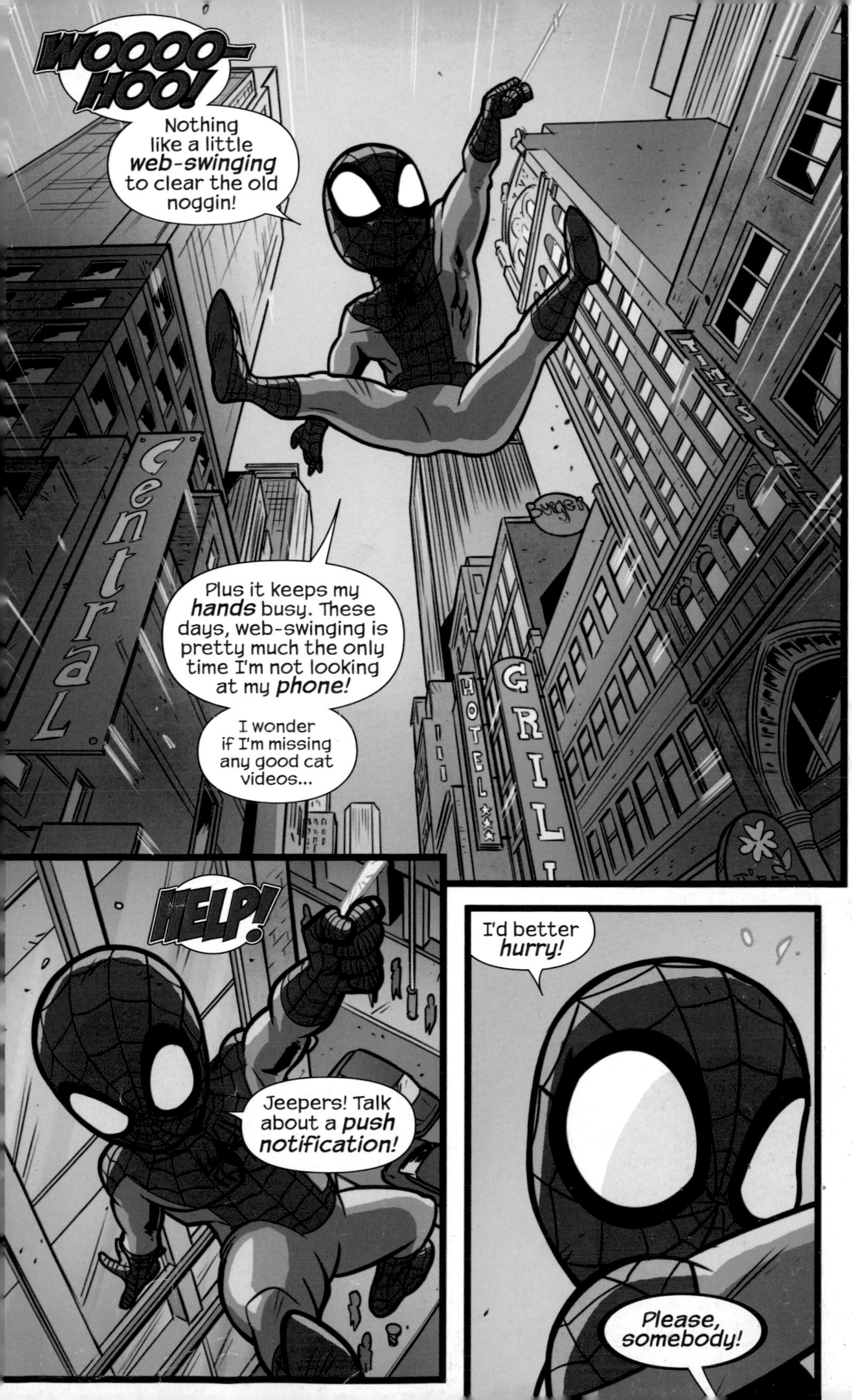
WOOOO-HOO!
Nothing like a little web-swinging to clear the old noggin!
Central
Burger
HOTEL
GRILL
Plus it keeps my hands busy. These days, web-swinging is pretty much the only time I'm not looking at my phone!
I wonder if I'm missing any good cat videos...
HELP!
Jeepers! Talk about a push notification!
I'd better hurry!
Please, somebody!

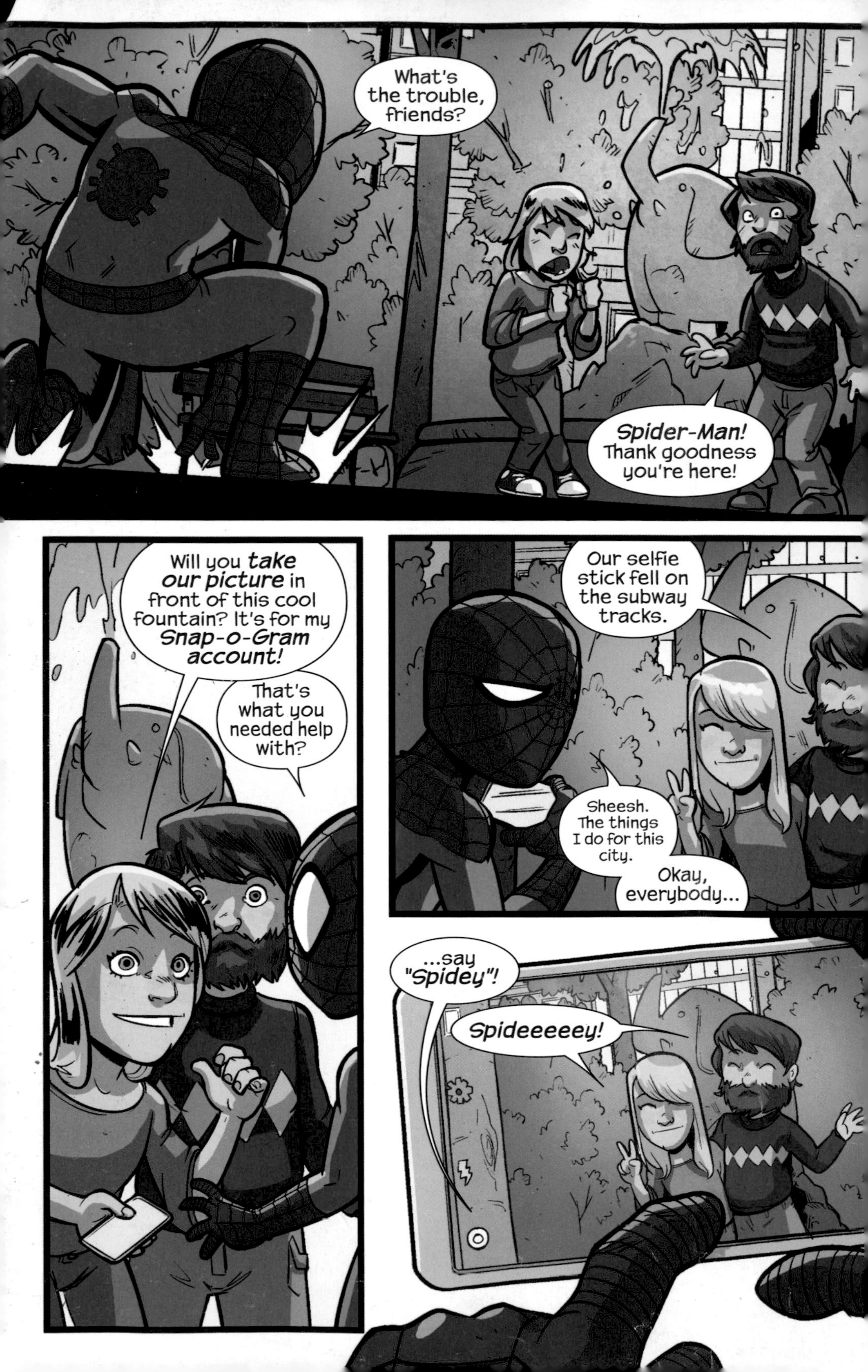

What's the trouble, friends?
Spider-Man! Thank goodness you're here!
Will you take our picture in front of this cool fountain? It's for my Snap-o-Gram account!
That's what you needed help with?
Our selfie stick fell on the subway tracks.
Sheesh. The things I do for this city.
Okay, everybody...
...say "Spidey"!
Spideeeeey!

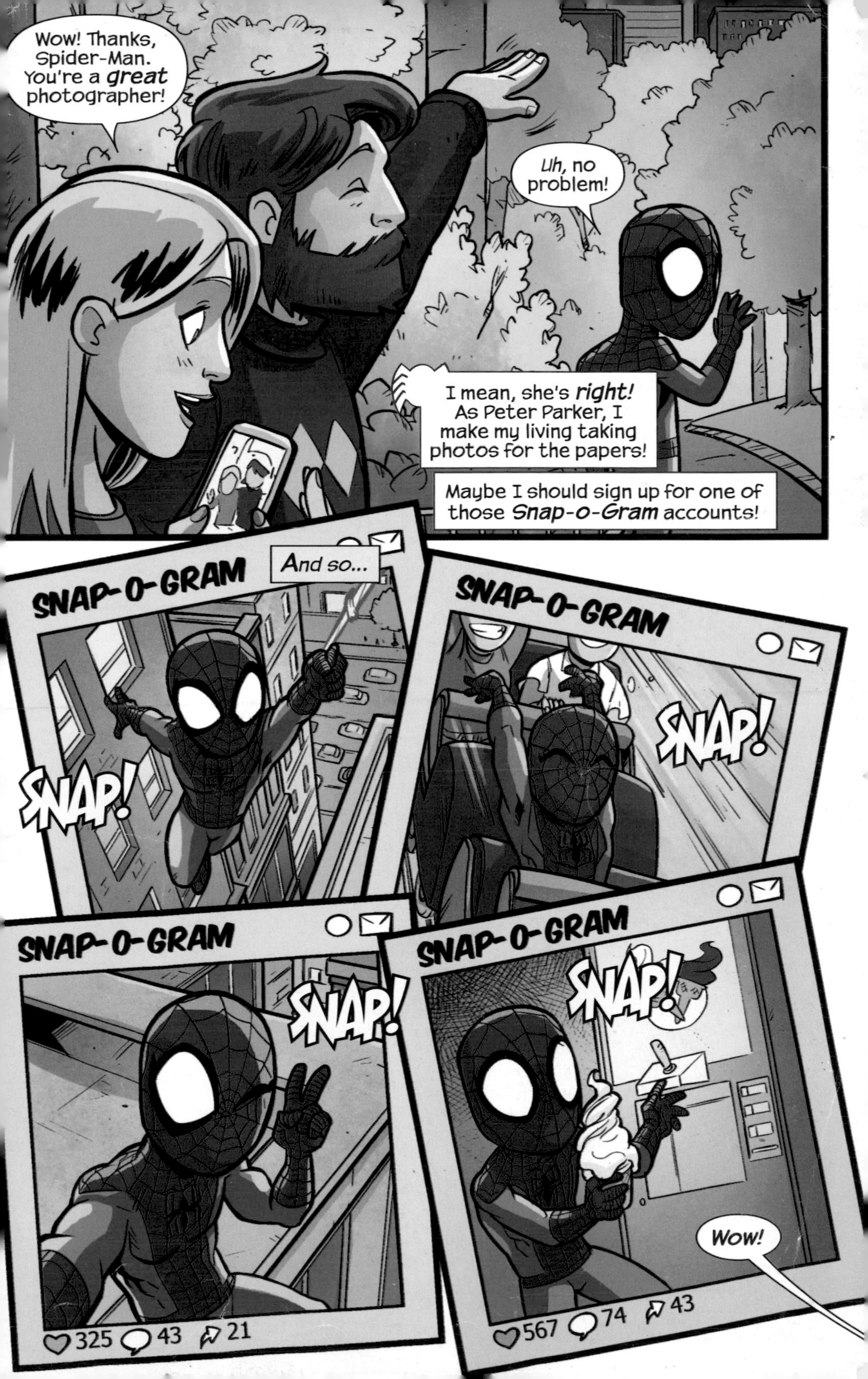
Wow! Thanks, Spider-Man. You're a great photographer!
Uh, no problem!
I mean, she's right! As Peter Parker, I make my living taking photos for the papers!
Maybe I should sign up for one of those Snap-o-Gram accounts!
SNAP-O-GRAM
And so...
SNAP!
SNAP-O-GRAM
SNAP!
SNAP-O-GRAM
SNAP!
325 43 21
SNAP-O-GRAM
SNAP!
Wow!
567 74 43

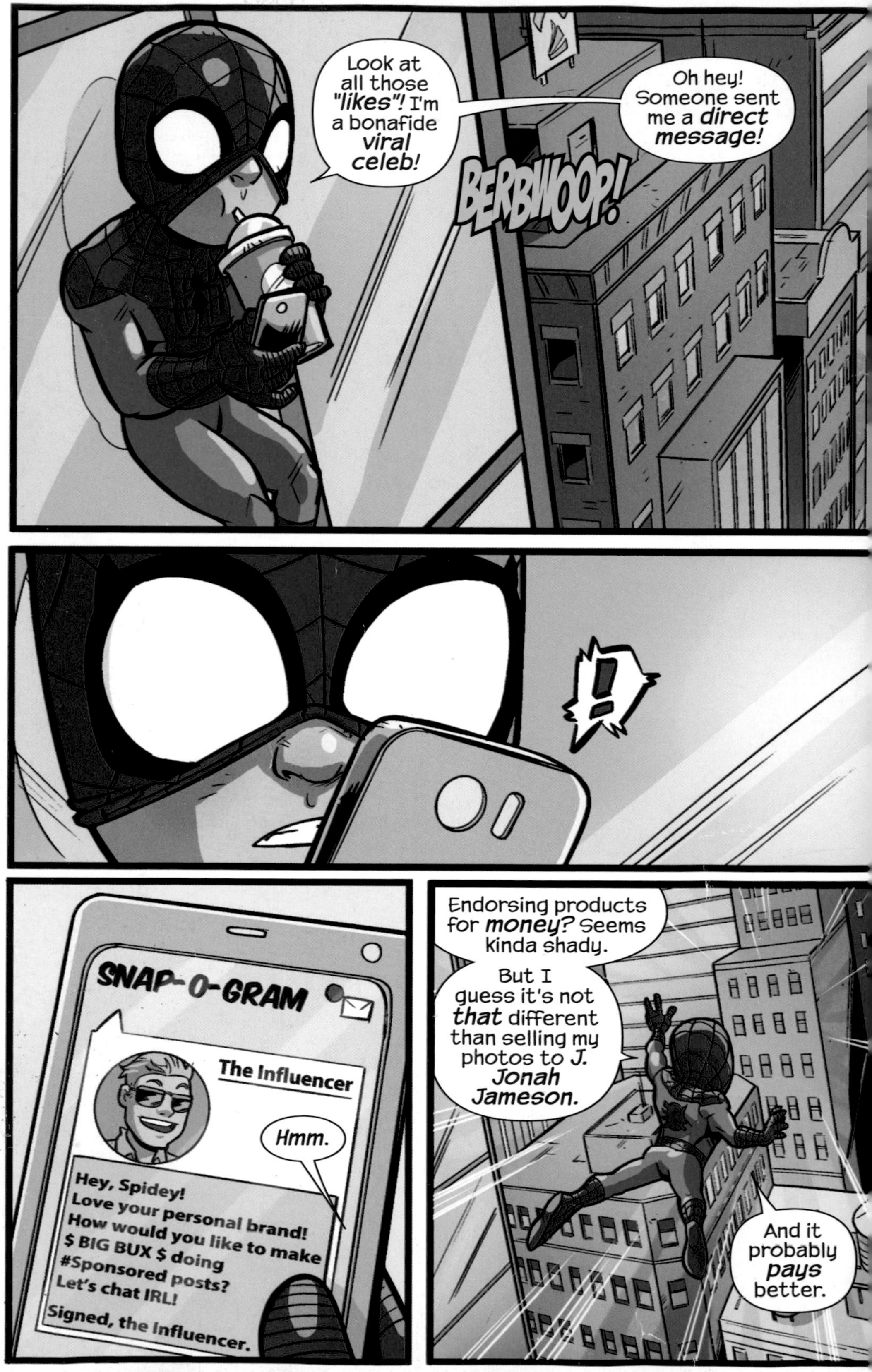

Look at all those "likes"! I'm a bonafide viral celeb!
BERBWOOP!
Oh hey! Someone sent me a direct message!
!
SNAP-O-GRAM
The Influencer
Hey, Spidey!
Love your personal brand!
How would you like to make
$ BIG BUX $ doing
#Sponsored posts?
Let's chat IRL!
Signed, the Influencer.
Hmm.
Endorsing products for money? Seems kinda shady.
But I guess it's not that different than selling my photos to J. Jonah Jameson.
And it probably pays better.

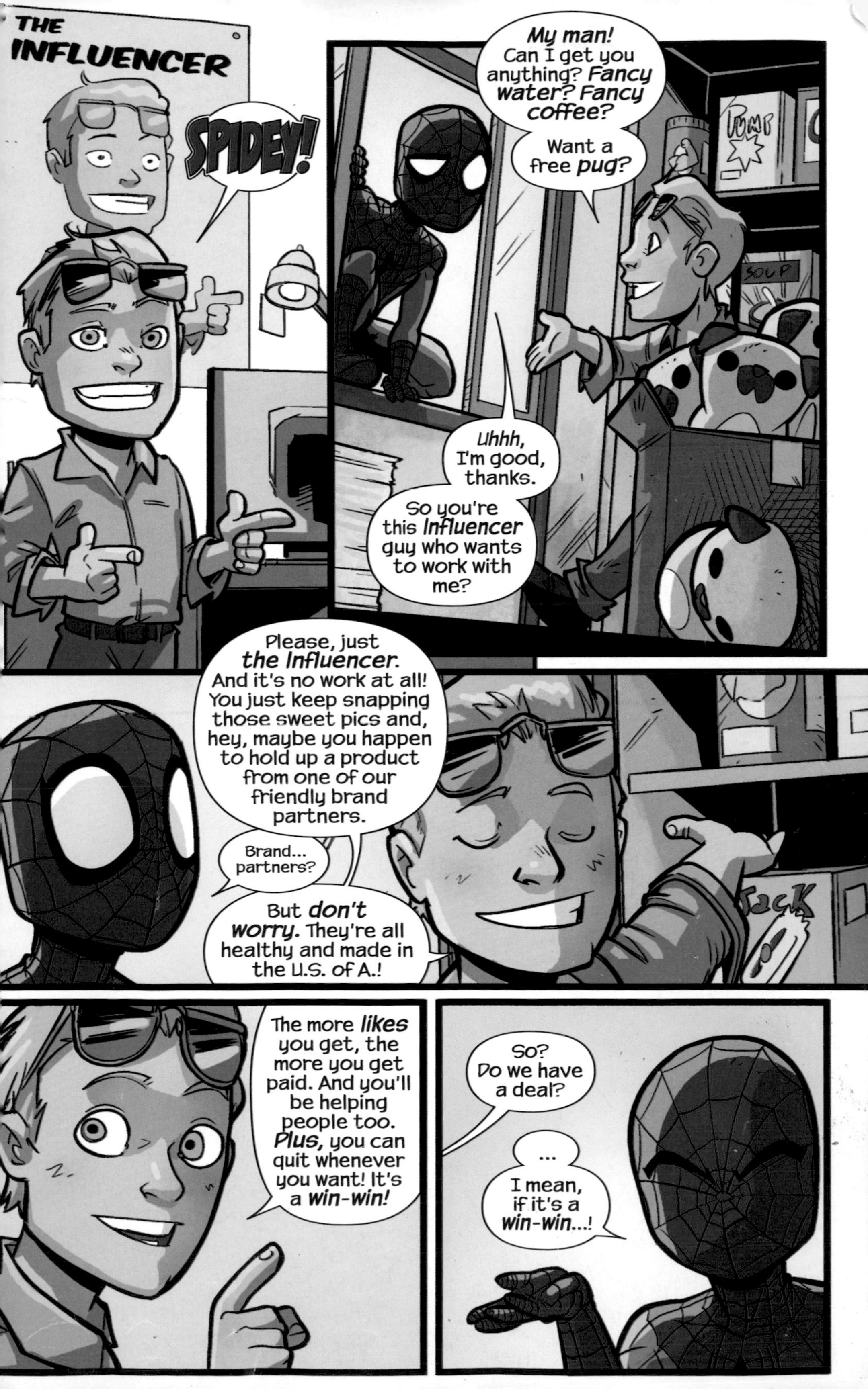
THE INFLUENCER
SPIDEY!
My man! Can I get you anything? Fancy water? Fancy coffee?
Want a free pug?
Uhhh, I'm good, thanks.
So you're this Influencer guy who wants to work with me?
Please, just the Influencer. And it's no work at all! You just keep snapping those sweet pics and, hey, maybe you happen to hold up a product from one of our friendly brand partners.
Brand... partners?
But don't worry. They're all healthy and made in the U.S. of A.!
The more likes you get, the more you get paid. And you'll be helping people too. Plus, you can quit whenever you want! It's a win-win!
So? Do we have a deal?
...
I mean, if it's a win-win...!

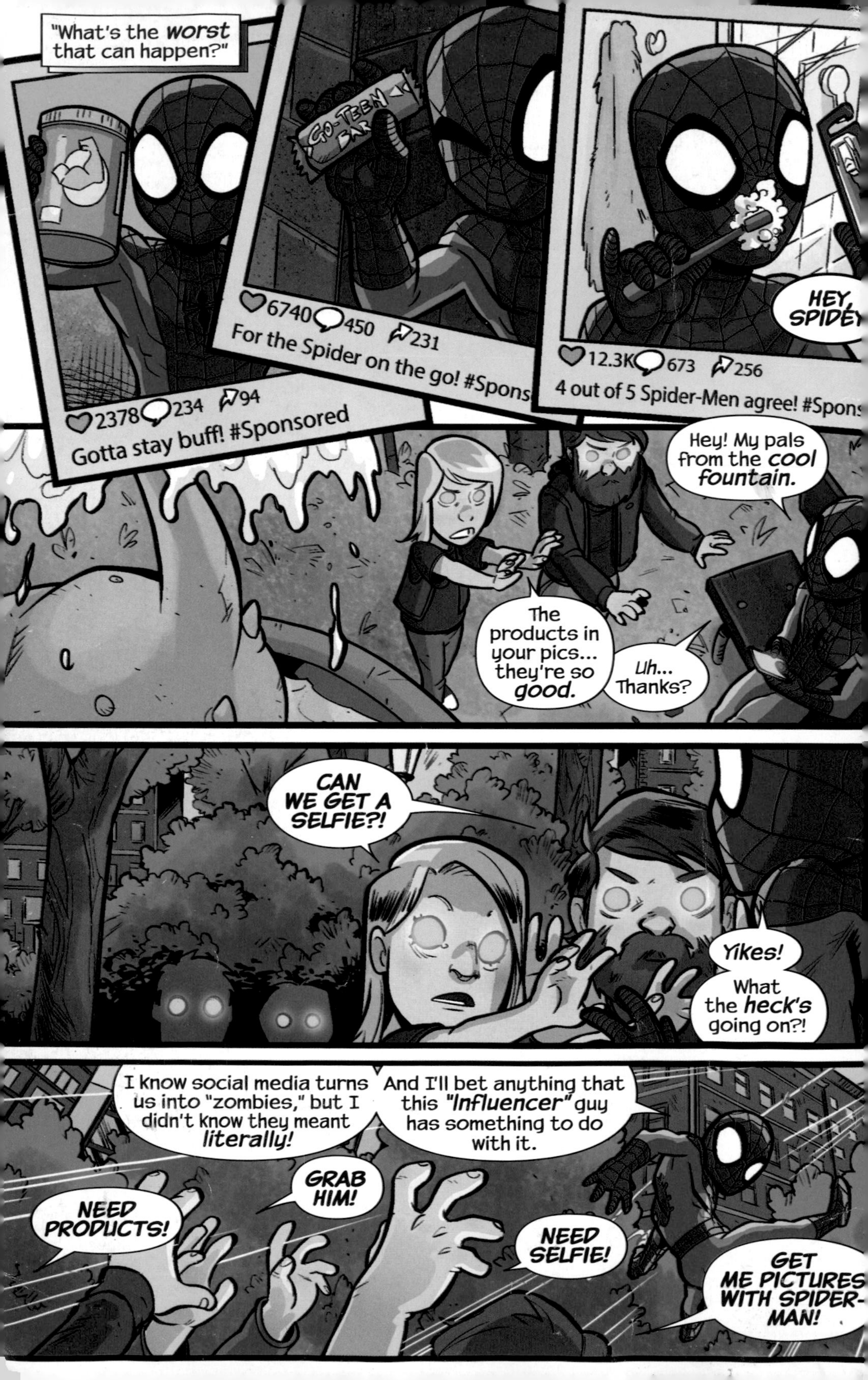
"What's the worst that can happen?"
GO-TEEN BAR
2378 234 94
Gotta stay buff! #Sponsored
6740 450 231
For the Spider on the go! #Spons
12.3K 673 256
4 out of 5 Spider-Men agree! #Spons
HEY, SPIDEY
Hey! My pals from the cool fountain.
The products in your pics... they're so good.
Uh... Thanks?
CAN WE GET A SELFIE?!
Yikes!
What the heck's going on?!
I know social media turns us into "zombies," but I didn't know they meant literally!
And I'll bet anything that this "Influencer" guy has something to do with it.
NEED PRODUCTS!
GRAB HIM!
NEED SELFIE!
GET ME PICTURES WITH SPIDER-MAN!

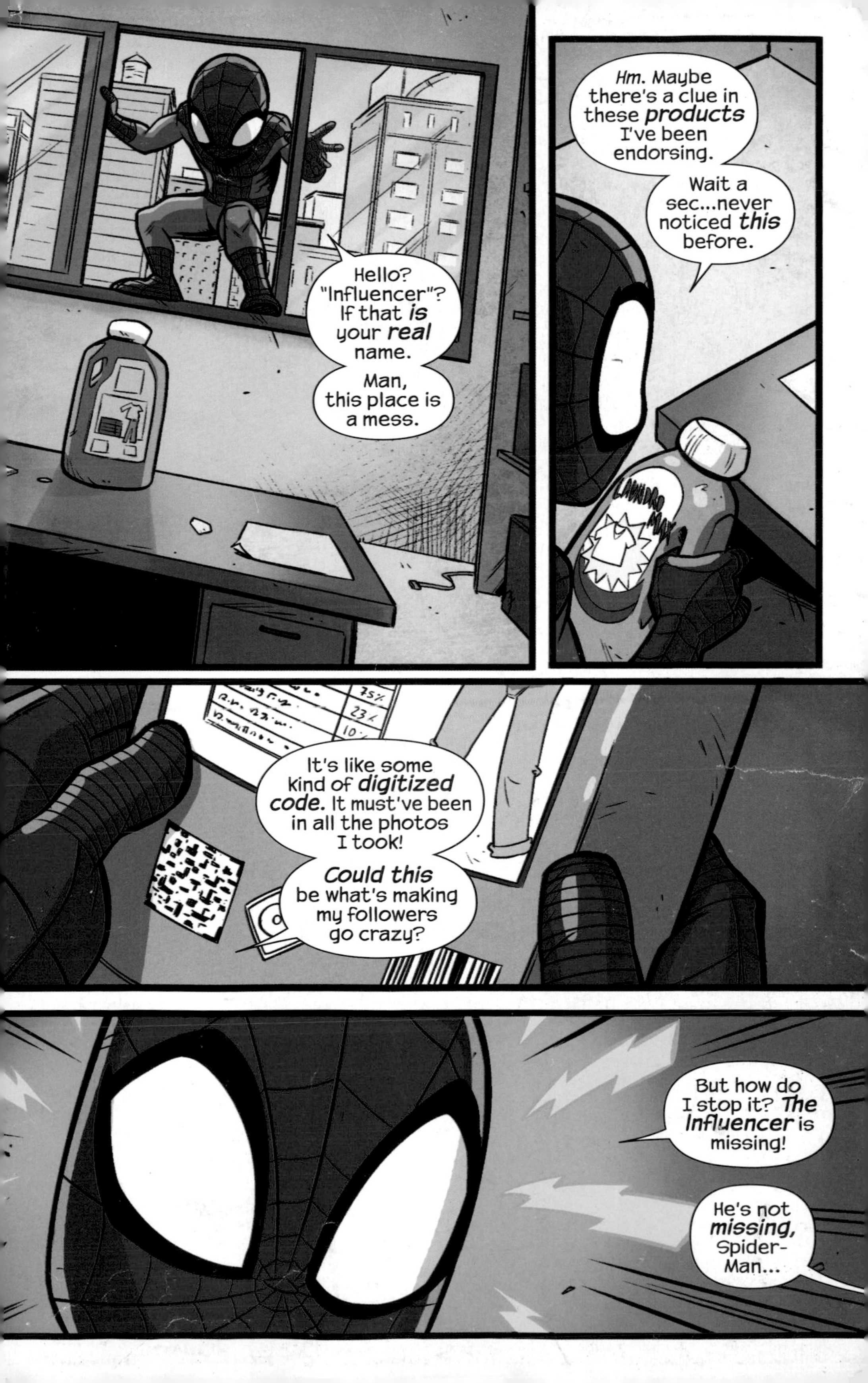
Hello? "Influencer"? If that *is* your *real* name.
Man, this place is a mess.
Hm. Maybe there's a clue in these *products* I've been endorsing.
Wait a sec...never noticed *this* before.
LAUNDRO MAX
It's like some kind of *digitized code.* It must've been in all the photos I took!
Could this be what's making my followers go crazy?
But how do I stop it? *The Influencer* is missing!
He's not *missing,* Spider-Man...

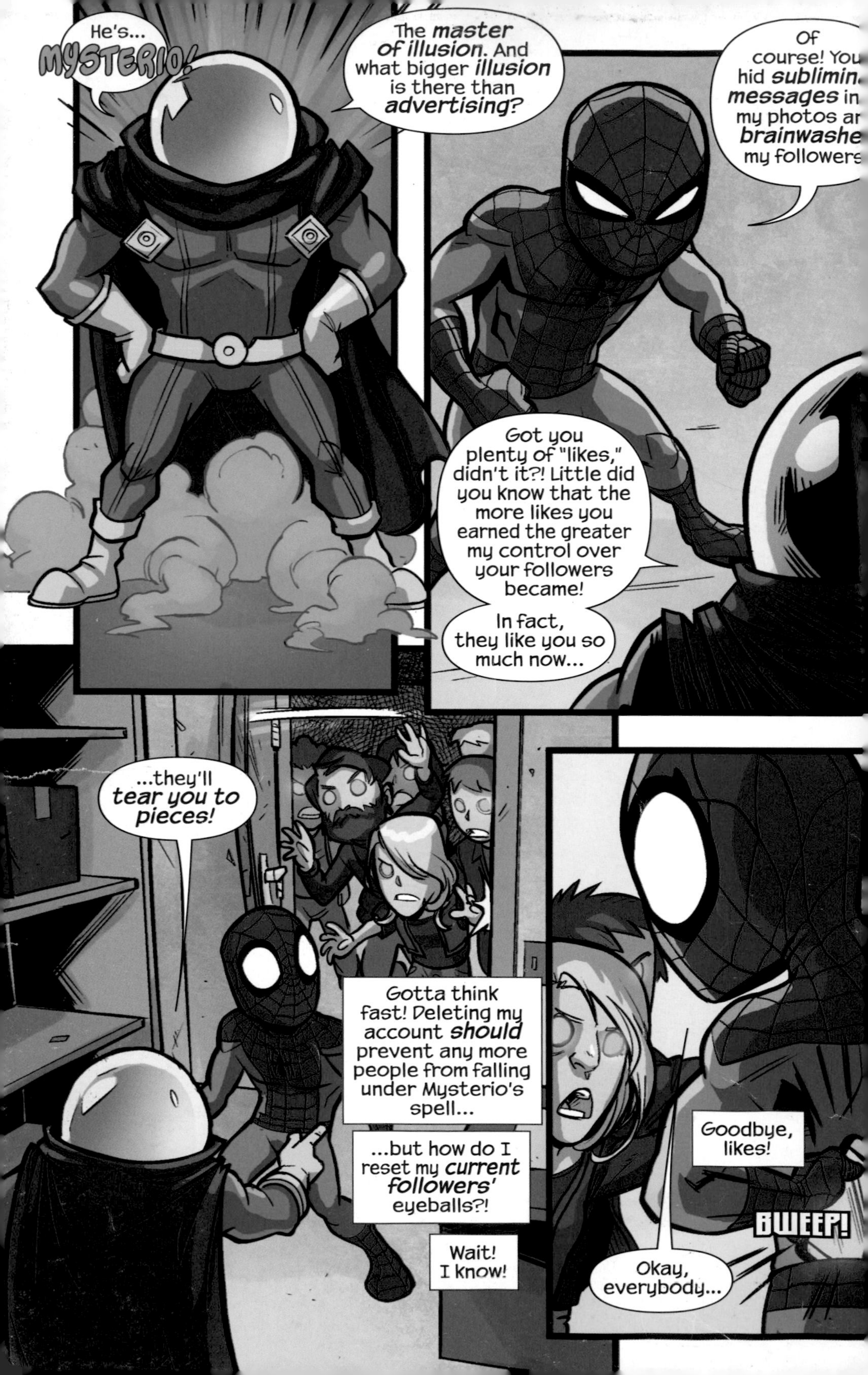
He's... MYSTERIO!
The master of illusion. And what bigger illusion is there than advertising?
Of course! You hid sublimin messages in my photos ar brainwashe my followers
Got you plenty of "likes," didn't it?! Little did you know that the more likes you earned the greater my control over your followers became!
In fact, they like you so much now...
...they'll tear you to pieces!
Gotta think fast! Deleting my account should prevent any more people from falling under Mysterio's spell...
...but how do I reset my current followers' eyeballs?!
Wait! I know!
Goodbye, likes!
BWEEP!
Okay, everybody...

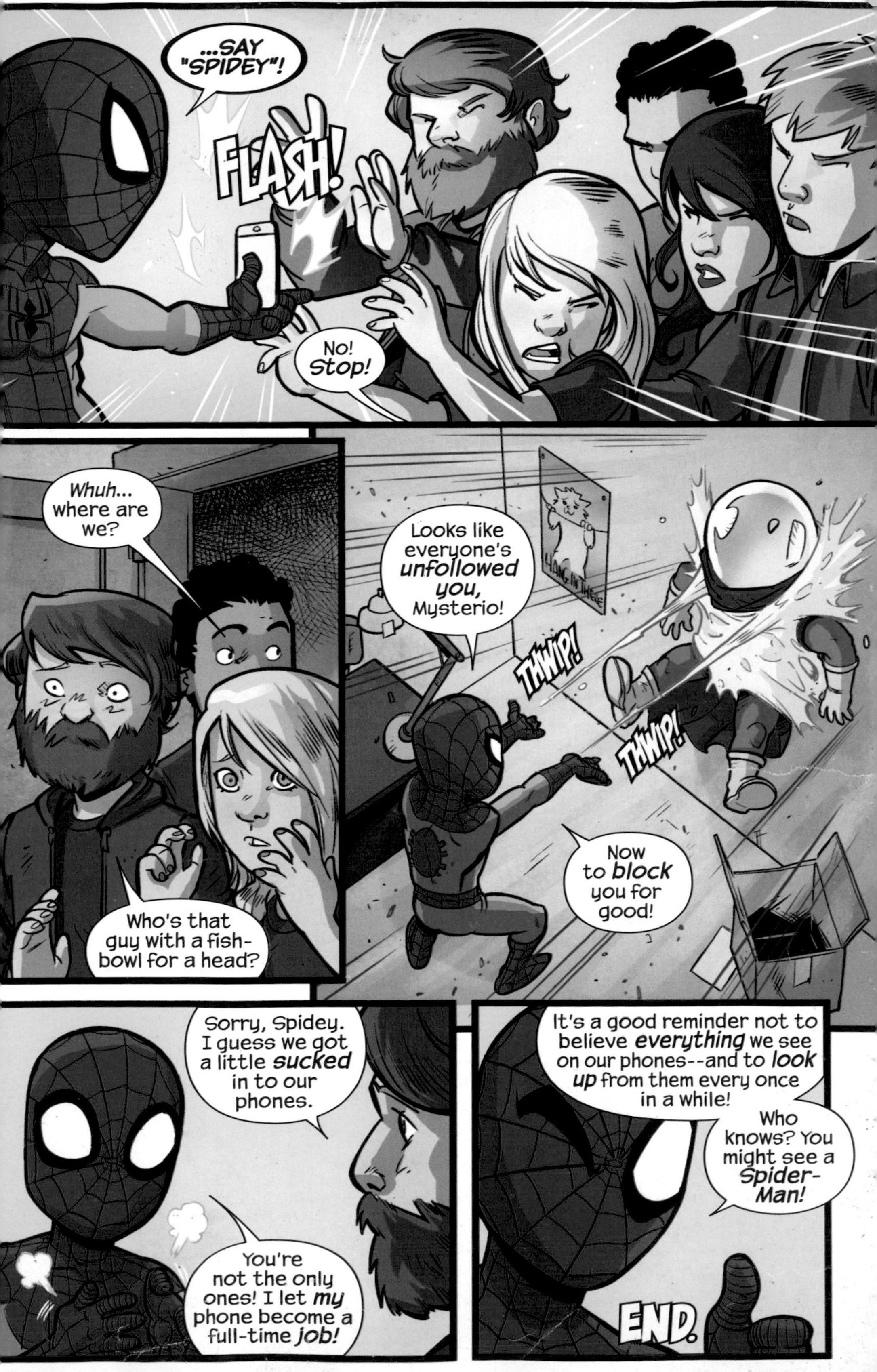
...SAY "SPIDEY"!
FLASH!
No! Stop!
Whuh... where are we?
Who's that guy with a fish-bowl for a head?
Looks like everyone's unfollowed you, Mysterio!
THWIP!
THWIP!
Now to block you for good!
Sorry, Spidey. I guess we got a little sucked in to our phones.
You're not the only ones! I let my phone become a full-time job!
It's a good reminder not to believe everything we see on our phones--and to look up from them every once in a while!
Who knows? You might see a Spider-Man!
END.

DAILY BUGLE

NEW YORK'S FUNNIEST DAILY NEWSPAPER

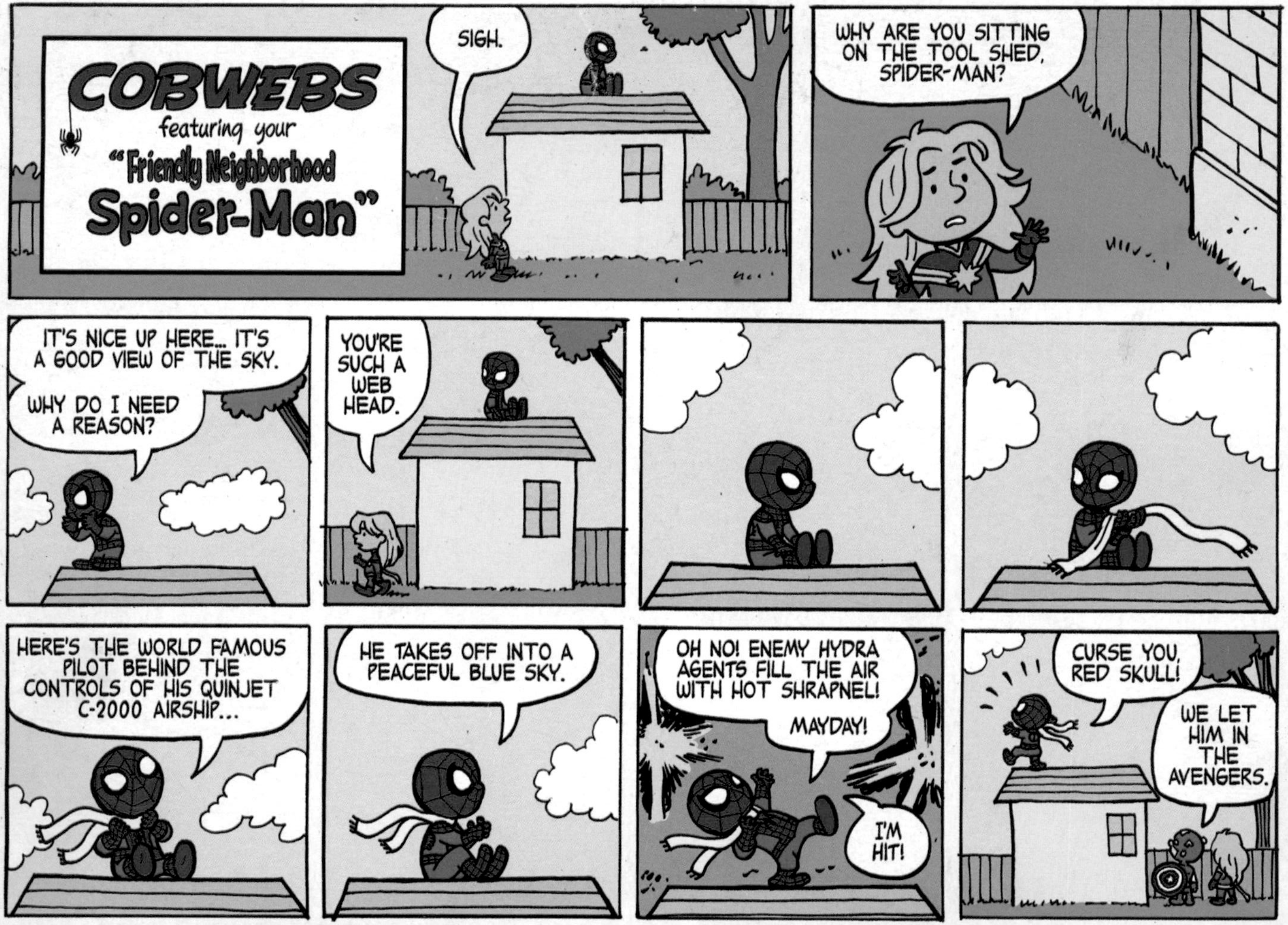

COBWEBS
featuring your "Friendly Neighborhood Spider-Man"
SIGH.
WHY ARE YOU SITTING ON THE TOOL SHED, SPIDER-MAN?
IT'S NICE UP HERE... IT'S A GOOD VIEW OF THE SKY.
WHY DO I NEED A REASON?
YOU'RE SUCH A WEB HEAD.
HERE'S THE WORLD FAMOUS PILOT BEHIND THE CONTROLS OF HIS QUINJET C-2000 AIRSHIP...
HE TAKES OFF INTO A PEACEFUL BLUE SKY.
OH NO! ENEMY HYDRA AGENTS FILL THE AIR WITH HOT SHRAPNEL!
MAYDAY!
I'M HIT!
CURSE YOU, RED SKULL!
WE LET HIM IN THE AVENGERS.

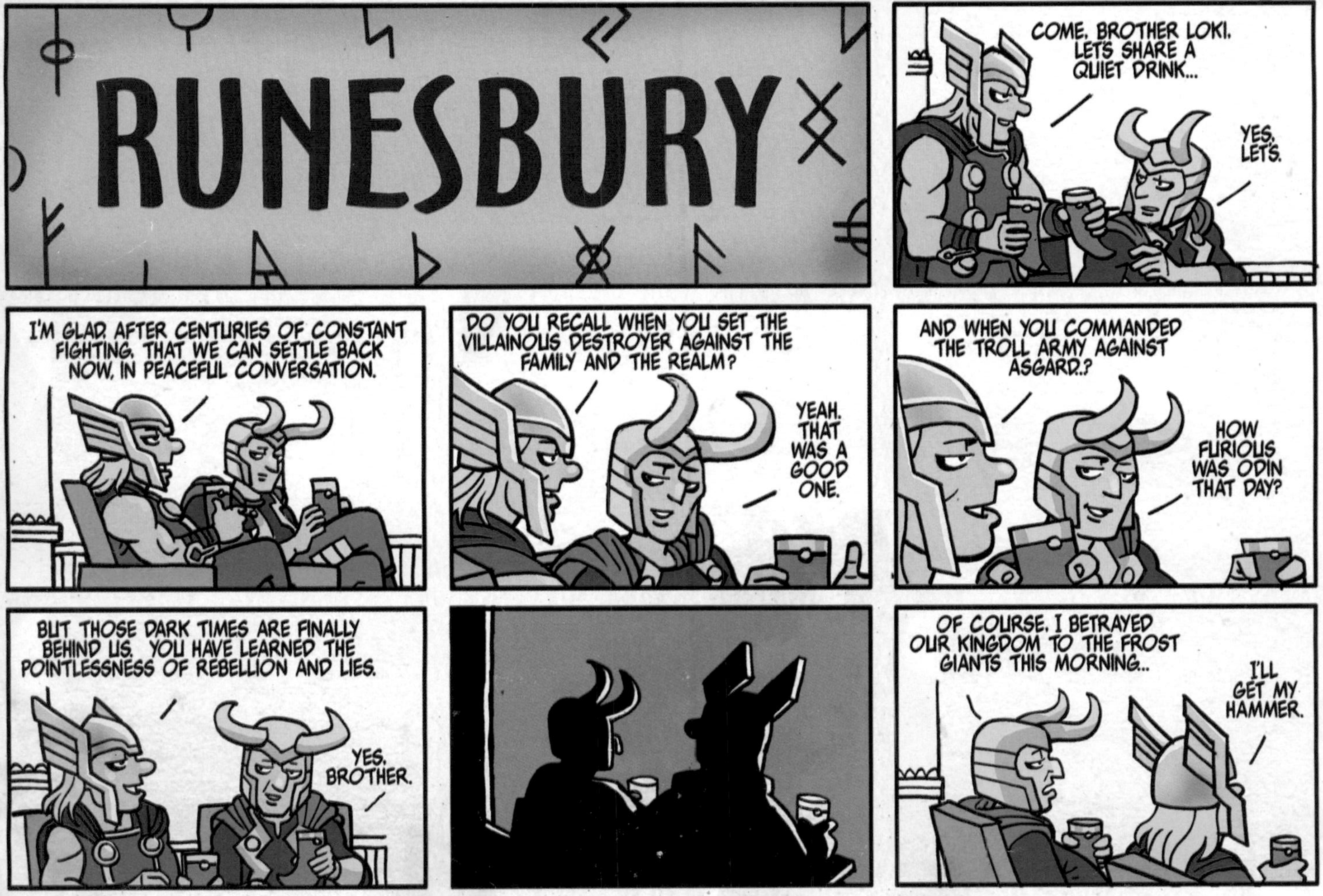
RUNESBURY
COME, BROTHER LOKI. LET'S SHARE A QUIET DRINK...
YES, LET'S.
I'M GLAD, AFTER CENTURIES OF CONSTANT FIGHTING, THAT WE CAN SETTLE BACK NOW, IN PEACEFUL CONVERSATION.
DO YOU RECALL WHEN YOU SET THE VILLAINOUS DESTROYER AGAINST THE FAMILY AND THE REALM?
YEAH. THAT WAS A GOOD ONE.
AND WHEN YOU COMMANDED THE TROLL ARMY AGAINST ASGARD..?
HOW FURIOUS WAS ODIN THAT DAY?
BUT THOSE DARK TIMES ARE FINALLY BEHIND US. YOU HAVE LEARNED THE POINTLESSNESS OF REBELLION AND LIES.
YES, BROTHER.
OF COURSE, I BETRAYED OUR KINGDOM TO THE FROST GIANTS THIS MORNING...
I'LL GET MY HAMMER.

DAILY BUGLE
NEW YORK'S FUNNIEST DAILY NEWSPAPER

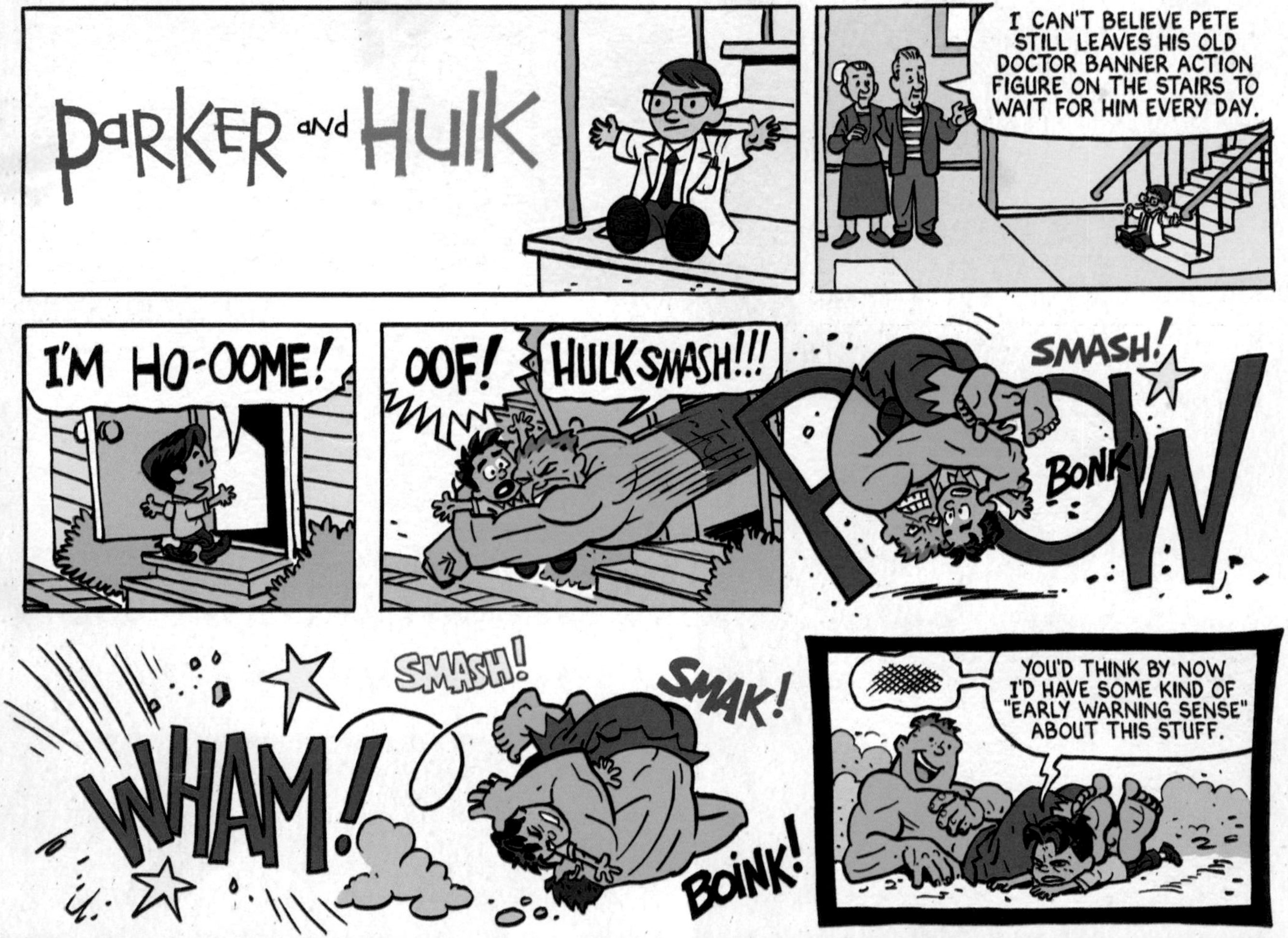
PARKER and HULK
I CAN'T BELIEVE PETE STILL LEAVES HIS OLD DOCTOR BANNER ACTION FIGURE ON THE STAIRS TO WAIT FOR HIM EVERY DAY.
I'M HO-OOME!
OOF!
HULK SMASH!!!
POW
SMASH!
BONK
WHAM!
SMASH!
SMAK!
BOINK!
YOU'D THINK BY NOW I'D HAVE SOME KIND OF "EARLY WARNING SENSE" ABOUT THIS STUFF.

DAILY BUGLE

NEW YORK'S FUNNIEST DAILY NEWSPAPER

the Strange Side

Making s'more-mammus.

Marvel Dog

Forget it. Last time I shooed him off the couch, he teleported me to Brazil.

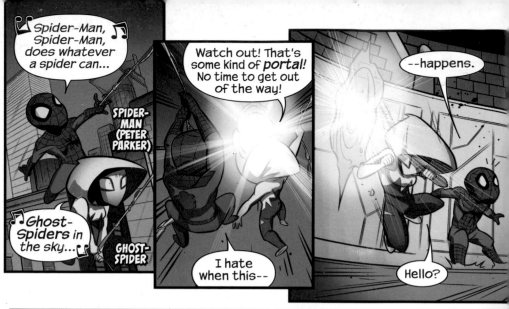

♪ Spider-Man, Spider-Man, does whatever a spider can... ♪

SPIDER-MAN (PETER PARKER)

♪ Ghost-Spiders in the sky... ♪

GHOST-SPIDER

Watch out! That's some kind of *portal*! No time to get out of the way!

I hate when this--

--happens.

Hello?

"Anyone home?"

Quiet day today...

SPIDER-WOMAN

...of course, I could be wrong!

What--?

SILK

What about my hot dooooogg?

SPIDER-GIRL

You want relish on that?

...

Lady?

Another day, another crimina--

Huh?

SPIDER-MAN (MILES MORALES)

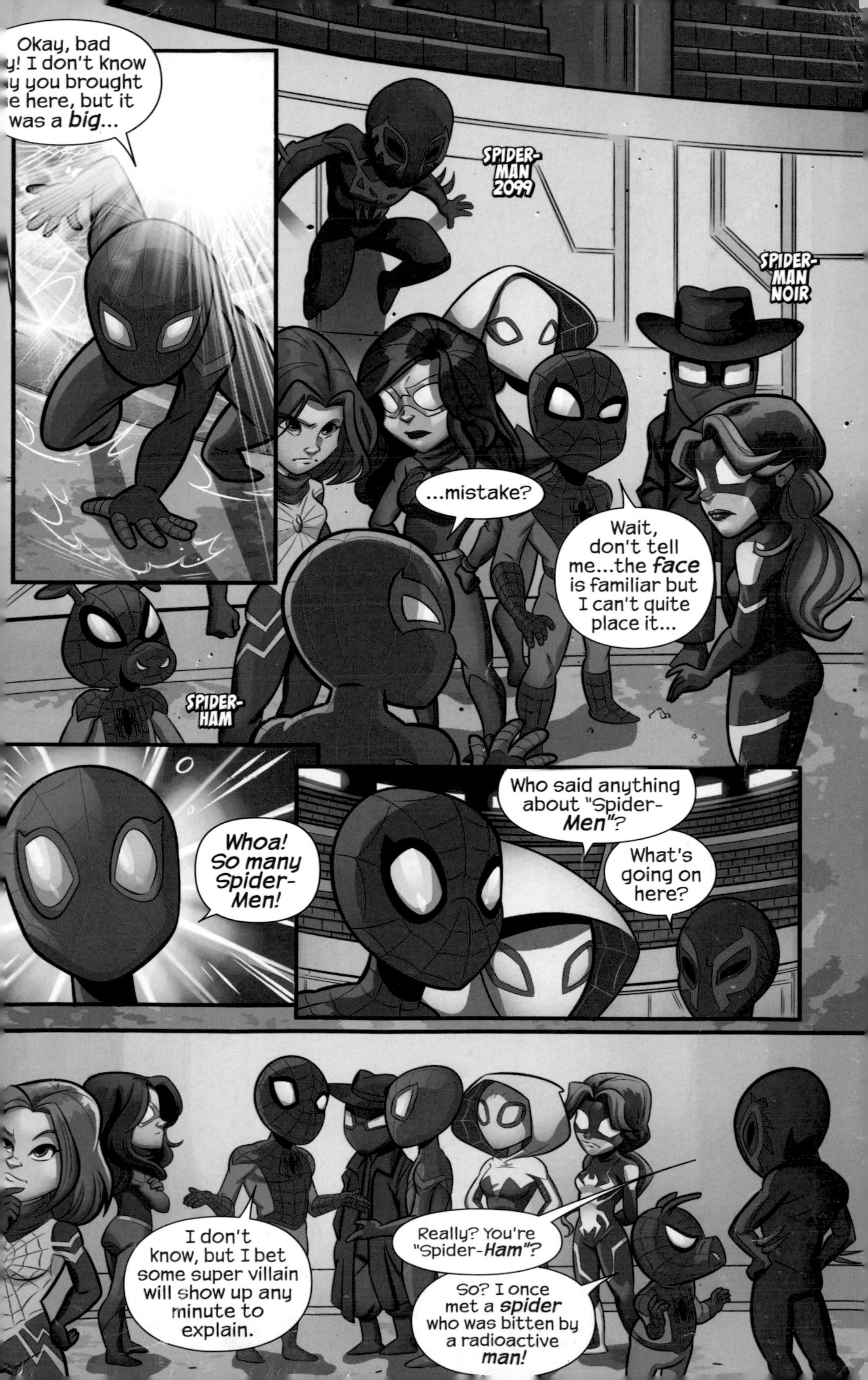

Okay, bad y! I don't know y you brought e here, but it was a big...
SPIDER-MAN 2099
SPIDER-MAN NOIR
...mistake?
Wait, don't tell me...the face is familiar but I can't quite place it...
SPIDER-HAM
Whoa! So many Spider-Men!
Who said anything about "Spider-Men"?
What's going on here?
I don't know, but I bet some super villain will show up any minute to explain.
Really? You're "Spider-Ham"?
So? I once met a spider who was bitten by a radioactive man!

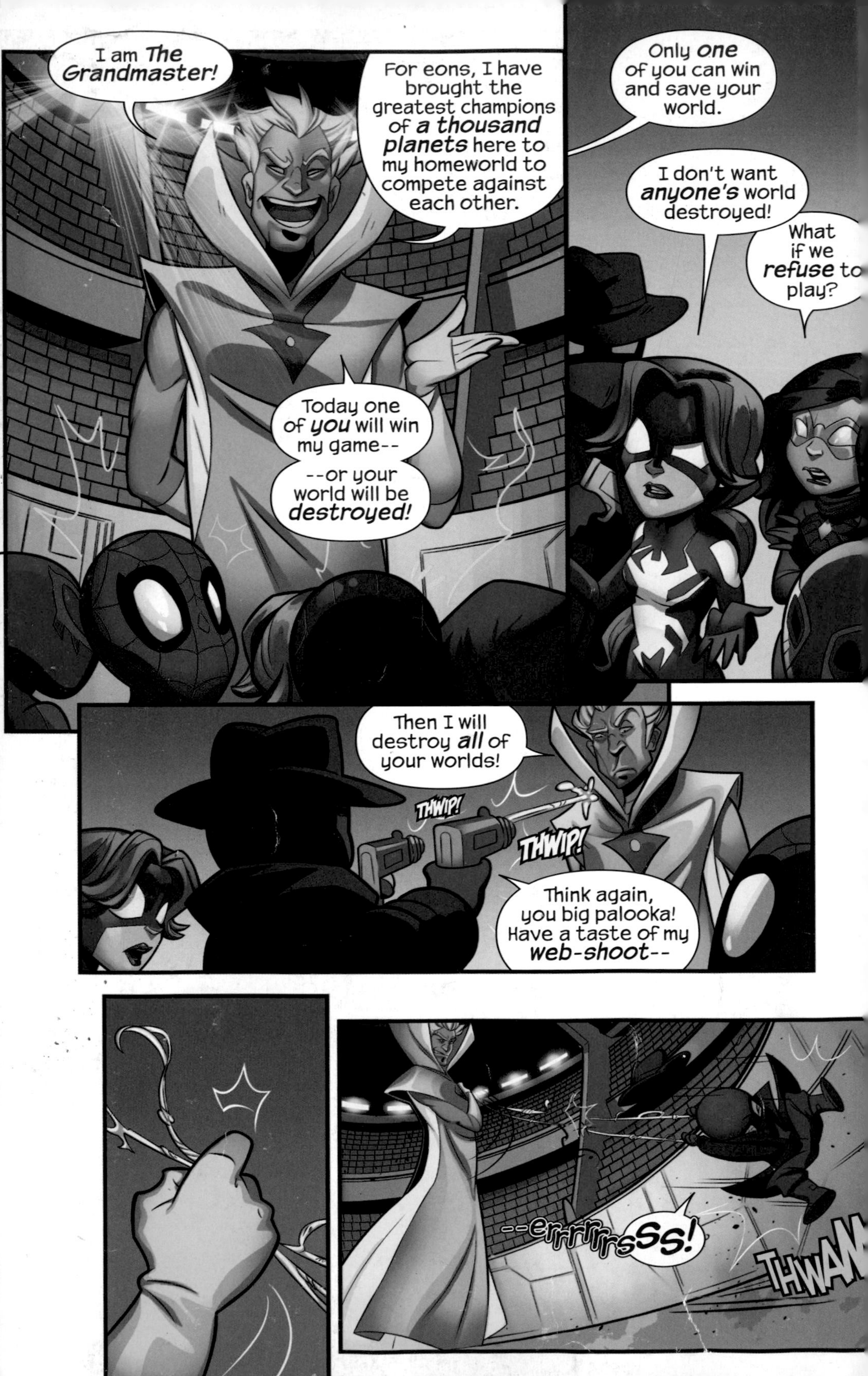
I am The Grandmaster!
For eons, I have brought the greatest champions of a thousand planets here to my homeworld to compete against each other.
Today one of you will win my game--
--or your world will be destroyed!
Only one of you can win and save your world.
I don't want anyone's world destroyed!
What if we refuse to play?
Then I will destroy all of your worlds!
THWIP!
THWIP!
Think again, you big palooka! Have a taste of my web-shoot--
--errrrrrsSS!
THWAM

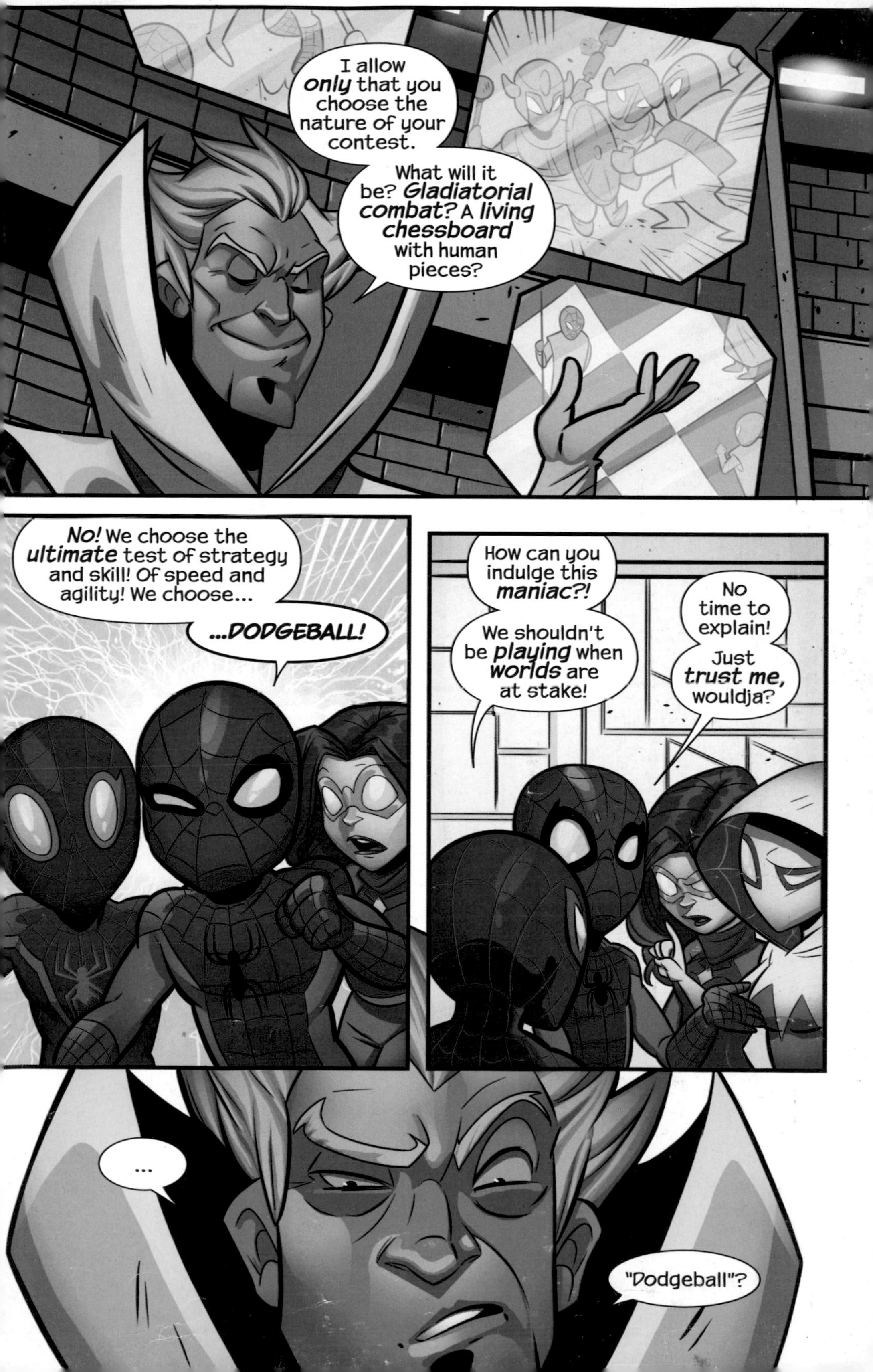
I allow only that you choose the nature of your contest.
What will it be? Gladiatorial combat? A living chessboard with human pieces?
No! We choose the ultimate test of strategy and skill! Of speed and agility! We choose...
...DODGEBALL!
How can you indulge this maniac?!
We shouldn't be playing when worlds are at stake!
No time to explain!
Just trust me, wouldja?
...
"Dodgeball"?

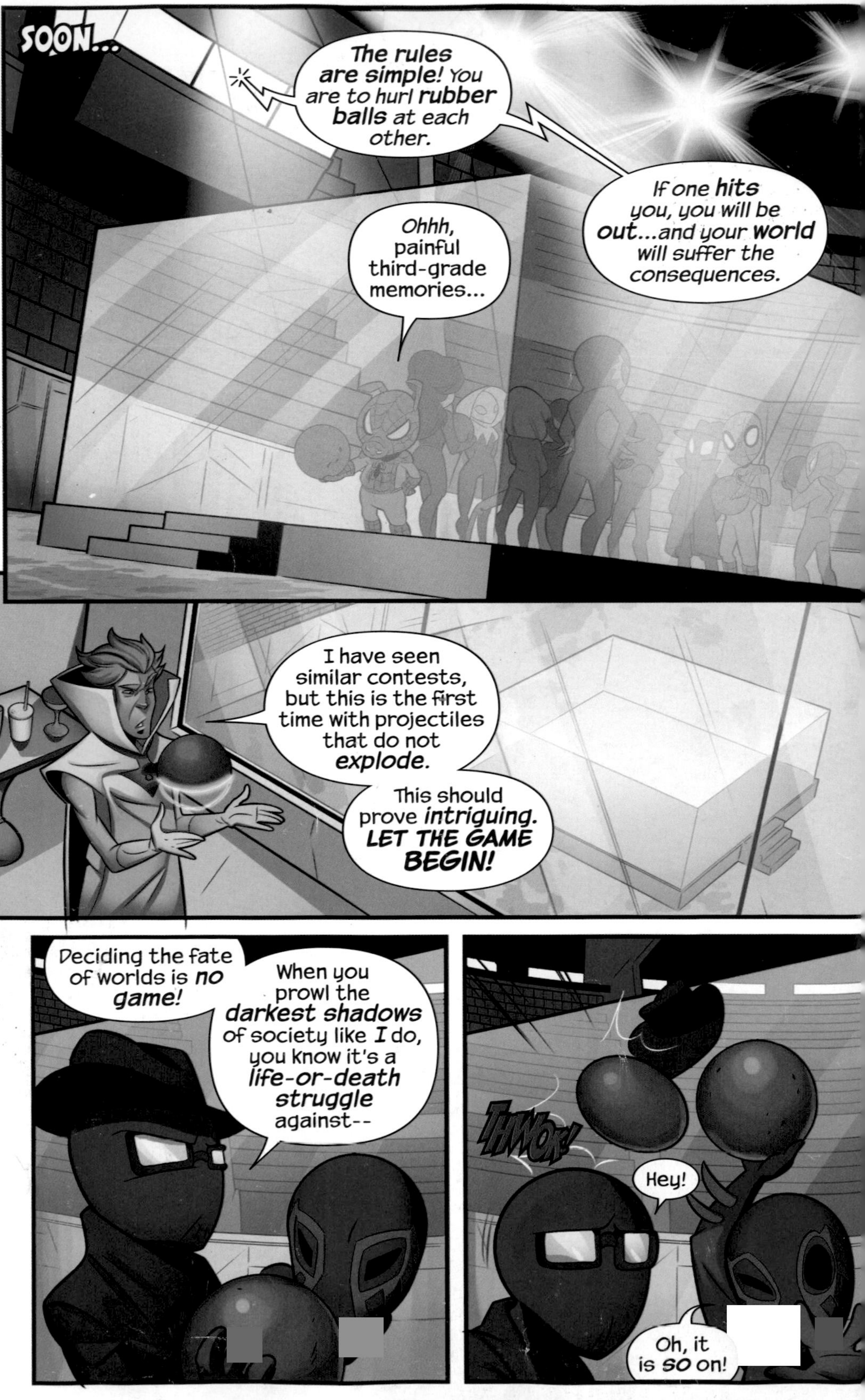
SOON...
The rules are simple! You are to hurl rubber balls at each other.
If one hits you, you will be out...and your world will suffer the consequences.
Ohhh, painful third-grade memories...
I have seen similar contests, but this is the first time with projectiles that do not explode.
This should prove intriguing. LET THE GAME BEGIN!
Deciding the fate of worlds is no game!
When you prowl the darkest shadows of society like I do, you know it's a life-or-death struggle against--
THWOK!
Hey!
Oh, it is SO on!

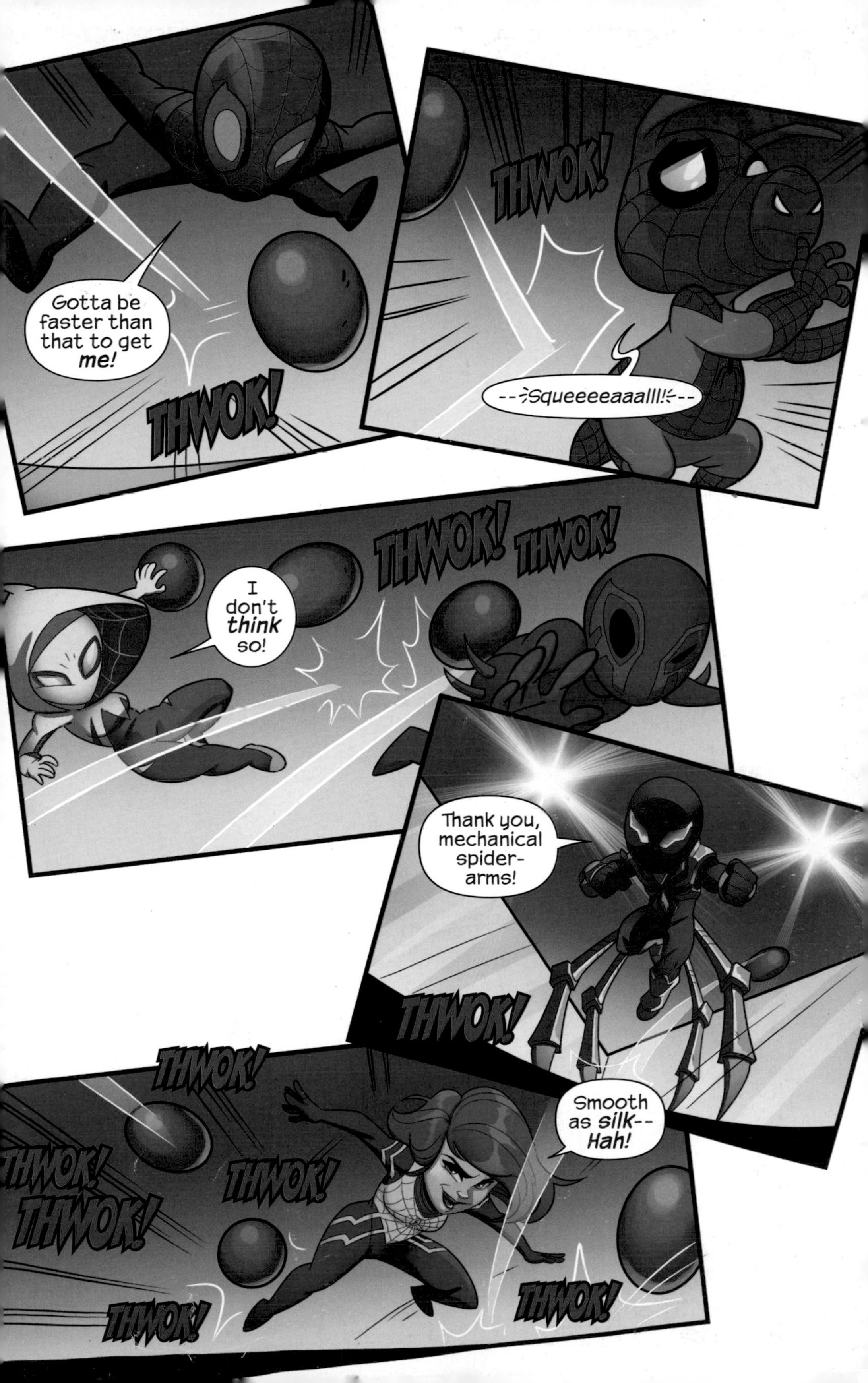

Gotta be faster than that to get *me!*
THWOK!
THWOK!
--Squeeeeaaalll!--
I don't *think* so!
THWOK!
THWOK!
Thank you, mechanical spider-arms!
THWOK!
THWOK!
THWOK!
THWOK!
THWOK!
Smooth as *silk*-- *Hah!*
THWOK!
THWOK!

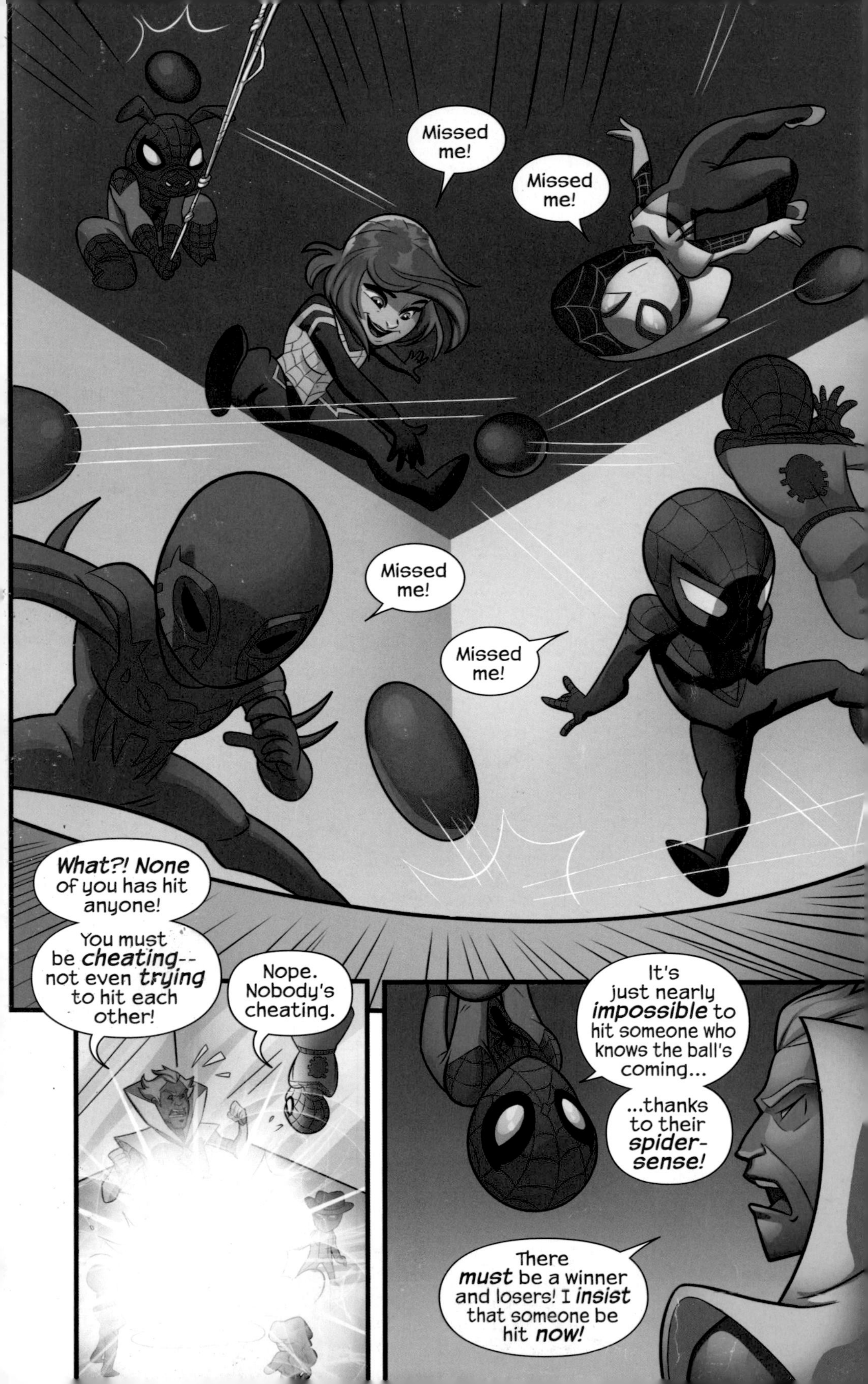
Missed me!
Missed me!
Missed me!
Missed me!
What?! None of you has hit anyone!
You must be cheating--not even trying to hit each other!
Nope. Nobody's cheating.
It's just nearly impossible to hit someone who knows the ball's coming...
...thanks to their spider-sense!
There must be a winner and losers! I insist that someone be hit now!

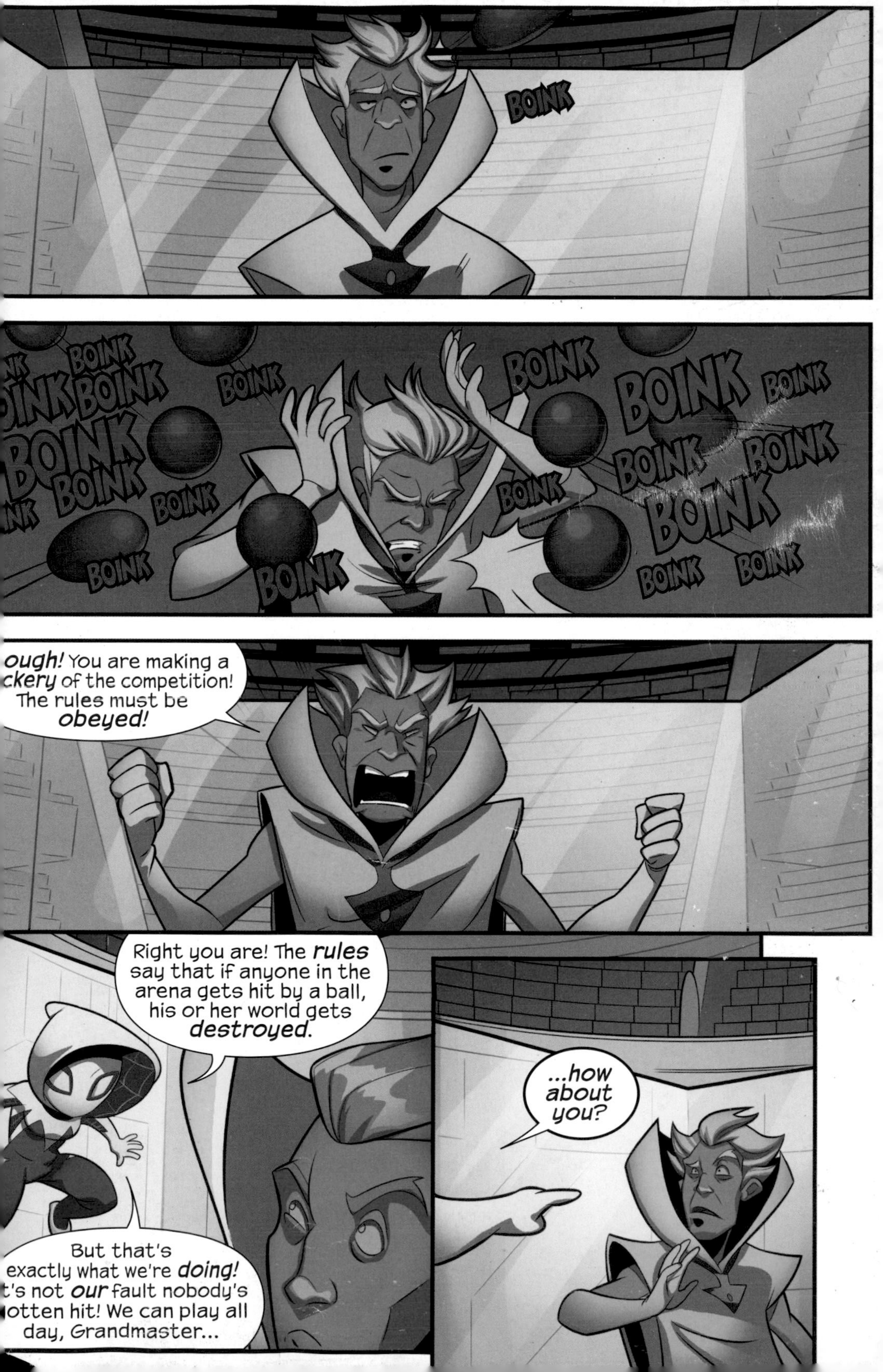
BOINK
BOINK
BOINK
BOINK
BOINK
BOINK
BOINK
BOINK
BOINK
BOINK
BOINK
BOINK
BOINK
BOINK
BOINK
BOINK
BOINK
BOINK
BOINK
ough! You are making a ckery of the competition! The rules must be obeyed!
Right you are! The rules say that if anyone in the arena gets hit by a ball, his or her world gets destroyed.
But that's exactly what we're doing! t's not our fault nobody's otten hit! We can play all day, Grandmaster...
...how about you?

It is true. The failure is my own for not knowing the skills of my combatants... and for that, *I* am the loser of this contest!

Very well. I shall destroy my world.

Whoa!

You mean *this* world? That we're *standing* on?

The rules demand it.

Not necessarily!

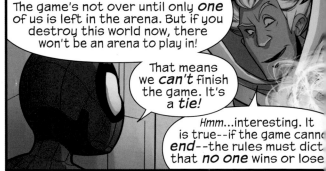

The game's not over until only **one** of us is left in the arena. But if you destroy this world now, there won't be an arena to play in!

That means we *can't* finish the game. It's a *tie!*

Hmm...interesting. It is true--if the game canno[t] **end**--the rules must dict[ate] that **no one** wins or lose[s]

Very well! I declare this contest a *tie*-- and *return* you to your worlds!

Pretty *smart thinking,* Spidey.

Thanks, other Spidey.

Home again--and Earth isn't even *destroyed!*

Saving the world is *exhausting!* I can't wait to go stretch out on my couch.

Or grab some *pizza!*

Sounds good. But *first...*

Anyone for a *rematch?*

EN[D]

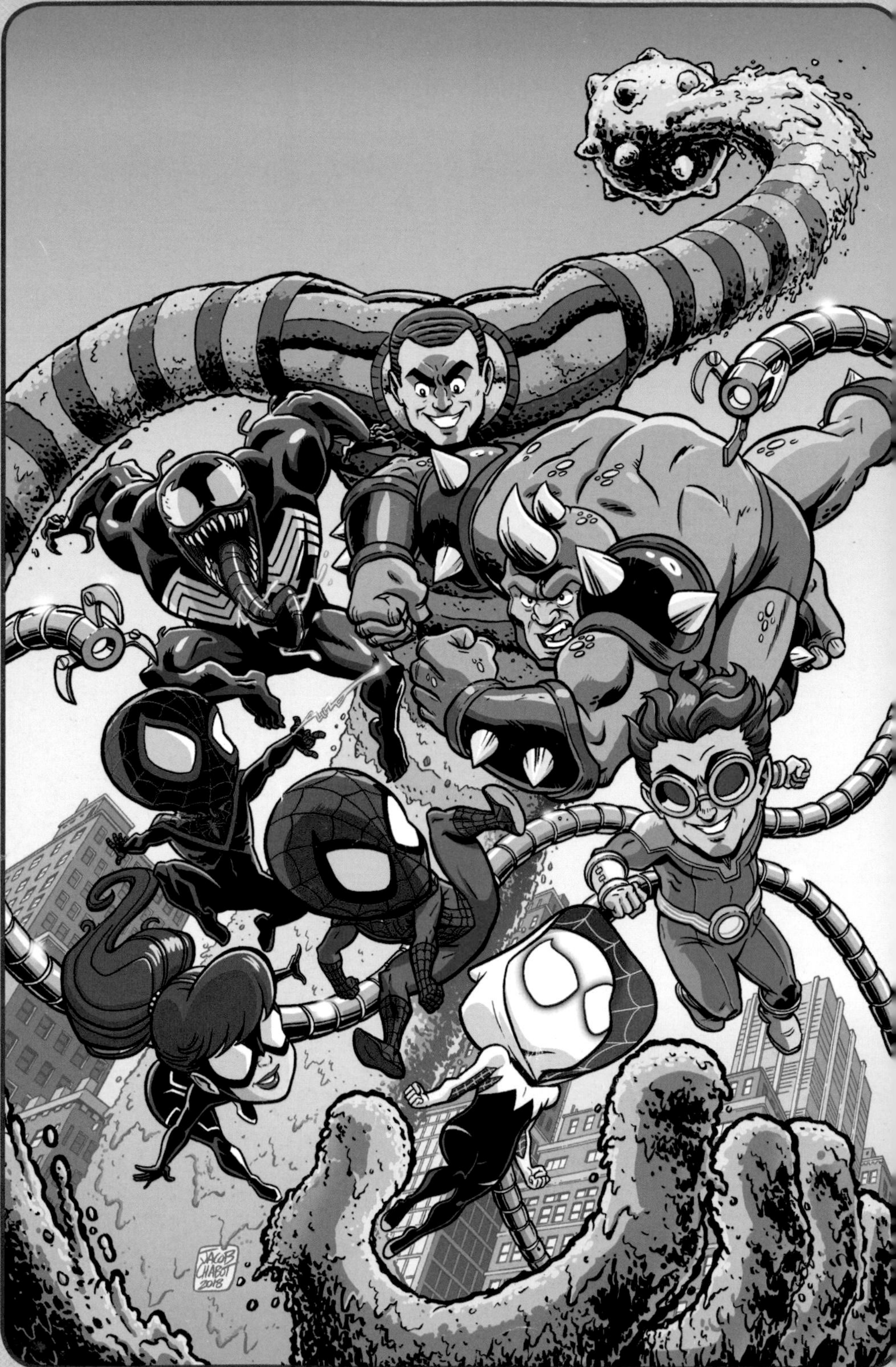
JACOB CHABOT 2018

Web of Intrigue

cover by Jacob Chabot

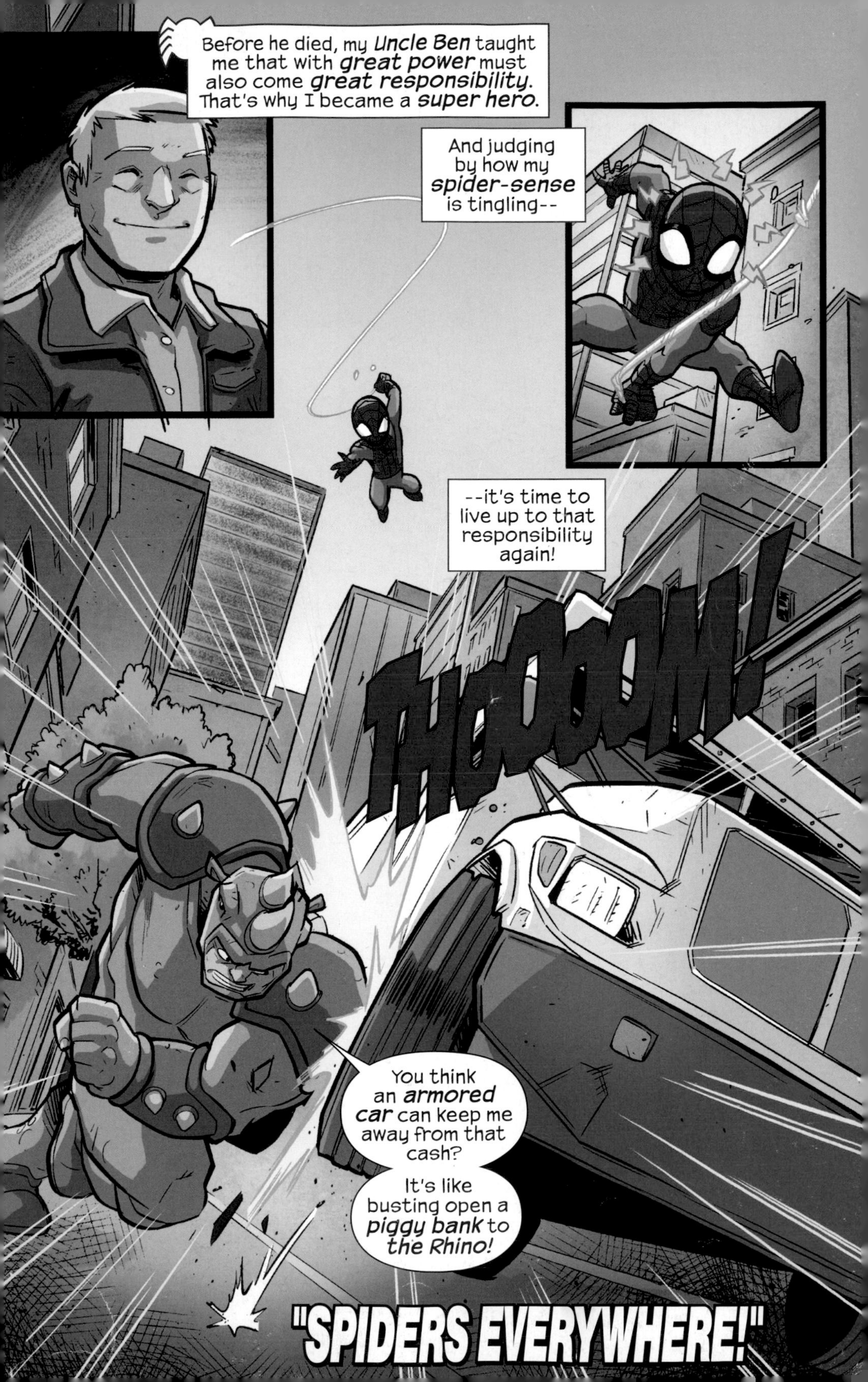
Before he died, my Uncle Ben taught me that with great power must also come great responsibility. That's why I became a super hero.
And judging by how my spider-sense is tingling--
--it's time to live up to that responsibility again!
THOOOOM!
You think an armored car can keep me away from that cash?
It's like busting open a piggy bank to the Rhino!
"SPIDERS EVERYWHERE!"

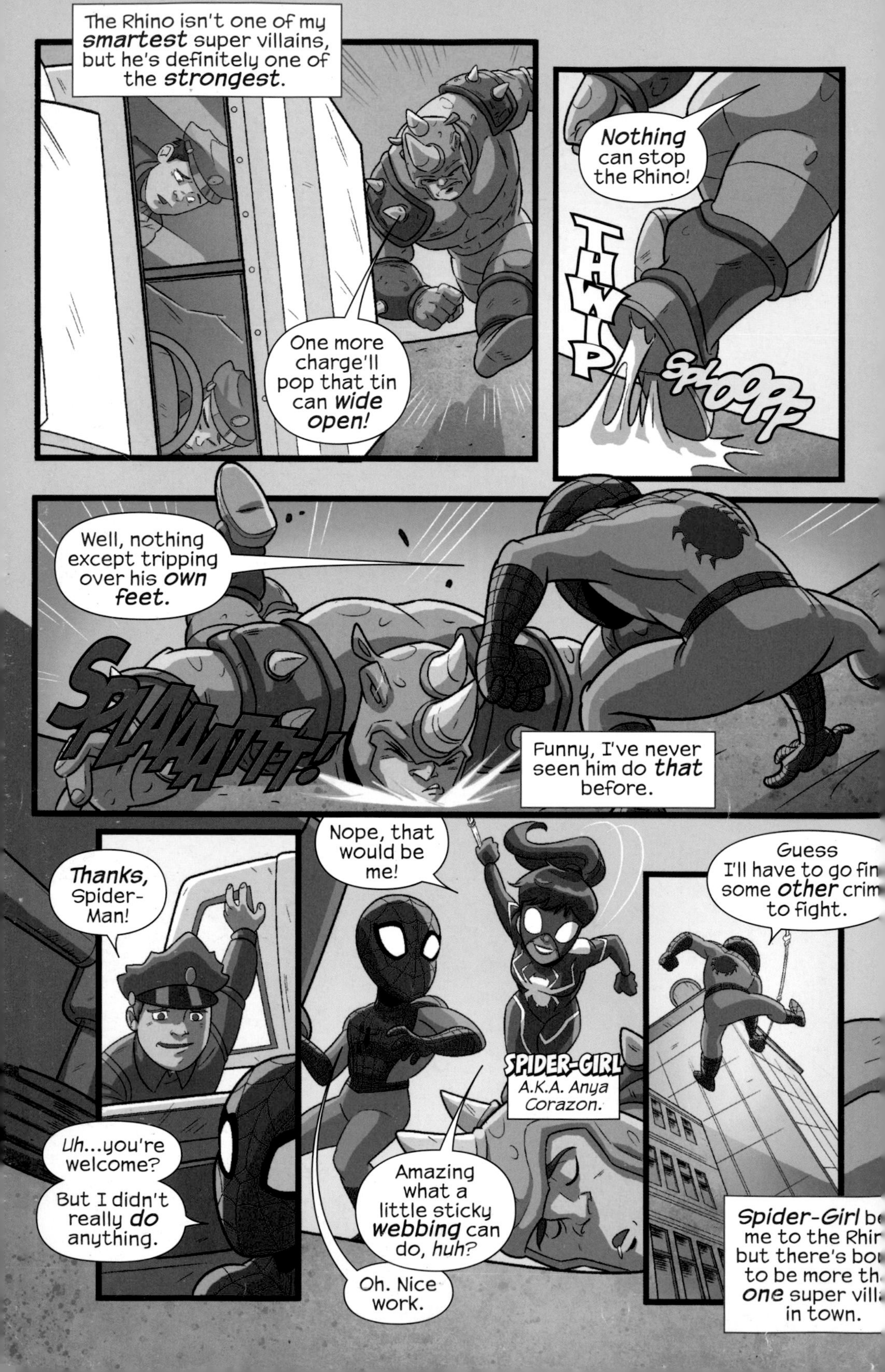

The Rhino isn't one of my smartest super villains, but he's definitely one of the strongest.
One more charge'll pop that tin can wide open!
Nothing can stop the Rhino!
THWIP
SPLOOP
Well, nothing except tripping over his own feet.
SPLAAATTT!
Funny, I've never seen him do that before.
Thanks, Spider-Man!
Uh...you're welcome?
But I didn't really do anything.
Nope, that would be me!
SPIDER-GIRL
A.K.A. Anya Corazon.
Amazing what a little sticky webbing can do, huh?
Oh. Nice work.
Guess I'll have to go fin some other crim to fight.
Spider-Girl be me to the Rhir but there's bo to be more th one super vill in town.

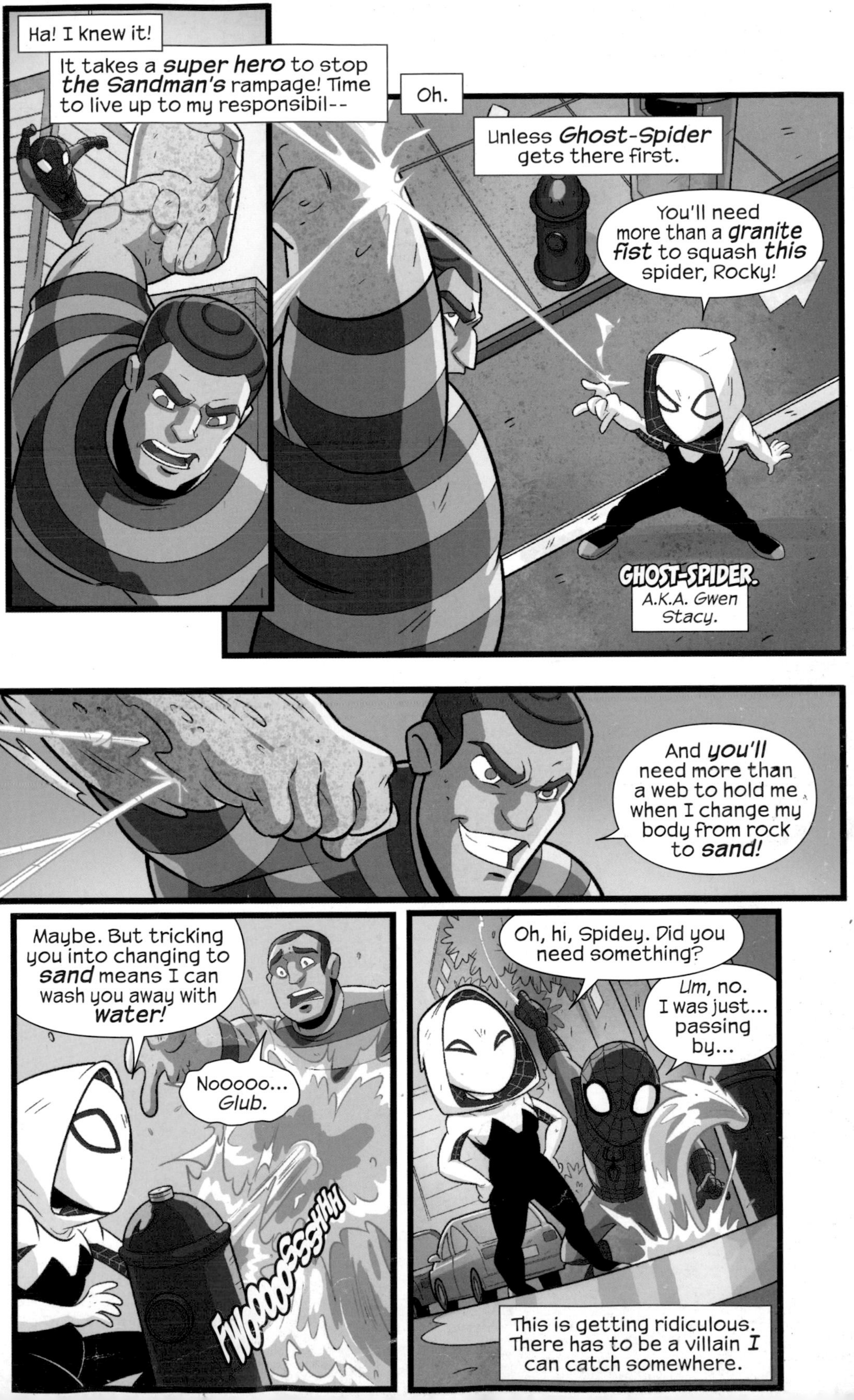

Ha! I knew it!
It takes a *super hero* to stop *the Sandman's* rampage! Time to live up to my responsibil--
Oh.
Unless *Ghost-Spider* gets there first.
You'll need more than a *granite fist* to squash *this* spider, Rocky!
GHOST-SPIDER.
A.K.A. Gwen Stacy.
And *you'll* need more than a web to hold me when I change my body from rock to *sand!*
Maybe. But tricking you into changing to *sand* means I can wash you away with *water!*
Nooooo... Glub.
FWOOOOSSSHHH
Oh, hi, Spidey. Did you need something?
Um, no. I was just... passing by...
This is getting ridiculous. There has to be a villain *I* can catch somewhere.

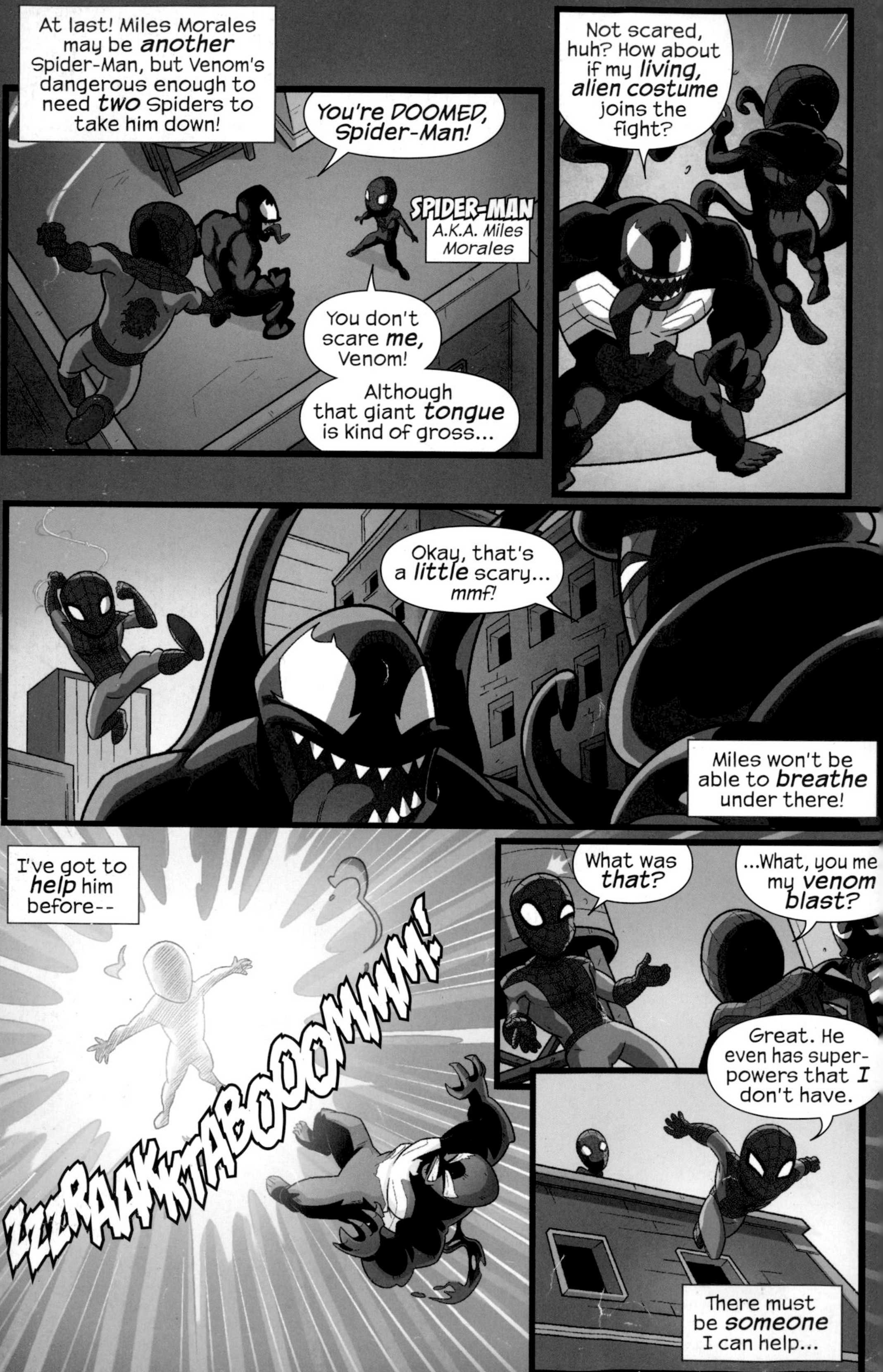
At last! Miles Morales may be *another* Spider-Man, but Venom's dangerous enough to need *two* Spiders to take him down!
You're DOOMED, Spider-Man!
SPIDER-MAN
A.K.A. Miles Morales
You don't scare *me,* Venom!
Although that giant *tongue* is kind of gross...
Not scared, huh? How about if my *living, alien costume* joins the fight?
Okay, that's a *little* scary... *mmf!*
Miles won't be able to *breathe* under there!
I've got to *help* him before--
ZZZRAAKKTABOOOMMM!
What was *that?*
...What, you me my *venom blast?*
Great. He even has super-powers that *I* don't have.
There must be *someone* I can help...

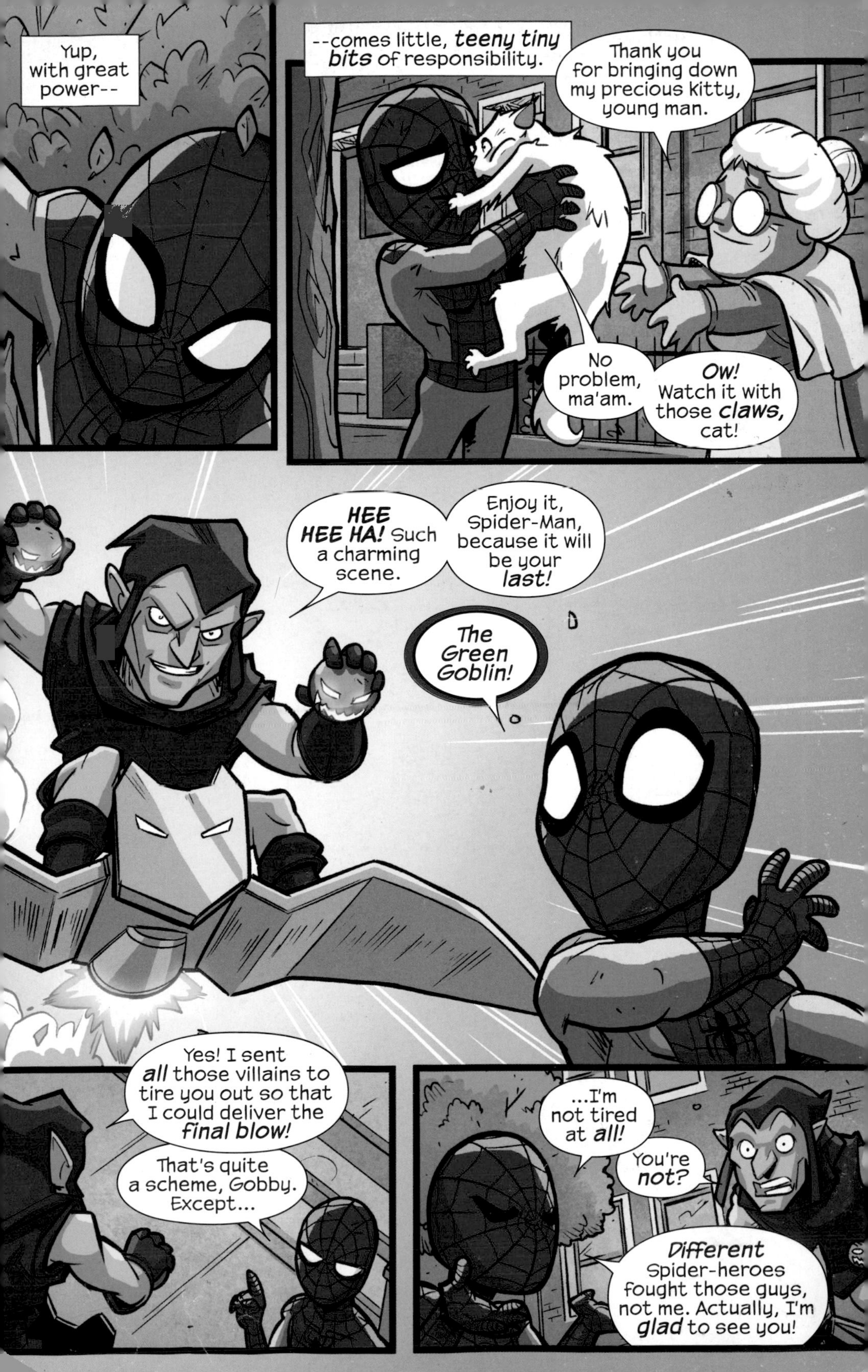
Yup, with great power--
--comes little, teeny tiny bits of responsibility.
Thank you for bringing down my precious kitty, young man.
No problem, ma'am.
Ow! Watch it with those claws, cat!
HEE HEE HA! Such a charming scene.
Enjoy it, Spider-Man, because it will be your last!
The Green Goblin!
Yes! I sent all those villains to tire you out so that I could deliver the final blow!
That's quite a scheme, Gobby. Except...
...I'm not tired at all!
You're not?
Different Spider-heroes fought those guys, not me. Actually, I'm glad to see you!

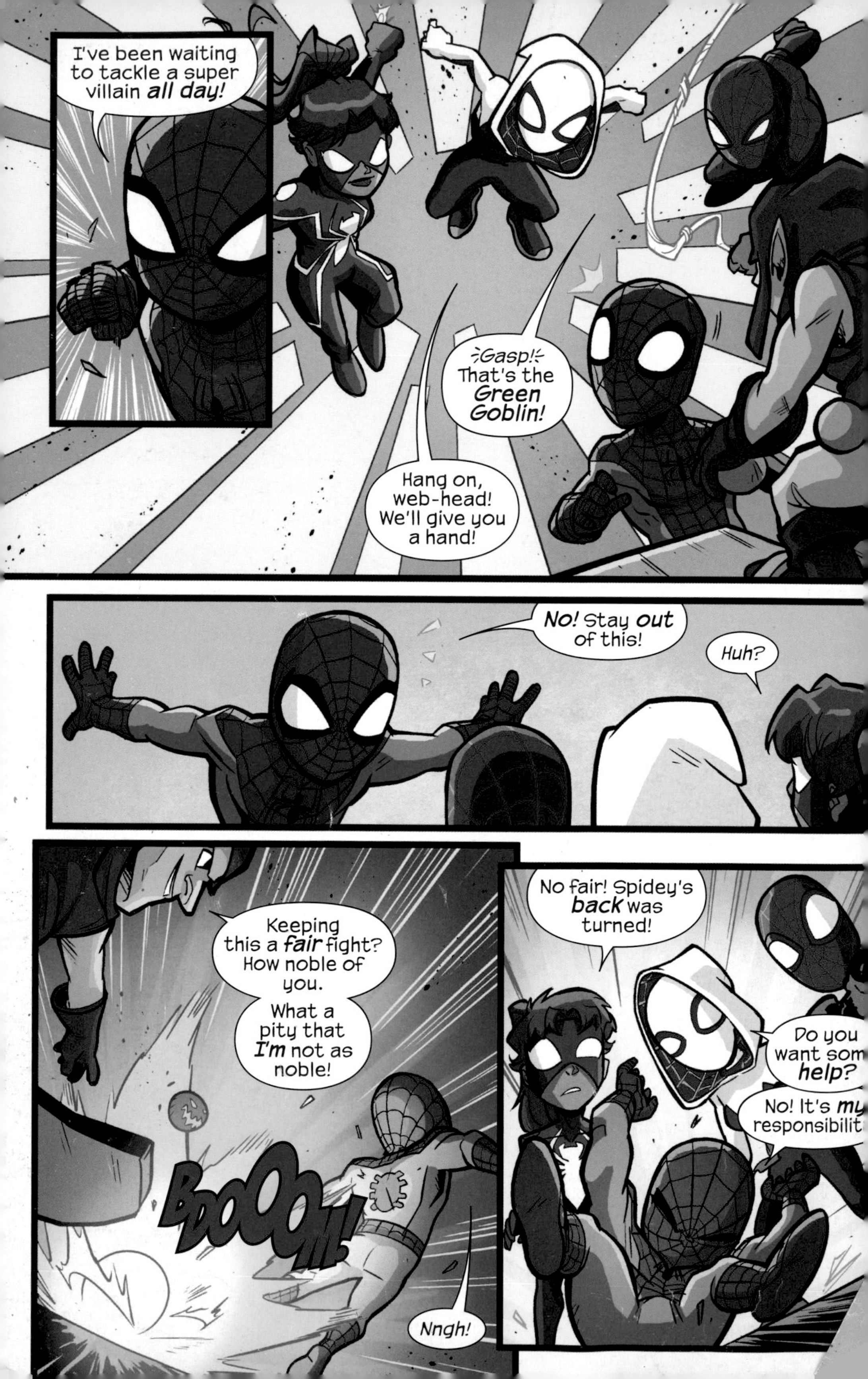
I've been waiting to tackle a super villain *all day!*
⁝Gasp!⁝ That's the *Green Goblin!*
Hang on, web-head! We'll give you a hand!
No! Stay *out* of this!
Huh?
Keeping this a *fair* fight? How noble of you.
What a pity that *I'm* not as noble!
BOOOOM!
Nngh!
No fair! Spidey's *back* was turned!
Do you want som *help?*
No! It's *my* responsibilit

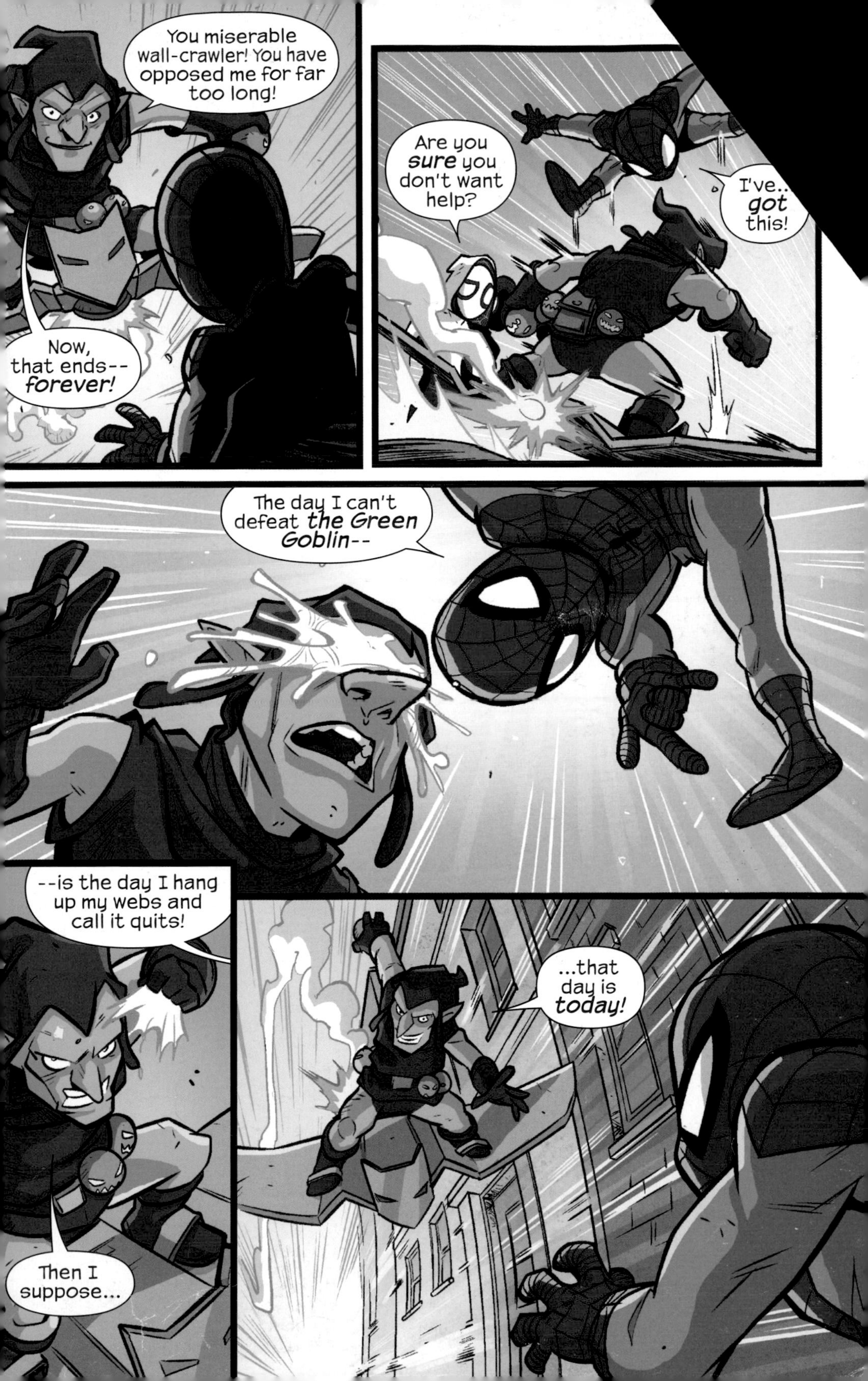

You miserable wall-crawler! You have opposed me for far too long!
Now, that ends-- *forever!*
Are you *sure* you don't want help?
I've... *got* this!
The day I can't defeat *the Green Goblin*--
--is the day I hang up my webs and call it quits!
Then I suppose...
...that day is *today!*

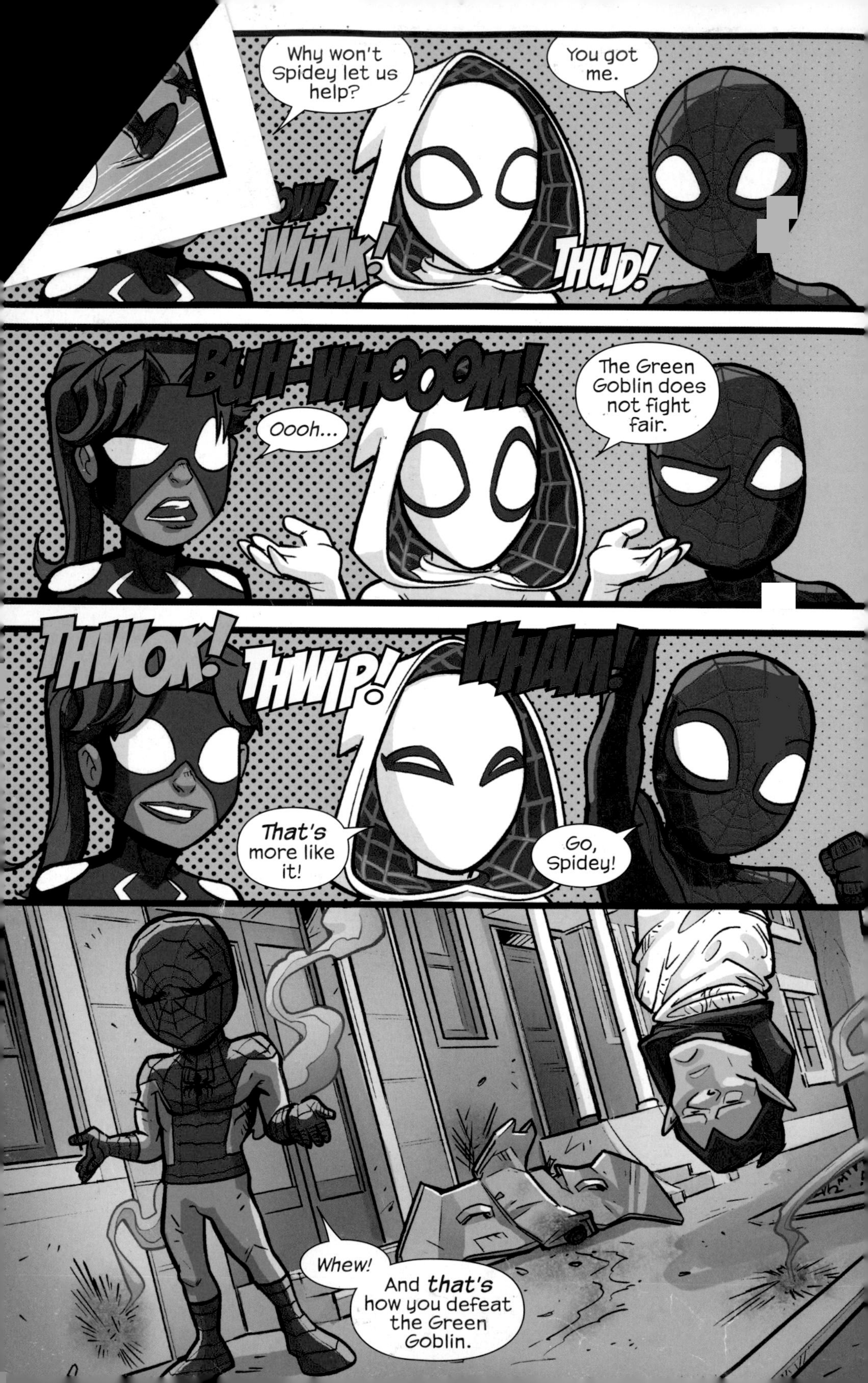
Why won't Spidey let us help?
You got me.
WHAK!
THUD!
BUH-WHOOOM!
Oooh...
The Green Goblin does not fight fair.
THWOK!
THWIP!
WHAM!
That's more like it!
Go, Spidey!
Whew!
And that's how you defeat the Green Goblin.

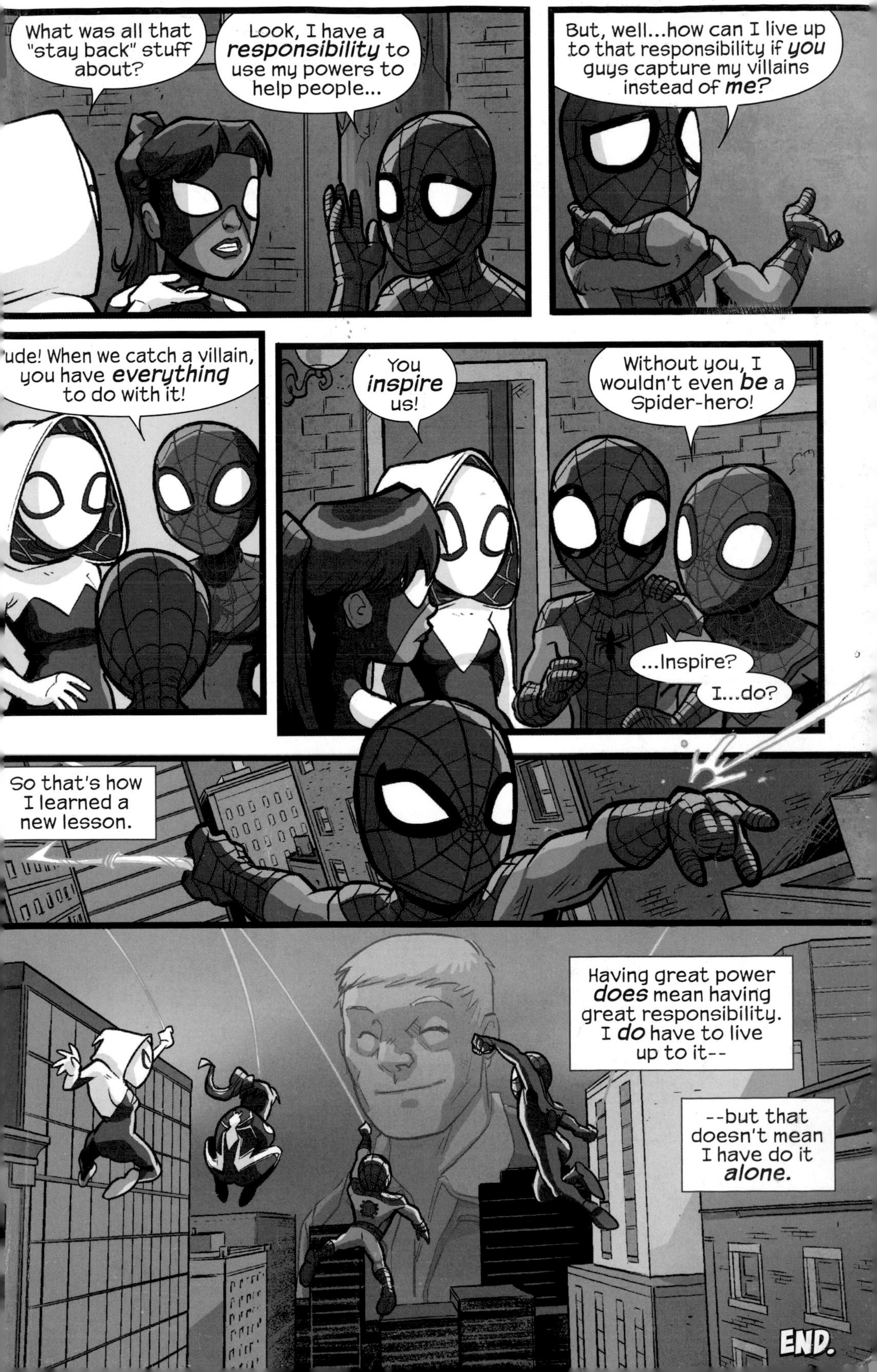

What was all that "stay back" stuff about?
Look, I have a responsibility to use my powers to help people...
But, well...how can I live up to that responsibility if you guys capture my villains instead of me?
ude! When we catch a villain, you have everything to do with it!
You inspire us!
Without you, I wouldn't even be a Spider-hero!
...Inspire?
I...do?
So that's how I learned a new lesson.
Having great power does mean having great responsibility. I do have to live up to it--
--but that doesn't mean I have do it alone.
END.

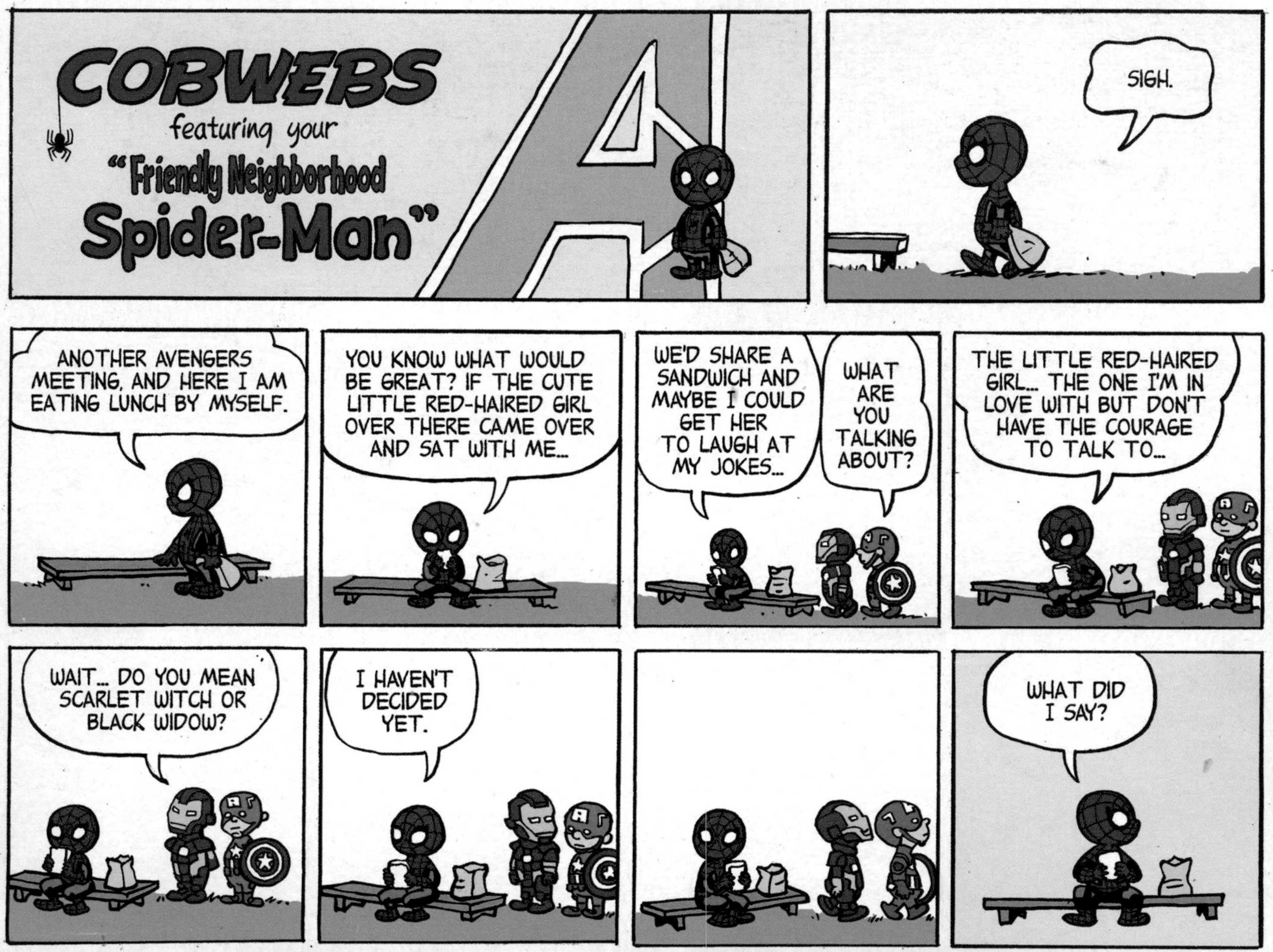
COBWEBS
featuring your
"Friendly Neighborhood
Spider-Man"
SIGH.
ANOTHER AVENGERS MEETING, AND HERE I AM EATING LUNCH BY MYSELF.
YOU KNOW WHAT WOULD BE GREAT? IF THE CUTE LITTLE RED-HAIRED GIRL OVER THERE CAME OVER AND SAT WITH ME...
WE'D SHARE A SANDWICH AND MAYBE I COULD GET HER TO LAUGH AT MY JOKES...
WHAT ARE YOU TALKING ABOUT?
THE LITTLE RED-HAIRED GIRL... THE ONE I'M IN LOVE WITH BUT DON'T HAVE THE COURAGE TO TALK TO...
WAIT... DO YOU MEAN SCARLET WITCH OR BLACK WIDOW?
I HAVEN'T DECIDED YET.
WHAT DID I SAY?

DAILY BUGLE
NEW YORK'S FUNNIEST DAILY NEWSPAPER

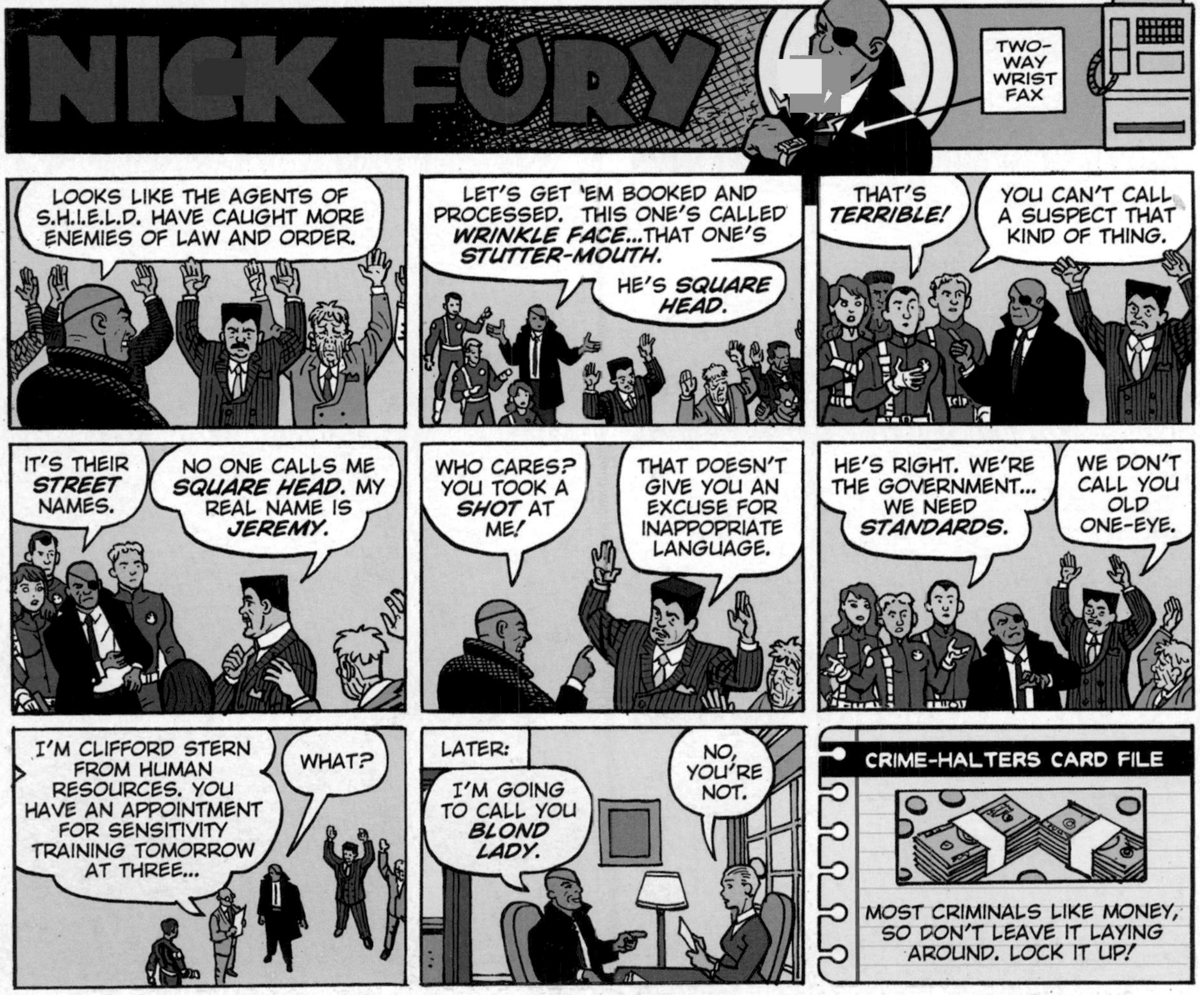
NICK FURY
TWO-WAY WRIST FAX
LOOKS LIKE THE AGENTS OF S.H.I.E.L.D. HAVE CAUGHT MORE ENEMIES OF LAW AND ORDER.
LET'S GET 'EM BOOKED AND PROCESSED. THIS ONE'S CALLED WRINKLE FACE...THAT ONE'S STUTTER-MOUTH.
HE'S SQUARE HEAD.
THAT'S TERRIBLE!
YOU CAN'T CALL A SUSPECT THAT KIND OF THING.
IT'S THEIR STREET NAMES.
NO ONE CALLS ME SQUARE HEAD. MY REAL NAME IS JEREMY.
WHO CARES? YOU TOOK A SHOT AT ME!
THAT DOESN'T GIVE YOU AN EXCUSE FOR INAPPROPRIATE LANGUAGE.
HE'S RIGHT. WE'RE THE GOVERNMENT... WE NEED STANDARDS.
WE DON'T CALL YOU OLD ONE-EYE.
I'M CLIFFORD STERN FROM HUMAN RESOURCES. YOU HAVE AN APPOINTMENT FOR SENSITIVITY TRAINING TOMORROW AT THREE...
WHAT?
LATER:
I'M GOING TO CALL YOU BLOND LADY.
NO, YOU'RE NOT.
CRIME-HALTERS CARD FILE
MOST CRIMINALS LIKE MONEY, SO DON'T LEAVE IT LAYING AROUND. LOCK IT UP!

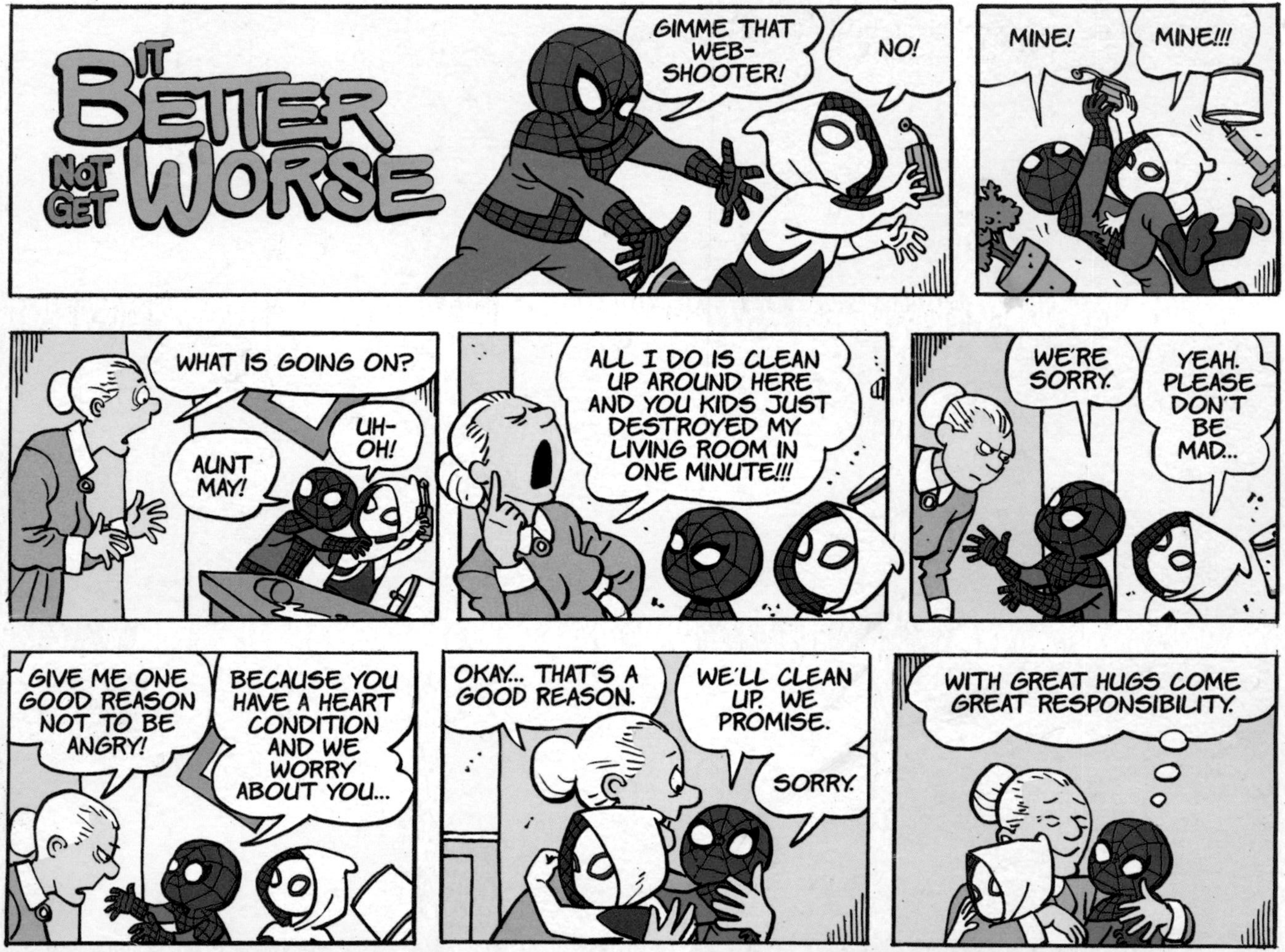
IT BETTER NOT GET WORSE
GIMME THAT WEB-SHOOTER!
NO!
MINE!
MINE!!!
WHAT IS GOING ON?
AUNT MAY!
UH-OH!
ALL I DO IS CLEAN UP AROUND HERE AND YOU KIDS JUST DESTROYED MY LIVING ROOM IN ONE MINUTE!!!
WE'RE SORRY.
YEAH. PLEASE DON'T BE MAD...
GIVE ME ONE GOOD REASON NOT TO BE ANGRY!
BECAUSE YOU HAVE A HEART CONDITION AND WE WORRY ABOUT YOU...
OKAY... THAT'S A GOOD REASON.
WE'LL CLEAN UP. WE PROMISE.
SORRY.
WITH GREAT HUGS COME GREAT RESPONSIBILITY.

DAILY BUGLE

NEW YORK'S FUNNIEST DAILY NEWSPAPER

the Strange Side

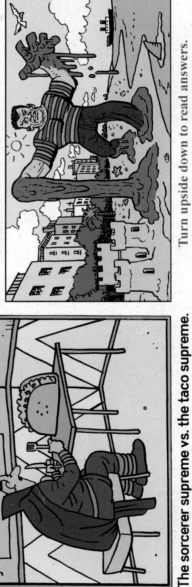

The sorcerer supreme vs. the taco supreme.

SPOT THE DIFFERENCES!

THE OBSERVATION GAME

HOW MANY DIFFERENCES CAN YOU FIND IN THE PICTURE BELOW?

In the top panel, Sandman is made of Atlantic sand.
In the bottom panel it's Pacific sand.

In the second panel, Sandman is humming to himself

Turn upside down to read answers.

script and art: Ty Templeton
colors: Keiren Smith

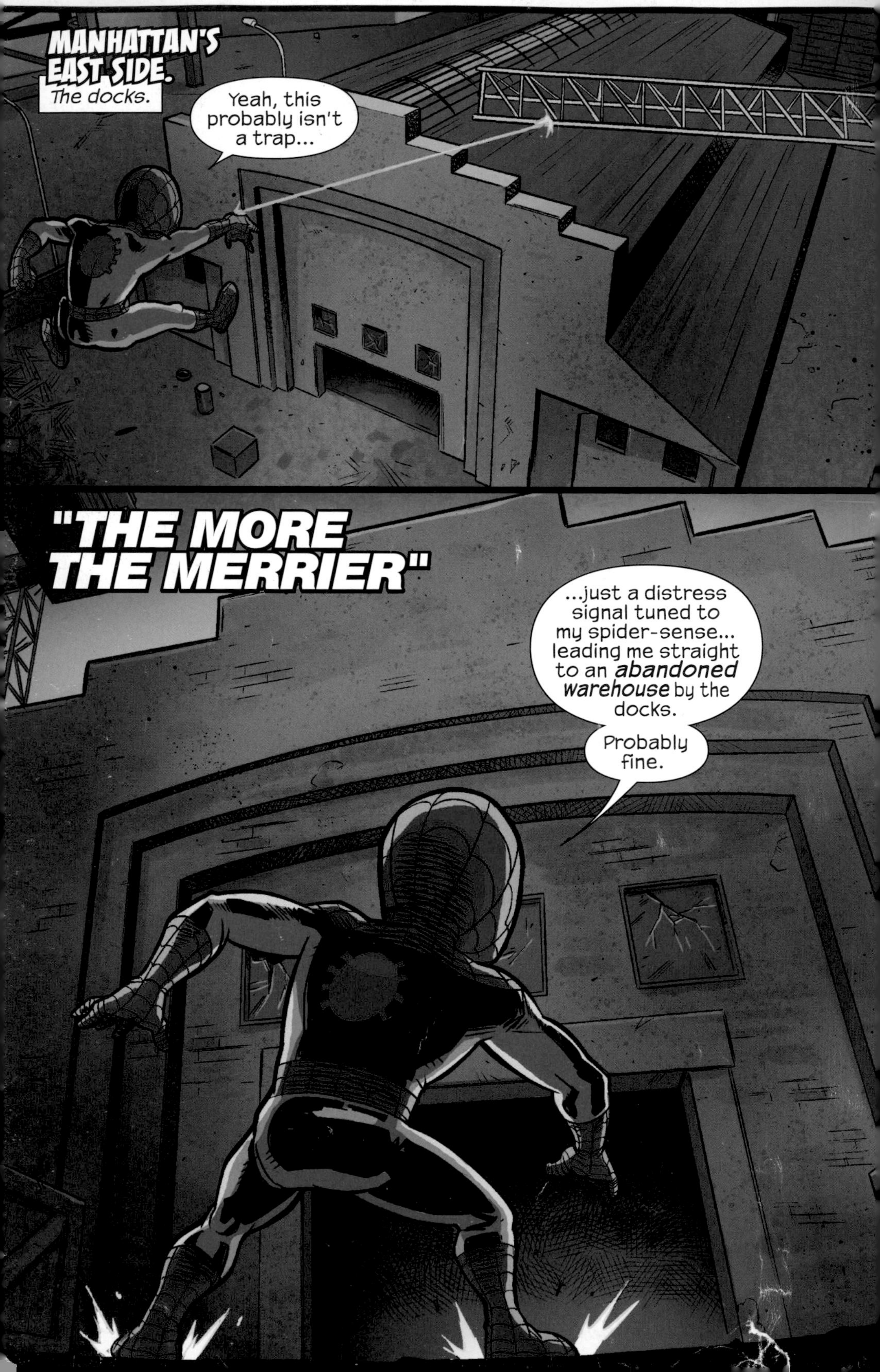
MANHATTAN'S EAST SIDE.
The docks.
Yeah, this probably isn't a trap...
"THE MORE THE MERRIER"
...just a distress signal tuned to my spider-sense... leading me straight to an *abandoned warehouse* by the docks.
Probably fine.

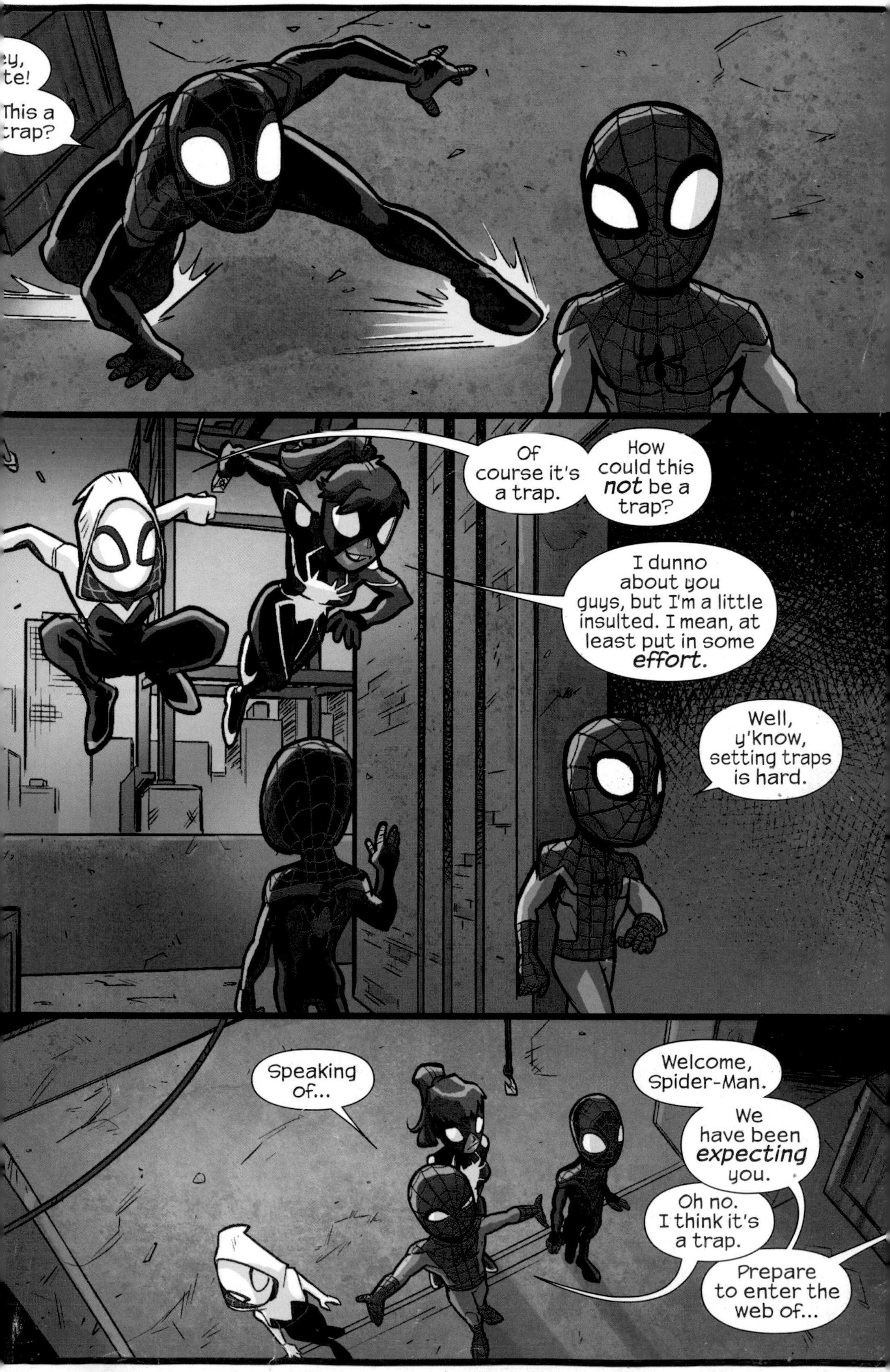

ey,
te!
This a
trap?
Of course it's a trap.
How could this *not* be a trap?
I dunno about you guys, but I'm a little insulted. I mean, at least put in some *effort.*
Well, y'know, setting traps is hard.
Speaking of...
Welcome, Spider-Man.
We have been *expecting* you.
Oh no. I think it's a trap.
Prepare to enter the web of...

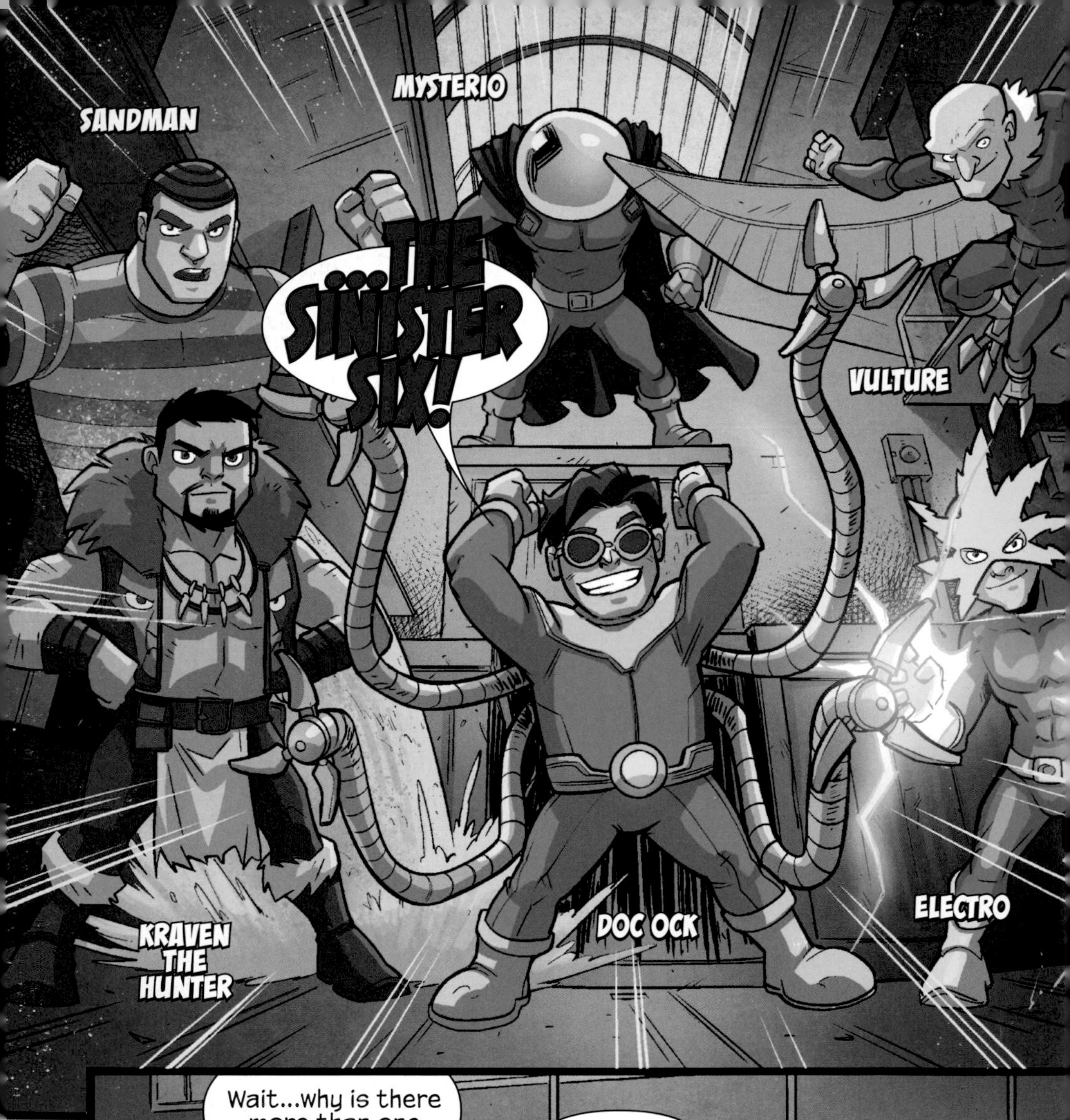
SANDMAN
MYSTERIO
...THE SINISTER SIX!
VULTURE
ELECTRO
DOC OCK
KRAVEN THE HUNTER

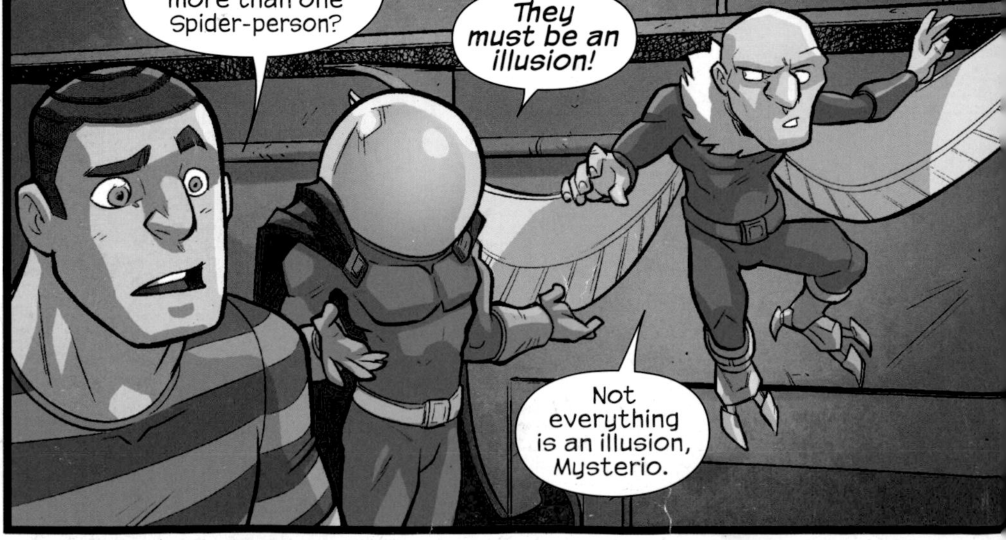
Wait...why is there more than one Spider-person?
They must be an illusion!
Not everything is an illusion, Mysterio.

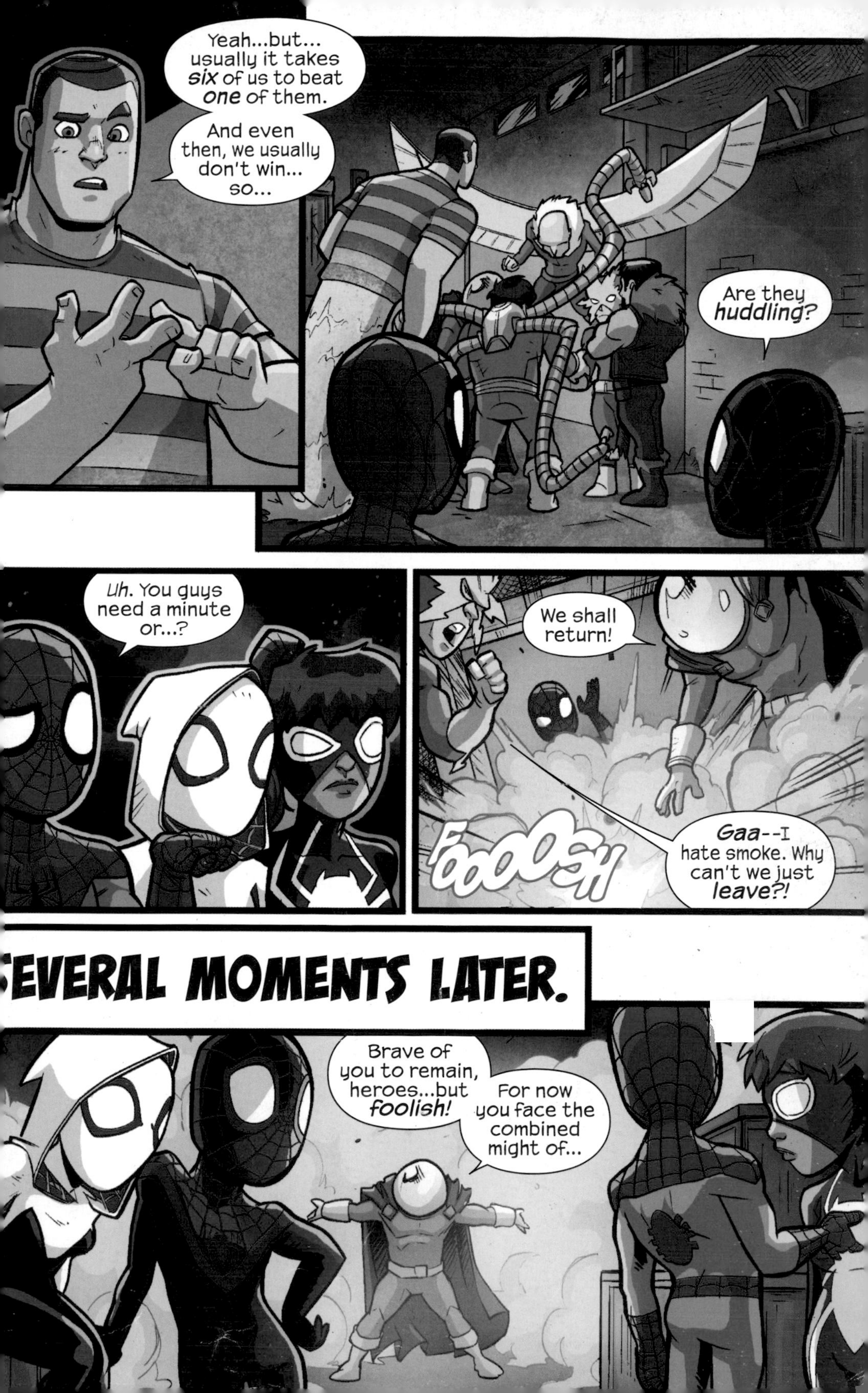
Yeah...but... usually it takes *six* of us to beat *one* of them.
And even then, we usually don't win... so...
Are they *huddling?*
Uh. You guys need a minute or...?
We shall return!
FOOOOSH
Gaa--I hate smoke. Why can't we just *leave?!*
SEVERAL MOMENTS LATER.
Brave of you to remain, heroes...but *foolish!*
For now you face the combined might of...

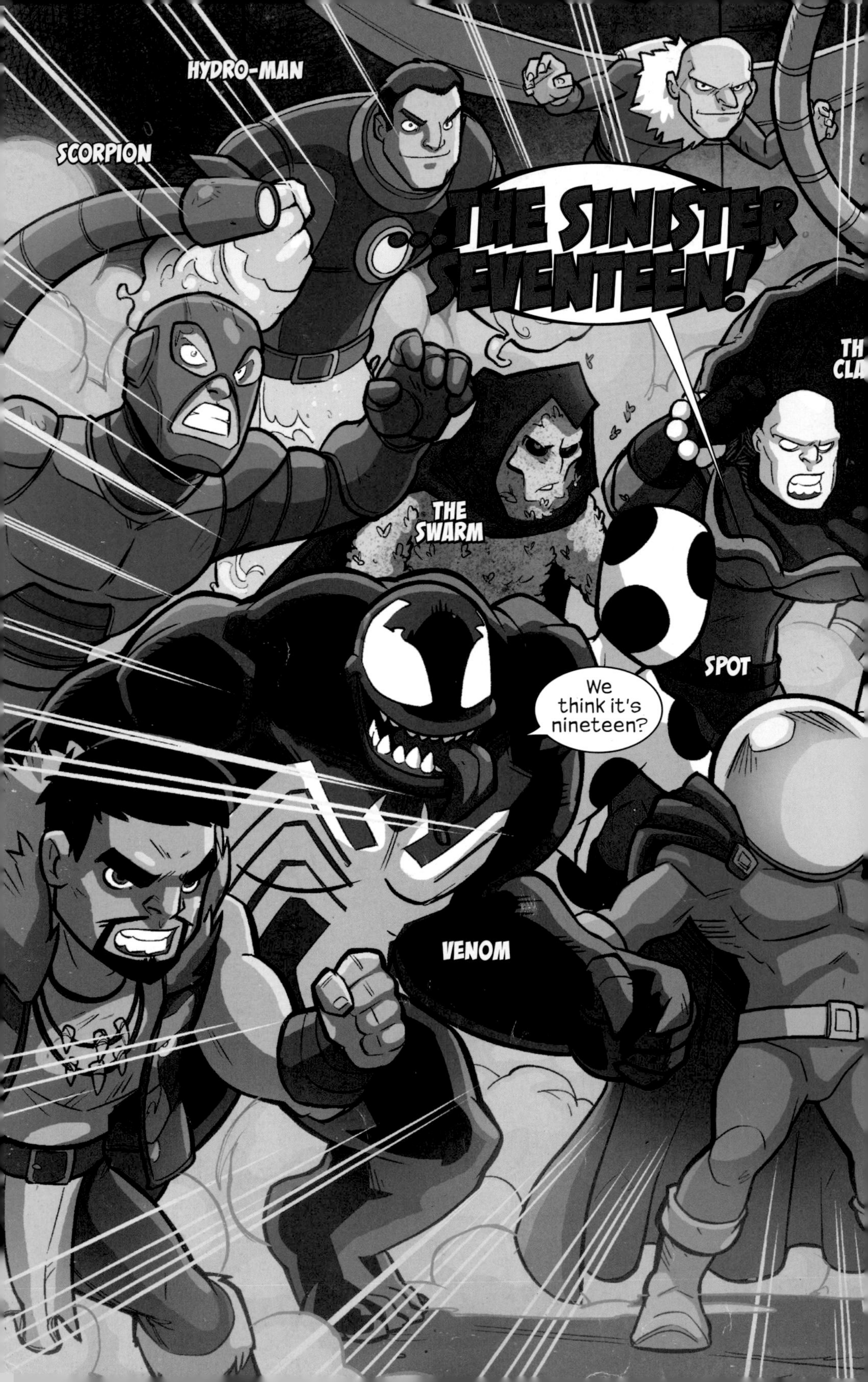
HYDRO-MAN
SCORPION
...THE SINISTER SEVENTEEN!
TH
CLA
THE SWARM
SPOT
We think it's nineteen?
VENOM

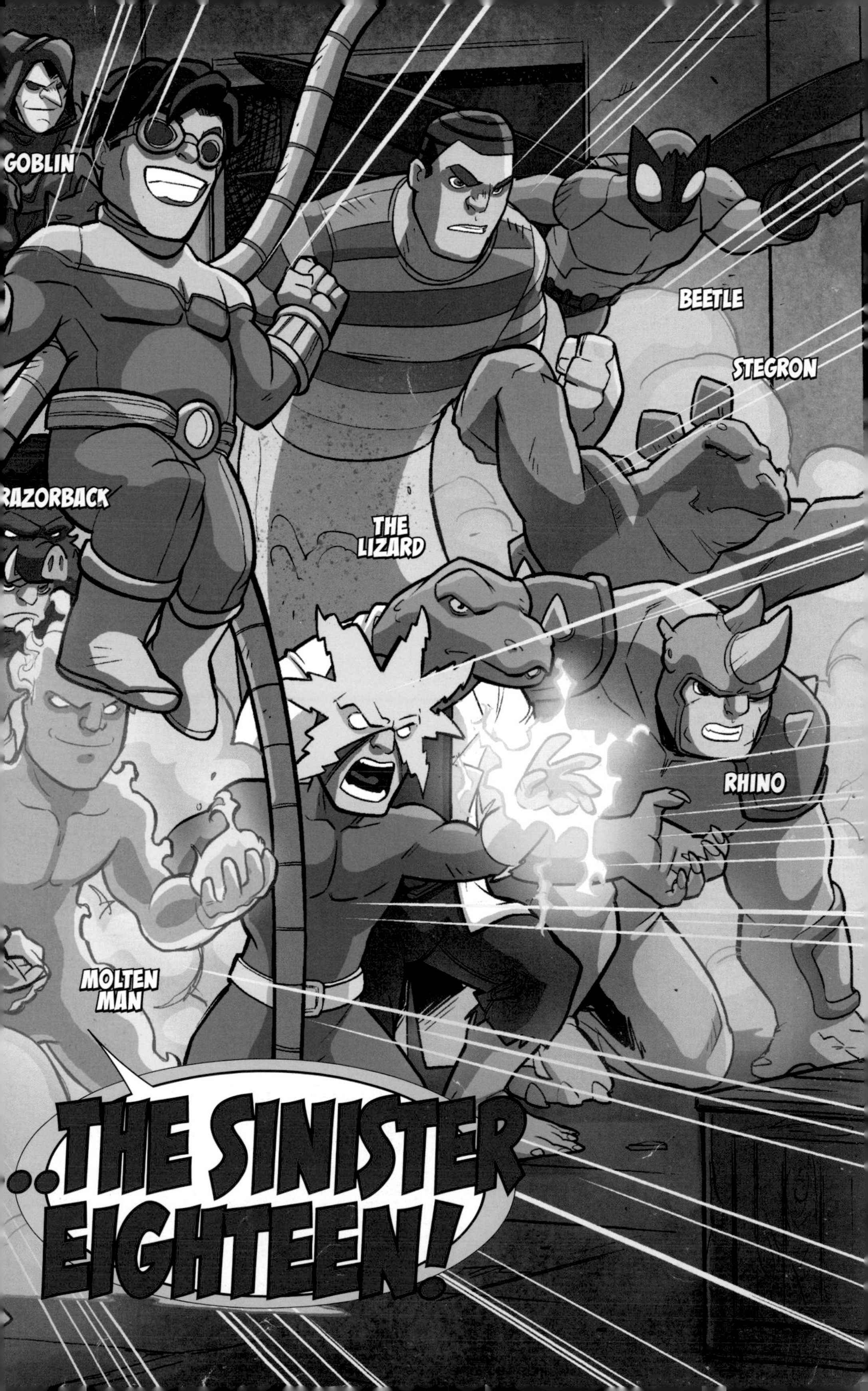
GOBLIN
BEETLE
STEGRON
RAZORBACK
THE LIZARD
RHINO
MOLTEN MAN
...THE SINISTER EIGHTEEN!

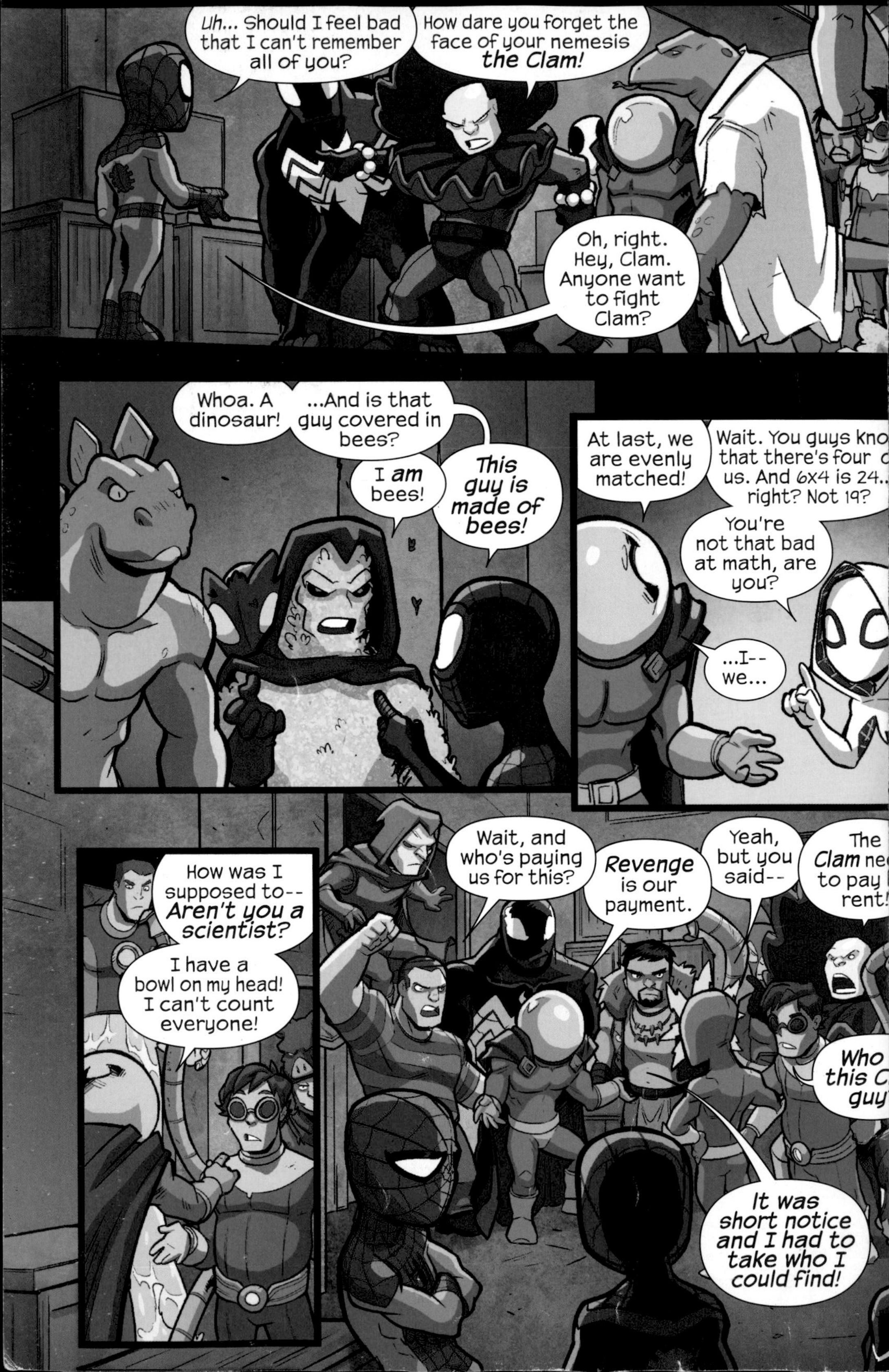

Uh... Should I feel bad that I can't remember all of you?
How dare you forget the face of your nemesis the Clam!
Oh, right. Hey, Clam. Anyone want to fight Clam?
Whoa. A dinosaur!
...And is that guy covered in bees?
I am bees!
This guy is made of bees!
At last, we are evenly matched!
Wait. You guys kno that there's four c us. And 6x4 is 24... right? Not 19?
You're not that bad at math, are you?
...I-- we...
How was I supposed to-- Aren't you a scientist?
I have a bowl on my head! I can't count everyone!
Wait, and who's paying us for this?
Revenge is our payment.
Yeah, but you said--
The Clam ne to pay rent!
Who this C guy
It was short notice and I had to take who I could find!

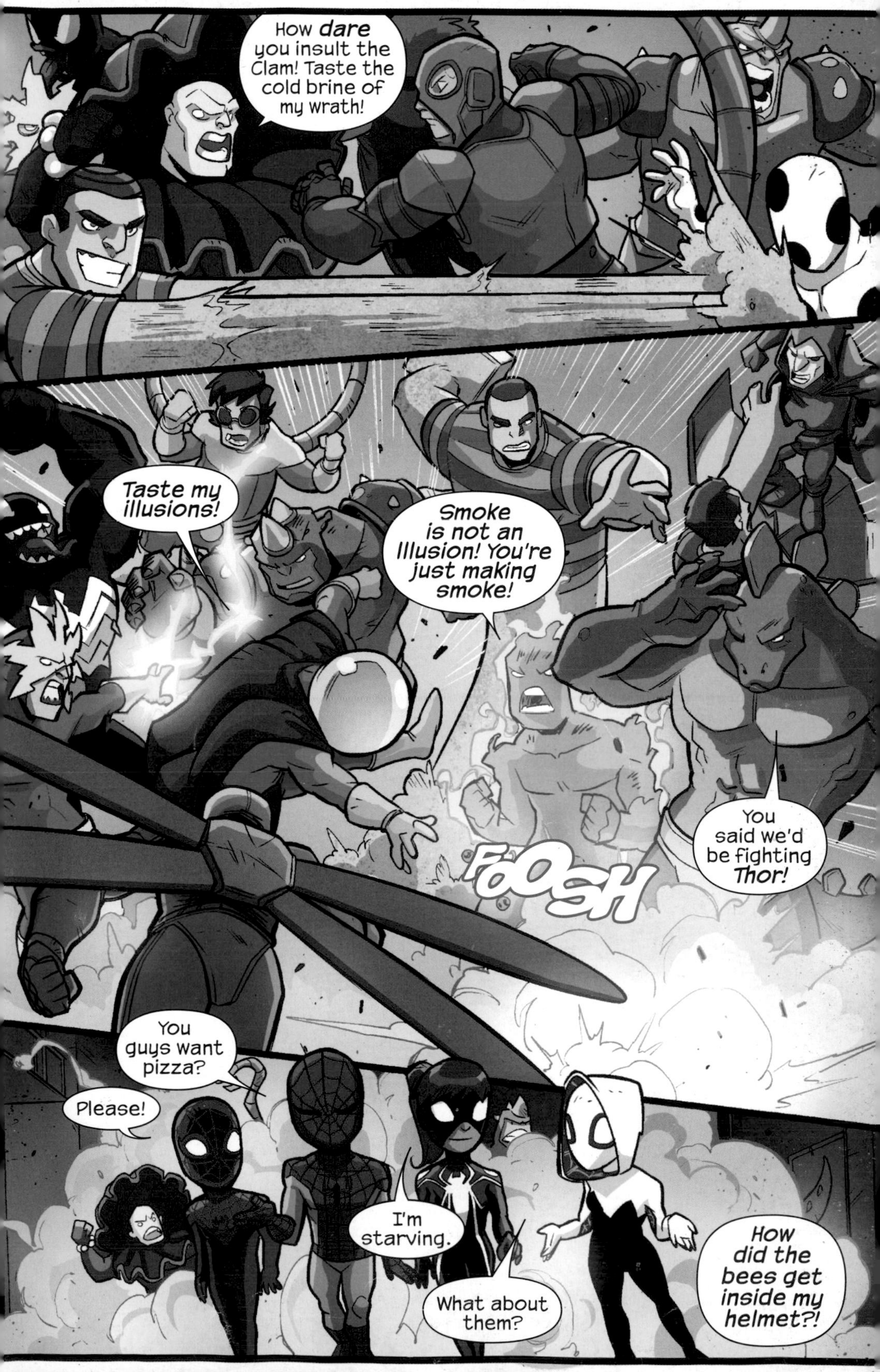
How dare you insult the Clam! Taste the cold brine of my wrath!
Taste my illusions!
Smoke is not an Illusion! You're just making smoke!
You said we'd be fighting Thor!
FOOSH
You guys want pizza?
Please!
I'm starving.
What about them?
How did the bees get inside my helmet?!

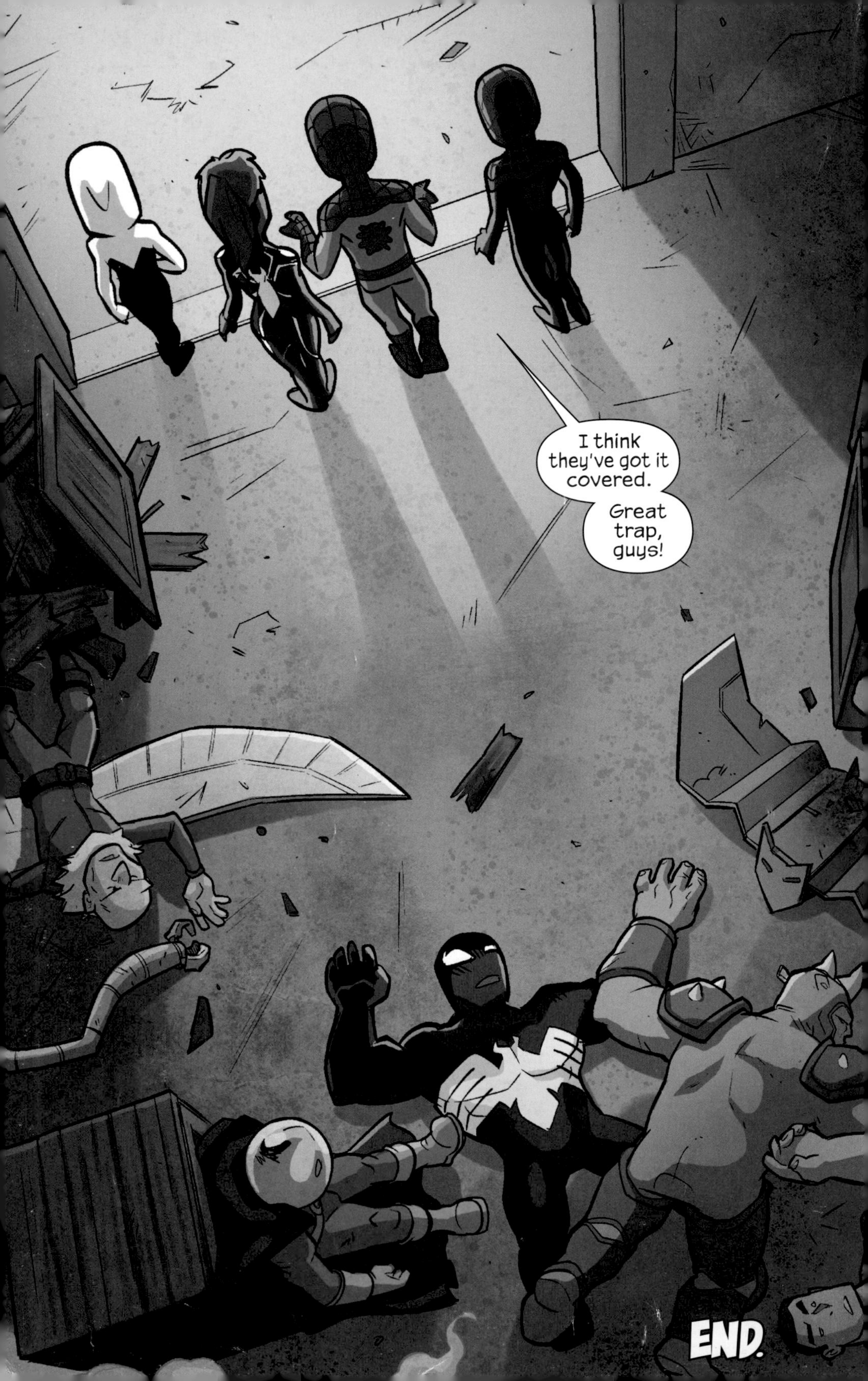
I think they've got it covered.
Great trap, guys!
END.

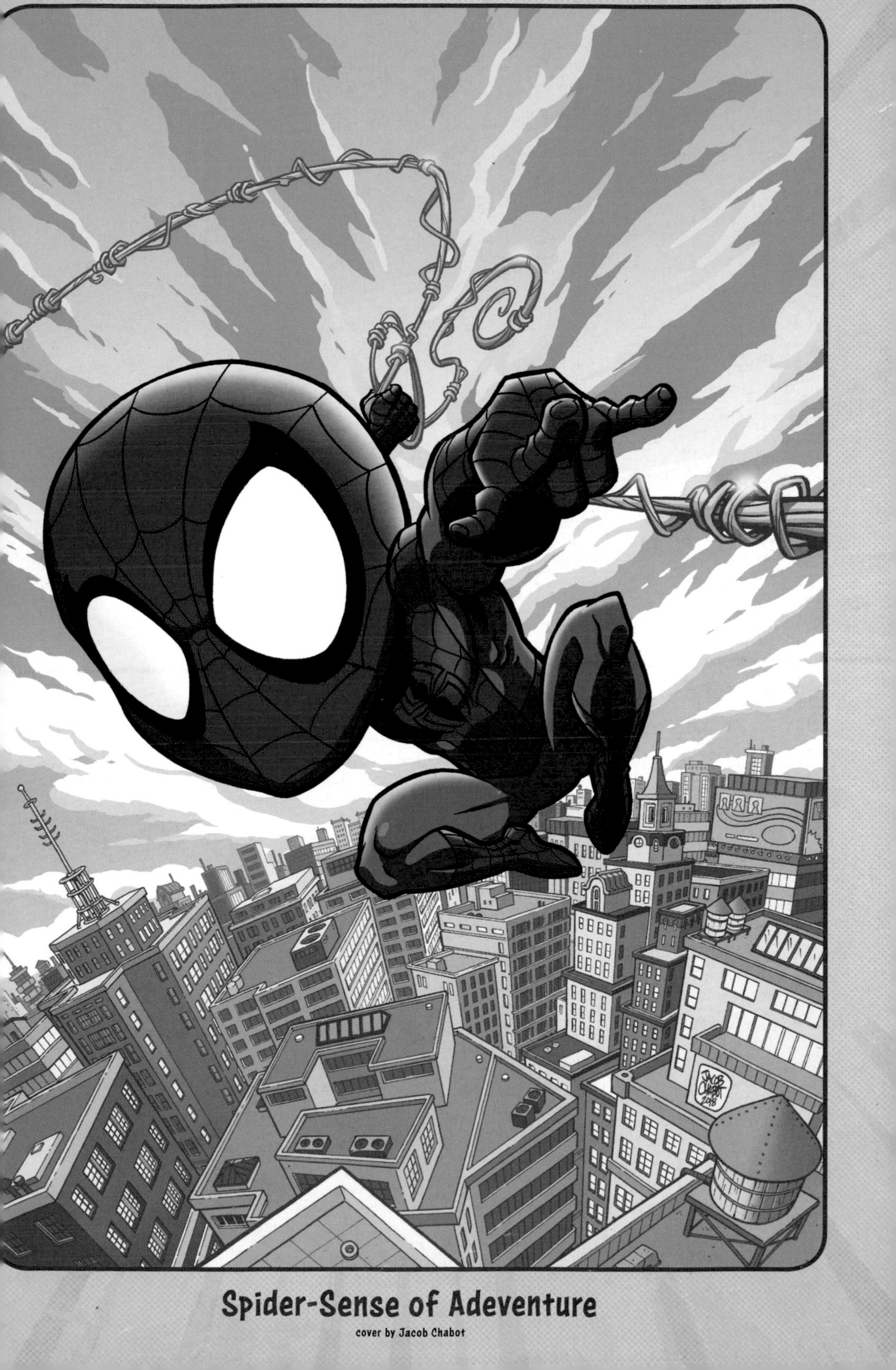

Spider-Sense of Adeventure

cover by Jacob Chabot

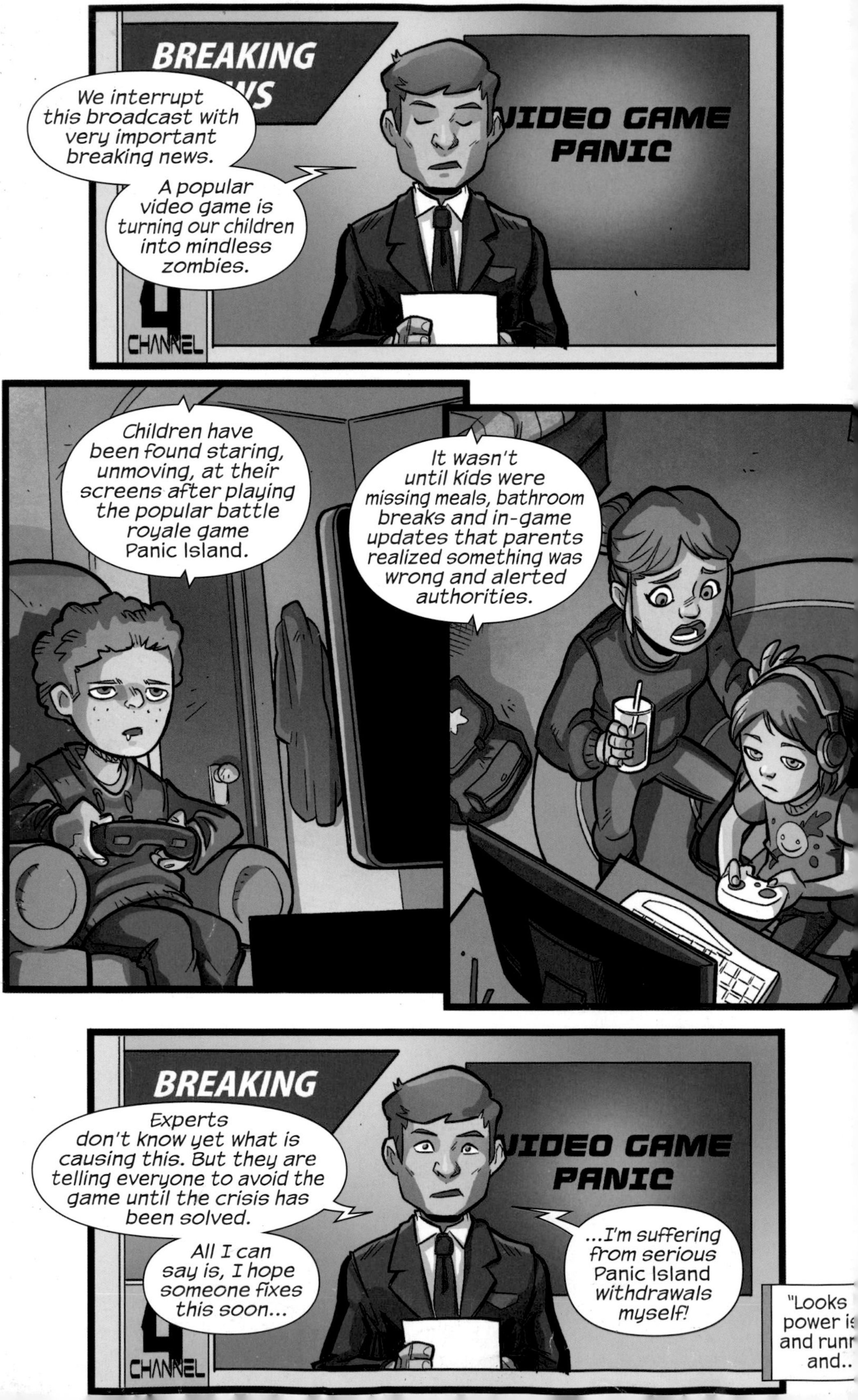
BREAKING NEWS
VIDEO GAME PANIC
We interrupt this broadcast with very important breaking news.
A popular video game is turning our children into mindless zombies.
CHANNEL 4
Children have been found staring, unmoving, at their screens after playing the popular battle royale game Panic Island.
It wasn't until kids were missing meals, bathroom breaks and in-game updates that parents realized something was wrong and alerted authorities.
BREAKING
VIDEO GAME PANIC
Experts don't know yet what is causing this. But they are telling everyone to avoid the game until the crisis has been solved.
All I can say is, I hope someone fixes this soon...
...I'm suffering from serious Panic Island withdrawals myself!
CHANNEL 4

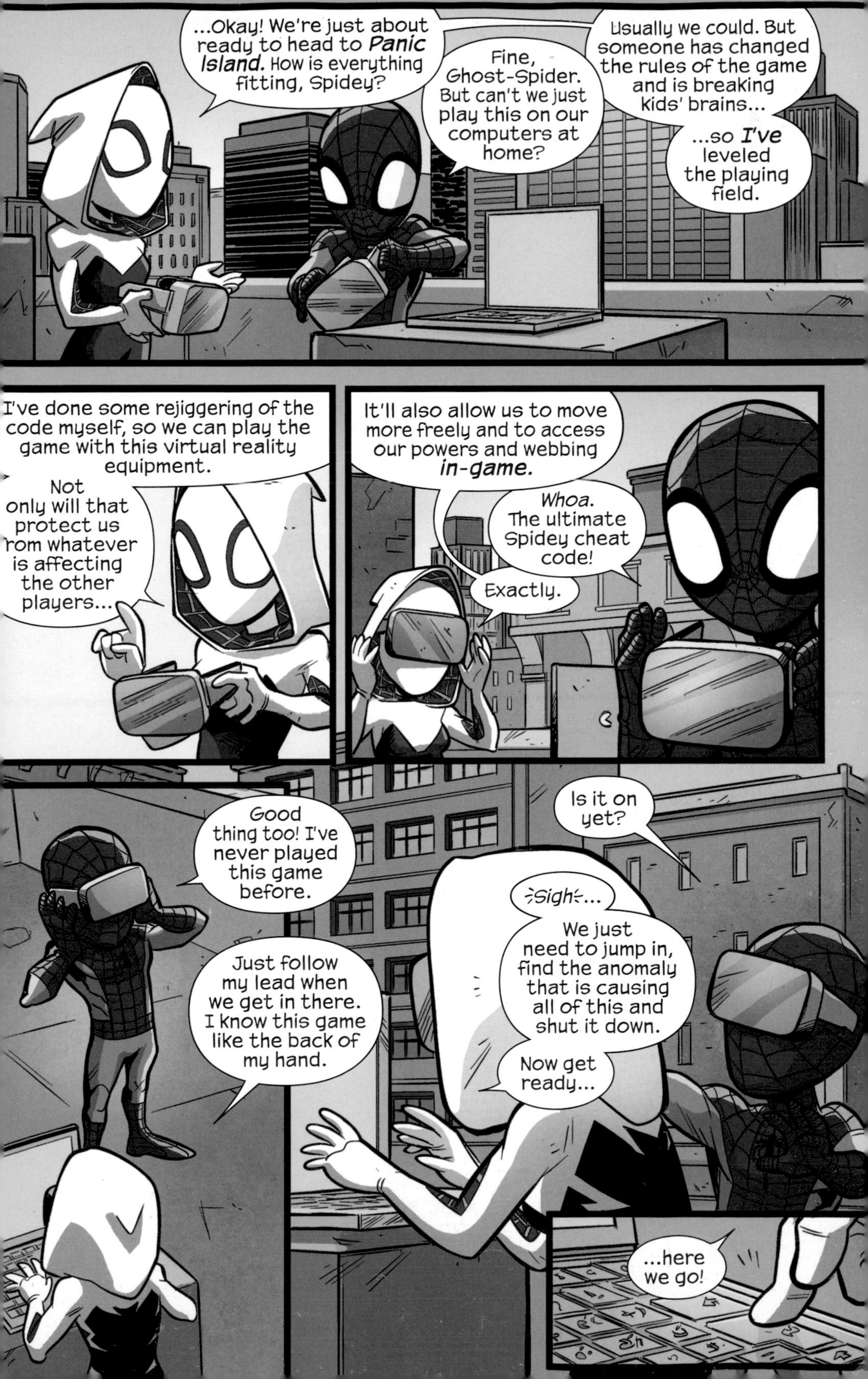

...Okay! We're just about ready to head to *Panic Island.* How is everything fitting, Spidey?
Fine, Ghost-Spider. But can't we just play this on our computers at home?
Usually we could. But someone has changed the rules of the game and is breaking kids' brains...
...so *I've* leveled the playing field.
I've done some rejiggering of the code myself, so we can play the game with this virtual reality equipment.
Not only will that protect us rom whatever is affecting the other players...
It'll also allow us to move more freely and to access our powers and webbing *in-game.*
Whoa. The ultimate Spidey cheat code!
Exactly.
Good thing too! I've never played this game before.
Just follow my lead when we get in there. I know this game like the back of my hand.
Is it on yet?
Sigh...
We just need to jump in, find the anomaly that is causing all of this and shut it down.
Now get ready...
...here we go!

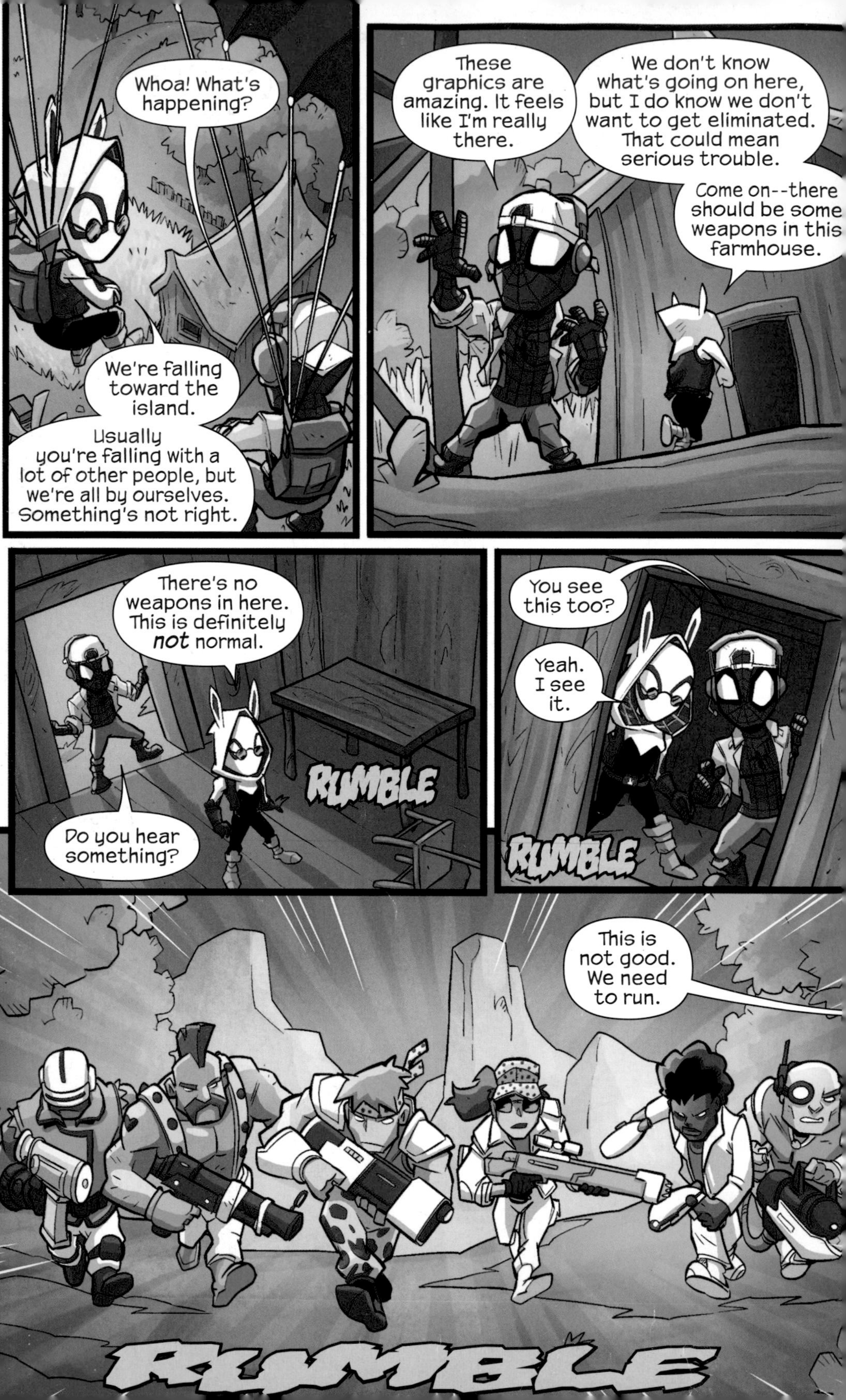
Whoa! What's happening?
We're falling toward the island.
Usually you're falling with a lot of other people, but we're all by ourselves. Something's not right.
These graphics are amazing. It feels like I'm really there.
We don't know what's going on here, but I do know we don't want to get eliminated. That could mean serious trouble.
Come on--there should be some weapons in this farmhouse.
There's no weapons in here. This is definitely *not* normal.
RUMBLE
Do you hear something?
You see this too?
Yeah. I see it.
RUMBLE
This is not good. We need to run.
RUMBLE

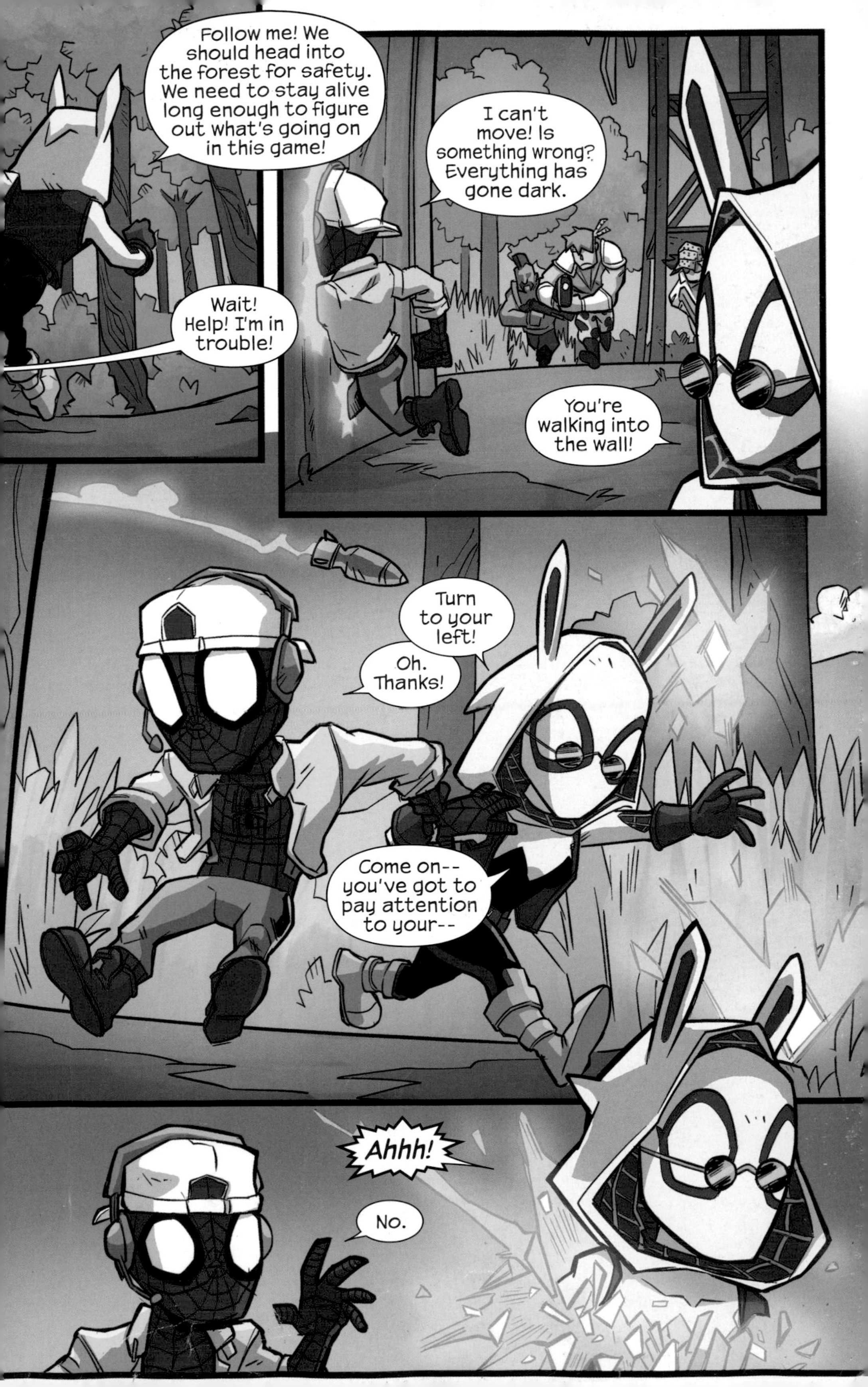
Follow me! We should head into the forest for safety. We need to stay alive long enough to figure out what's going on in this game!
Wait! Help! I'm in trouble!
I can't move! Is something wrong? Everything has gone dark.
You're walking into the wall!
Turn to your left!
Oh. Thanks!
Come on--you've got to pay attention to your--
Ahhh!
No.

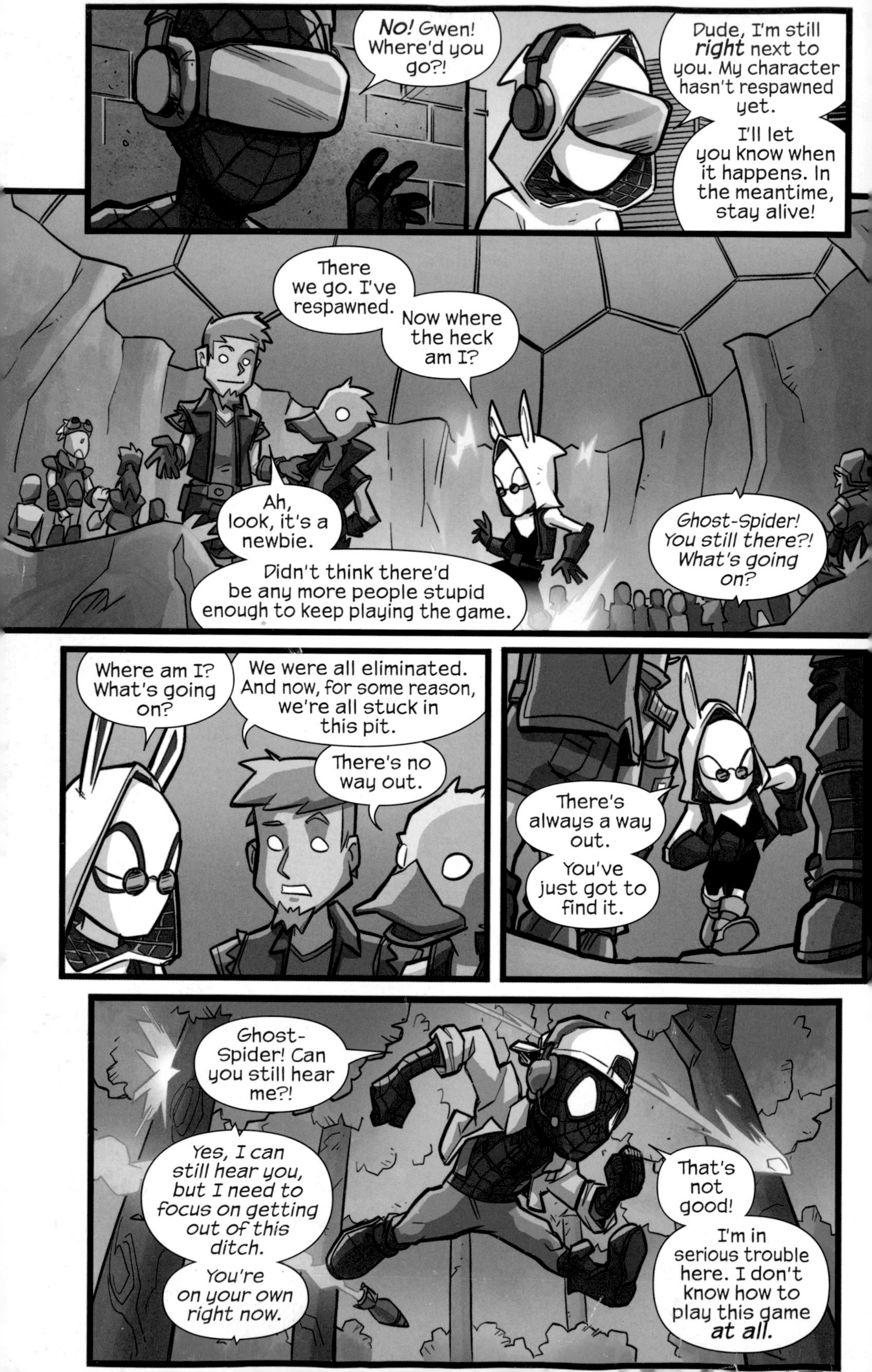

No! Gwen! Where'd you go?!
Dude, I'm still right next to you. My character hasn't respawned yet.
I'll let you know when it happens. In the meantime, stay alive!
There we go. I've respawned.
Now where the heck am I?
Ah, look, it's a newbie.
Didn't think there'd be any more people stupid enough to keep playing the game.
Ghost-Spider! You still there?! What's going on?
Where am I? What's going on?
We were all eliminated. And now, for some reason, we're all stuck in this pit.
There's no way out.
There's always a way out.
You've just got to find it.
Ghost-Spider! Can you still hear me?!
Yes, I can still hear you, but I need to focus on getting out of this ditch.
You're on your own right now.
That's not good!
I'm in serious trouble here. I don't know how to play this game at all.

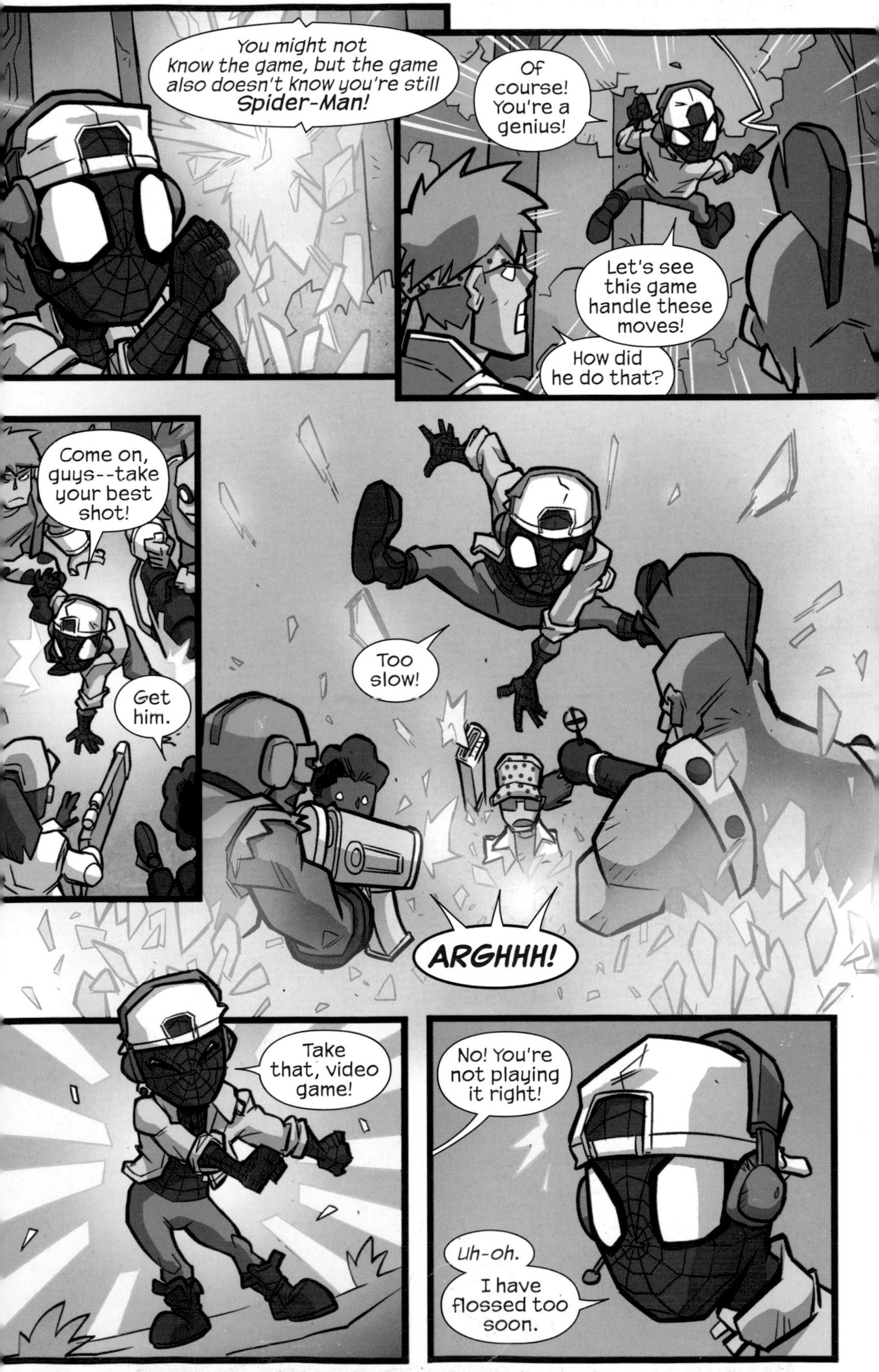
You might not know the game, but the game also doesn't know you're still **Spider-Man!**
Of course! You're a genius!
Let's see this game handle these moves!
How did he do that?
Come on, guys--take your best shot!
Get him.
Too slow!
ARGHHH!
Take that, video game!
No! You're not playing it right!
Uh-oh.
I have flossed too soon.

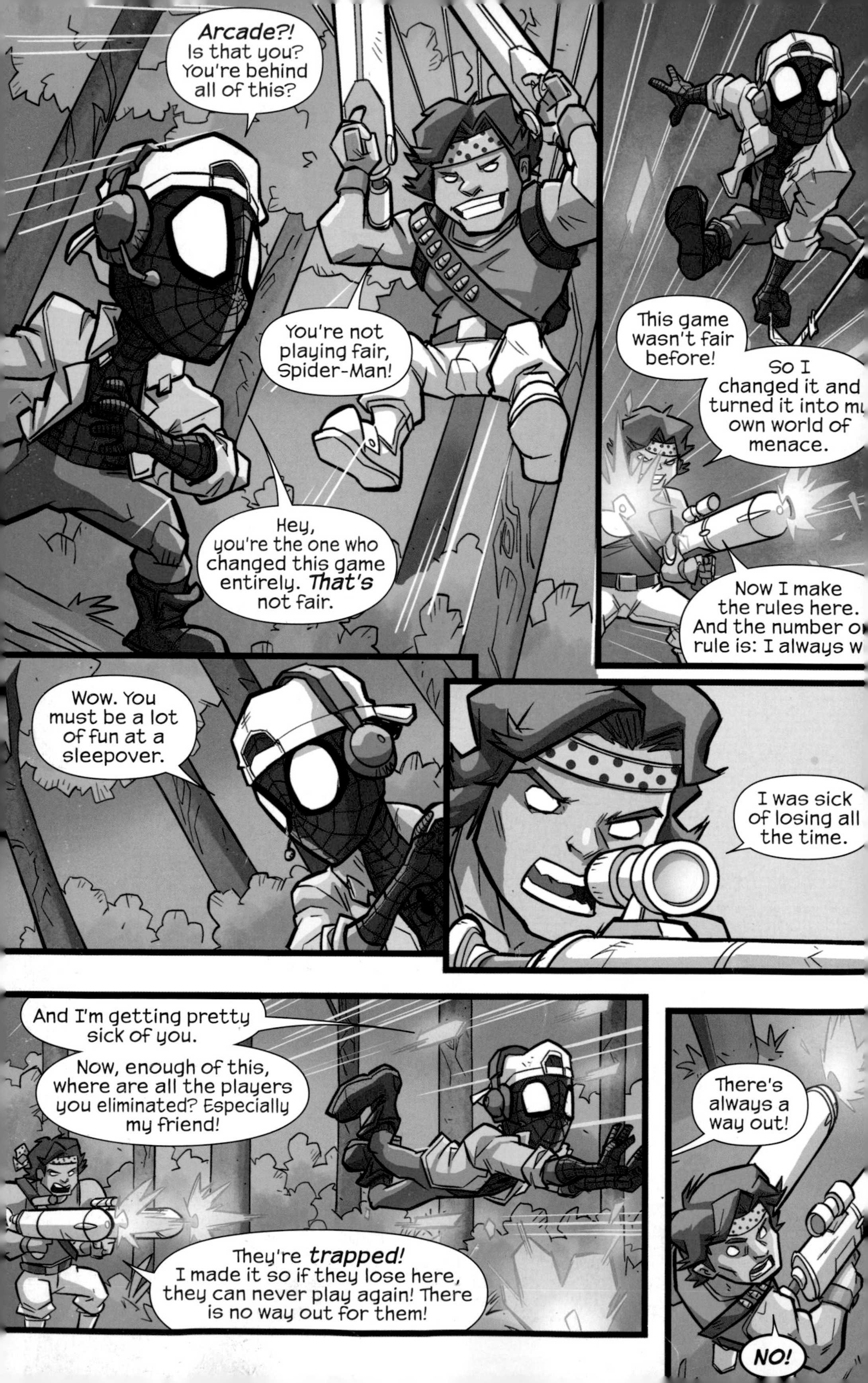

Arcade?! Is that you? You're behind all of this?
You're not playing fair, Spider-Man!
Hey, you're the one who changed this game entirely. ***That's*** not fair.
This game wasn't fair before!
So I changed it and turned it into m own world of menace.
Now I make the rules here. And the number o rule is: I always w
Wow. You must be a lot of fun at a sleepover.
I was sick of losing all the time.
And I'm getting pretty sick of you.
Now, enough of this, where are all the players you eliminated? Especially my friend!
They're ***trapped!*** I made it so if they lose here, they can never play again! There is no way out for them!
There's always a way out!
NO!

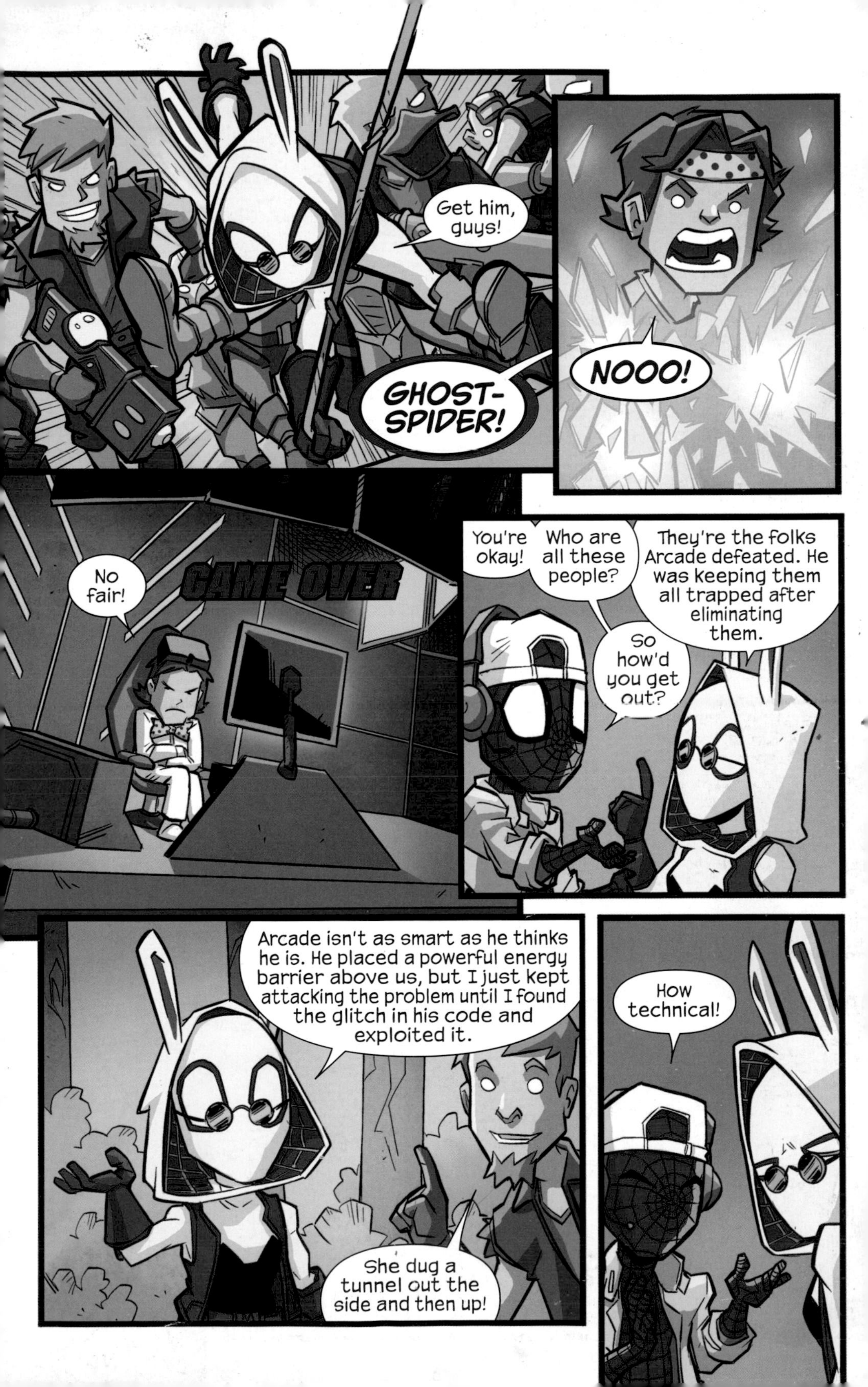
Get him, guys!
GHOST-SPIDER!
NOOO!
GAME OVER
No fair!
You're okay!
Who are all these people?
They're the folks Arcade defeated. He was keeping them all trapped after eliminating them.
So how'd you get out?
Arcade isn't as smart as he thinks he is. He placed a powerful energy barrier above us, but I just kept attacking the problem until I found the glitch in his code and exploited it.
She dug a tunnel out the side and then up!
How technical!

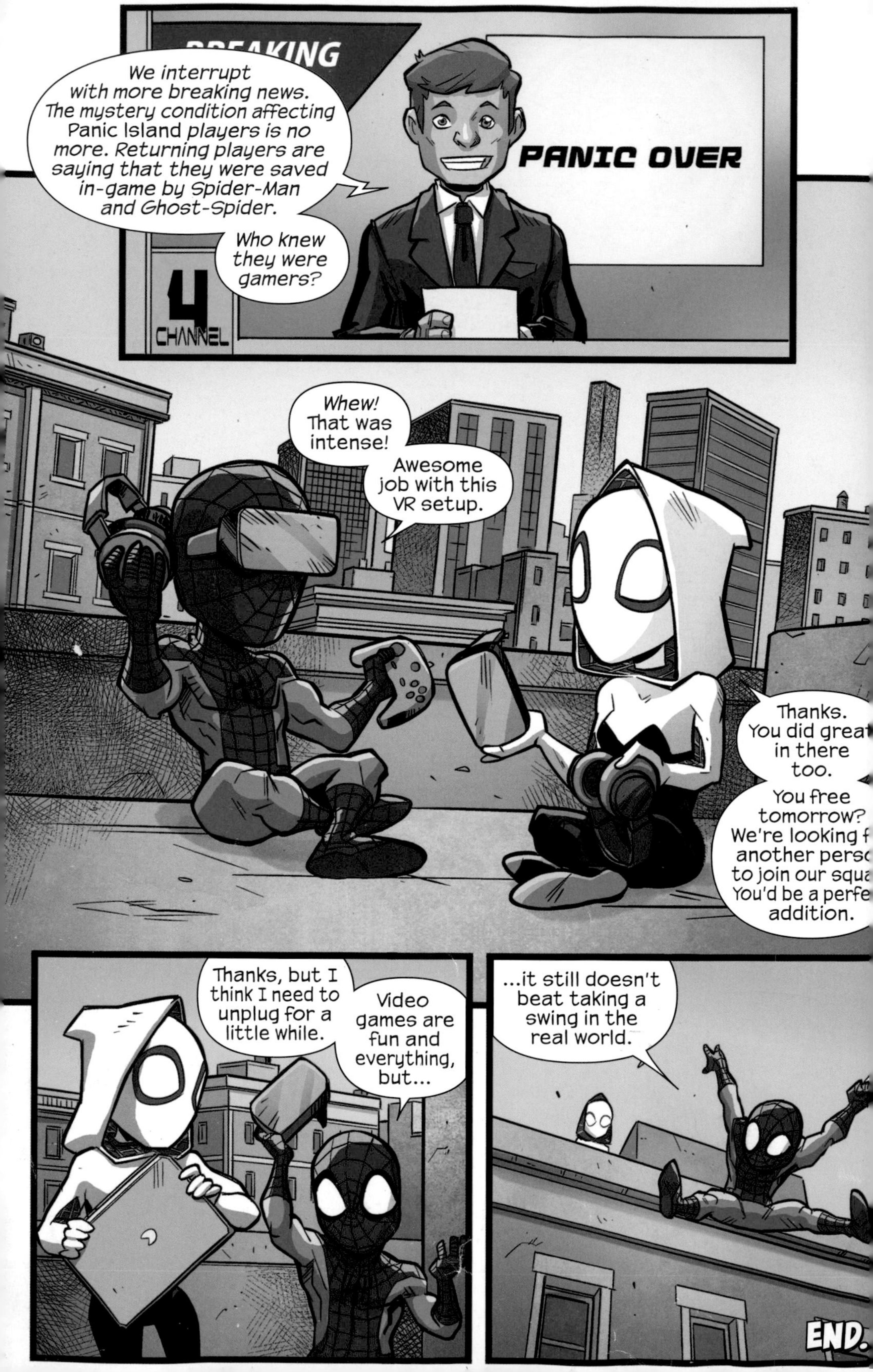
BREAKING
We interrupt with more breaking news. The mystery condition affecting Panic Island players is no more. Returning players are saying that they were saved in-game by Spider-Man and Ghost-Spider.
PANIC OVER
Who knew they were gamers?
CHANNEL
Whew! That was intense!
Awesome job with this VR setup.
Thanks. You did grea in there too.
You free tomorrow? We're looking another pers to join our squ You'd be a perf addition.
Thanks, but I think I need to unplug for a little while.
Video games are fun and everything, but...
...it still doesn't beat taking a swing in the real world.
END.

DAILY BUGLE
NEW YORK'S FUNNIEST DAILY NEWSPAPER

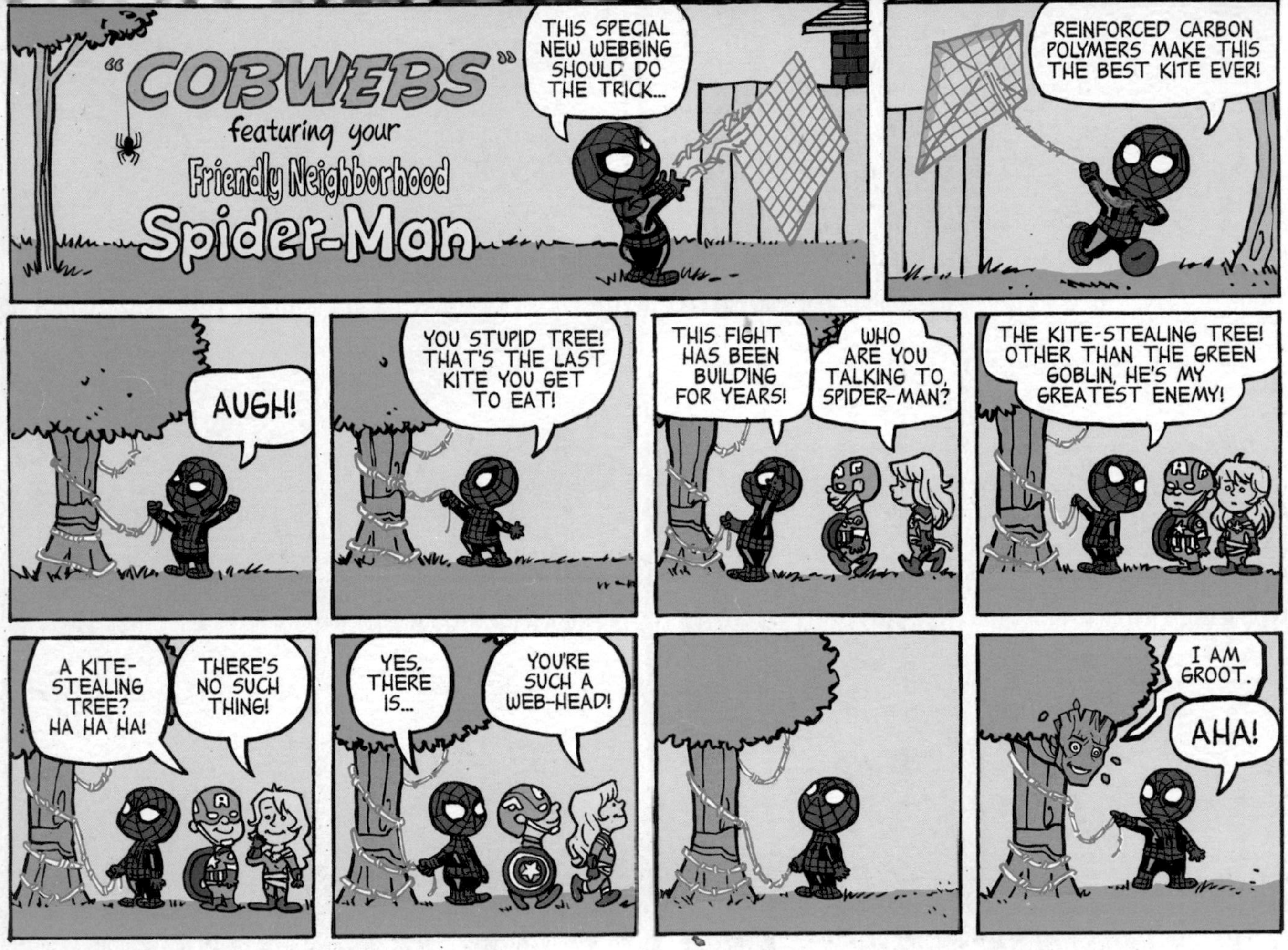
"COBWEBS"
featuring your
Friendly Neighborhood
Spider-Man
THIS SPECIAL NEW WEBBING SHOULD DO THE TRICK...
REINFORCED CARBON POLYMERS MAKE THIS THE BEST KITE EVER!
AUGH!
YOU STUPID TREE! THAT'S THE LAST KITE YOU GET TO EAT!
THIS FIGHT HAS BEEN BUILDING FOR YEARS!
WHO ARE YOU TALKING TO, SPIDER-MAN?
THE KITE-STEALING TREE! OTHER THAN THE GREEN GOBLIN, HE'S MY GREATEST ENEMY!
A KITE-STEALING TREE? HA HA HA!
THERE'S NO SUCH THING!
YES, THERE IS...
YOU'RE SUCH A WEB-HEAD!
I AM GROOT.
AHA!

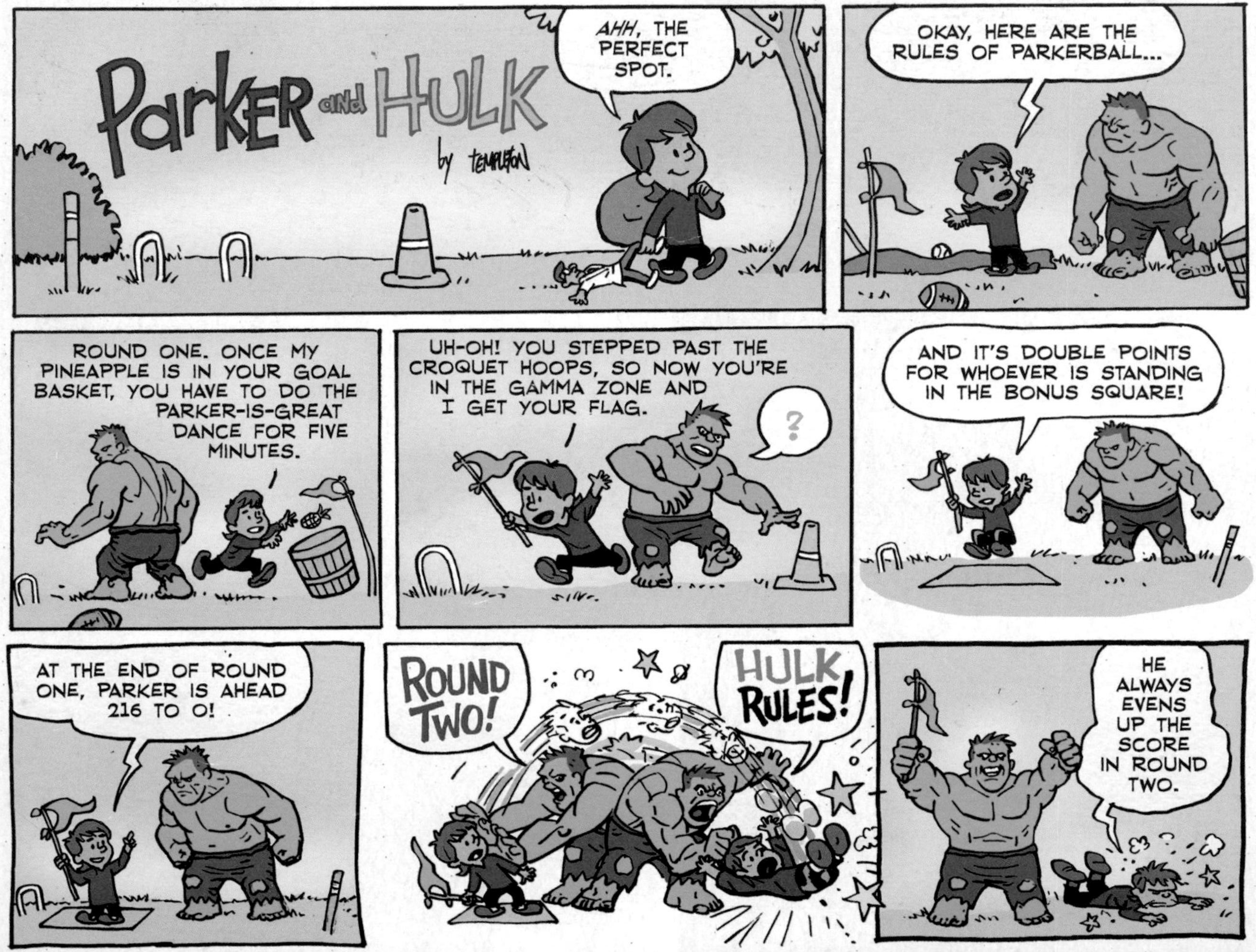
Parker and Hulk
by Templeton
AHH, THE PERFECT SPOT.
OKAY, HERE ARE THE RULES OF PARKERBALL...
ROUND ONE. ONCE MY PINEAPPLE IS IN YOUR GOAL BASKET, YOU HAVE TO DO THE PARKER-IS-GREAT DANCE FOR FIVE MINUTES.
UH-OH! YOU STEPPED PAST THE CROQUET HOOPS, SO NOW YOU'RE IN THE GAMMA ZONE AND I GET YOUR FLAG.
?
AND IT'S DOUBLE POINTS FOR WHOEVER IS STANDING IN THE BONUS SQUARE!
AT THE END OF ROUND ONE, PARKER IS AHEAD 216 TO 0!
ROUND TWO!
HULK RULES!
HE ALWAYS EVENS UP THE SCORE IN ROUND TWO.

OCTOR OCTOPUS in "THRILLING FILLING"

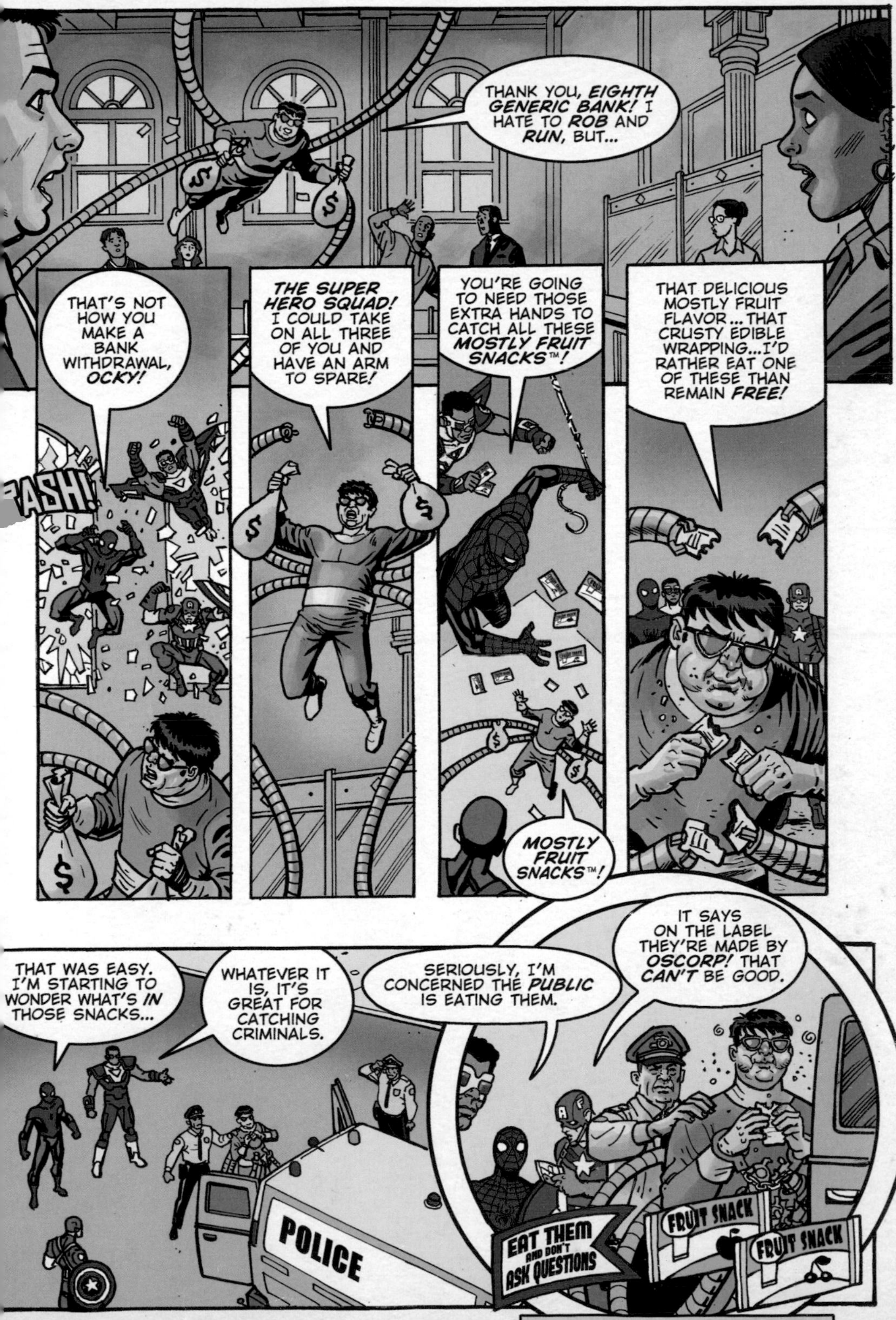

THANK YOU, EIGHTH GENERIC BANK! I HATE TO ROB AND RUN, BUT...
THAT'S NOT HOW YOU MAKE A BANK WITHDRAWAL, OCKY!
ASH!
THE SUPER HERO SQUAD! I COULD TAKE ON ALL THREE OF YOU AND HAVE AN ARM TO SPARE!
YOU'RE GOING TO NEED THOSE EXTRA HANDS TO CATCH ALL THESE MOSTLY FRUIT SNACKS™!
MOSTLY FRUIT SNACKS™!
THAT DELICIOUS MOSTLY FRUIT FLAVOR... THAT CRUSTY EDIBLE WRAPPING... I'D RATHER EAT ONE OF THESE THAN REMAIN FREE!
THAT WAS EASY. I'M STARTING TO WONDER WHAT'S IN THOSE SNACKS...
WHATEVER IT IS, IT'S GREAT FOR CATCHING CRIMINALS.
SERIOUSLY, I'M CONCERNED THE PUBLIC IS EATING THEM.
IT SAYS ON THE LABEL THEY'RE MADE BY OSCORP! THAT CAN'T BE GOOD.
POLICE
EAT THEM AND DON'T ASK QUESTIONS
FRUIT SNACK
FRUIT SNACK
A DIVISION OF OSCORP INDUSTRIES.

SCRIPT AND ART: TY TEMPLETON COLORS: KEIREN SMITH

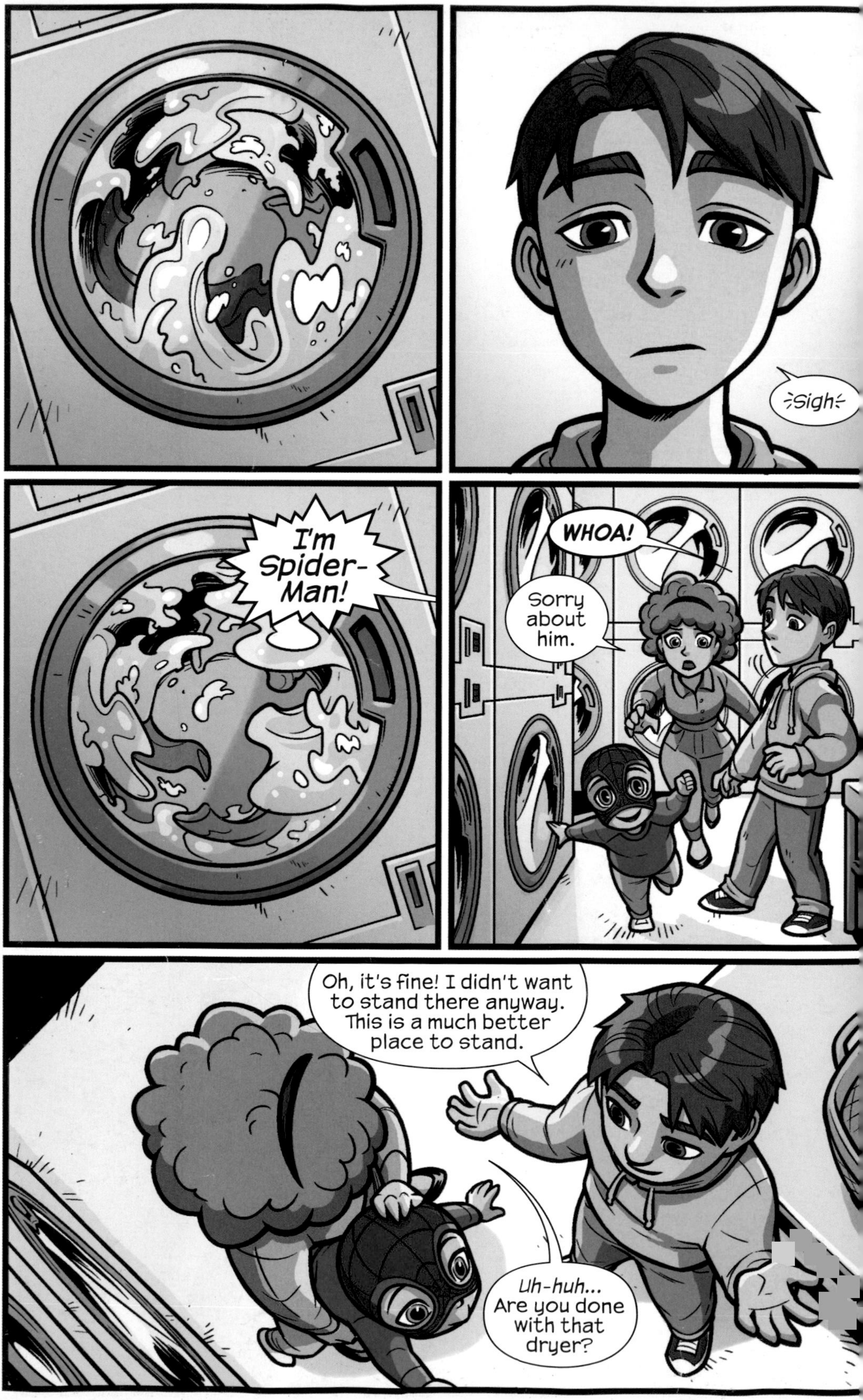
Sigh
I'm Spider-Man!
WHOA!
Sorry about him.
Oh, it's fine! I didn't want to stand there anyway. This is a much better place to stand.
Uh-huh... Are you done with that dryer?

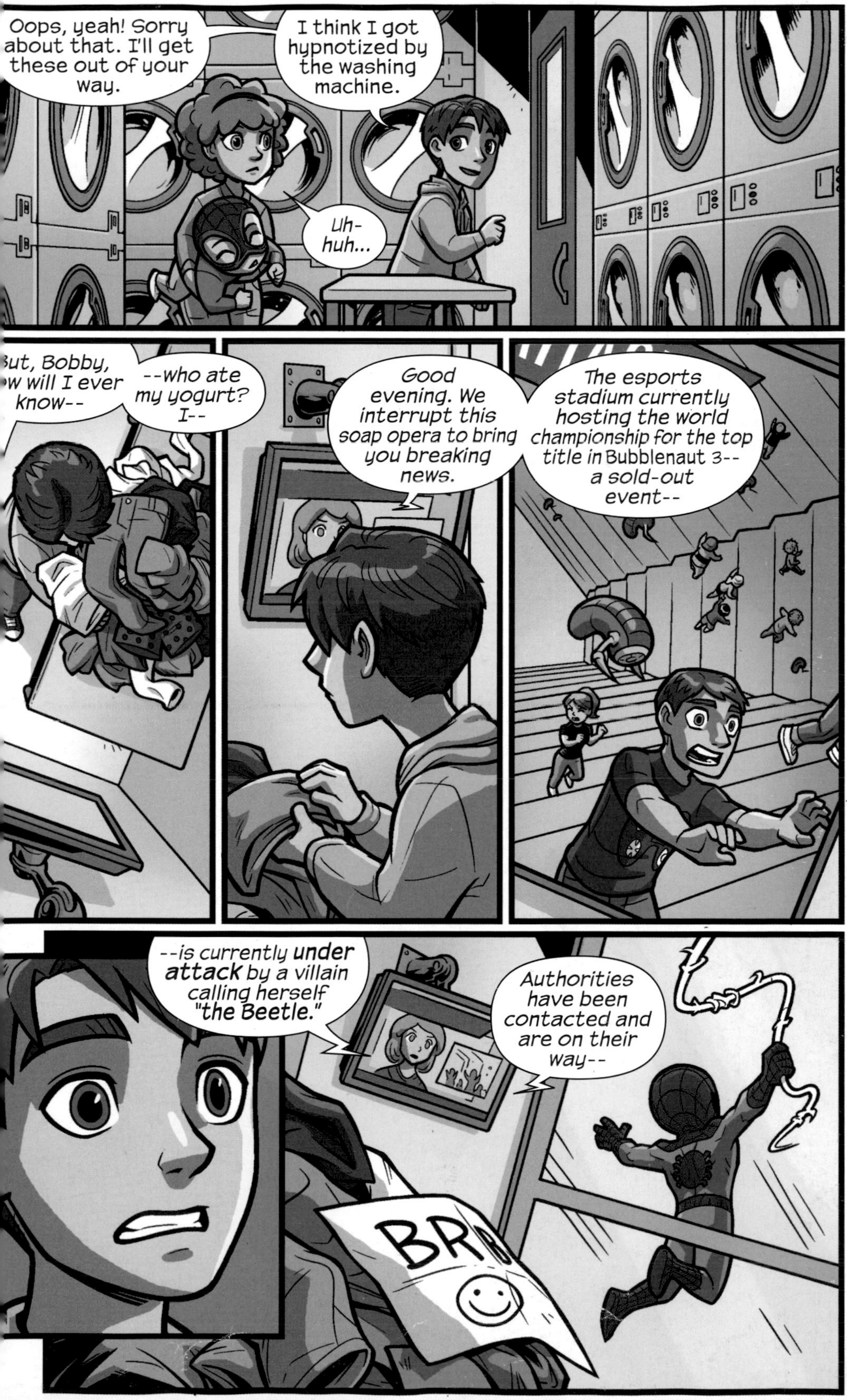
Oops, yeah! Sorry about that. I'll get these out of your way.
I think I got hypnotized by the washing machine.
Uh-huh...
ut, Bobby, w will I ever know--
--who ate my yogurt? I--
Good evening. We interrupt this soap opera to bring you breaking news.
The esports stadium currently hosting the world championship for the top title in Bubblenaut 3--a sold-out event--
--is currently **under attack** by a villain calling herself "the Beetle."
Authorities have been contacted and are on their way--
BR

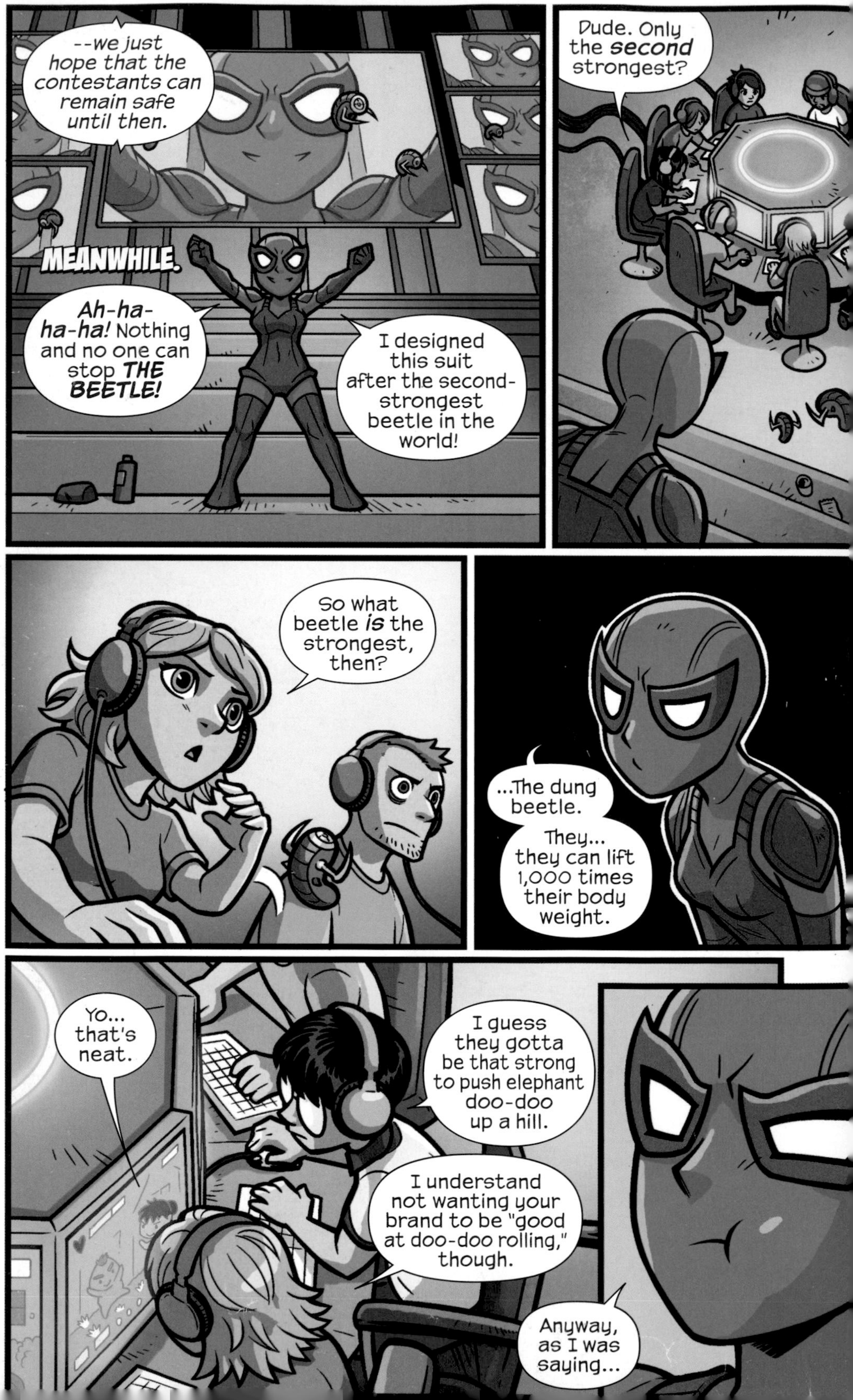
--we just hope that the contestants can remain safe until then.
MEANWHILE.
Ah-ha-ha-ha! Nothing and no one can stop THE BEETLE!
I designed this suit after the second-strongest beetle in the world!
Dude. Only the second strongest?
So what beetle is the strongest, then?
...The dung beetle.
They... they can lift 1,000 times their body weight.
Yo... that's neat.
I guess they gotta be that strong to push elephant doo-doo up a hill.
I understand not wanting your brand to be "good at doo-doo rolling," though.
Anyway, as I was saying...

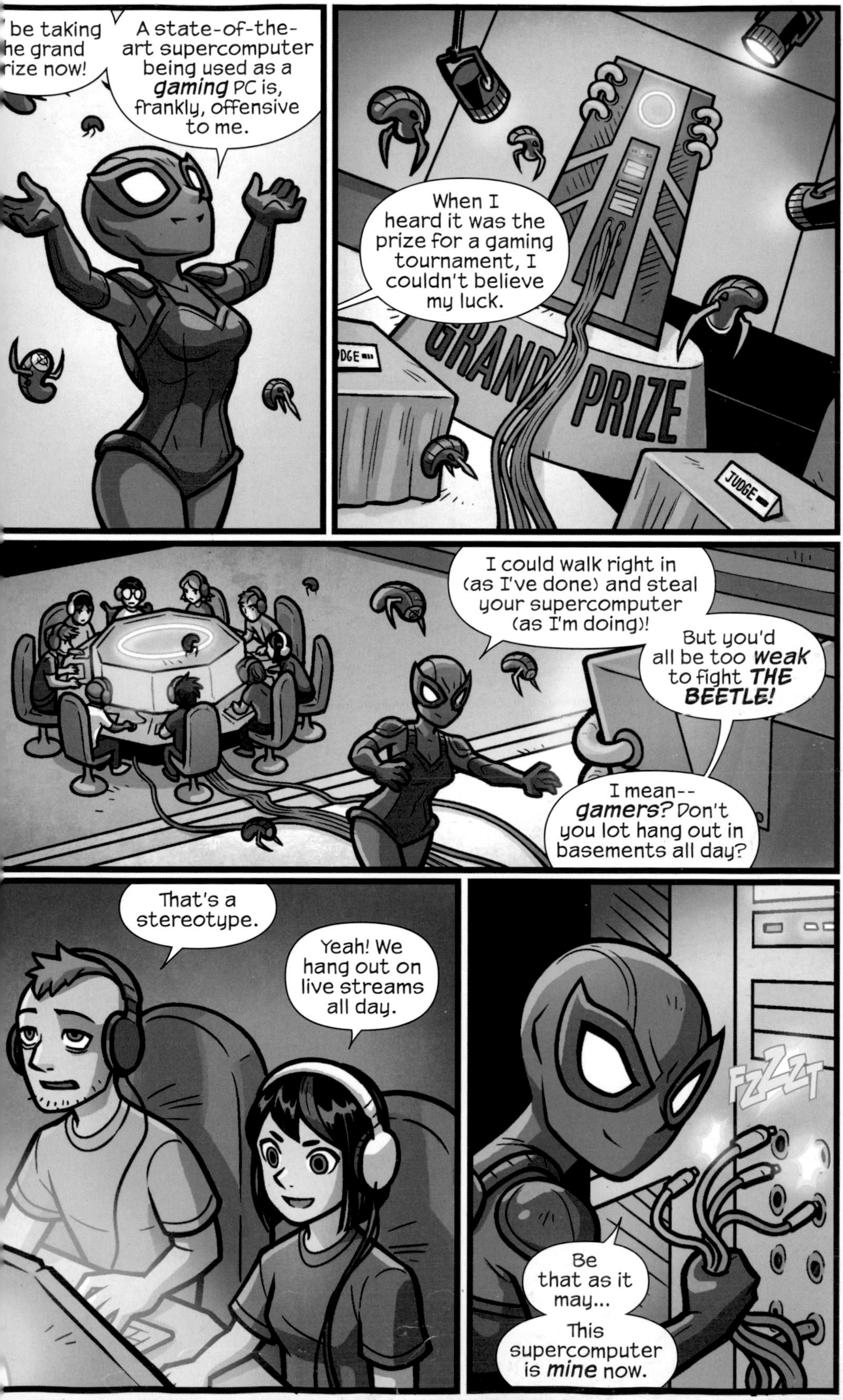

be taking he grand rize now!
A state-of-the-art supercomputer being used as a *gaming* PC is, frankly, offensive to me.
When I heard it was the prize for a gaming tournament, I couldn't believe my luck.
GRAND PRIZE
JUDGE
I could walk right in (as I've done) and steal your supercomputer (as I'm doing)!
But you'd all be too *weak* to fight *THE BEETLE!*
I mean-- *gamers?* Don't you lot hang out in basements all day?
That's a stereotype.
Yeah! We hang out on live streams all day.
FZZZT
Be that as it may...
This supercomputer is *mine* now.

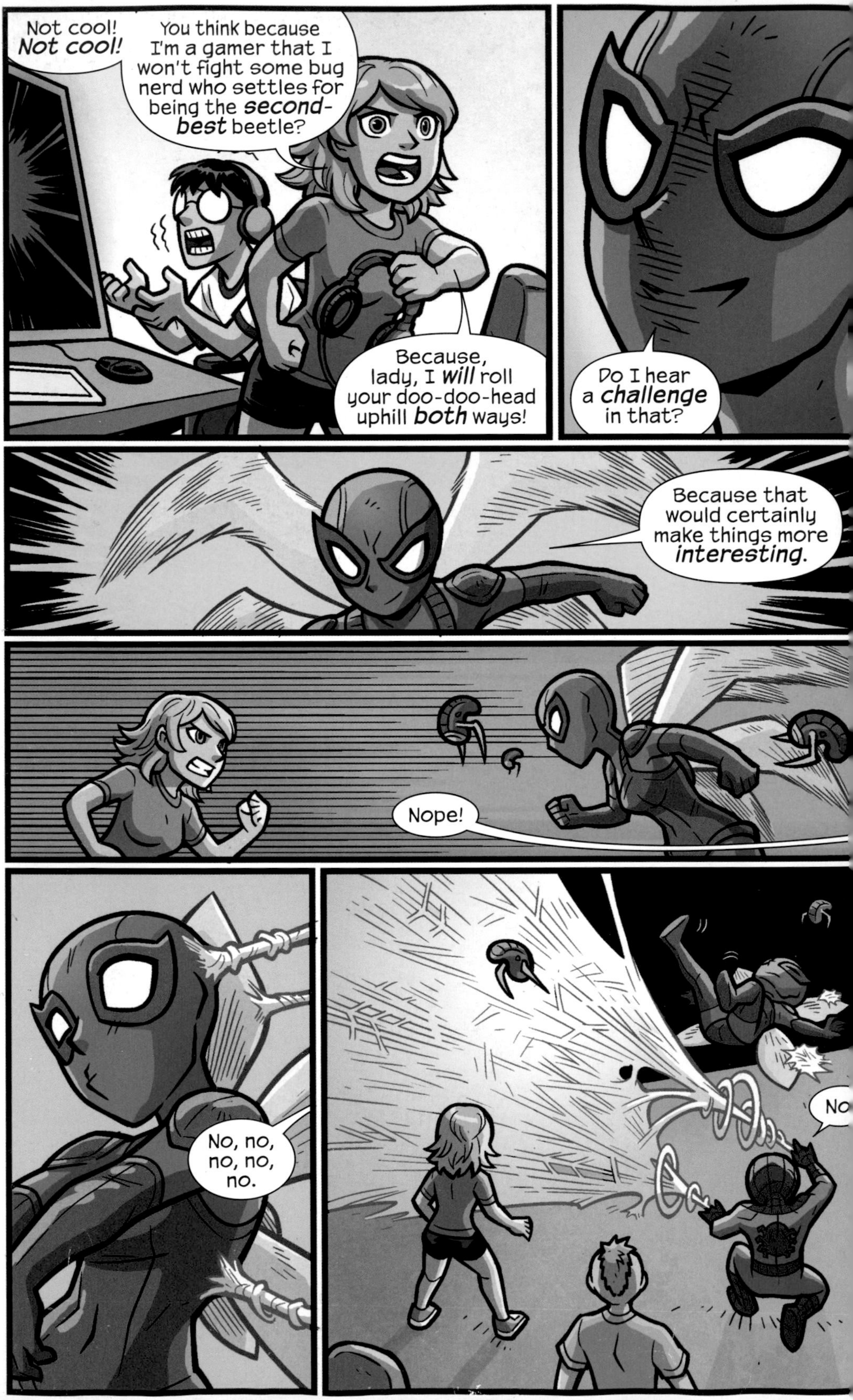
Not cool! *Not cool!*
You think because I'm a gamer that I won't fight some bug nerd who settles for being the *second-best* beetle?
Because, lady, I *will* roll your doo-doo-head uphill *both* ways!
Do I hear a *challenge* in that?
Because that would certainly make things more *interesting.*
Nope!
No, no, no, no, no.
No

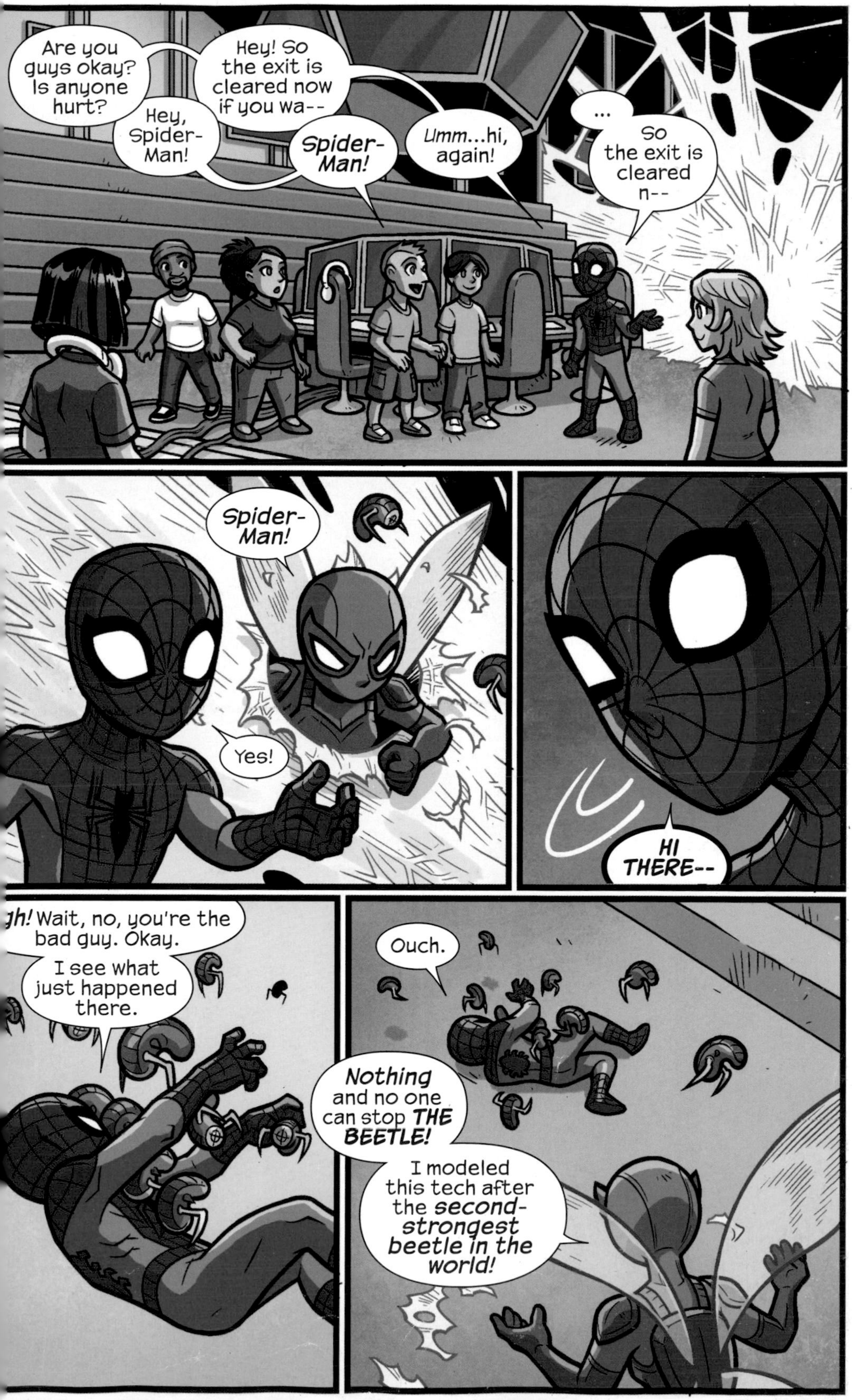
Are you guys okay? Is anyone hurt?
Hey, Spider-Man!
Hey! So the exit is cleared now if you wa--
Spider-Man!
Umm...hi, again!
...
So the exit is cleared n--
Spider-Man!
Yes!
HI THERE--
gh! Wait, no, you're the bad guy. Okay.
I see what just happened there.
Ouch.
Nothing and no one can stop THE BEETLE!
I modeled this tech after the second-strongest beetle in the world!

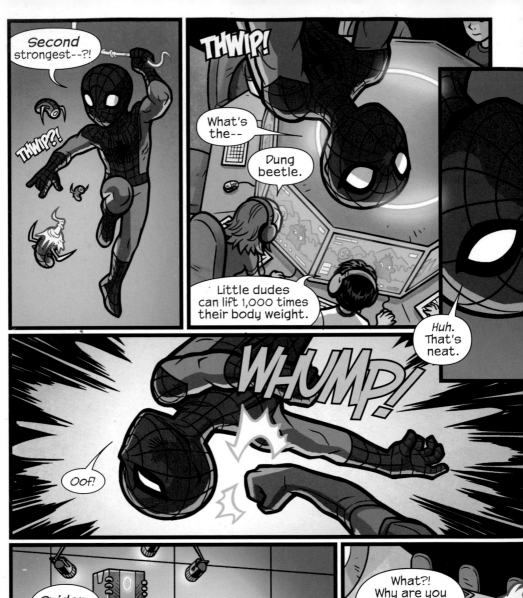

Second strongest--?!

THWIP?!

THWIP!

What's the--

Dung beetle.

Little dudes can lift 1,000 times their body weight.

Huh. That's neat.

WHUMP!

Oof!

Spider-Man!

Hey, buddy.

I fixed the computer!

What?! Why are you guys *still* here?! It's too dangerous!

THWIP!

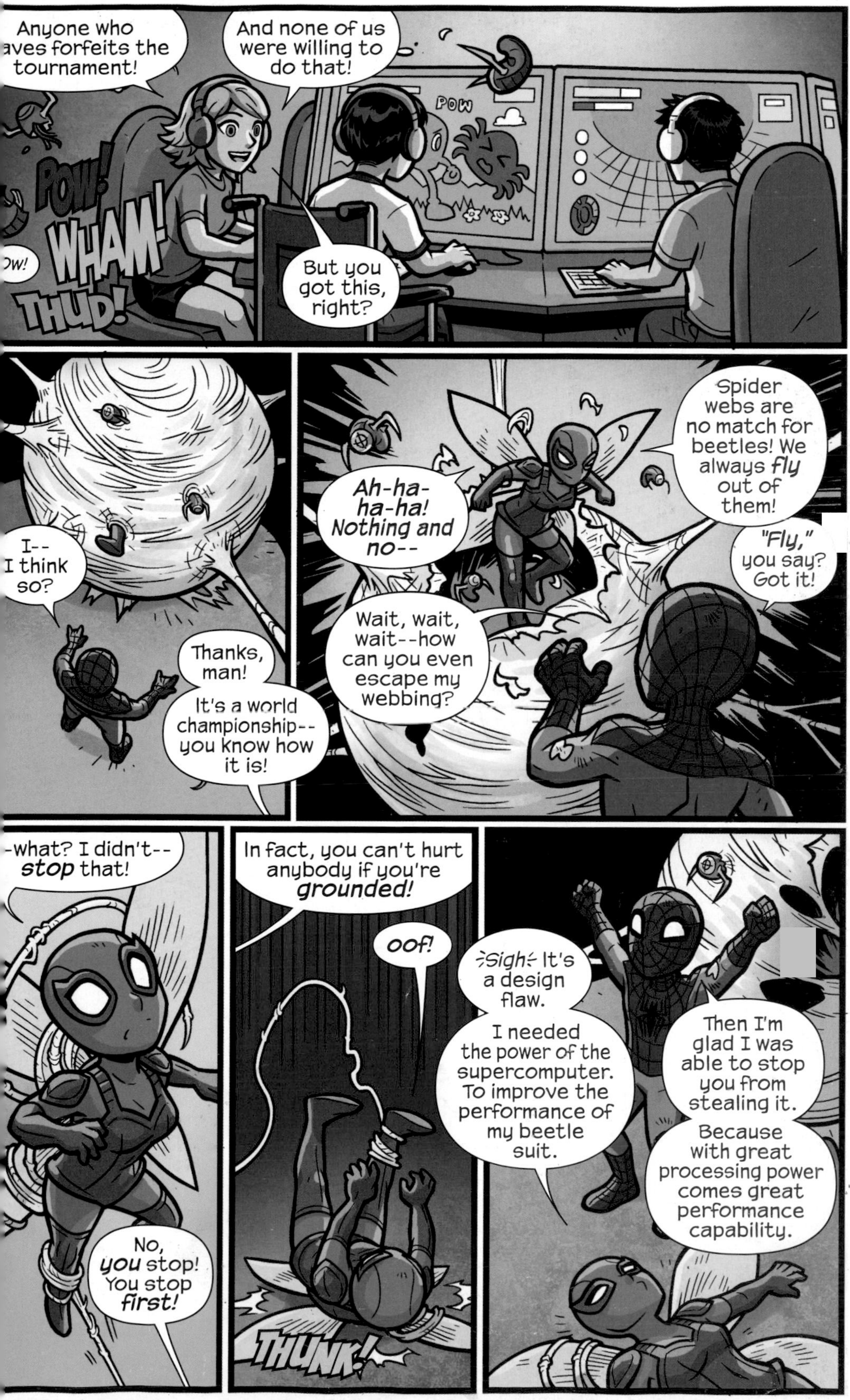
Anyone who aves forfeits the tournament!
And none of us were willing to do that!
POW
POW!
WHAM!
OW!
THUD!
But you got this, right?
I-- I think so?
Thanks, man!
It's a world championship-- you know how it is!
Ah-ha-ha-ha! Nothing and no--
Spider webs are no match for beetles! We always *fly* out of them!
"Fly," you say? Got it!
Wait, wait, wait--how can you even escape my webbing?
-what? I didn't-- *stop* that!
No, *you* stop! You stop *first!*
In fact, you can't hurt anybody if you're *grounded!*
oof!
THUNK!
Sigh It's a design flaw.
I needed the power of the supercomputer. To improve the performance of my beetle suit.
Then I'm glad I was able to stop you from stealing it.
Because with great processing power comes great performance capability.

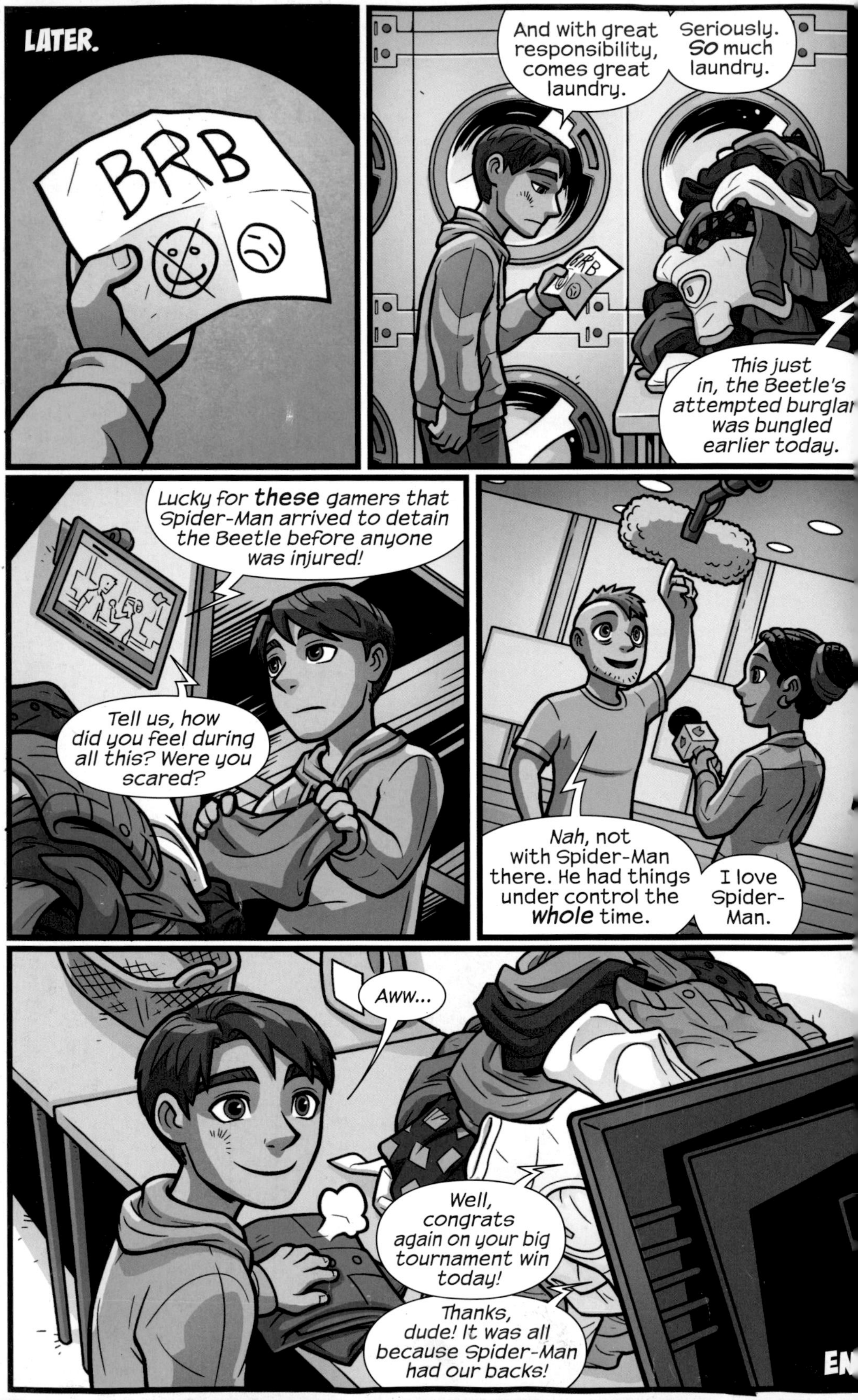
LATER.
BRB
And with great responsibility, comes great laundry.
Seriously. SO much laundry.
This just in, the Beetle's attempted burgla
was bungled earlier today.
Lucky for these gamers that Spider-Man arrived to detain the Beetle before anyone was injured!
Tell us, how did you feel during all this? Were you scared?
Nah, not with Spider-Man there. He had things under control the whole time.
I love Spider-Man.
Aww...
Well, congrats again on your big tournament win today!
Thanks, dude! It was all because Spider-Man had our backs!
EN

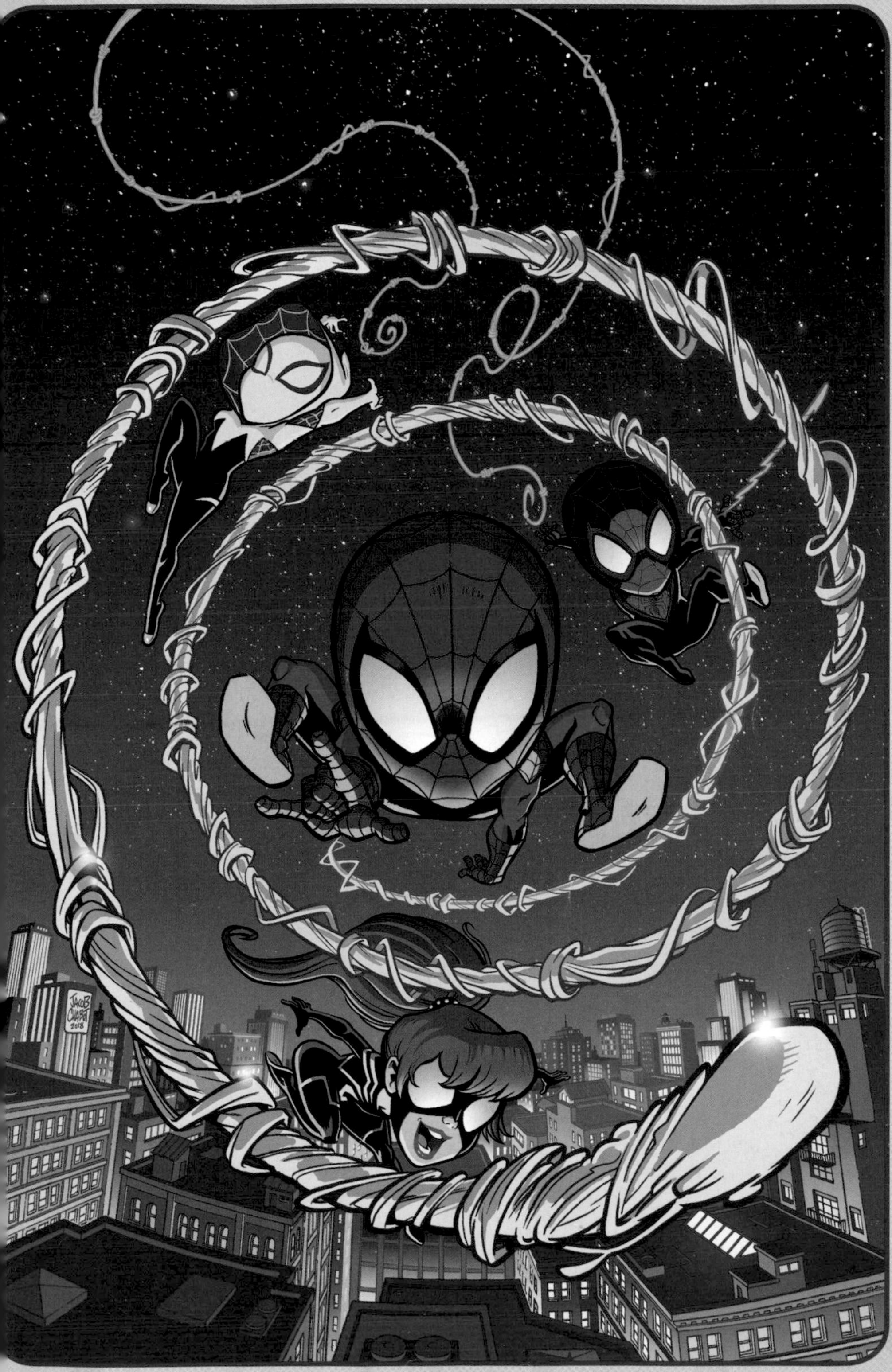

Web Designers

cover by Jacob Chabot

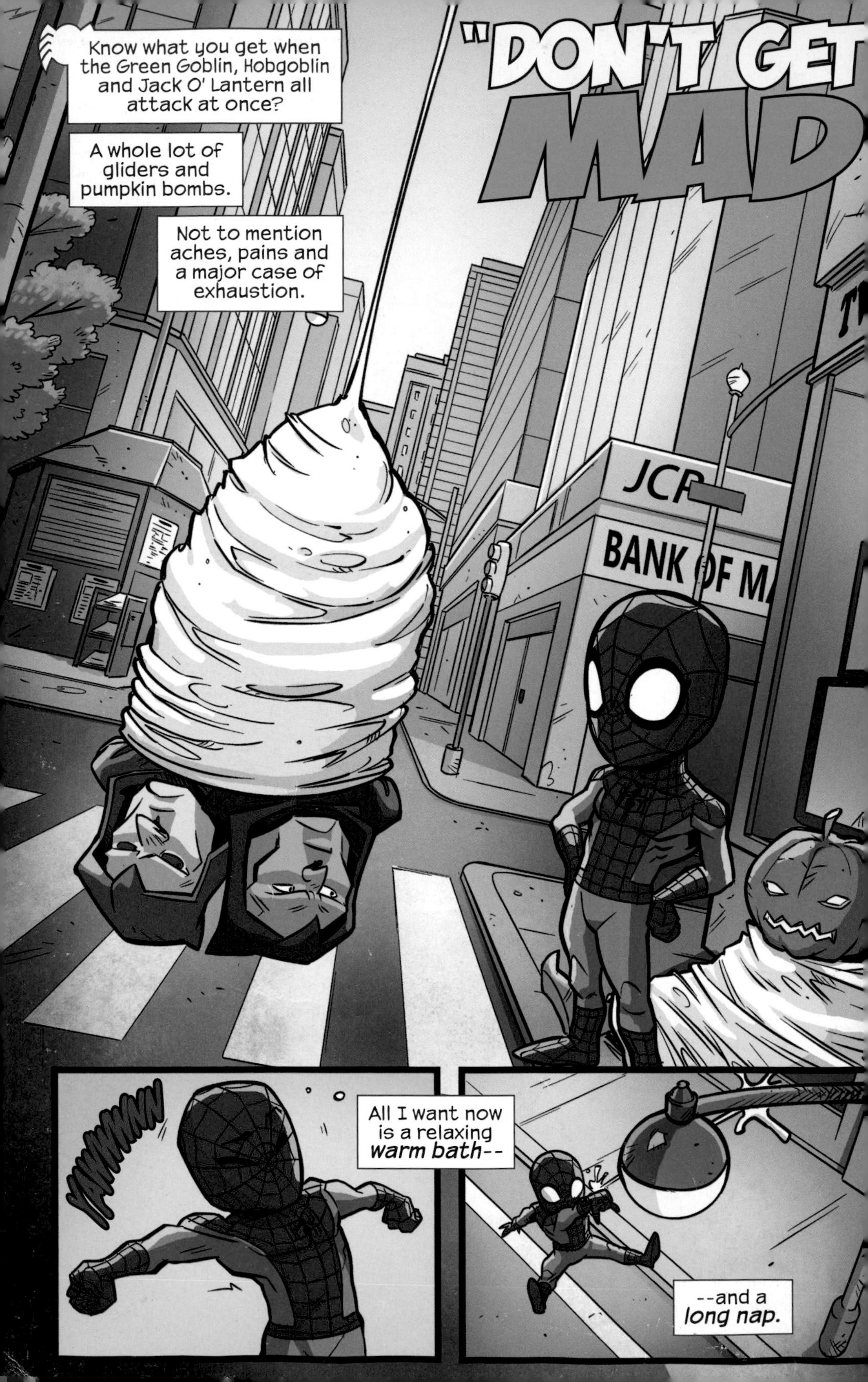
"DON'T GET MAD
Know what you get when the Green Goblin, Hobgoblin and Jack O' Lantern all attack at once?
A whole lot of gliders and pumpkin bombs.
Not to mention aches, pains and a major case of exhaustion.
JCP
BANK OF MA
YAWWWNN
All I want now is a relaxing *warm bath*--
--and a *long nap.*

Whoops! No rest for the weary!

My **spider-sense** is signaling danger! I don't see anyth--

Wha--? An **earthquake?!**

But New York doesn't **have** earthquakes!

Thin

RUMMMMMMMMB8LLE

Not unless you're gettin' rocked by **the Shocker!**

Oh. No offense, Shockie, but after a gaggle of Goblins, I'm kind of **glad** that I'm just up against your vibration powers!

Plus, not a lot of bad guys can pull off a costume made from a **quilt.**

...Spider-annn!

...the ...ard ...0?

...hat is this, ...ional Gang Up ...Wall-Crawlers Day?

With the Lizard in the mix, this just got a lot more **dangerous!**

...**Spider-Man!**

And there's someone **else** too?

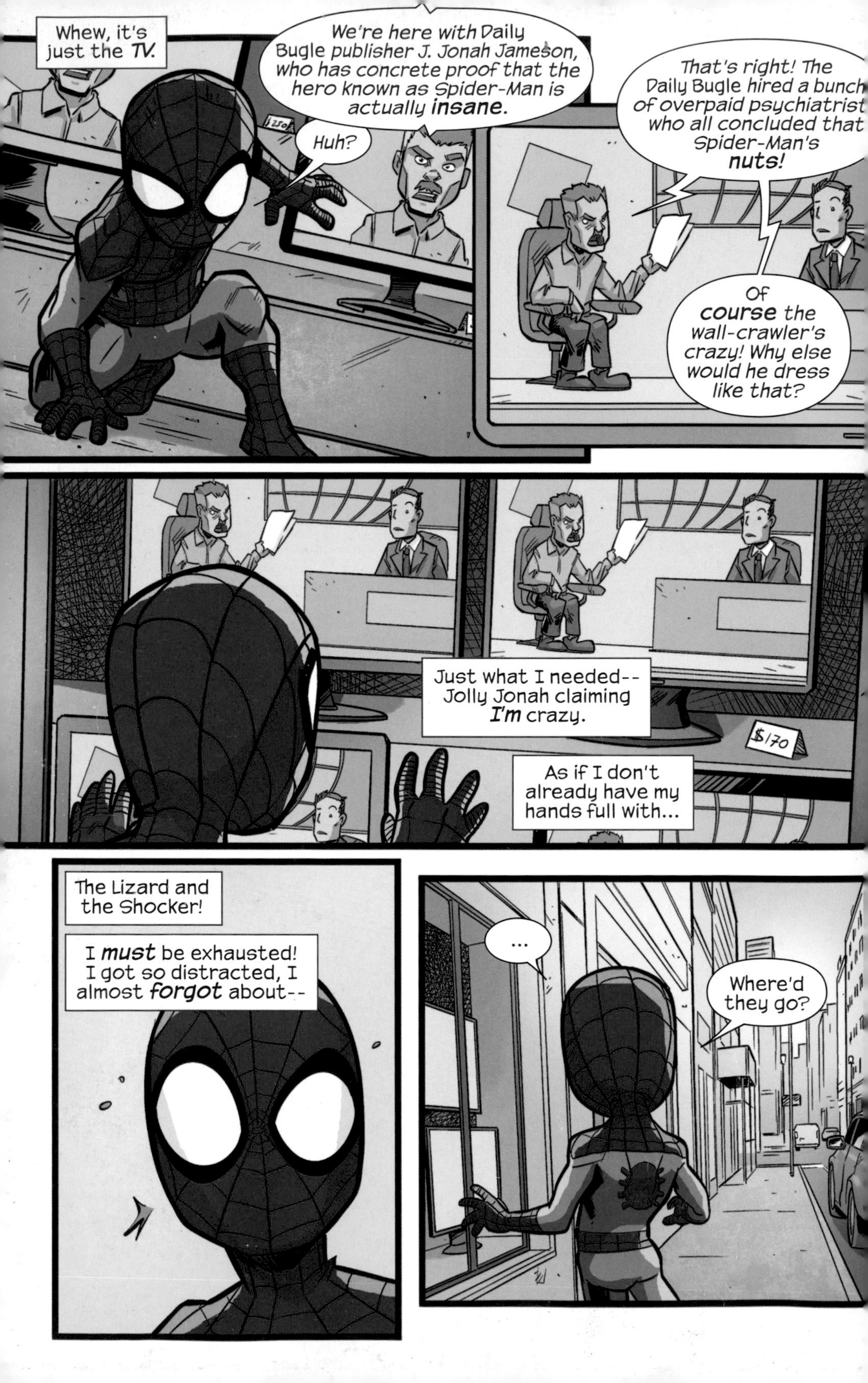
Whew, it's just the TV.
We're here with Daily Bugle publisher J. Jonah Jameson, who has concrete proof that the hero known as Spider-Man is actually insane.
Huh?
That's right! The Daily Bugle hired a bunch of overpaid psychiatrist who all concluded that Spider-Man's nuts!
Of course the wall-crawler's crazy! Why else would he dress like that?
$250
Just what I needed-- Jolly Jonah claiming I'm crazy.
$170
As if I don't already have my hands full with...
The Lizard and the Shocker!
I must be exhausted! I got so distracted, I almost forgot about--
...
Where'd they go?

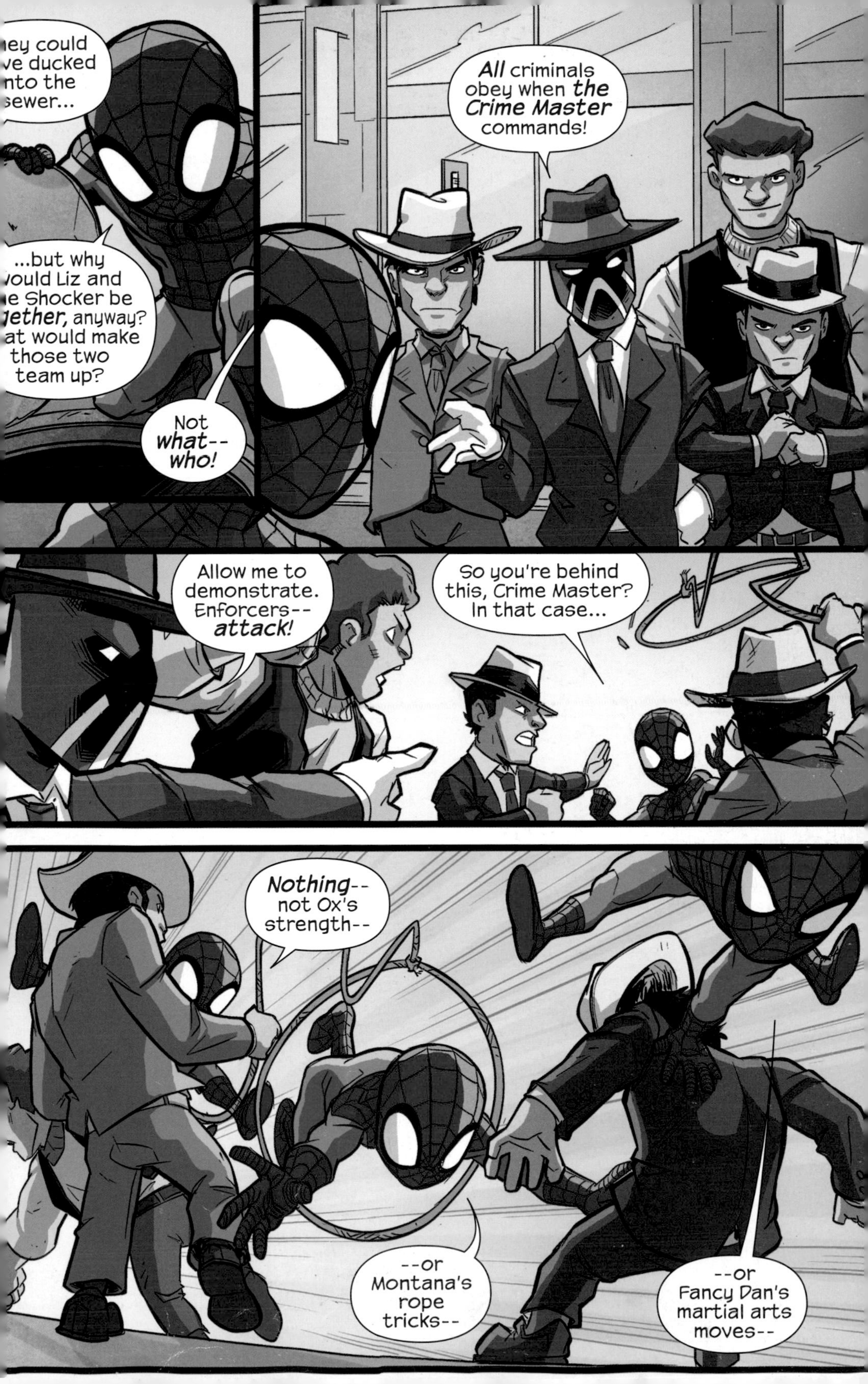

ey could ve ducked nto the sewer...
...but why vould Liz and e Shocker be ether, anyway? at would make those two team up?
Not what-- who!
All criminals obey when the Crime Master commands!
Allow me to demonstrate. Enforcers-- attack!
So you're behind this, Crime Master? In that case...
Nothing-- not Ox's strength--
--or Montana's rope tricks--
--or Fancy Dan's martial arts moves--

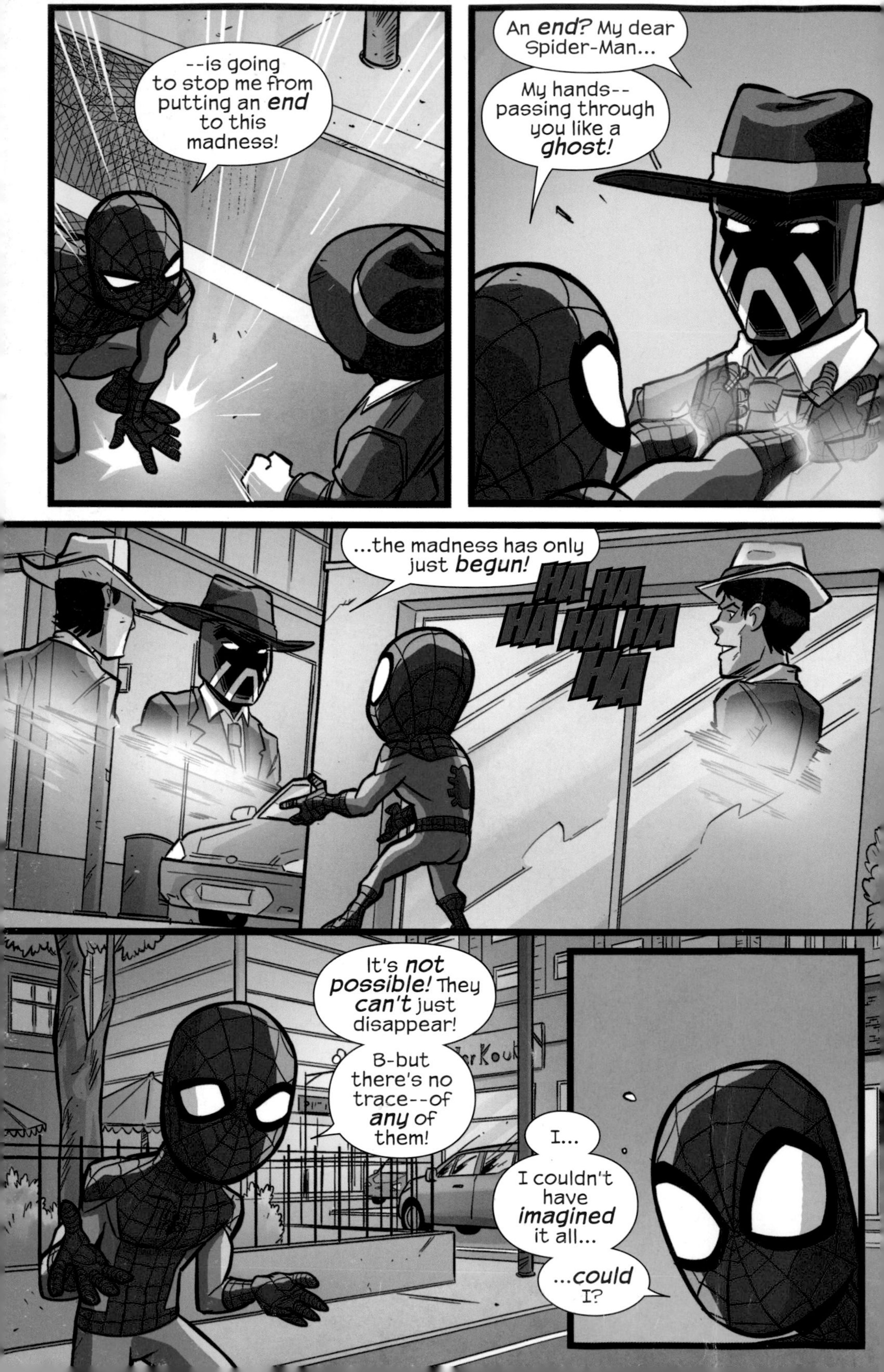
--is going to stop me from putting an end to this madness!
An end? My dear Spider-Man...
My hands--passing through you like a ghost!
...the madness has only just begun!
HA HA HA HA HA HA
It's not possible! They can't just disappear!
B-but there's no trace--of any of them!
I...
I couldn't have imagined it all...
...could I?

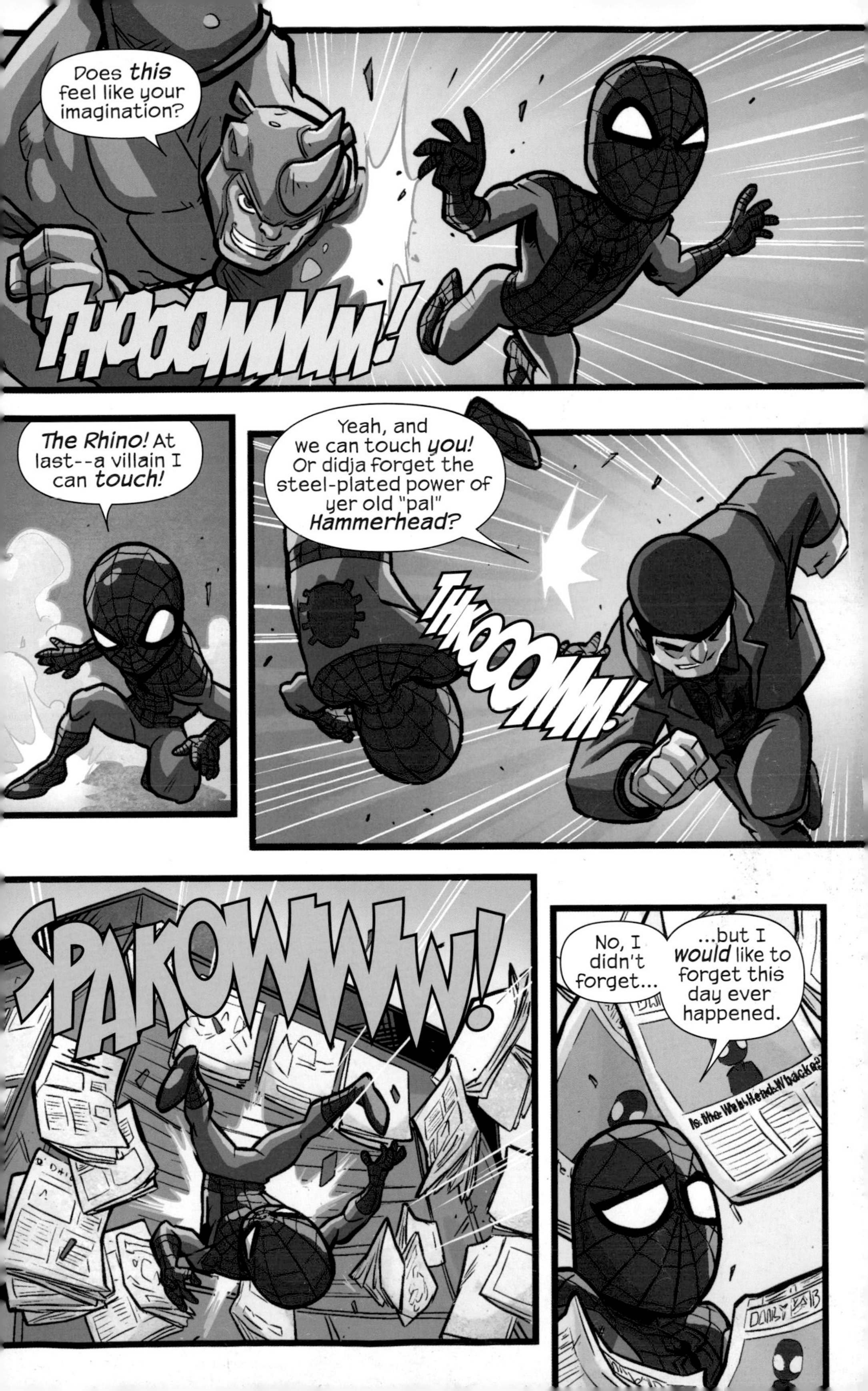
Does this feel like your imagination?
THOOOMMMM!
The Rhino! At last--a villain I can touch!
Yeah, and we can touch you! Or didja forget the steel-plated power of yer old "pal" Hammerhead?
THKOOOMM!
SPAKOWWW!
No, I didn't forget...
...but I would like to forget this day ever happened.

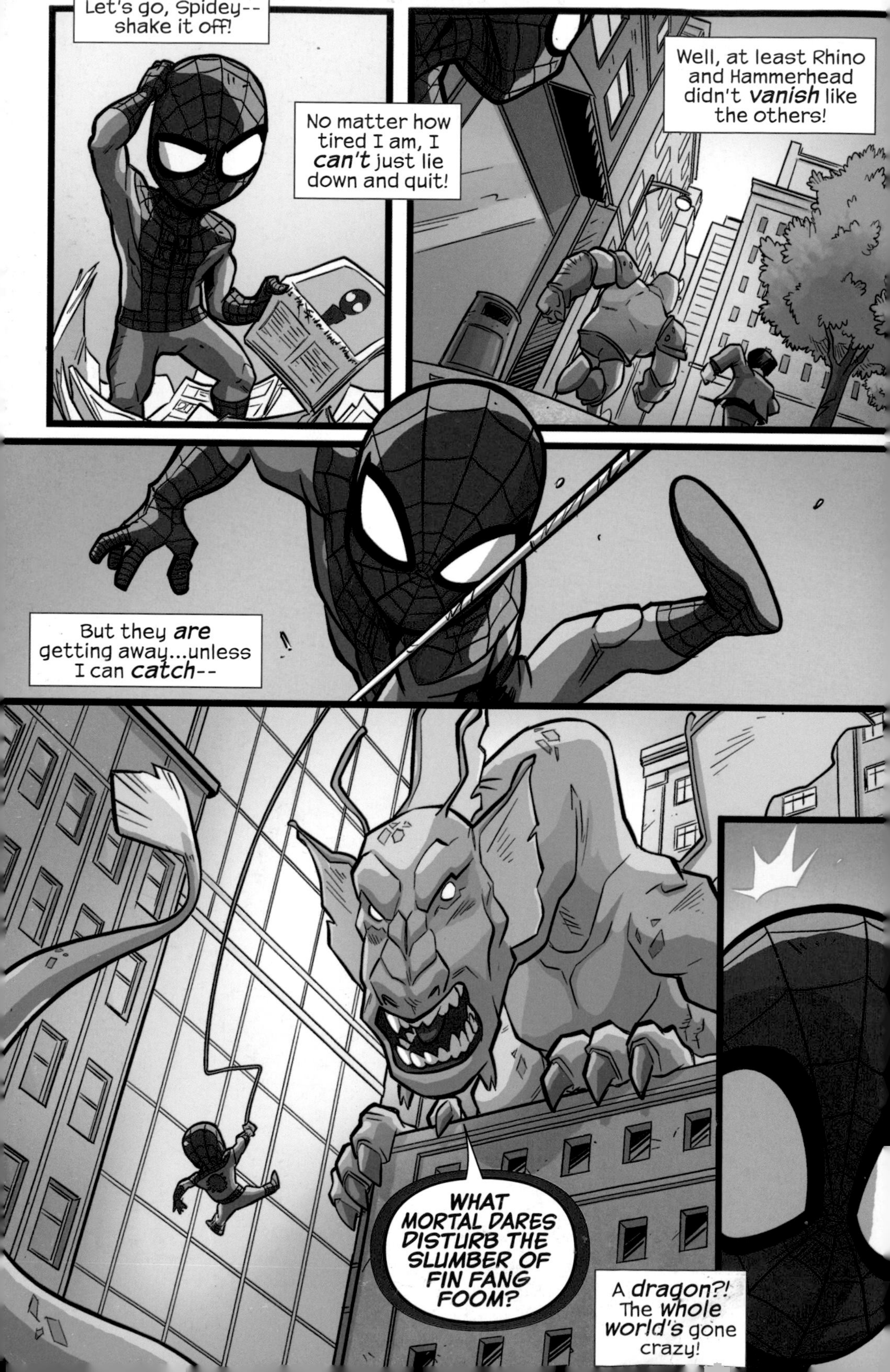
Let's go, Spidey--shake it off!
No matter how tired I am, I *can't* just lie down and quit!
Well, at least Rhino and Hammerhead didn't *vanish* like the others!
But they *are* getting away...unless I can *catch*--
WHAT MORTAL DARES DISTURB THE SLUMBER OF FIN FANG FOOM?
A *dragon?!* The *whole world's* gone crazy!

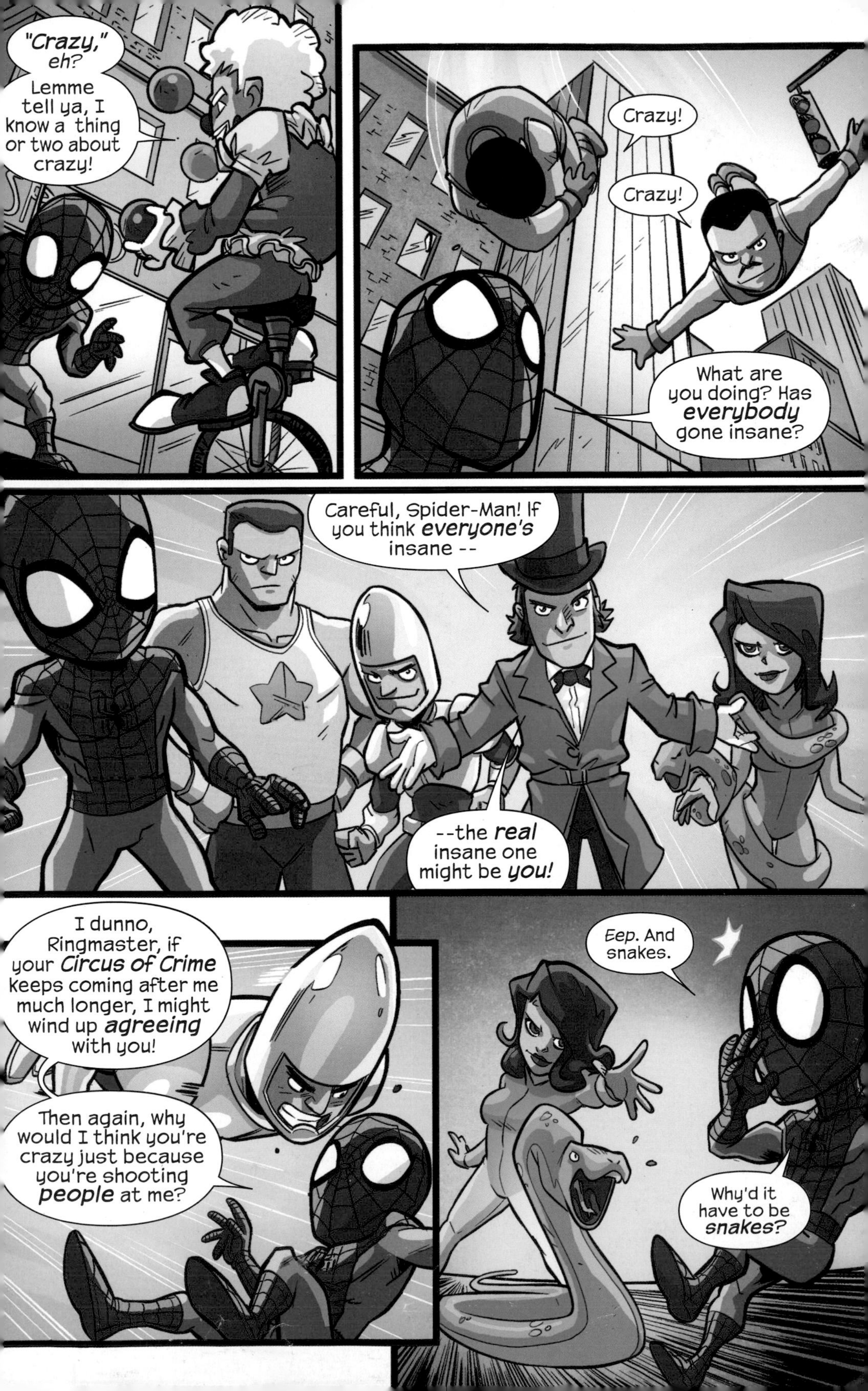
"Crazy," eh?
Lemme tell ya, I know a thing or two about crazy!
Crazy!
Crazy!
What are you doing? Has everybody gone insane?
Careful, Spider-Man! If you think everyone's insane --
--the real insane one might be you!
I dunno, Ringmaster, if your Circus of Crime keeps coming after me much longer, I might wind up agreeing with you!
Then again, why would I think you're crazy just because you're shooting people at me?
Eep. And snakes.
Why'd it have to be snakes?

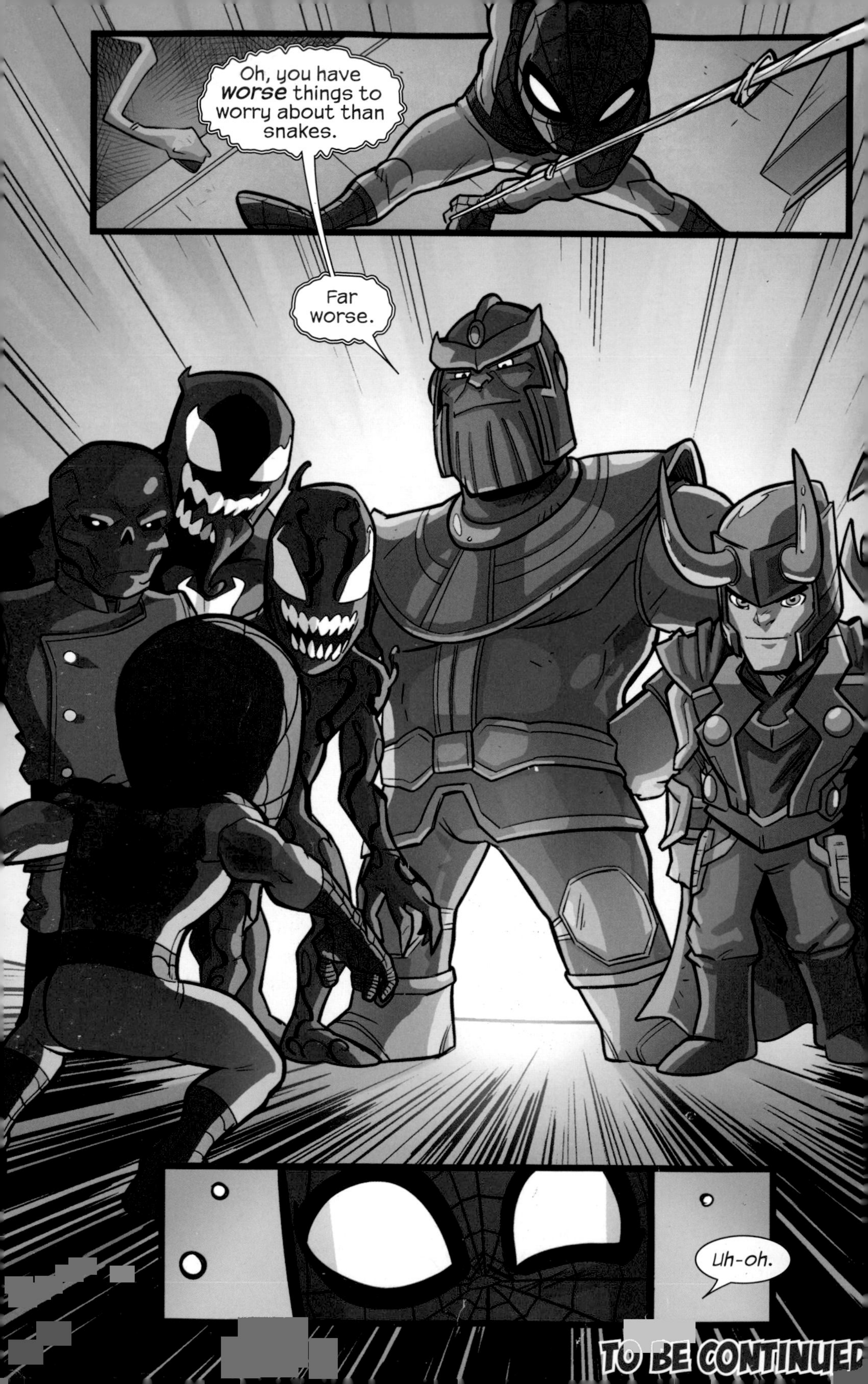
Oh, you have *worse* things to worry about than snakes.
Far worse.
Uh-oh.
TO BE CONTINUED

DAILY BUGLE

NEW YORK'S FUNNIEST DAILY NEWSPAPER

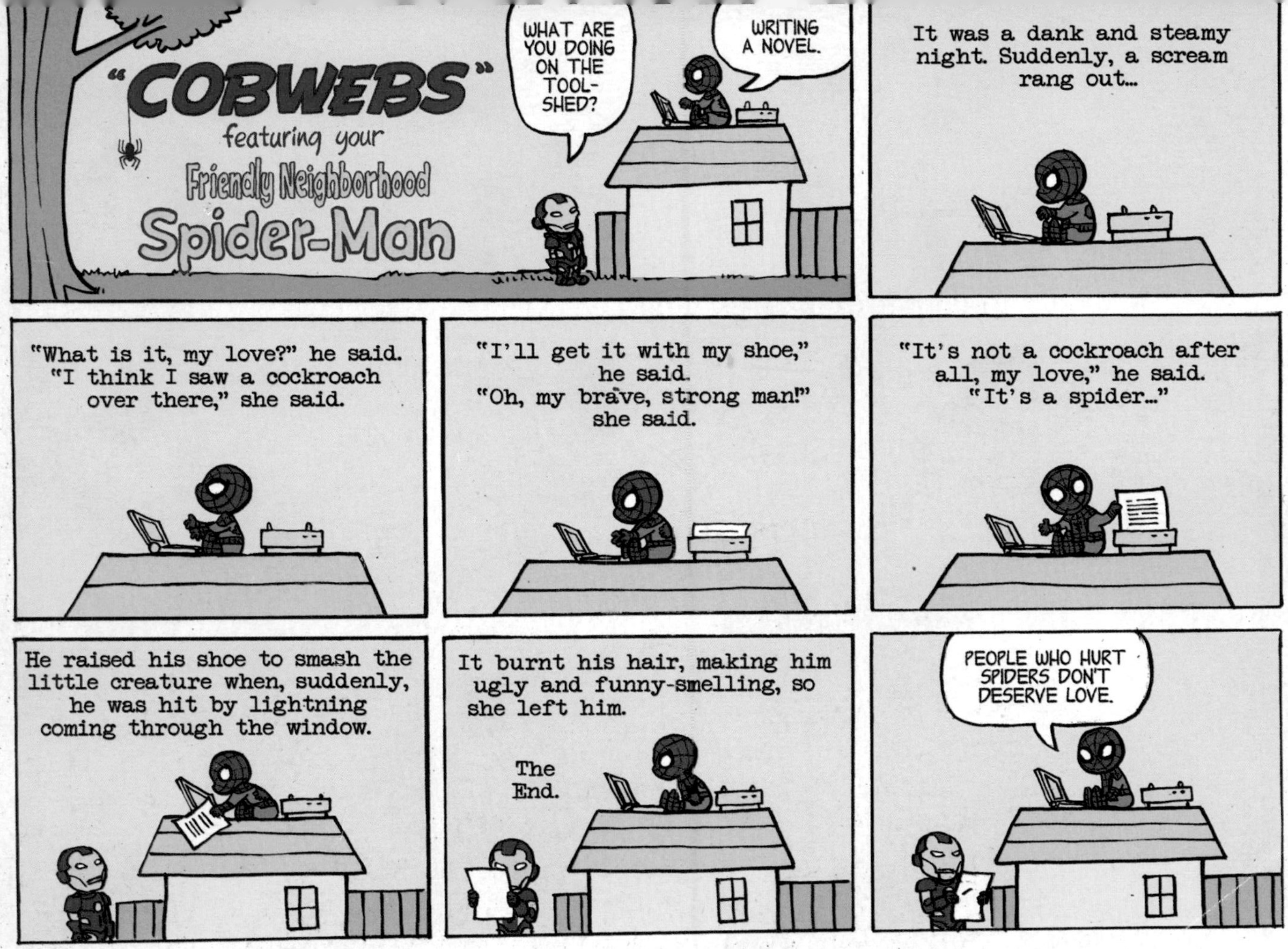

"COBWEBS"
featuring your
Friendly Neighborhood
Spider-Man
WHAT ARE YOU DOING ON THE TOOL-SHED?
WRITING A NOVEL.
It was a dank and steamy night. Suddenly, a scream rang out...
"What is it, my love?" he said. "I think I saw a cockroach over there," she said.
"I'll get it with my shoe," he said. "Oh, my brave, strong man!" she said.
"It's not a cockroach after all, my love," he said. "It's a spider..."
He raised his shoe to smash the little creature when, suddenly, he was hit by lightning coming through the window.
It burnt his hair, making him ugly and funny-smelling, so she left him.
The End.
PEOPLE WHO HURT SPIDERS DON'T DESERVE LOVE.

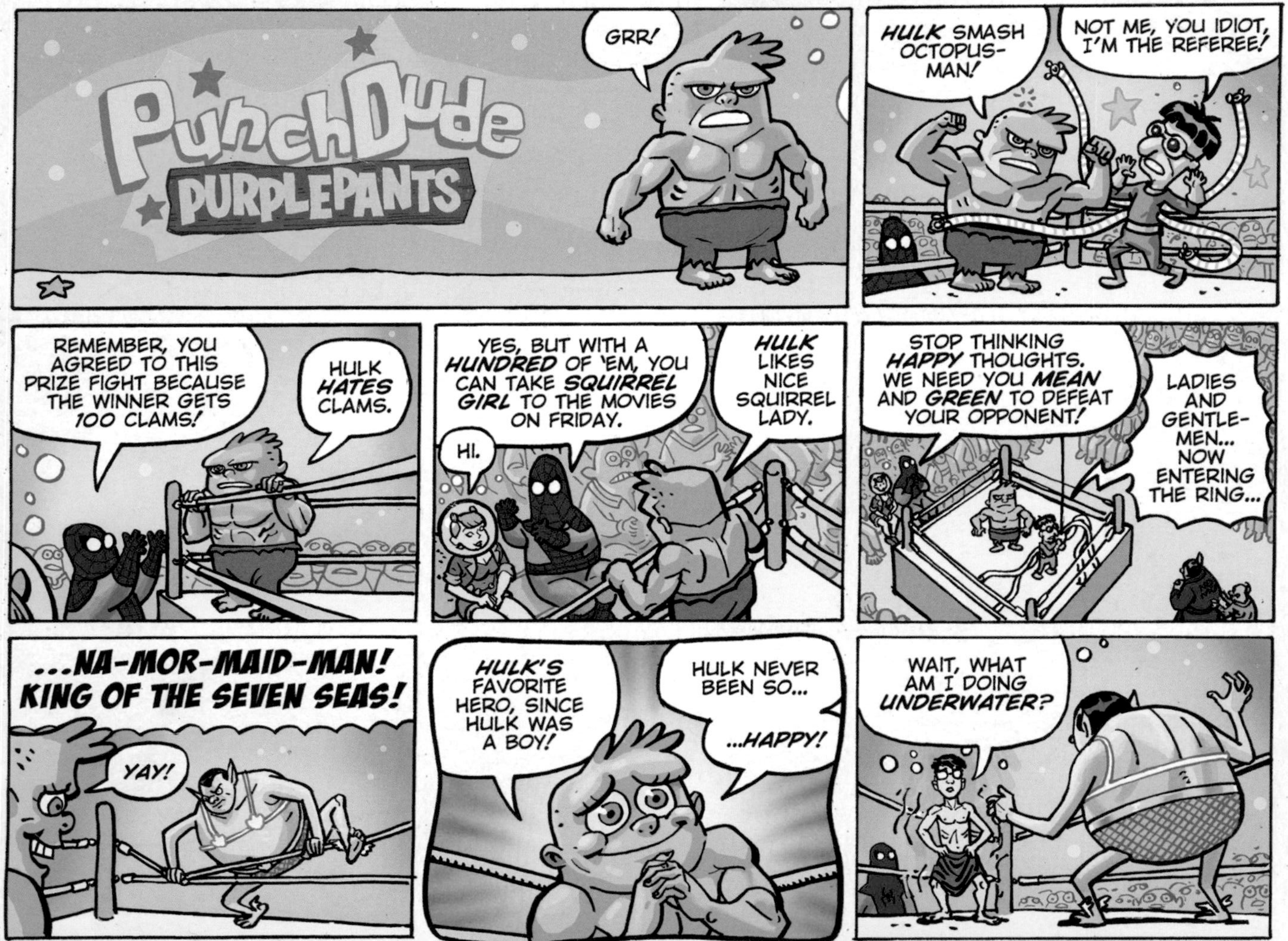
PunchDude PURPLEPANTS
GRR!
HULK SMASH OCTOPUS-MAN!
NOT ME, YOU IDIOT, I'M THE REFEREE!
REMEMBER, YOU AGREED TO THIS PRIZE FIGHT BECAUSE THE WINNER GETS 100 CLAMS!
HULK HATES CLAMS.
YES, BUT WITH A HUNDRED OF 'EM, YOU CAN TAKE SQUIRREL GIRL TO THE MOVIES ON FRIDAY.
HI.
HULK LIKES NICE SQUIRREL LADY.
STOP THINKING HAPPY THOUGHTS. WE NEED YOU MEAN AND GREEN TO DEFEAT YOUR OPPONENT!
LADIES AND GENTLE-MEN... NOW ENTERING THE RING...
...NA-MOR-MAID-MAN! KING OF THE SEVEN SEAS!
YAY!
HULK'S FAVORITE HERO, SINCE HULK WAS A BOY!
HULK NEVER BEEN SO...
...HAPPY!
WAIT, WHAT AM I DOING UNDERWATER?

DAILY BUGLE

NEW YORK'S FUNNIEST DAILY NEWSPAPER

Peter and Miles's New Super Hero

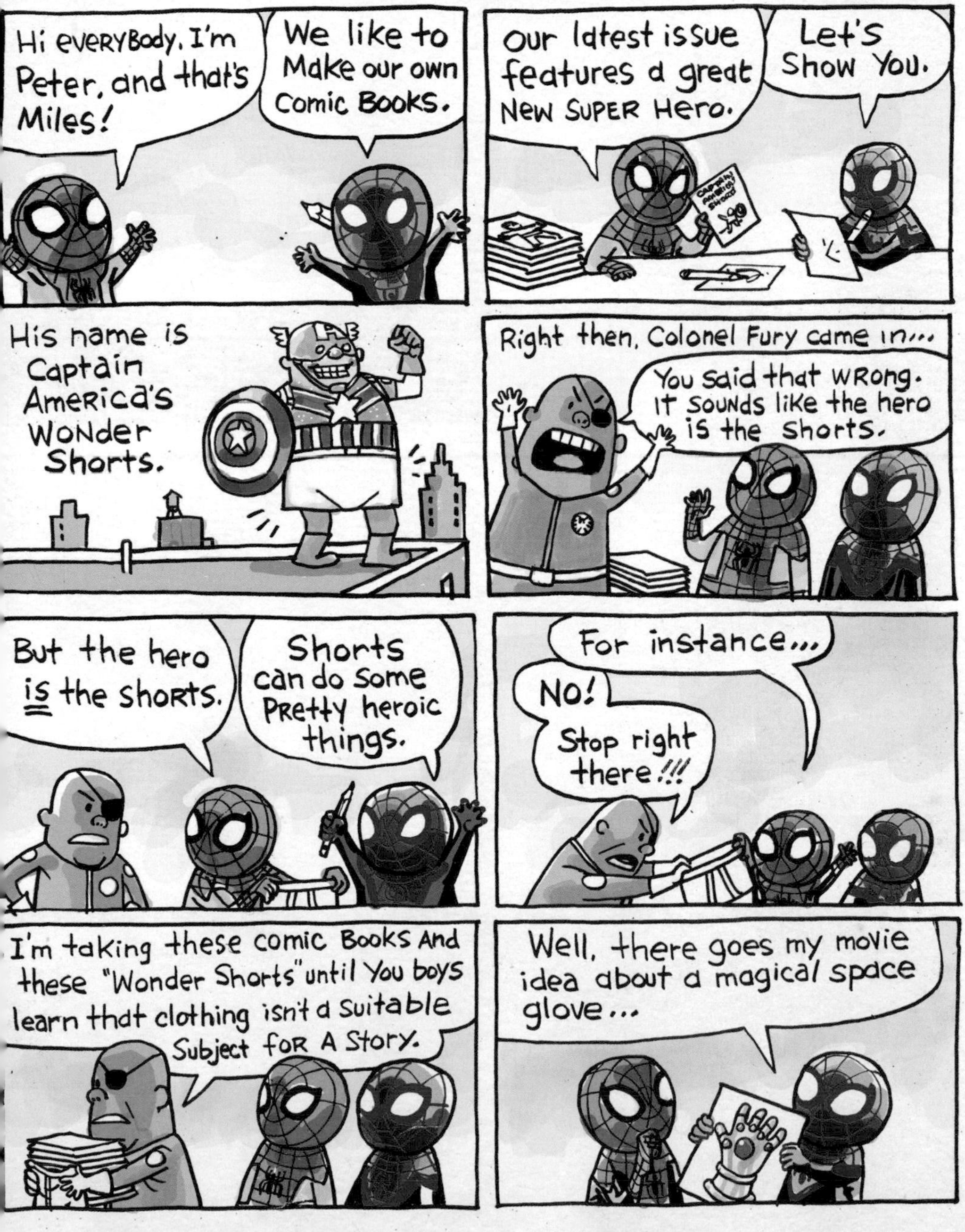

Hi everybody. I'm Peter, and that's Miles!
We like to make our own comic books.
Our latest issue features a great new super hero.
Let's show you.
His name is Captain America's Wonder Shorts.
Right then, Colonel Fury came in...
You said that wrong. It sounds like the hero is the shorts.
But the hero is the shorts.
Shorts can do some pretty heroic things.
For instance...
No! Stop right there!!!
I'm taking these comic books and these "Wonder Shorts" until you boys learn that clothing isn't a suitable subject for a story.
Well, there goes my movie idea about a magical space glove...

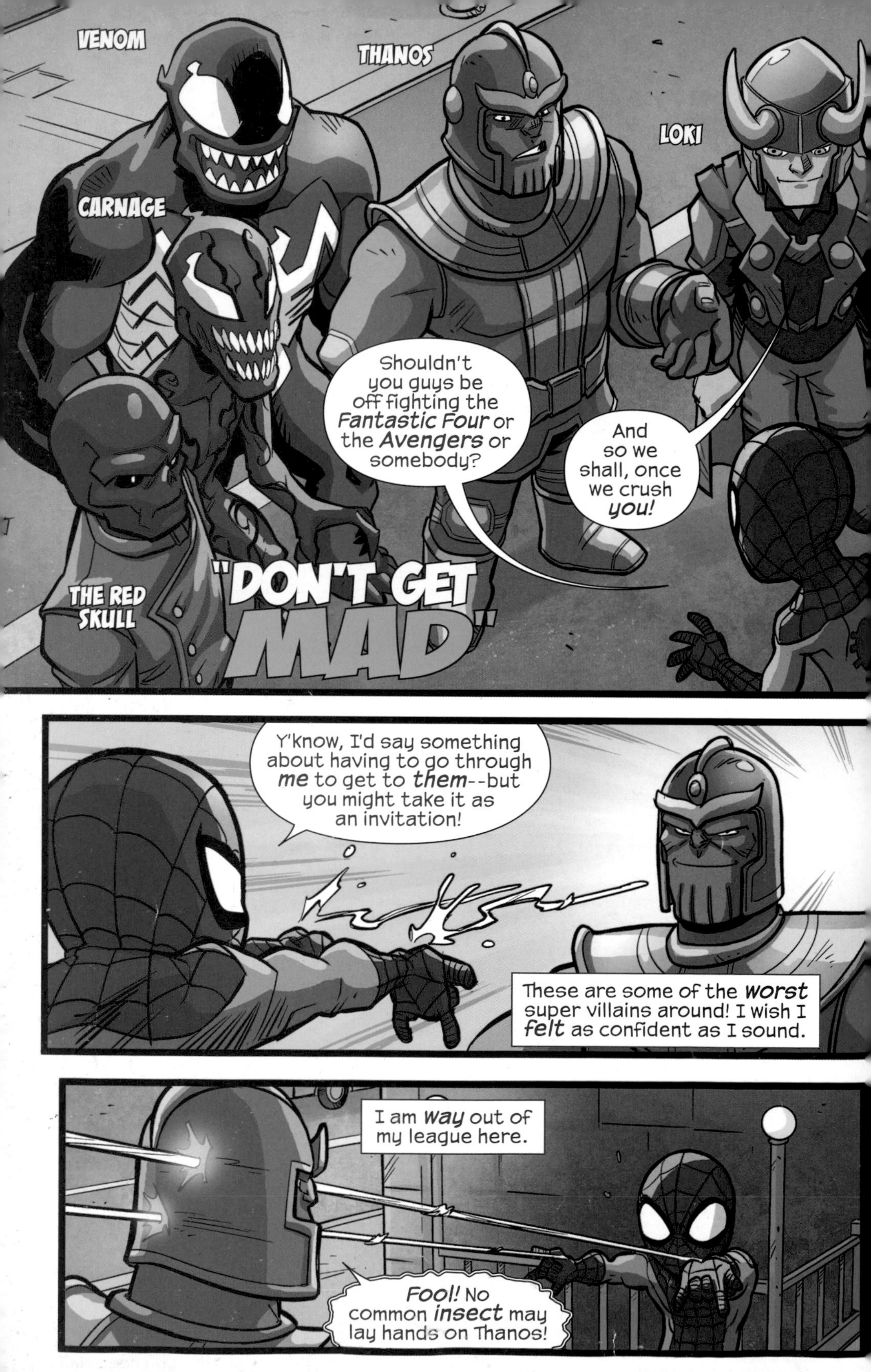
VENOM
THANOS
LOKI
CARNAGE
THE RED SKULL
"DON'T GET MAD"
Shouldn't you guys be off fighting the Fantastic Four or the Avengers or somebody?
And so we shall, once we crush you!
Y'know, I'd say something about having to go through me to get to them--but you might take it as an invitation!
These are some of the worst super villains around! I wish I felt as confident as I sound.
I am way out of my league here.
Fool! No common insect may lay hands on Thanos!

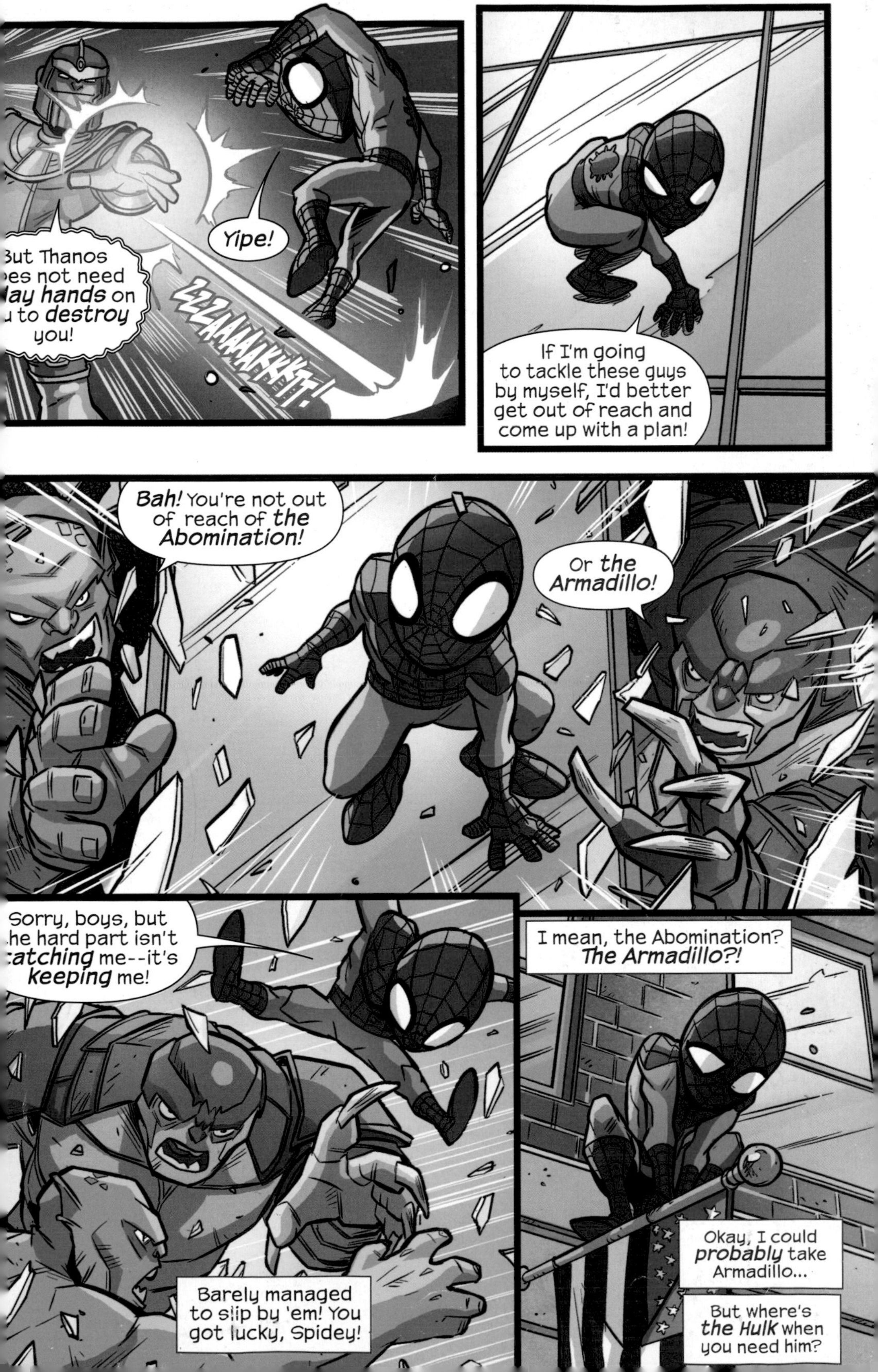
ut Thanos
es not need
lay hands on
to destroy
you!
Yipe!
ZZZAAAAAKKKT!
If I'm going
to tackle these guys
by myself, I'd better
get out of reach and
come up with a plan!
Bah! You're not out
of reach of the
Abomination!
Or the
Armadillo!
Sorry, boys, but
he hard part isn't
atching me--it's
keeping me!
Barely managed
to slip by 'em! You
got lucky, Spidey!
I mean, the Abomination?
The Armadillo?!
Okay, I could
probably take
Armadillo...
But where's
the Hulk when
you need him?

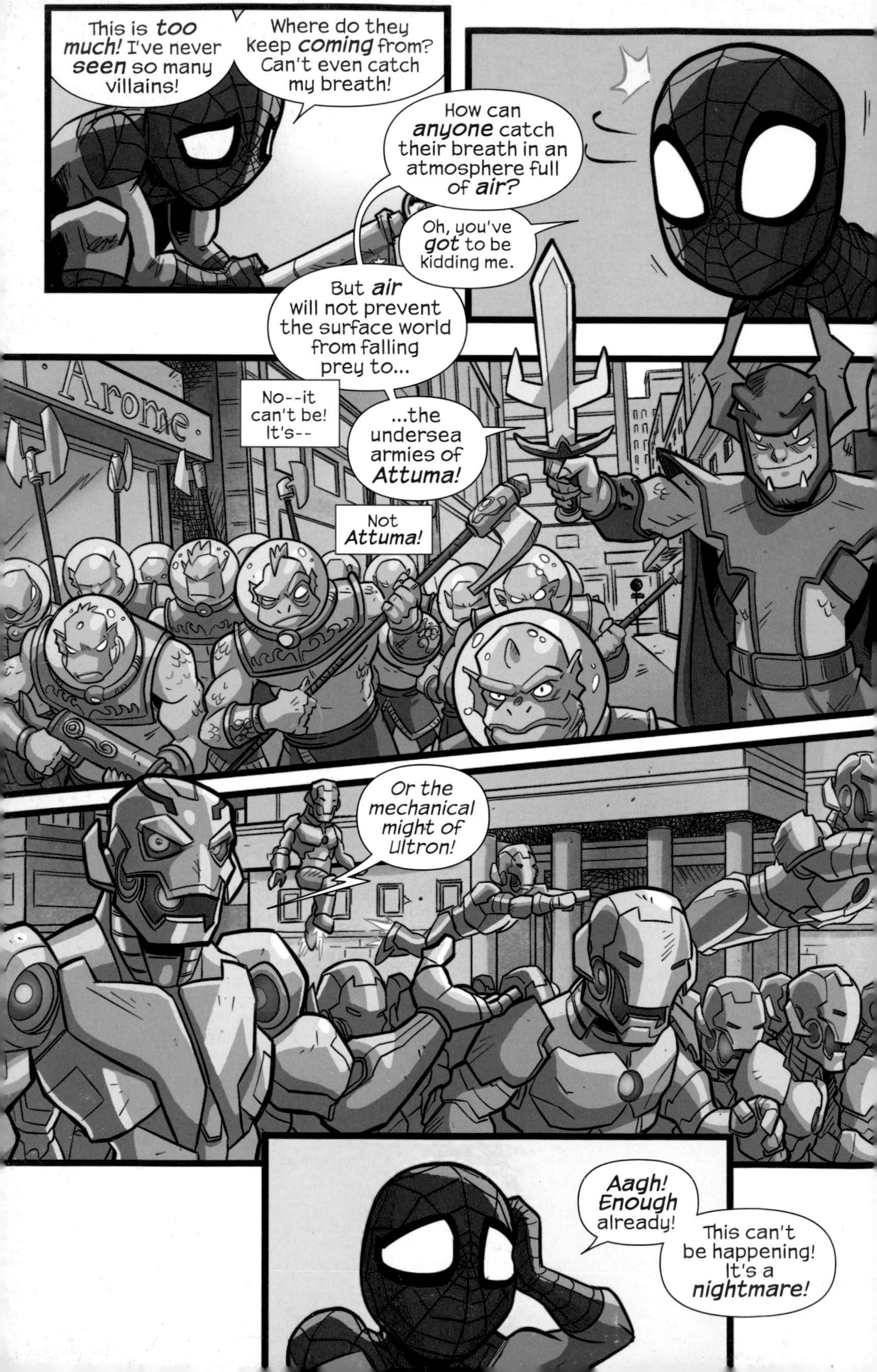
This is too much! I've never seen so many villains!
Where do they keep coming from? Can't even catch my breath!
How can anyone catch their breath in an atmosphere full of air?
Oh, you've got to be kidding me.
But air will not prevent the surface world from falling prey to...
Arome
No--it can't be! It's--
...the undersea armies of Attuma!
Not Attuma!
Or the mechanical might of Ultron!
Aagh! Enough already!
This can't be happening! It's a nightmare!

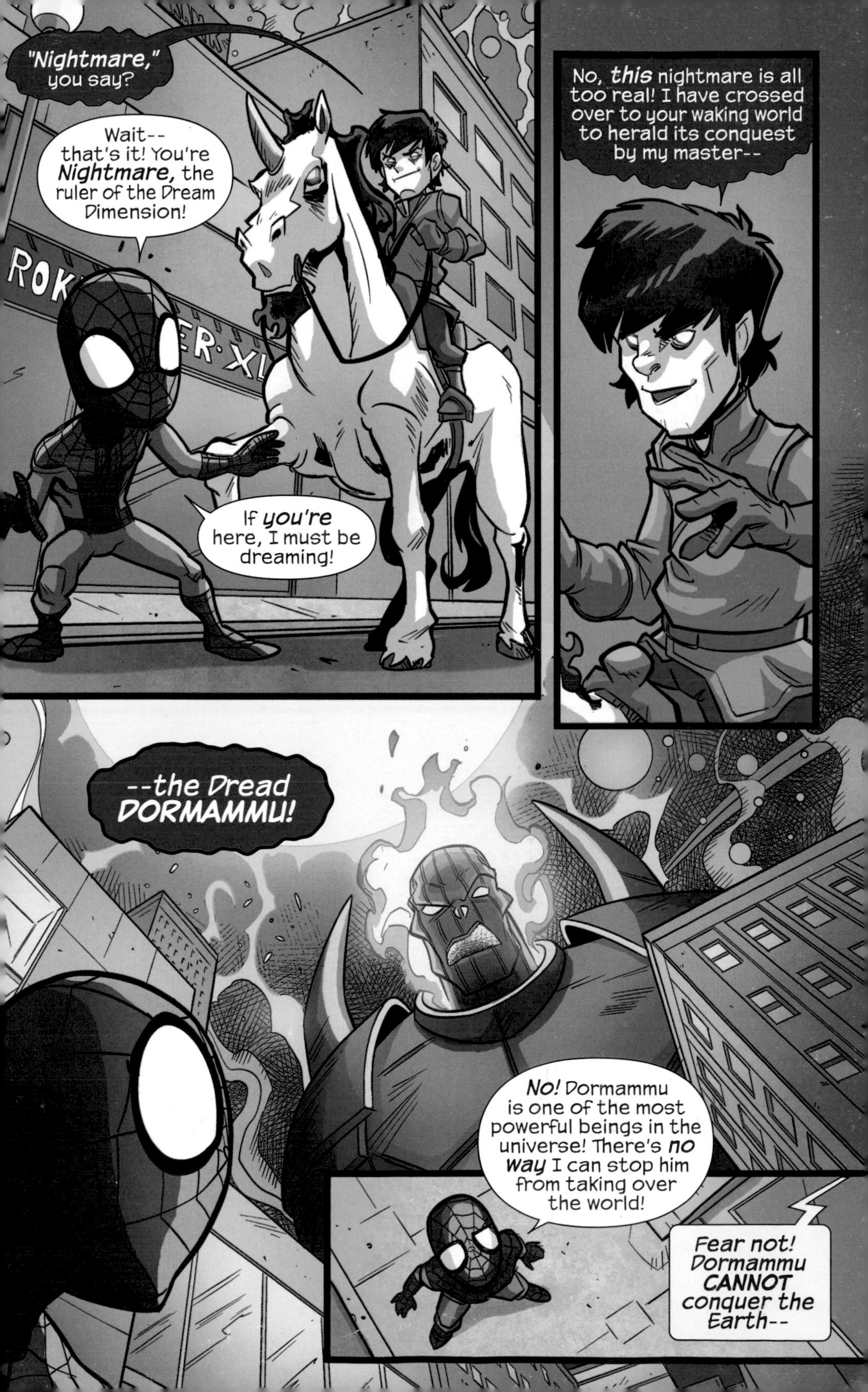
"Nightmare," you say?
Wait-- that's it! You're Nightmare, the ruler of the Dream Dimension!
If you're here, I must be dreaming!
No, this nightmare is all too real! I have crossed over to your waking world to herald its conquest by my master--
--the Dread DORMAMMU!
No! Dormammu is one of the most powerful beings in the universe! There's no way I can stop him from taking over the world!
Fear not! Dormammu CANNOT conquer the Earth--

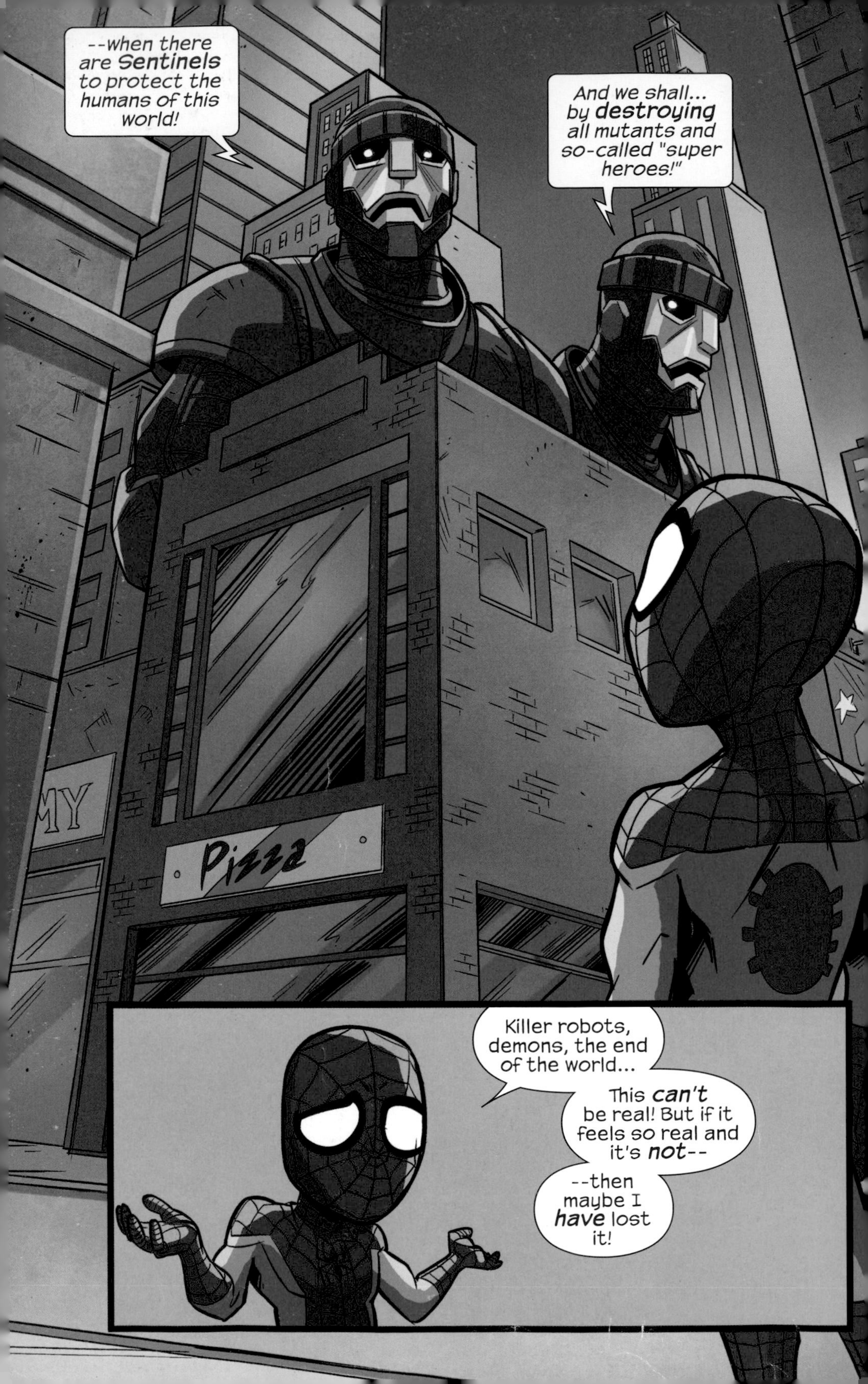
--when there are Sentinels to protect the humans of this world!
And we shall... by destroying all mutants and so-called "super heroes!"
MY
Pizza
Killer robots, demons, the end of the world...
This can't be real! But if it feels so real and it's not--
--then maybe I have lost it!

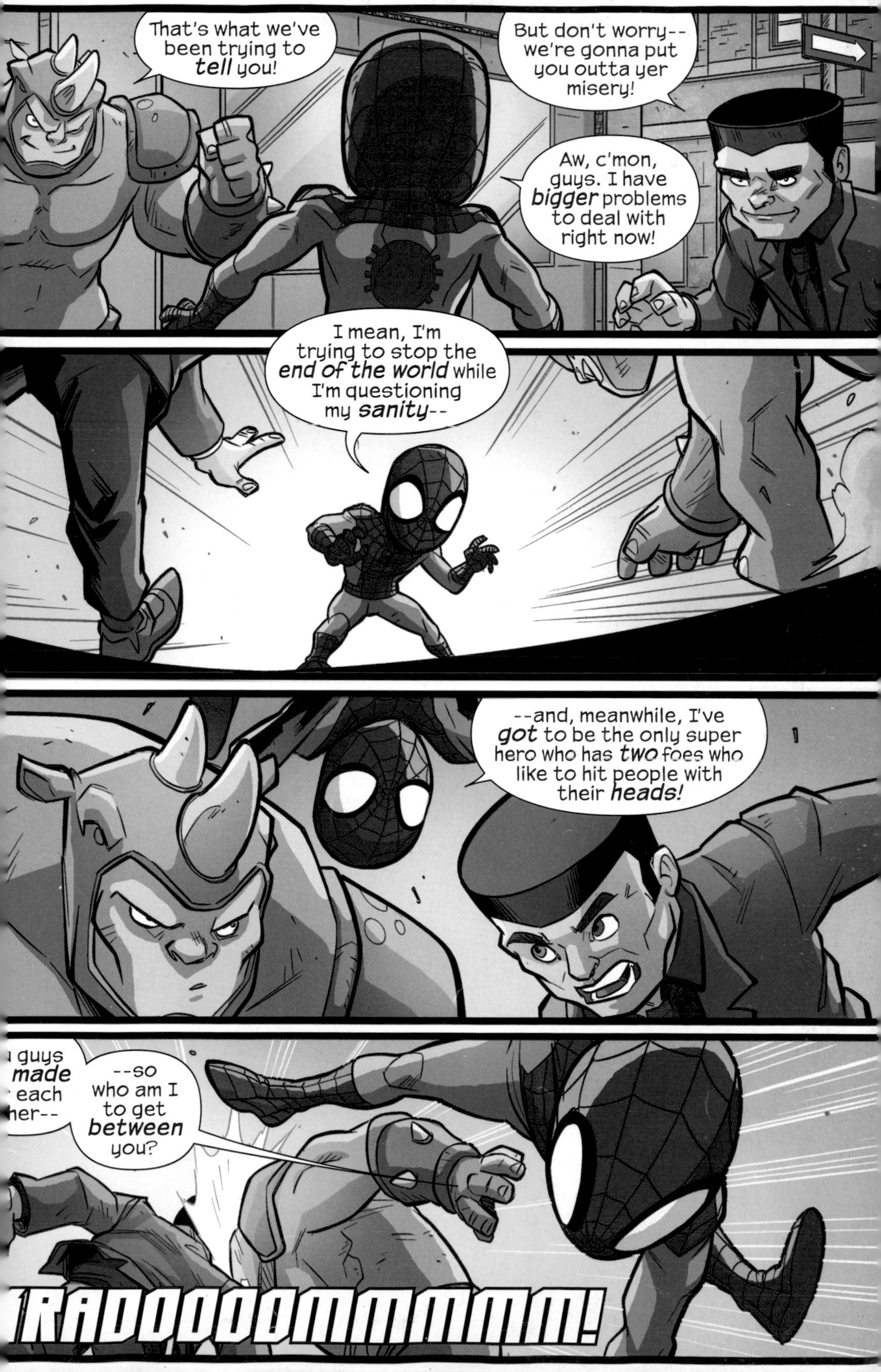
That's what we've been trying to *tell* you!
But don't worry-- we're gonna put you outta yer misery!
Aw, c'mon, guys. I have *bigger* problems to deal with right now!
I mean, I'm trying to stop the *end of the world* while I'm questioning my *sanity*--
--and, meanwhile, I've *got* to be the only super hero who has *two* foes who like to hit people with their *heads!*
guys *made* each her--
--so who am I to get *between* you?
RADOOOMMMMMM!

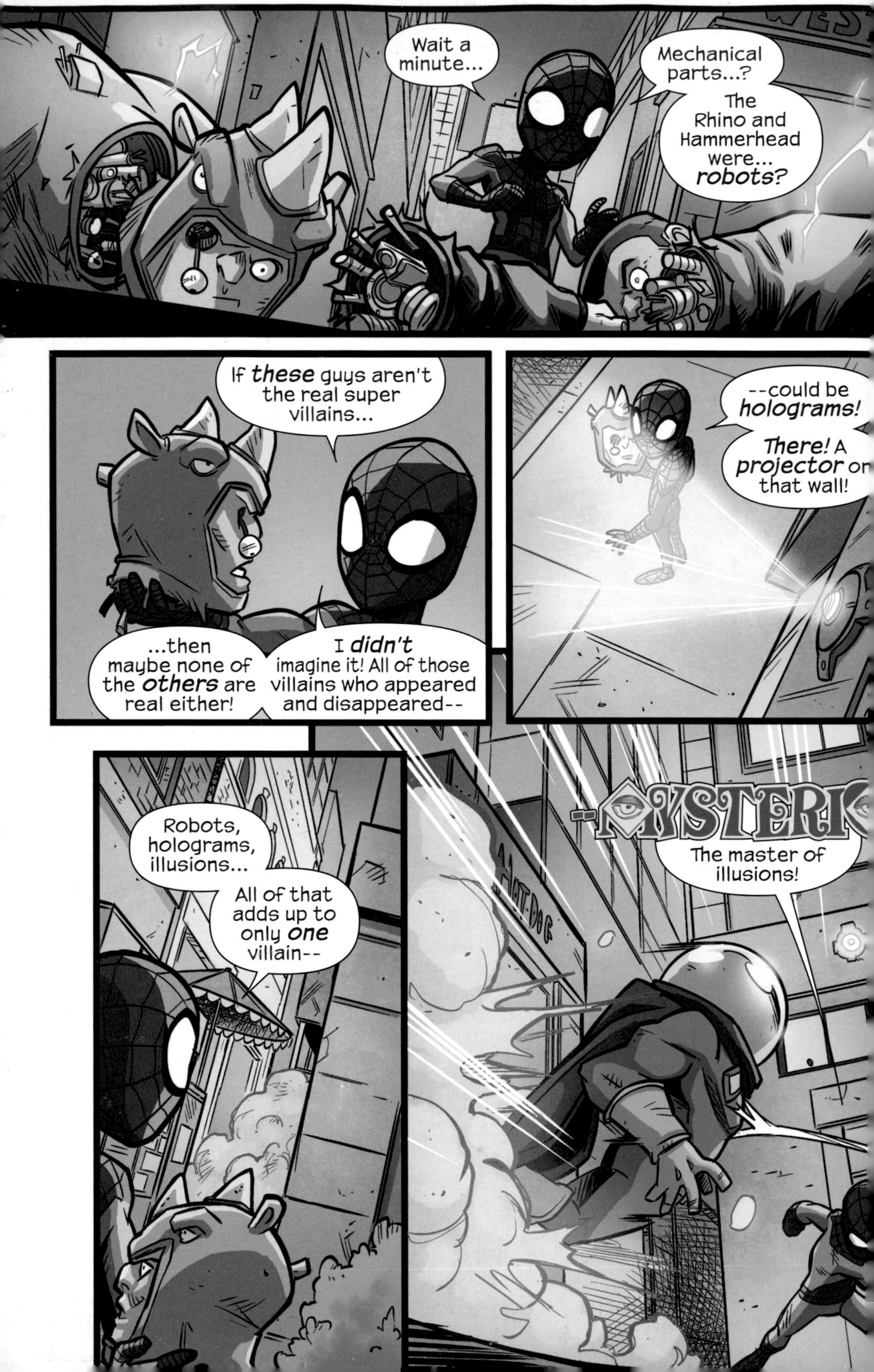
Wait a minute...
Mechanical parts...?
The Rhino and Hammerhead were... robots?
If these guys aren't the real super villains...
...then maybe none of the others are real either!
I didn't imagine it! All of those villains who appeared and disappeared--
--could be holograms!
There! A projector on that wall!
Robots, holograms, illusions...
All of that adds up to only one villain--
MYSTERIO
The master of illusions!

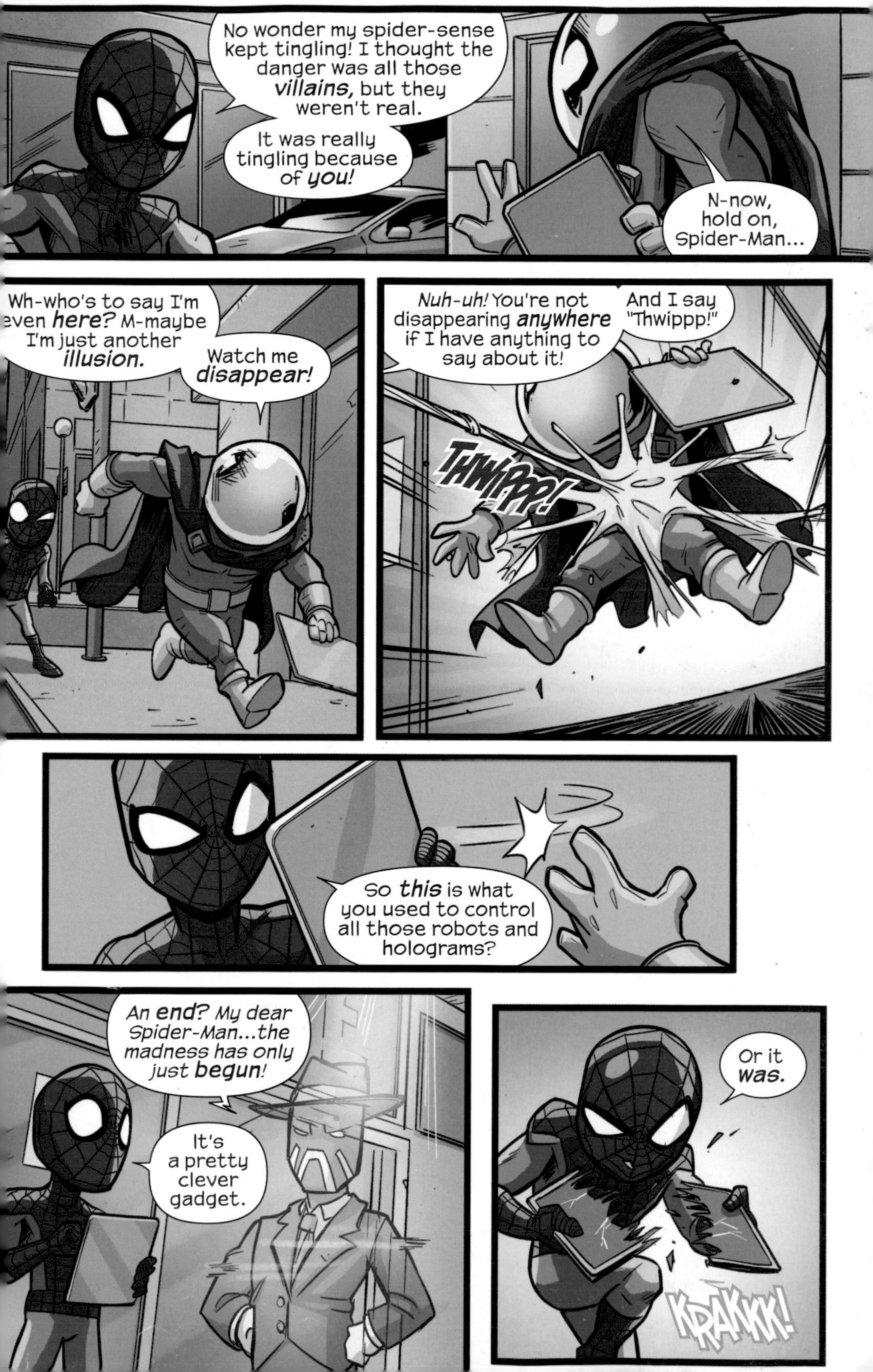
No wonder my spider-sense kept tingling! I thought the danger was all those villains, but they weren't real.
It was really tingling because of you!
N-now, hold on, Spider-Man...
Wh-who's to say I'm even here? M-maybe I'm just another illusion.
Watch me disappear!
Nuh-uh! You're not disappearing anywhere if I have anything to say about it!
And I say "Thwippp!"
THWIPPP!
So this is what you used to control all those robots and holograms?
An end? My dear Spider-Man...the madness has only just begun!
It's a pretty clever gadget.
Or it was.
KRAKKK!

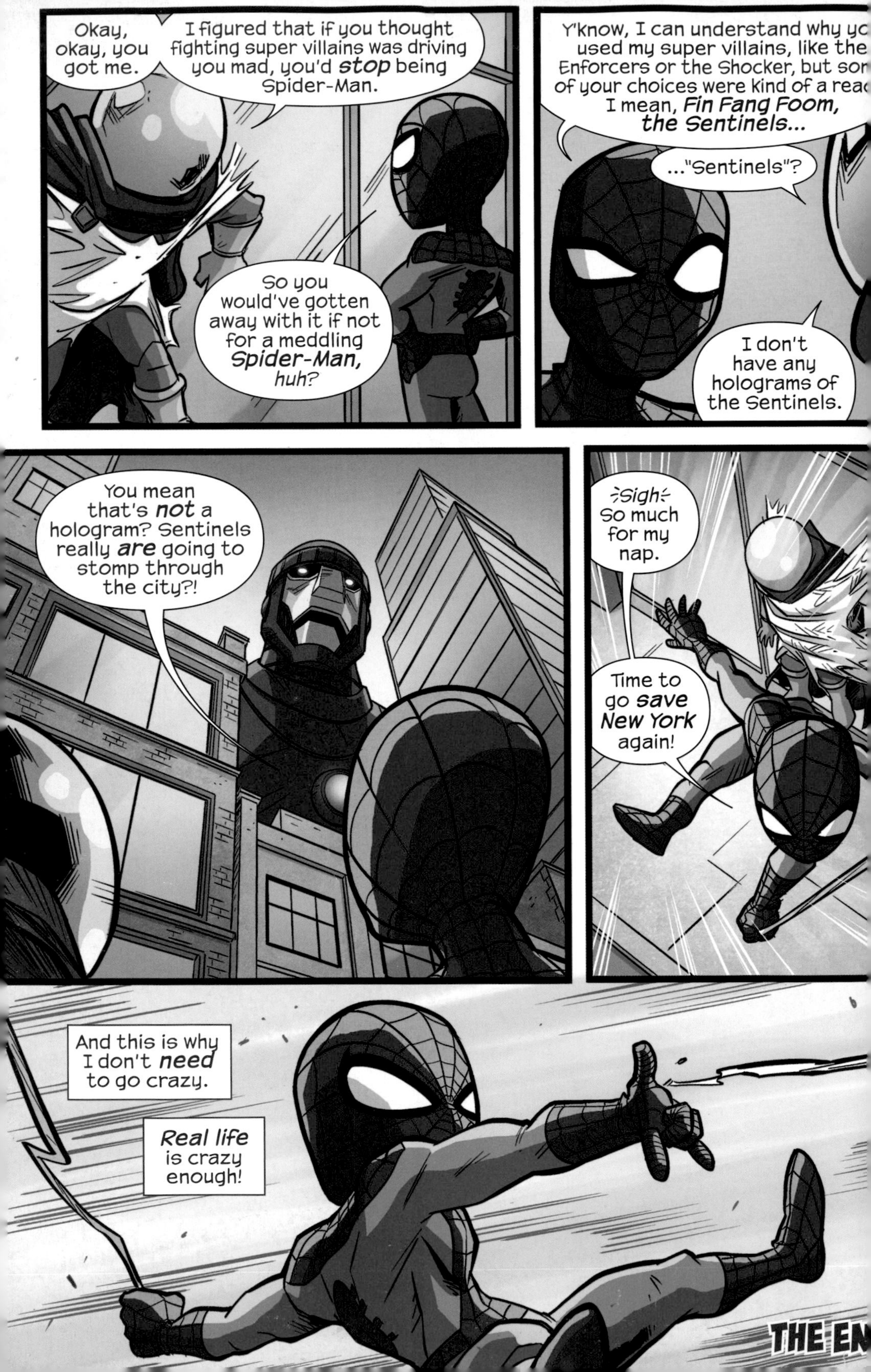
Okay, okay, you got me.
I figured that if you thought fighting super villains was driving you mad, you'd *stop* being Spider-Man.
So you would've gotten away with it if not for a meddling *Spider-Man,* huh?
Y'know, I can understand why yo used my super villains, like the Enforcers or the Shocker, but som of your choices were kind of a rea I mean, *Fin Fang Foom, the Sentinels...*
..."Sentinels"?
I don't have any holograms of the Sentinels.
You mean that's *not* a hologram? Sentinels really *are* going to stomp through the city?!
Sigh So much for my nap.
Time to go *save New York* again!
And this is why I don't *need* to go crazy.
Real life is crazy enough!
THE EN

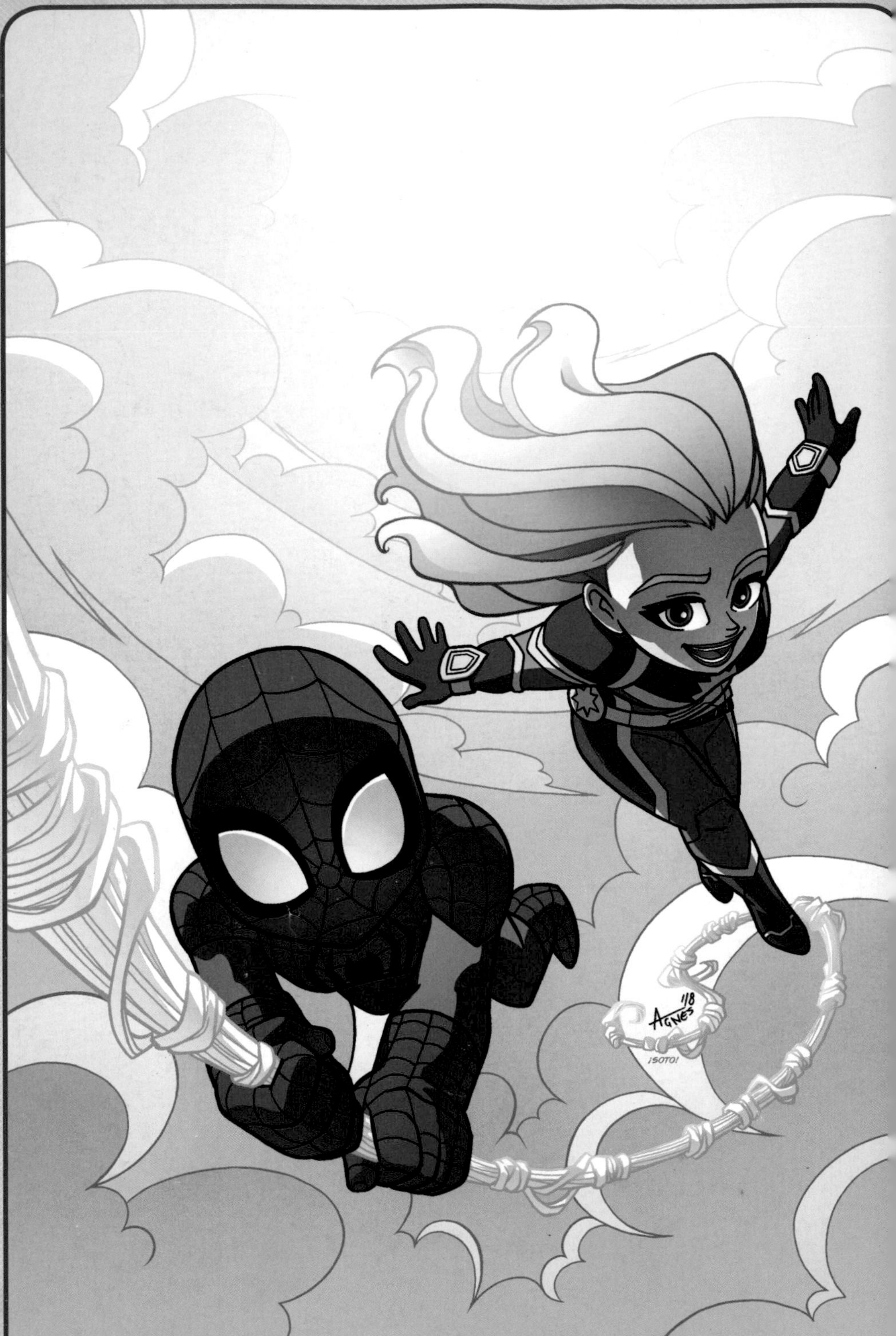

AGNES '18
¡SOTO!

First Day of School

cover by Agnes Garbowska & Chris Sotomayor

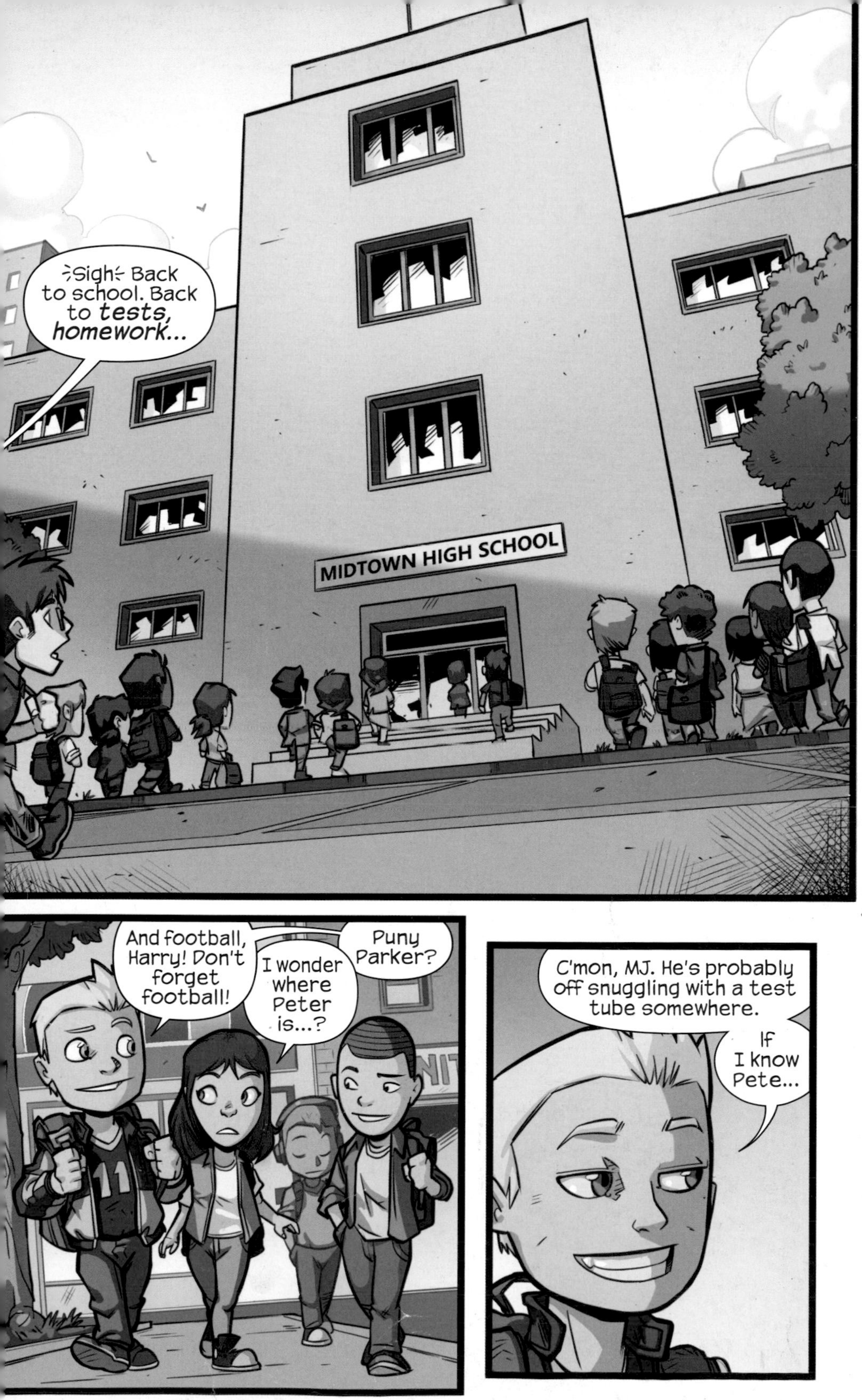

⫶Sigh⫶ Back to school. Back to *tests, homework...*
MIDTOWN HIGH SCHOOL
And football, Harry! Don't forget football!
Puny Parker?
I wonder where Peter is...?
C'mon, MJ. He's probably off snuggling with a test tube somewhere.
If I know Pete...

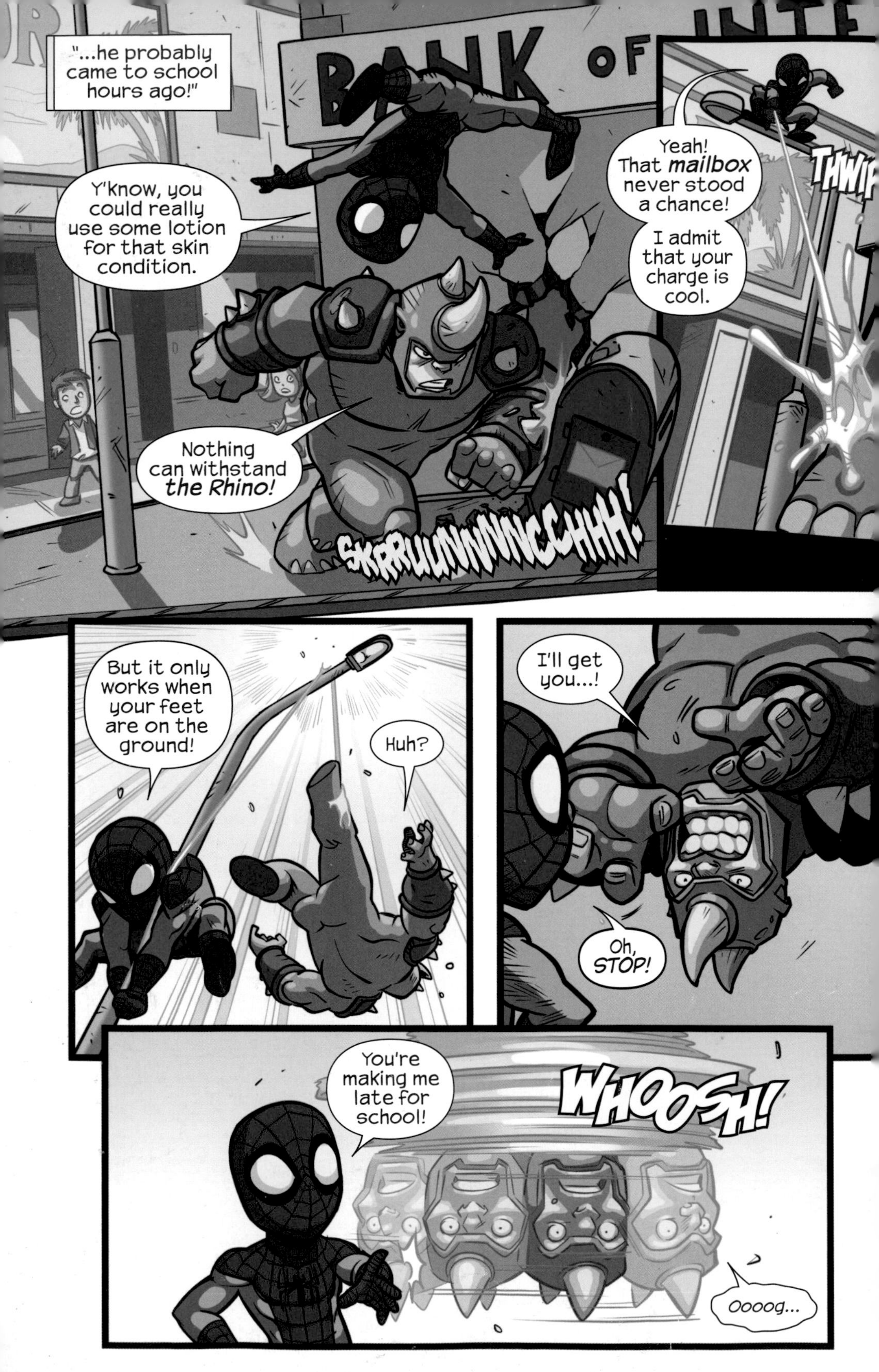
BANK OF INTE
"...he probably came to school hours ago!"
Y'know, you could really use some lotion for that skin condition.
Yeah! That *mailbox* never stood a chance!
I admit that your charge is cool.
THWIP
Nothing can withstand *the Rhino!*
SKRRUUNNNNCCHHH!
But it only works when your feet are on the ground!
Huh?
I'll get you...!
Oh, STOP!
You're making me late for school!
WHOOSH!
Oooog...

No time to walk to school as *Peter Parker!*

Uh-oh! Typical Parker luck--always bad!

But with a little web-swinging as *Spider-Man,* I might make it.

My *spider-sense* is tingling like crazy! There must be danger nearby--*big danger!*

Yikes! Must be that *meteor* about to hit the city...

...and my *SCHOOL!*

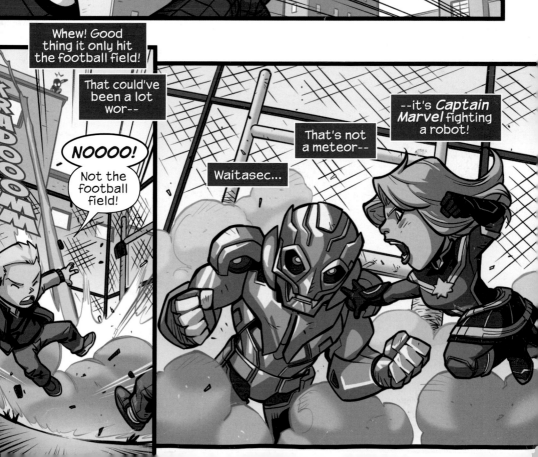

Whew! Good thing it only hit the football field!

That could've been a lot wor--

KA-BOOOOM!

NOOOO!

Not the football field!

Waitasec...

That's not a meteor--

--it's *Captain Marvel* fighting a robot!

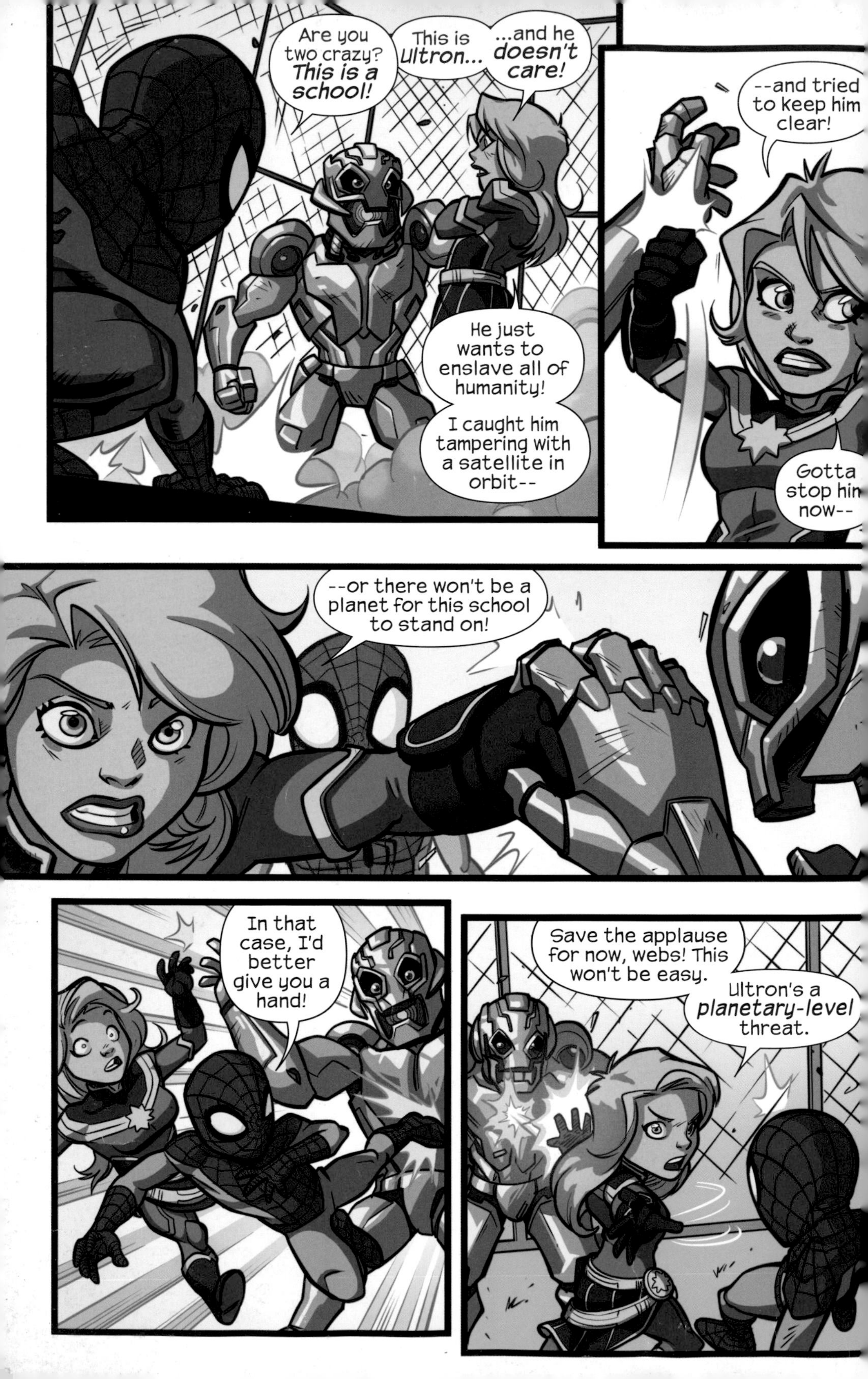
Are you two crazy? This is a school!
This is Ultron...
...and he doesn't care!
He just wants to enslave all of humanity!
I caught him tampering with a satellite in orbit--
--and tried to keep him clear!
Gotta stop him now--
--or there won't be a planet for this school to stand on!
In that case, I'd better give you a hand!
Save the applause for now, webs! This won't be easy.
Ultron's a planetary-level threat.

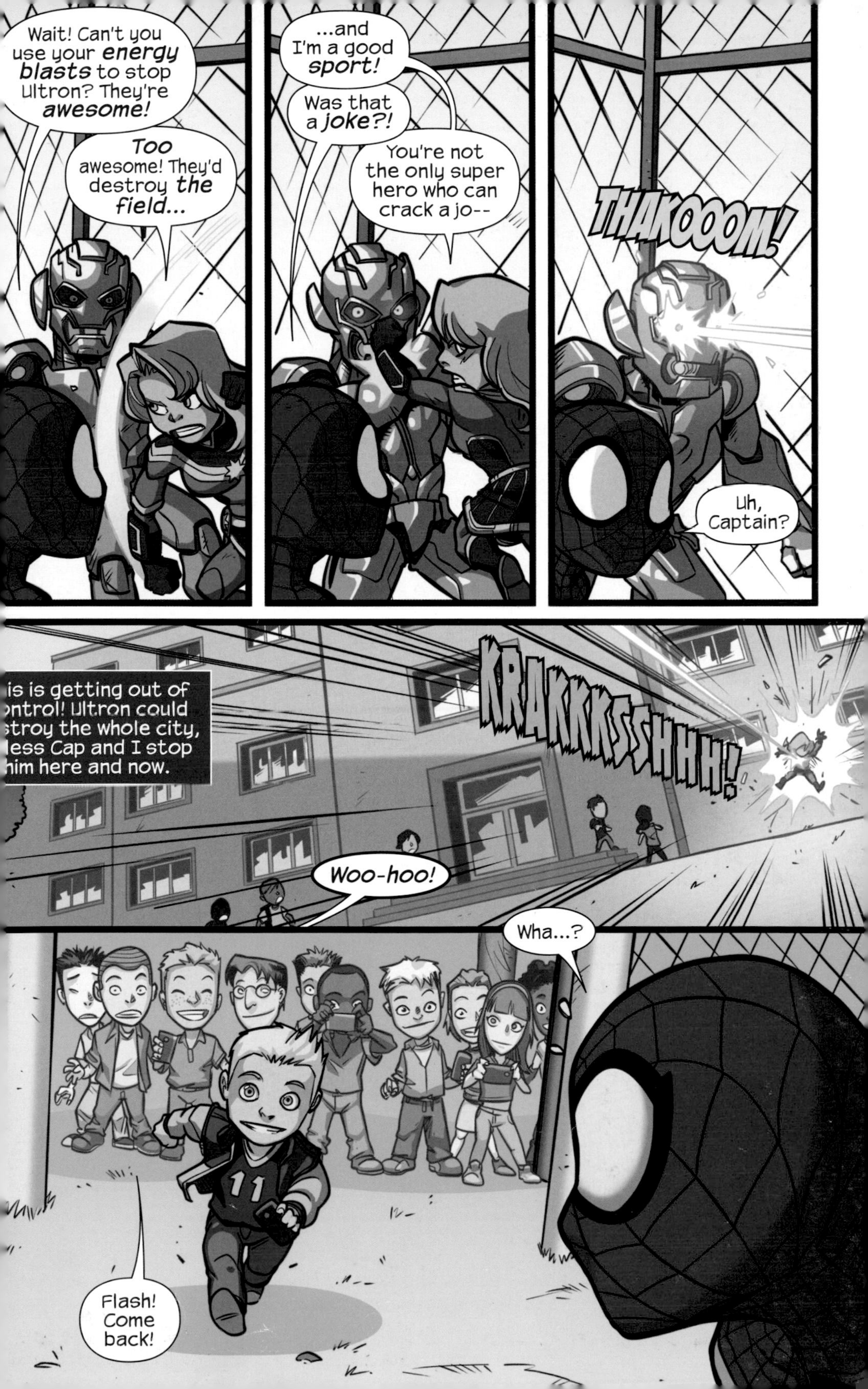
Wait! Can't you use your energy blasts to stop Ultron? They're awesome!
Too awesome! They'd destroy the field...
...and I'm a good sport!
Was that a joke?!
You're not the only super hero who can crack a jo--
THAKOOOM!
Uh, Captain?
is is getting out of ontrol! Ultron could stroy the whole city, less Cap and I stop him here and now.
KRAKKKSSHHH!
Woo-hoo!
Wha...?
Flash! Come back!

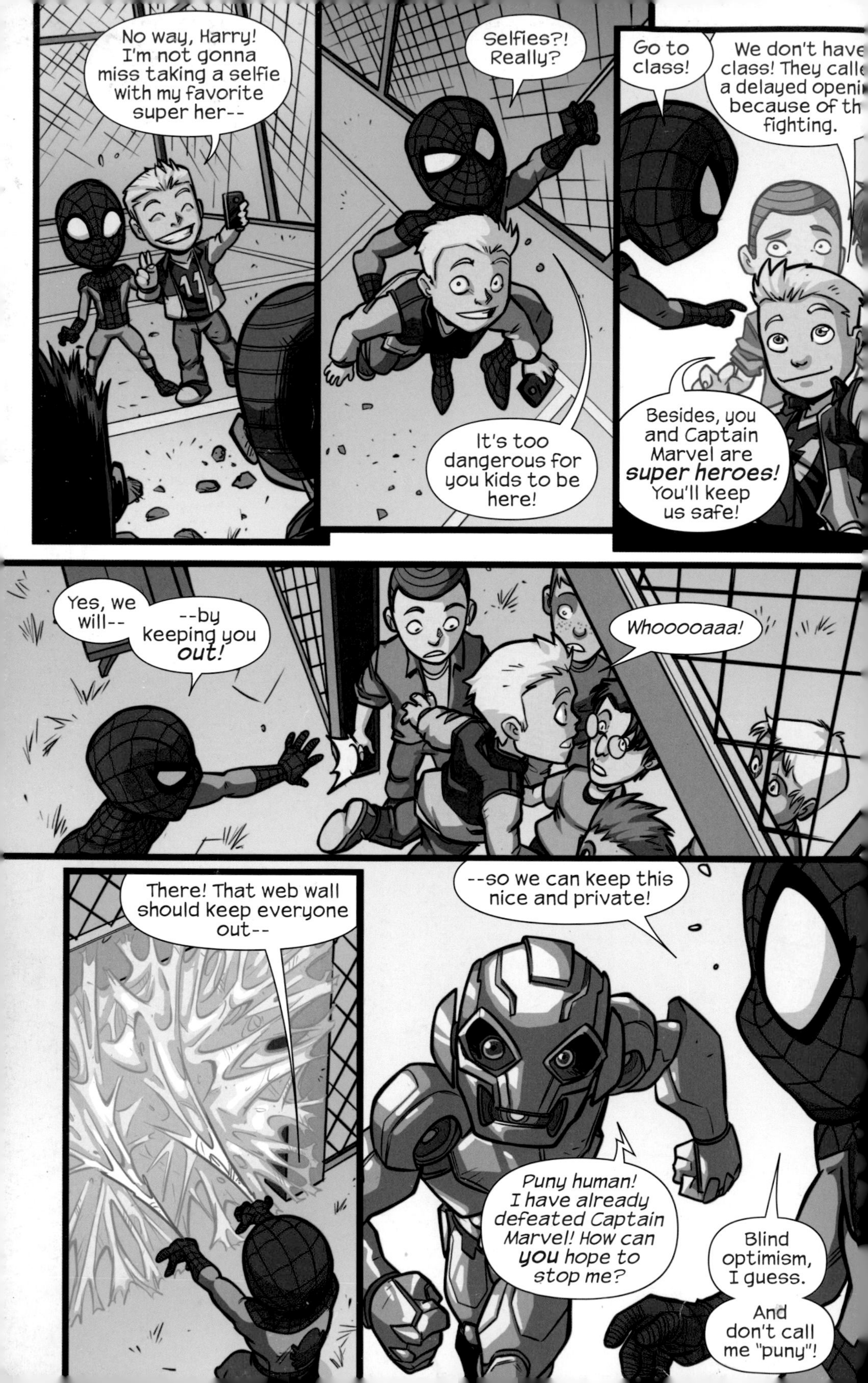

No way, Harry! I'm not gonna miss taking a selfie with my favorite super her--
Selfies?! Really?
It's too dangerous for you kids to be here!
Go to class!
We don't have class! They calle a delayed openi because of th fighting.
Besides, you and Captain Marvel are super heroes! You'll keep us safe!
Yes, we will--
--by keeping you out!
Whoooooaaa!
There! That web wall should keep everyone out--
--so we can keep this nice and private!
Puny human! I have already defeated Captain Marvel! How can you hope to stop me?
Blind optimism, I guess.
And don't call me "puny"!

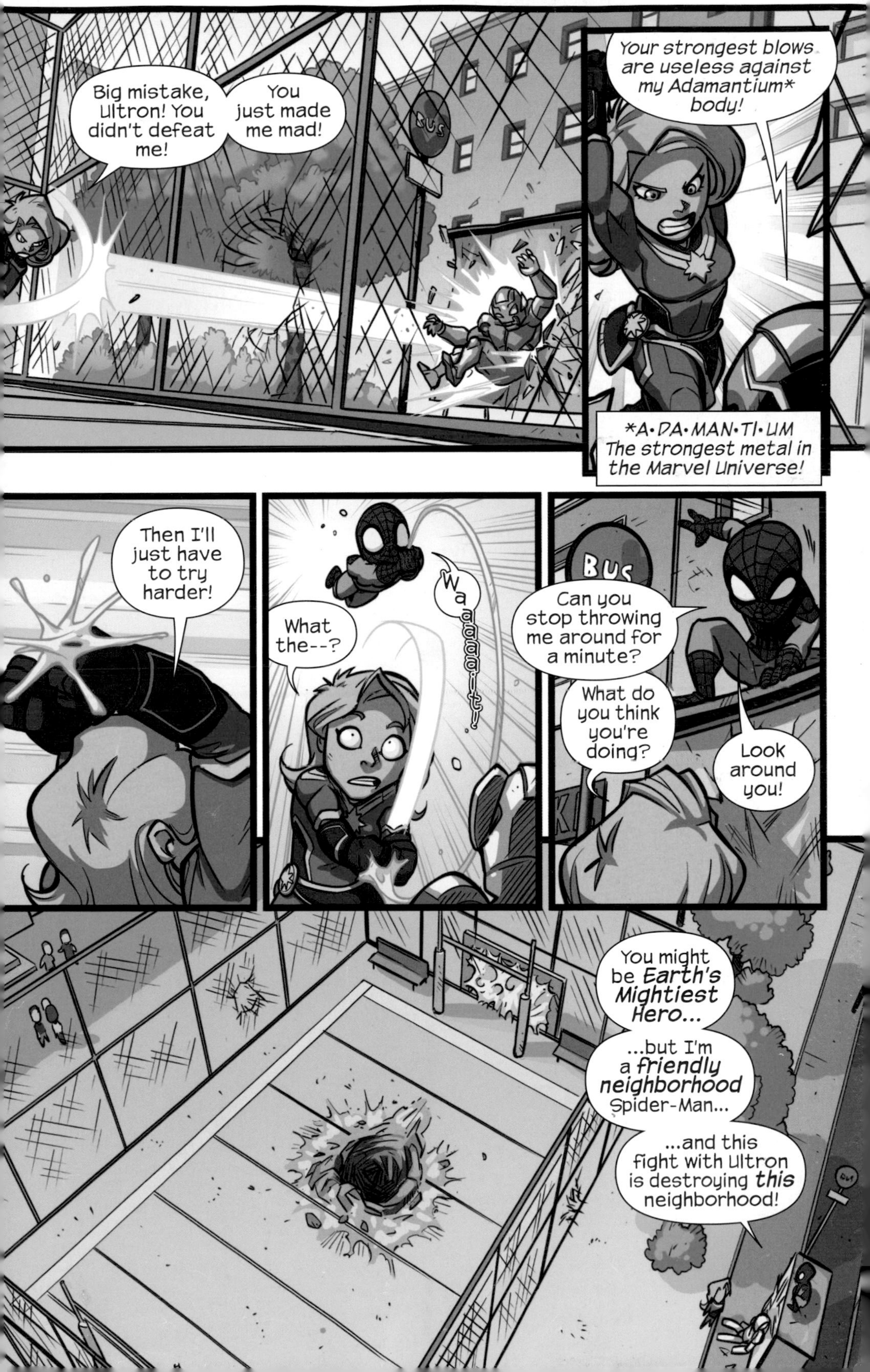

Big mistake, Ultron! You didn't defeat me!
You just made me mad!
BUS
Your strongest blows are useless against my Adamantium* body!
*A·DA·MAN·TI·UM The strongest metal in the Marvel Universe!
Then I'll just have to try harder!
What the--?
Waaaaaait!
BUS
Can you stop throwing me around for a minute?
What do you think you're doing?
Look around you!
You might be Earth's Mightiest Hero...
...but I'm a friendly neighborhood Spider-Man...
...and this fight with Ultron is destroying this neighborhood!

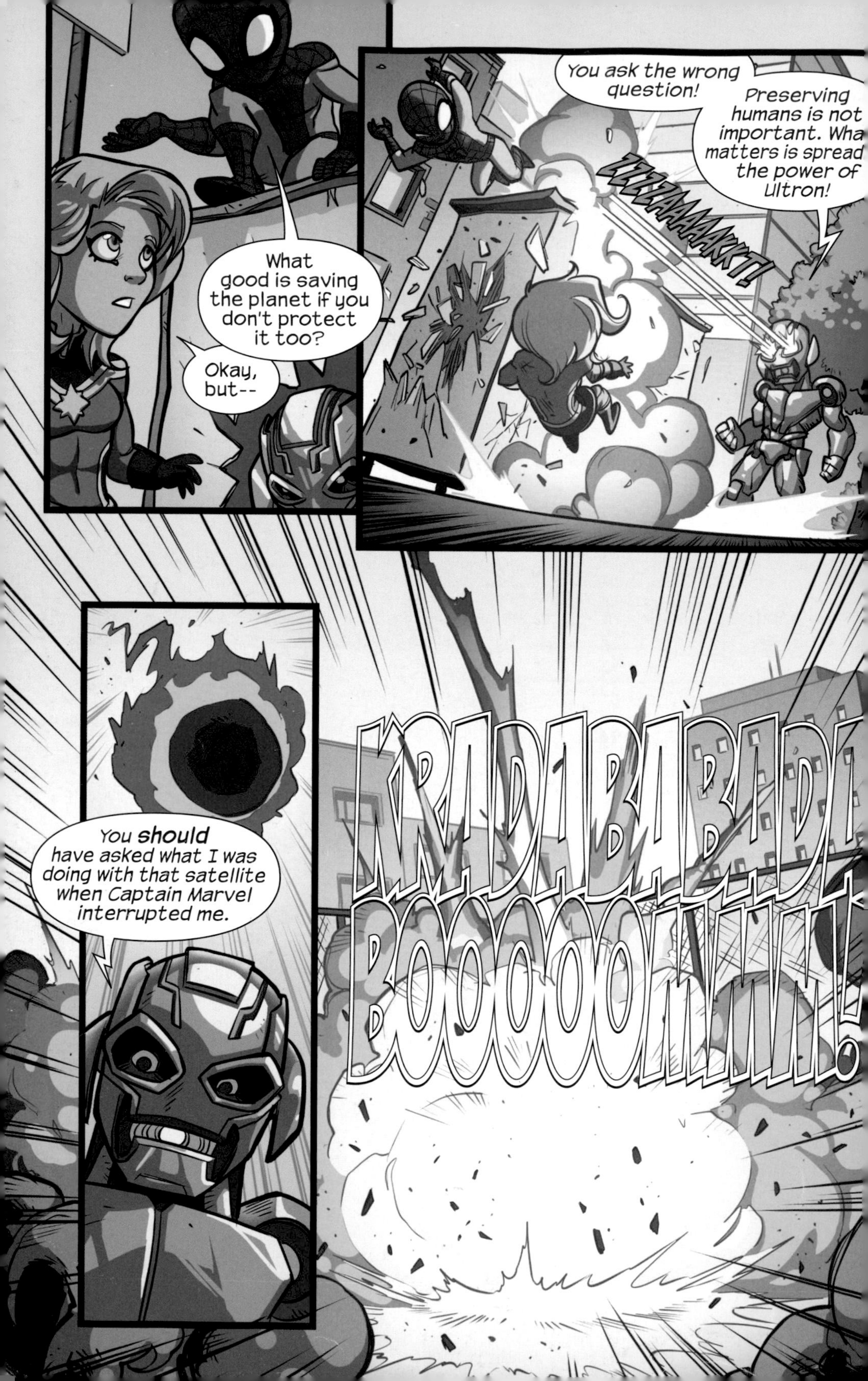

What good is saving the planet if you don't protect it too?
Okay, but--
You ask the wrong question!
Preserving humans is not important. Wha matters is spread the power of Ultron!
ZZZZAAAAAKKT!
You should have asked what I was doing with that satellite when Captain Marvel interrupted me.
KRADABABADI BOOOOOOMMMM!

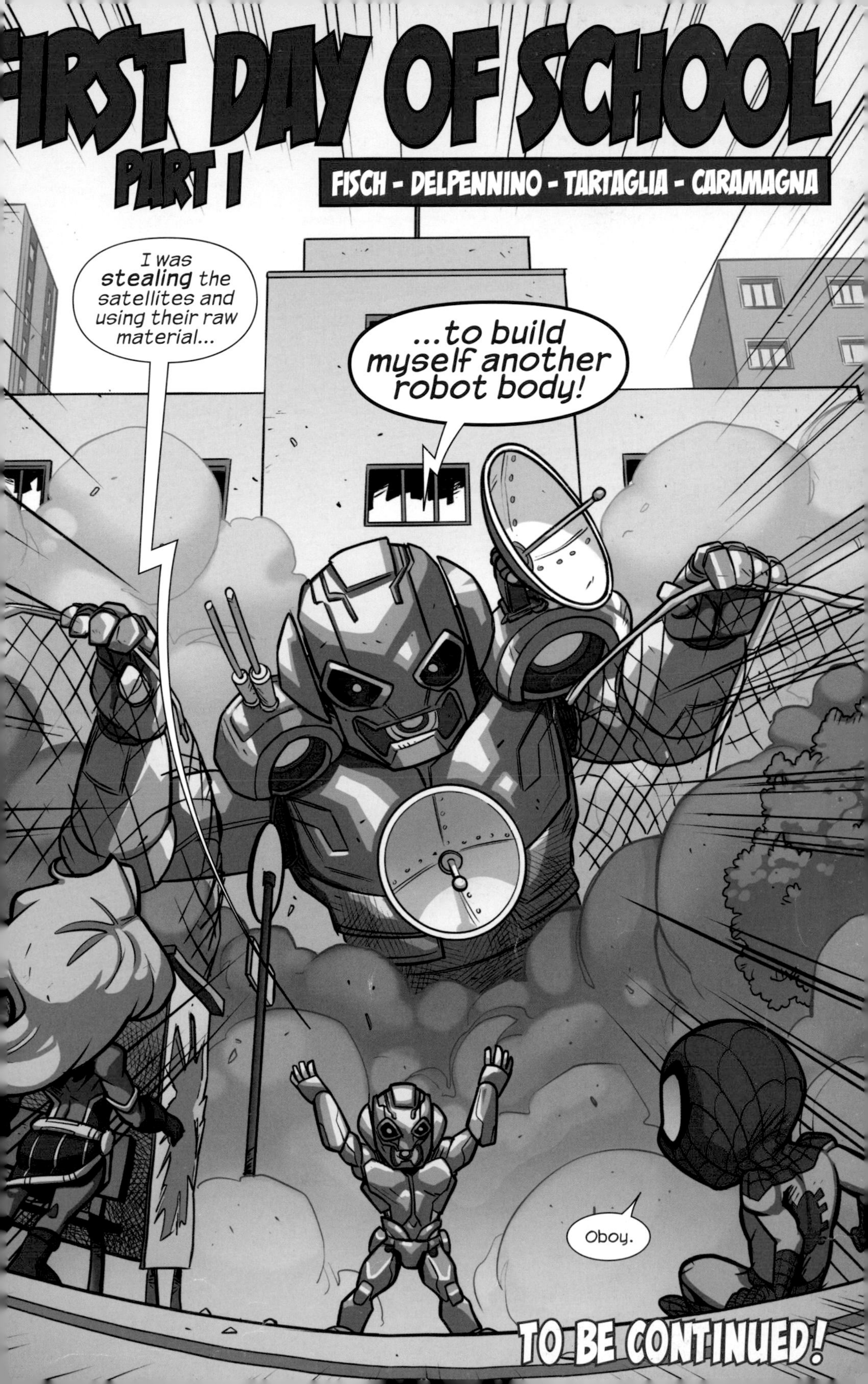
FIRST DAY OF SCHOOL
PART 1
FISCH - DELPENNINO - TARTAGLIA - CARAMAGNA
I was stealing the satellites and using their raw material...
...to build myself another robot body!
Oboy.
TO BE CONTINUED!

DAILY BUGLE

NEW YORK'S FUNNIEST DAILY NEWSPAPER

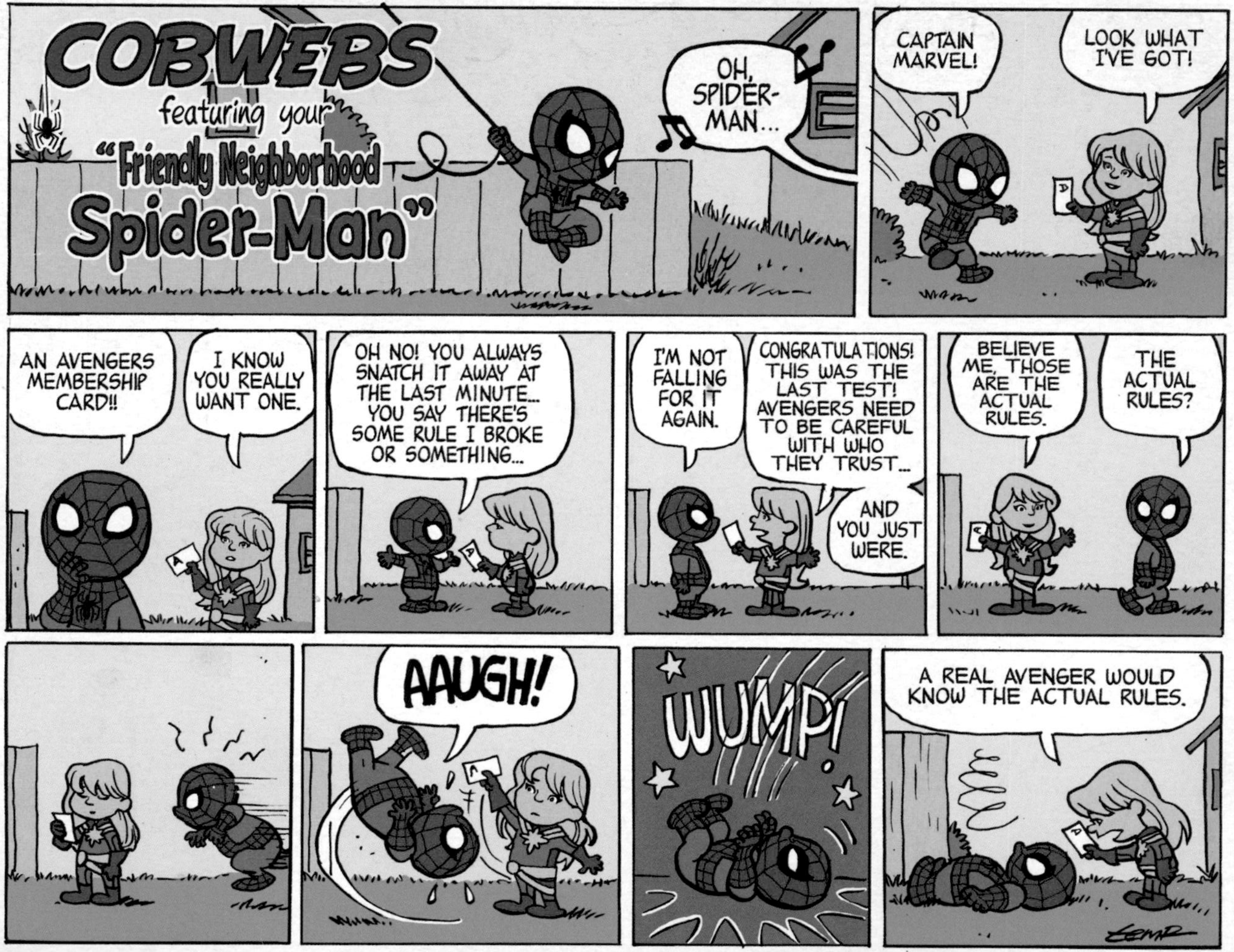
COBWEBS
featuring your "Friendly Neighborhood Spider-Man"
OH, SPIDER-MAN...
CAPTAIN MARVEL!
LOOK WHAT I'VE GOT!
AN AVENGERS MEMBERSHIP CARD!!
I KNOW YOU REALLY WANT ONE.
OH NO! YOU ALWAYS SNATCH IT AWAY AT THE LAST MINUTE... YOU SAY THERE'S SOME RULE I BROKE OR SOMETHING...
I'M NOT FALLING FOR IT AGAIN.
CONGRATULATIONS! THIS WAS THE LAST TEST! AVENGERS NEED TO BE CAREFUL WITH WHO THEY TRUST...
AND YOU JUST WERE.
BELIEVE ME, THOSE ARE THE ACTUAL RULES.
THE ACTUAL RULES?
AAUGH!
WUMP!
A REAL AVENGER WOULD KNOW THE ACTUAL RULES.

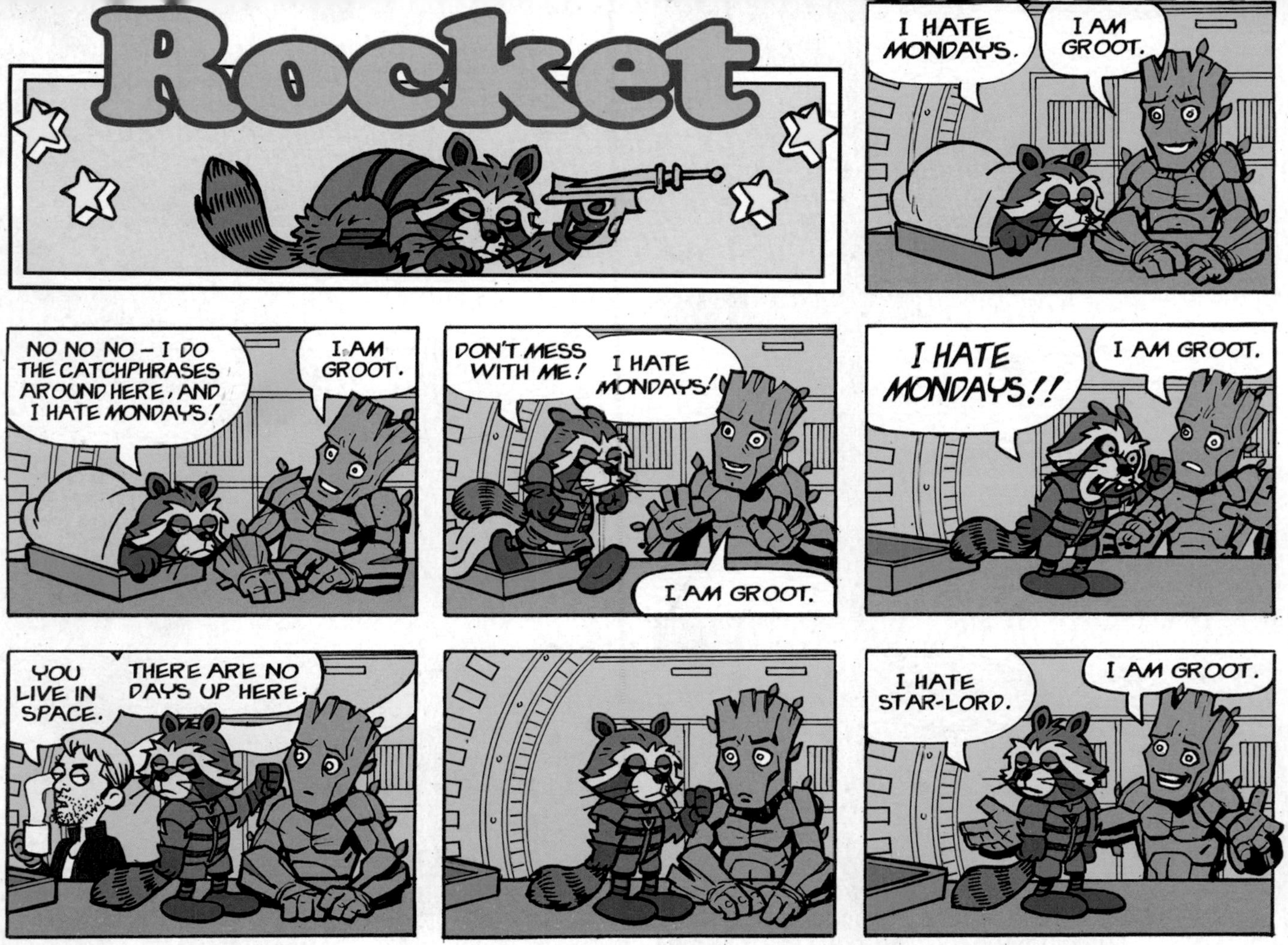
Rocket
I HATE MONDAYS.
I AM GROOT.
I HATE MONDAYS!!
I AM GROOT.
NO NO NO – I DO THE CATCHPHRASES AROUND HERE, AND I HATE MONDAYS!
I AM GROOT.
DON'T MESS WITH ME!
I HATE MONDAYS!
I AM GROOT.
I HATE STAR-LORD.
I AM GROOT.
THERE ARE NO DAYS UP HERE.
YOU LIVE IN SPACE.

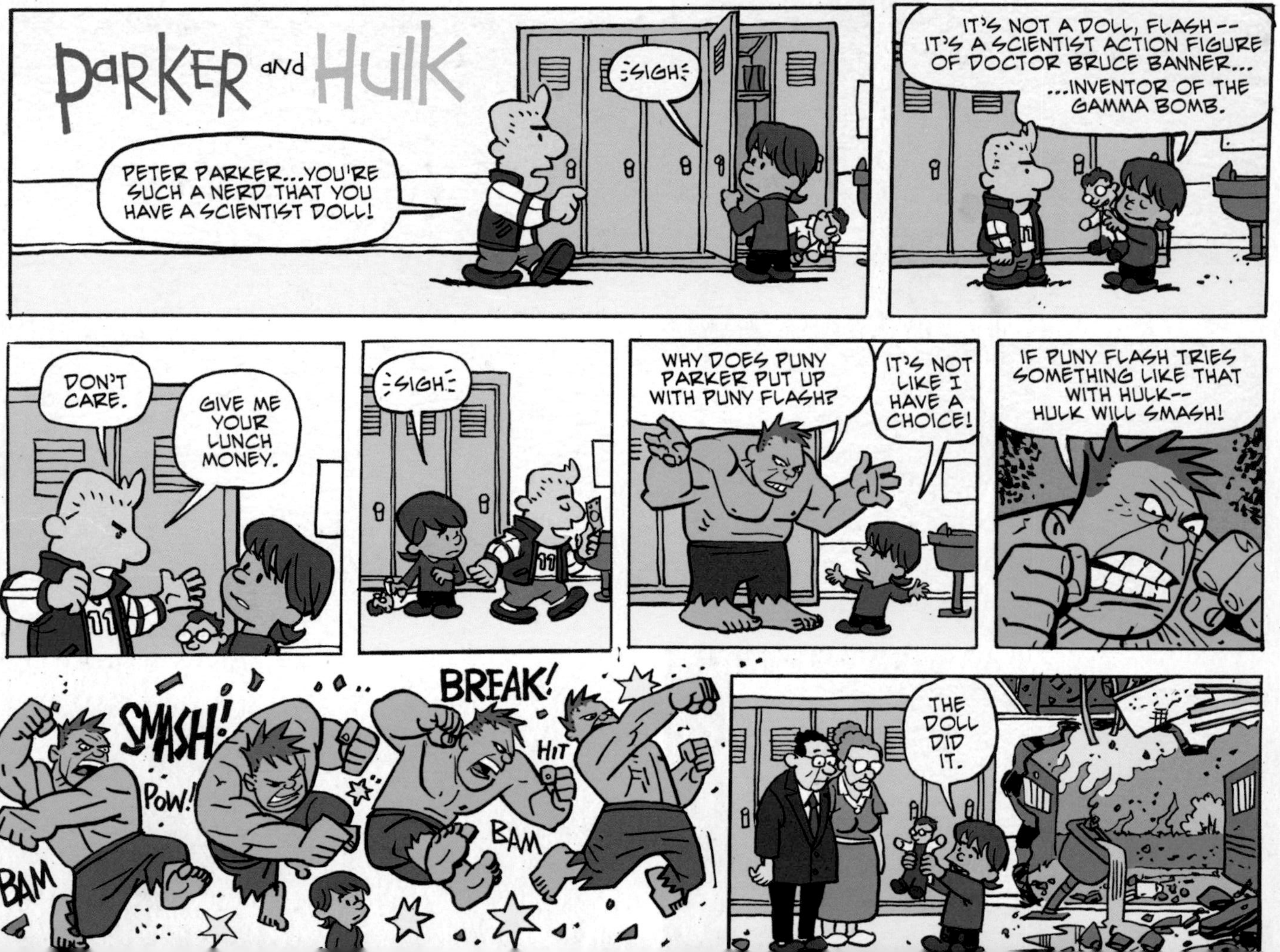
PARKER and HULK
PETER PARKER...YOU'RE SUCH A NERD THAT YOU HAVE A SCIENTIST DOLL!
SIGH
IT'S NOT A DOLL, FLASH -- IT'S A SCIENTIST ACTION FIGURE OF DOCTOR BRUCE BANNER...
...INVENTOR OF THE GAMMA BOMB.
DON'T CARE.
GIVE ME YOUR LUNCH MONEY.
SIGH
WHY DOES PUNY PARKER PUT UP WITH PUNY FLASH?
IT'S NOT LIKE I HAVE A CHOICE!
IF PUNY FLASH TRIES SOMETHING LIKE THAT WITH HULK-- HULK WILL SMASH!
SMASH!
BREAK!
HIT
POW!
BAM
BAM
THE DOLL DID IT.

Strange Side

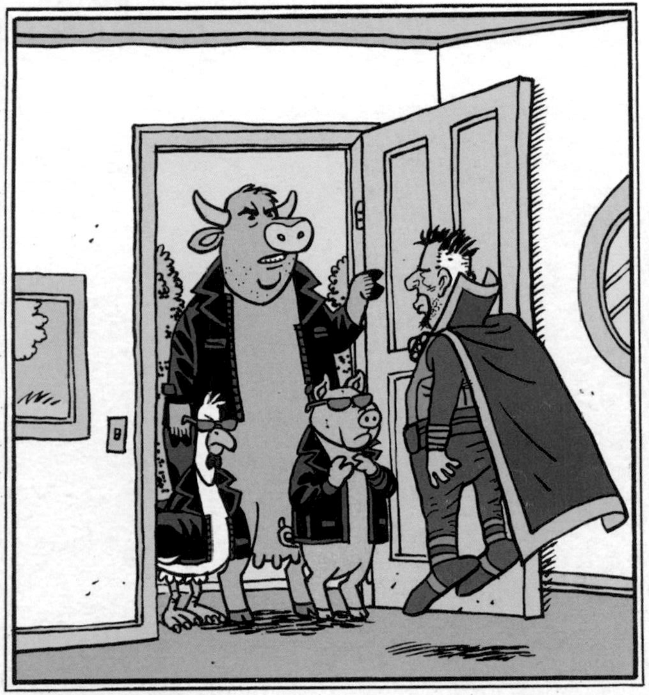

"We're from the farm next door.
You were spell casting in your sleep again."

The Villainy Circus

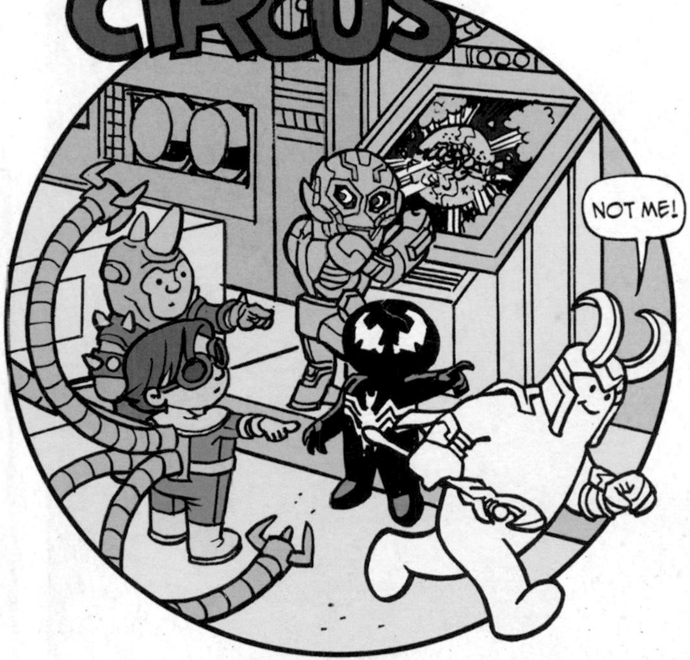
NOT ME!

"All right, WHO set off
my doomsday device?"

DAILY BUGLE

NEW YORK'S FUNNIEST DAILY NEWSPAPER

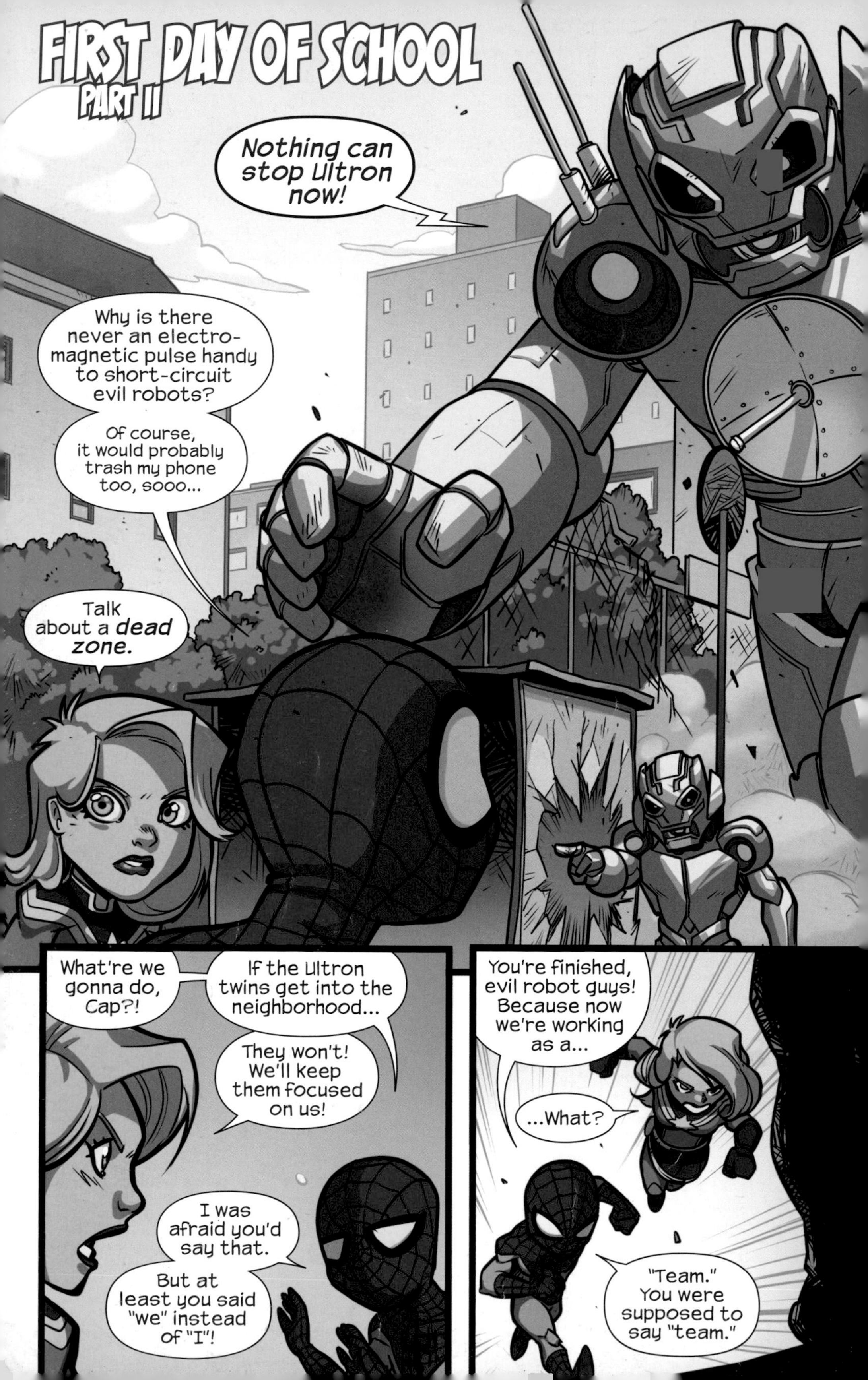
FIRST DAY OF SCHOOL
PART II
Nothing can stop Ultron now!
Why is there never an electro-magnetic pulse handy to short-circuit evil robots?
Of course, it would probably trash my phone too, sooo...
Talk about a *dead zone.*
What're we gonna do, Cap?!
If the Ultron twins get into the neighborhood...
They won't! We'll keep them focused on us!
I was afraid you'd say that.
But at least you said "we" instead of "I"!
You're finished, evil robot guys! Because now we're working as a...
...What?
"Team." You were supposed to say "team."

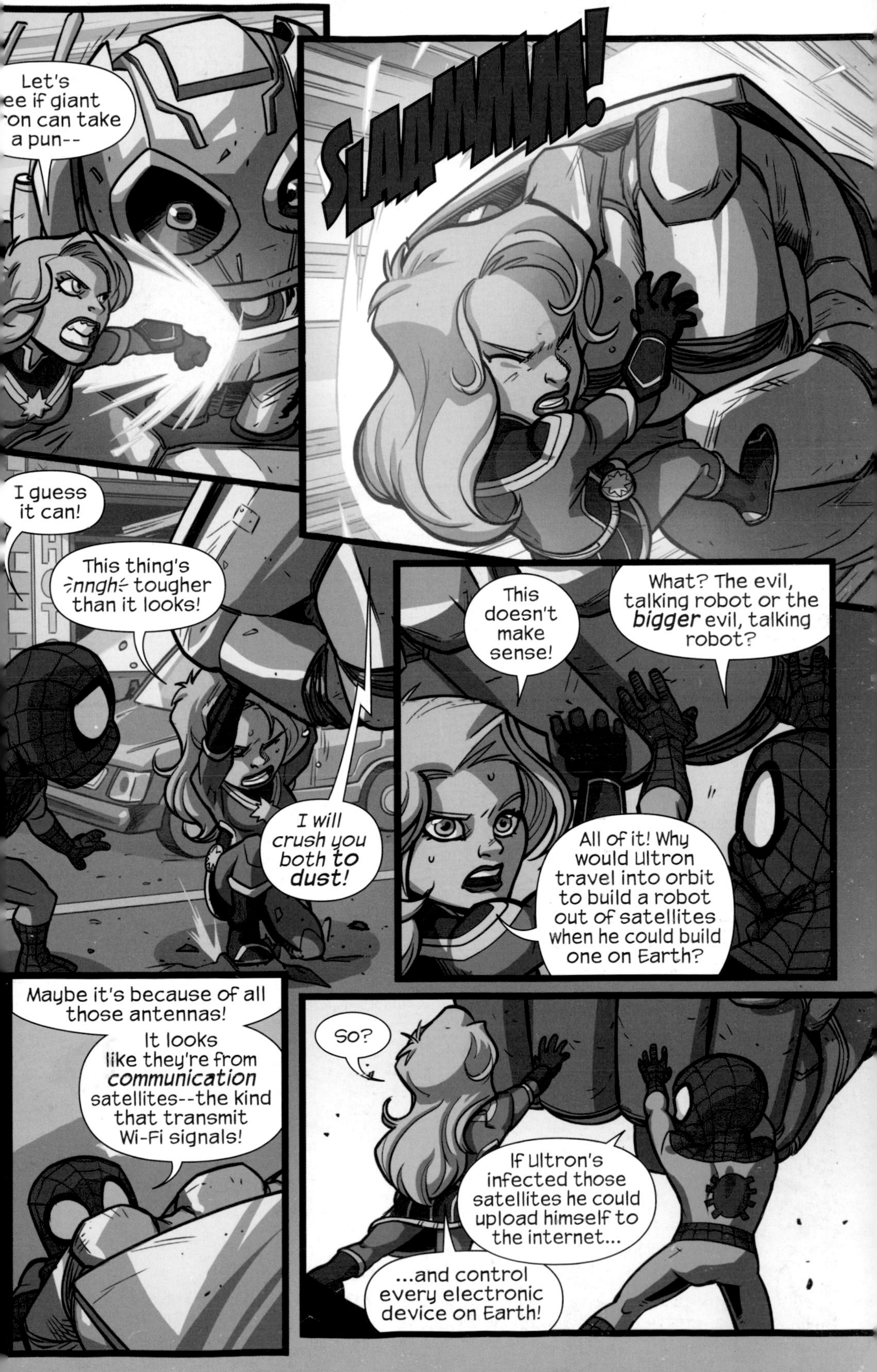
Let's ee if giant ron can take a pun--
SLAAMMMM!
I guess it can!
This thing's -nngh- tougher than it looks!
I will crush you both to dust!
This doesn't make sense!
What? The evil, talking robot or the bigger evil, talking robot?
All of it! Why would Ultron travel into orbit to build a robot out of satellites when he could build one on Earth?
Maybe it's because of all those antennas!
It looks like they're from communication satellites--the kind that transmit Wi-Fi signals!
So?
If Ultron's infected those satellites he could upload himself to the internet...
...and control every electronic device on Earth!

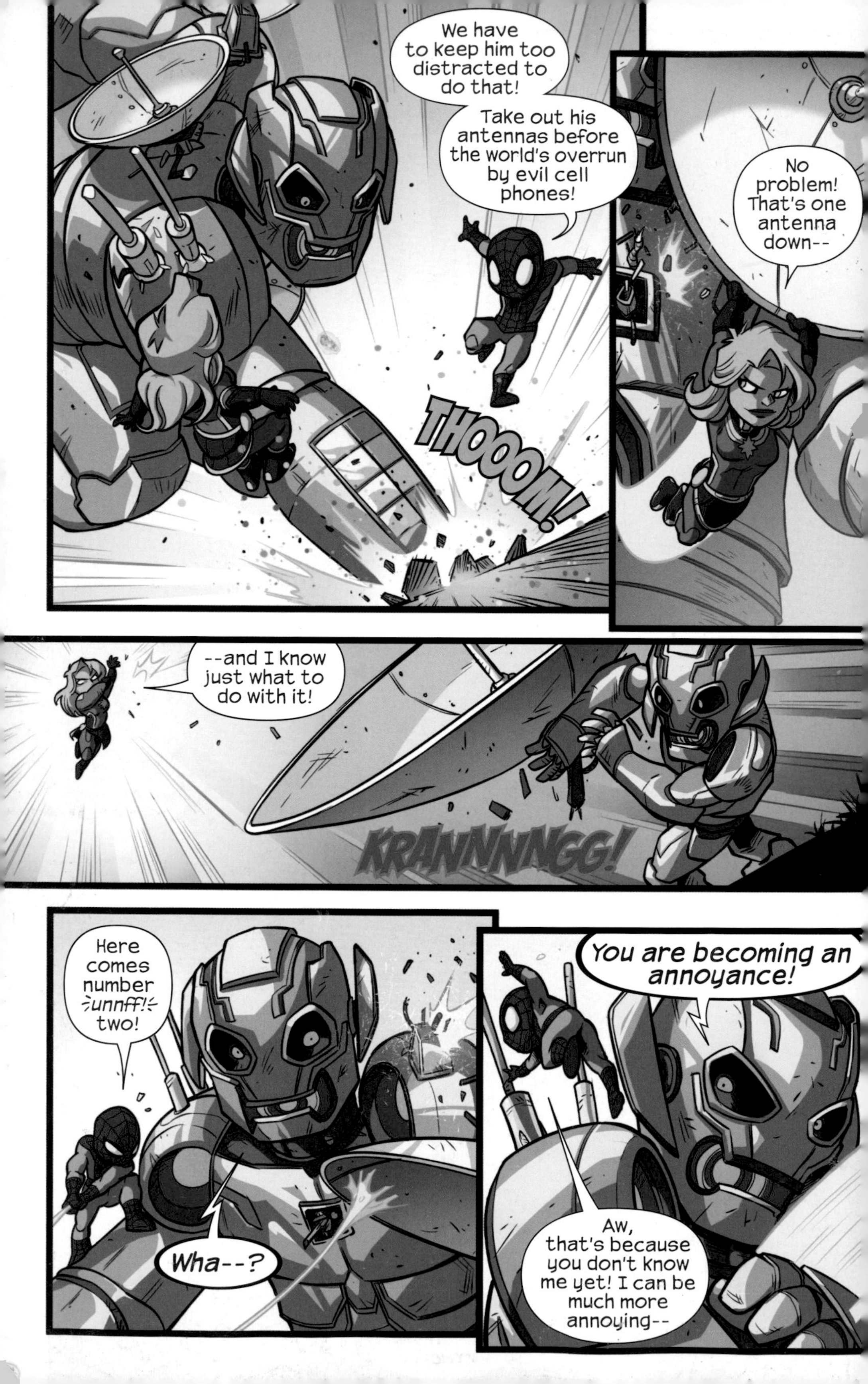
We have to keep him too distracted to do that!
Take out his antennas before the world's overrun by evil cell phones!
THOOOOM!
No problem! That's one antenna down--
--and I know just what to do with it!
KRANNNNGG!
Here comes number unnff! two!
Wha--?
You are becoming an annoyance!
Aw, that's because you don't know me yet! I can be much more annoying--

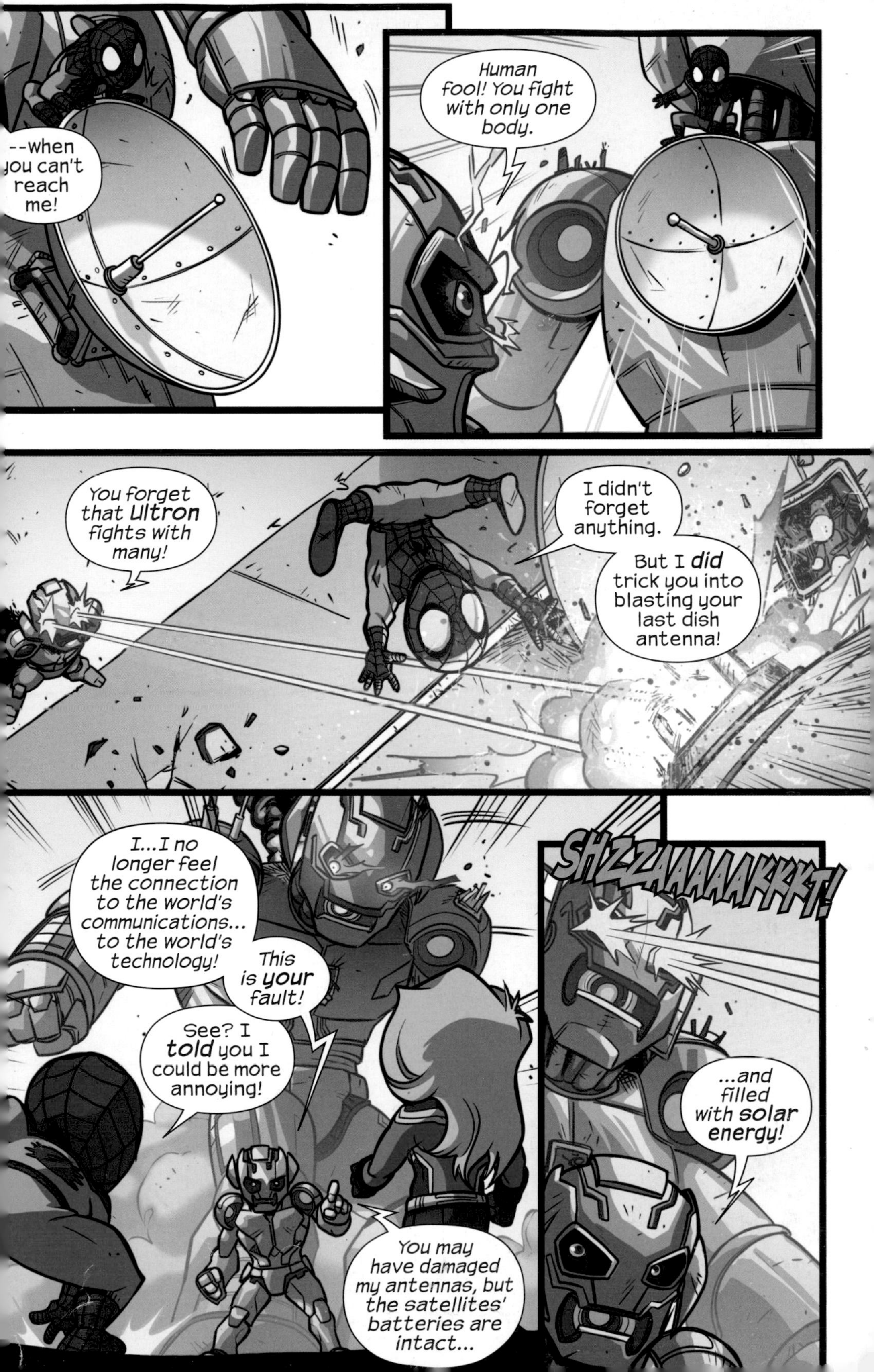
--when you can't reach me!
Human fool! You fight with only one body.
You forget that Ultron fights with many!
I didn't forget anything.
But I did trick you into blasting your last dish antenna!
I...I no longer feel the connection to the world's communications... to the world's technology!
This is your fault!
See? I told you I could be more annoying!
You may have damaged my antennas, but the satellites' batteries are intact...
SHZZAAAAAKKKT!
...and filled with solar energy!

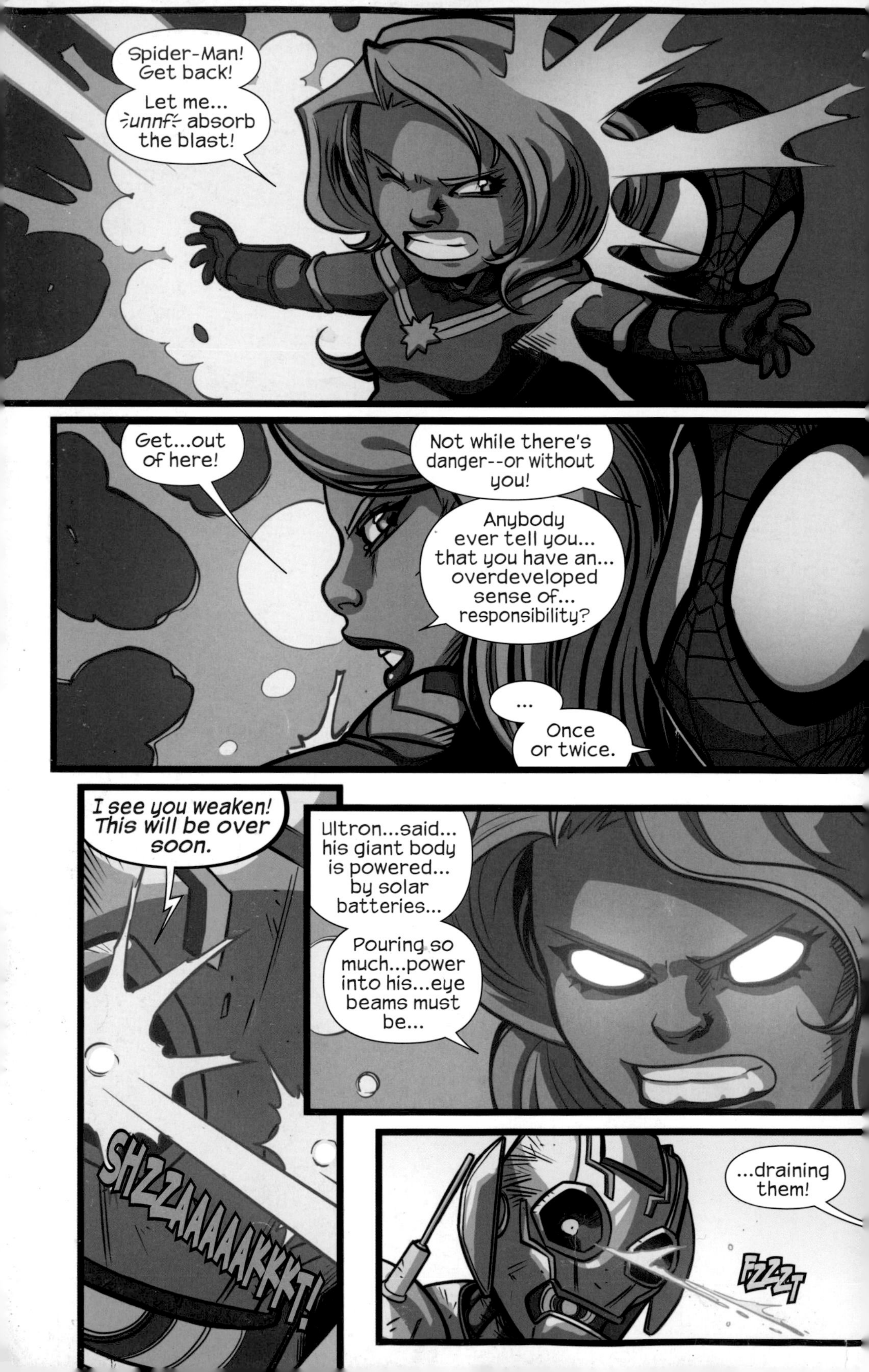
Spider-Man! Get back!
Let me... ≈unnf≈ absorb the blast!
Get...out of here!
Not while there's danger--or without you!
Anybody ever tell you... that you have an... overdeveloped sense of... responsibility?
...
Once or twice.
I see you weaken! This will be over soon.
Ultron...said... his giant body is powered... by solar batteries...
Pouring so much...power into his...eye beams must be...
SHZZAAAAAKKKT!
...draining them!
FZZZT

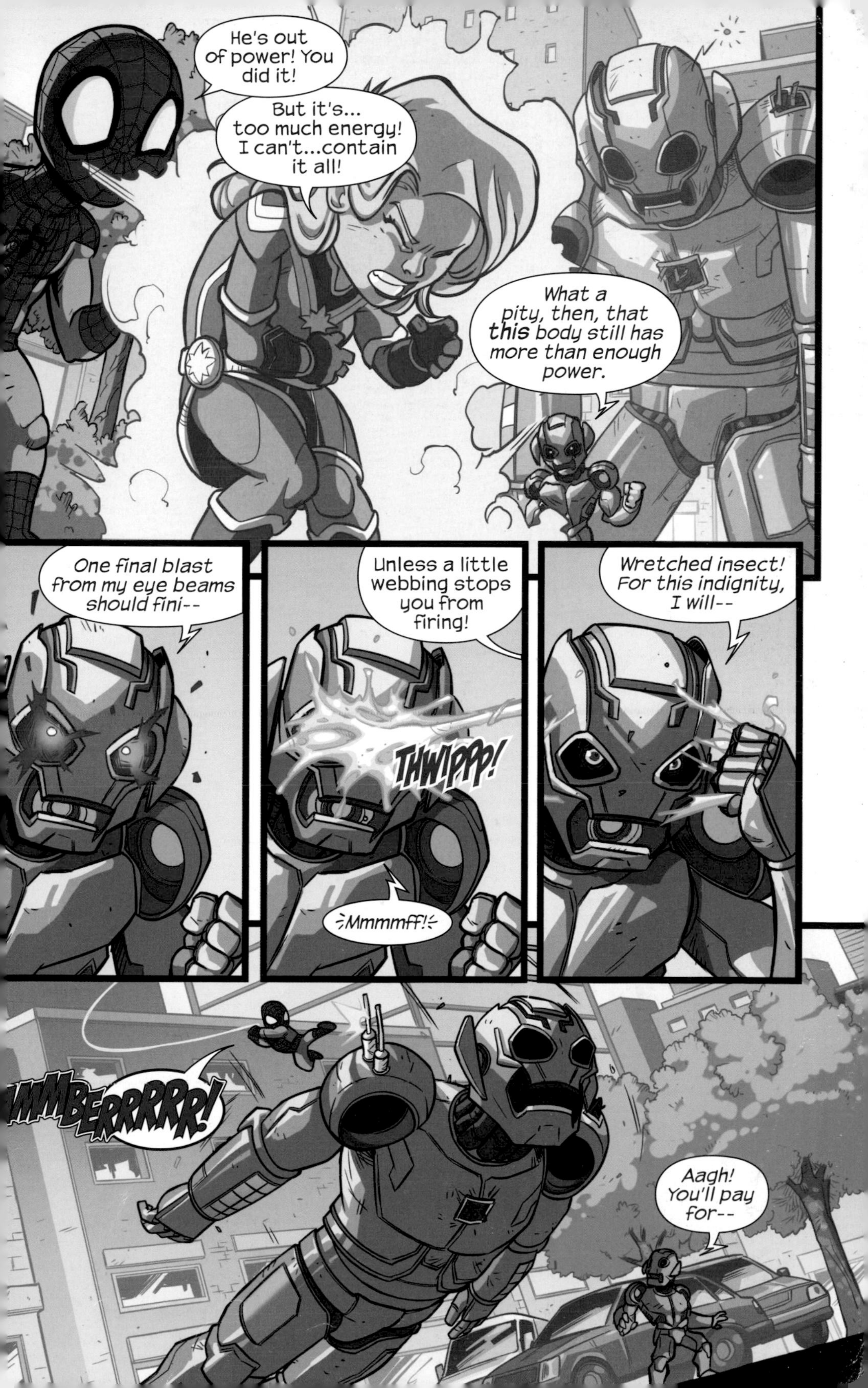
He's out of power! You did it!
But it's... too much energy! I can't...contain it all!
What a pity, then, that **this** body still has more than enough power.
One final blast from my eye beams should fini--
Unless a little webbing stops you from firing!
THWIPPP!
Mmmmff!
Wretched insect! For this indignity, I will--
MMBERRRRR!
Aagh! You'll pay for--

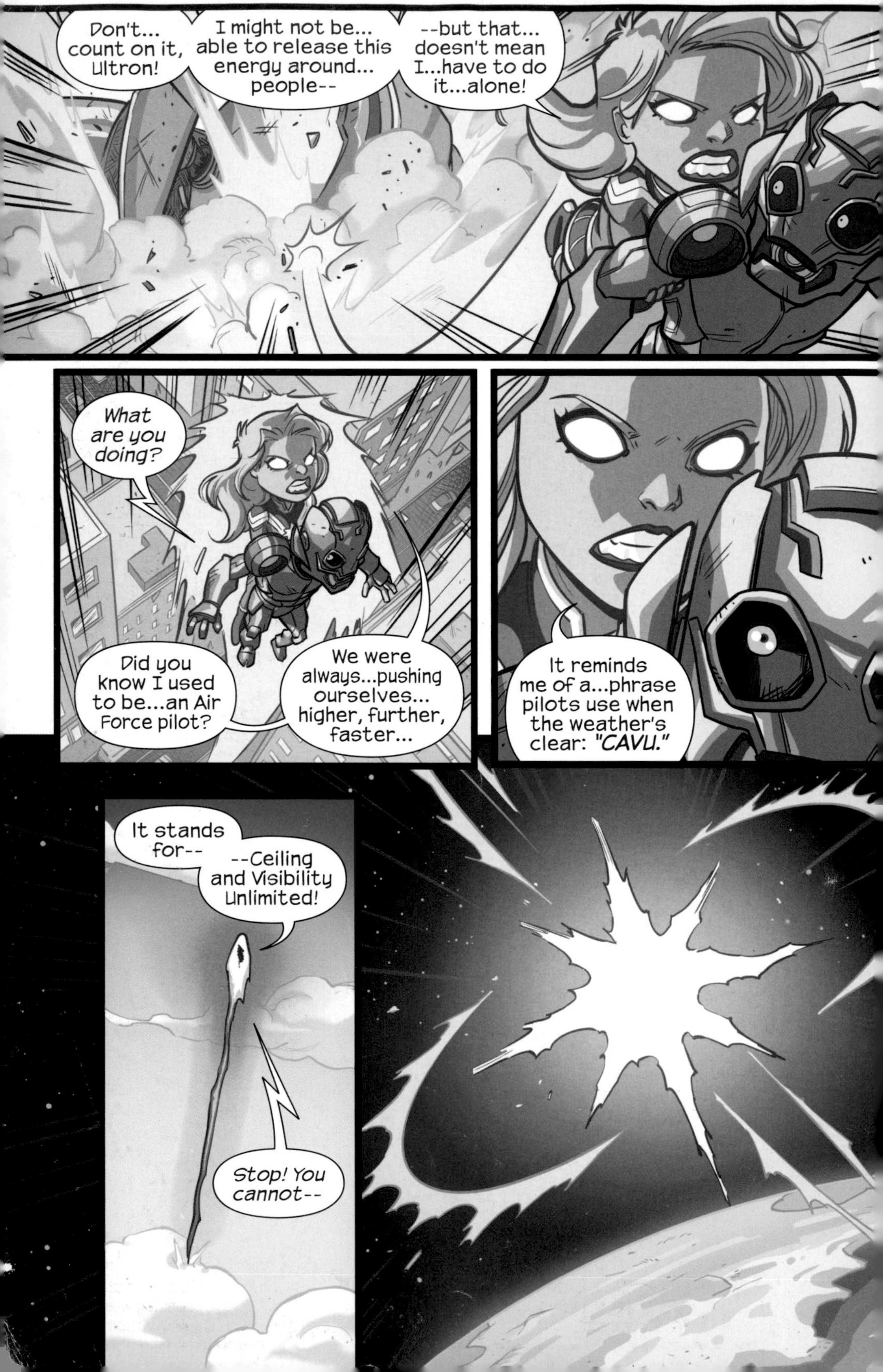
Don't... count on it, Ultron!
I might not be... able to release this energy around... people--
--but that... doesn't mean I...have to do it...alone!
What are you doing?
Did you know I used to be...an Air Force pilot?
We were always...pushing ourselves... higher, further, faster...
It reminds me of a...phrase pilots use when the weather's clear: "CAVU."
It stands for--
--Ceiling and Visibility Unlimited!
Stop! You cannot--

CAP! How could anyone survive that?

I just hope she's okay...

Nice of you to worry. But... I'm *Earth's Mightiest Hero*, remember?

You're all right! And you're not all glow-y anymore!

And Ultron's gone! My joke about the electromagnetic pulse gave me an idea.

When I released all that solar energy, it fried Ultron's circuits!

It'll take him a long time to pull himself back together.

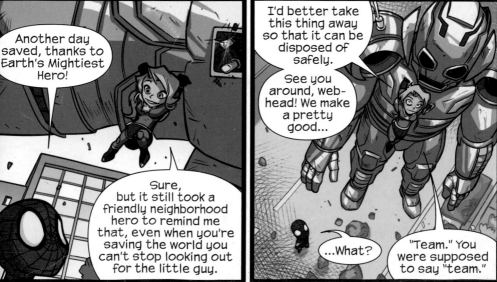

Another day saved, thanks to Earth's Mightiest Hero!

Sure, but it still took a friendly neighborhood hero to remind me that, even when you're saving the world you can't stop looking out for the little guy.

I'd better take this thing away so that it can be disposed of safely.

See you around, web-head! We make a pretty good...

...What?

"Team." You were supposed to say "team."

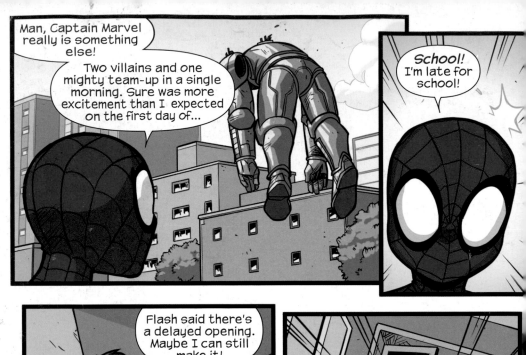

Man, Captain Marvel really is something else!

Two villains and one mighty team-up in a single morning. Sure was more excitement than I expected on the first day of...

School! I'm late for school!

Flash said there's a delayed opening. Maybe I can still make it!

Come on, come on, come on...

Almost there...

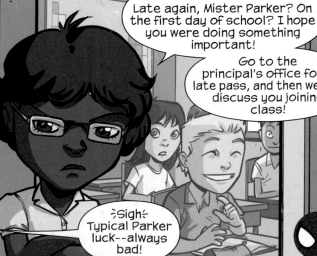

Late again, Mister Parker? On the first day of school? I hope you were doing something important!

Go to the principal's office for a late pass, and then we ca discuss you joining class!

≈Sigh≈ Typical Parker luck--always bad!

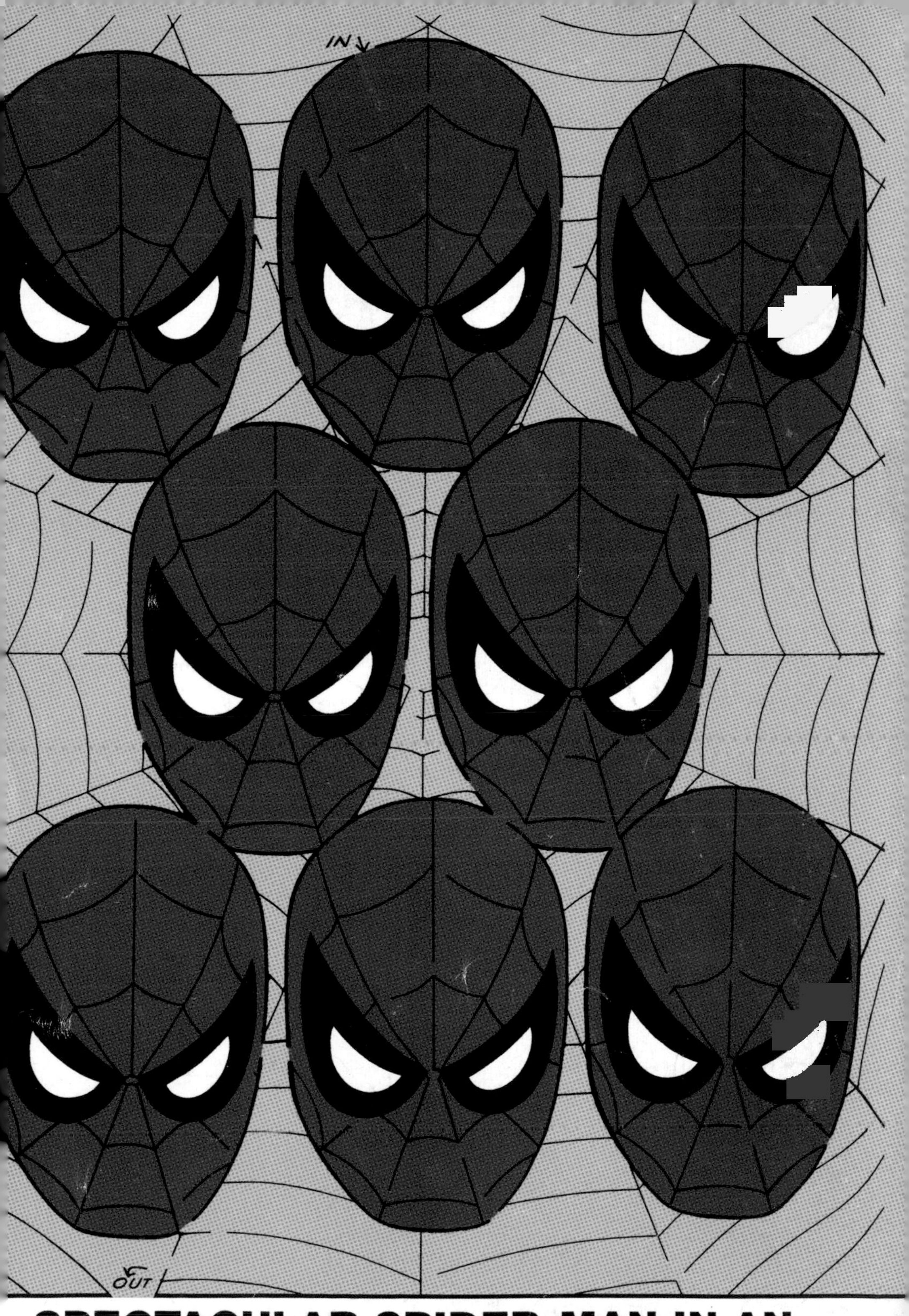
IN
OUT

SPECTACULAR SPIDER-MAN IN AN AMAZING SPIDER-MAZE!

Let your pencil do the walking, Spidey-lover!

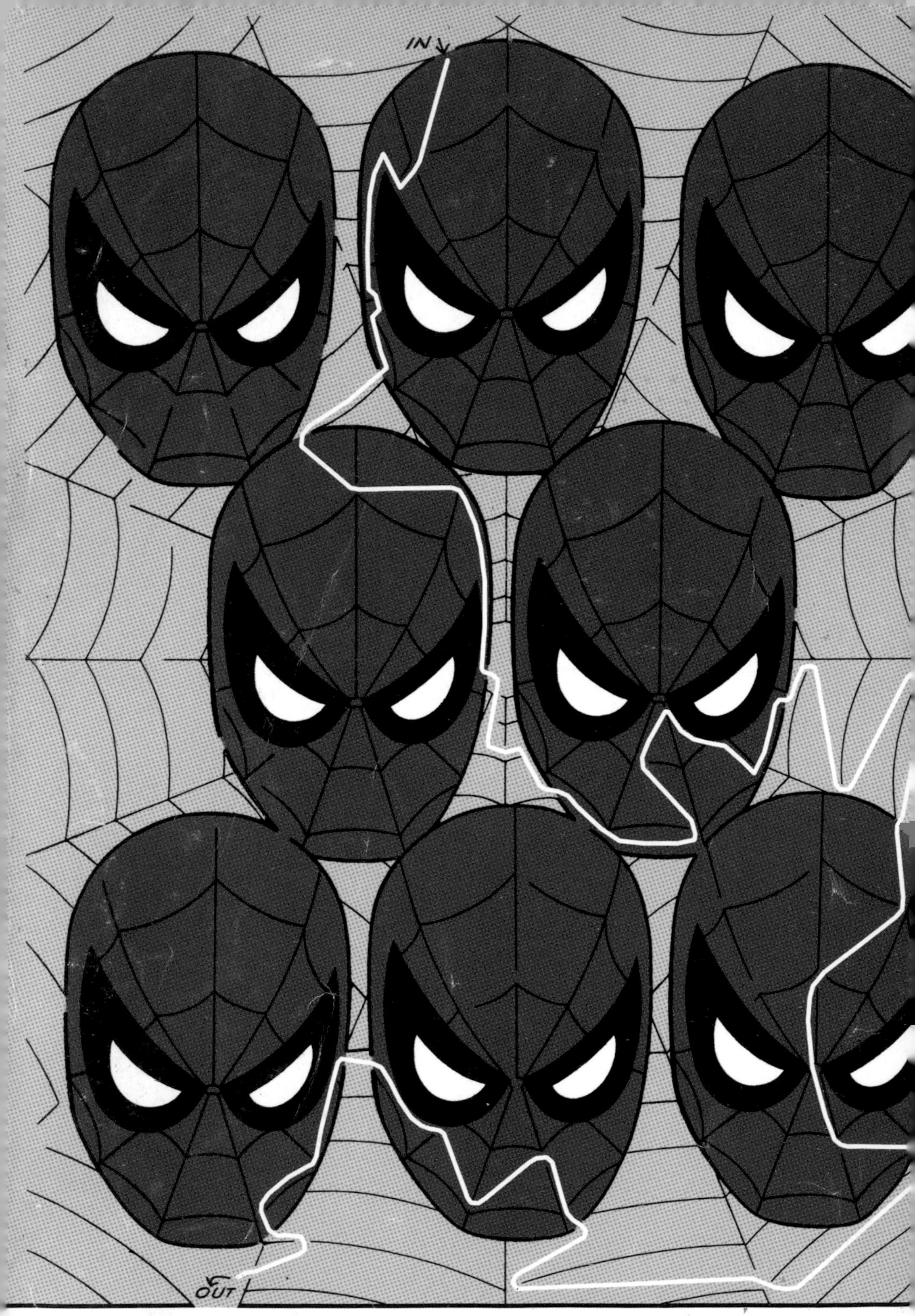
IN
OUT

SPECTACULAR SPIDER-MAN IN AN AMAZING SPIDER-MAZE!

Let your pencil do the walking, Spidey-lover!